THE SEVENTH TELLING

The Kabbalah of Moshe Katan

MITCHELL CHEFITZ

St. Martin's Griffin

New York

www.stmartins.com

Library of Congress Cataloging-in-Publication Data

Chefitz, Mitchell.
    The seventh telling : the kabbalah of Moshe Katan / Mitchell Chefitz.—1st ed.
      p. cm.
    ISBN 0-312-26645-6 (hc)
    ISBN 0-312-28922-7 (pbk)
    1. Cabala—Fiction. 2. Jews—United States—Fiction. I. Title.

PS3553.H34873 S48 2001
813'.6—dc21   00-046980

First St. Martin's Griffin Edition: January 2002

10 9 8 7 6 5 4 3 2 1

To Wallis

This book is a work of fiction. Those who know me may find some parallels between the progress of Moshe Katan's life and mine, but, please, know I am neither so competent nor so terrible as he. As for Rivkah, Moshe's wife, she is not my wife. My wife dances; Rivkah dances. That's where the similarity ends. So if you find yourself concerned for Rivkah's welfare, please do not transfer that concern to Walli.

This work is the product of thirty years of study and practice. To make a list of those who contributed to my growth, and therefore to the content of this book, would be to offend altogether too many whose names I would surely exclude, not by intention, but because I could not make the list adequately comprehensive. So I thank everyone in the Havurah, in the local and national communities. You have provided the fertile environment for study and prayer necessary to sustain me in my God-wrestling. You will see bits and pieces of your visions within.

Special thanks to special souls, each of whom redirected me into new channels of growth: Shlomo Carlebach (ז"ל), who gave me voice; Zalman Schachter-Shalomi, who gave me vision; Joseph Nicastri, who taught me the discipline of the artist; and Barbara Gelles (ע"ה), from whom I learned to cherish each day.

Many friends have been kind enough to help with the literary development of this book, reading the manuscript in its different incarnations and advising me something was missing. I thank all of you for your faith. Some of you were there from the very beginning and carried me through to the end: Bernard Eingold, who listened patiently before words were committed to paper; Irving Bolotin, who has been a mentor to me and my family; Jeffrey Reiss, who provided a foundation for each successive level; Jack Riemer, even more than my rabbi, my friend; and Eli Matalon, whose advice now transcends worlds.

Lastly I thank the professionals who have the extraordinary talent to nurture creativity to blossom without stemming it: my agent, Natasha Kern; my teacher, Lesley Kellas Payne; and my editor at St. Martin's, Michael Denneny. What a blessing to have a such a team! Ellen Frankel provided the initial push toward getting this book between hard covers, and Gideon Weil shed some light upon its ending.

Two studies in preparation for this work have appeared in print: "Reb Zalman's Story: God as Partner," in *Worlds of Jewish Prayer,* edited by Shohama Wiener and Jonathan Omer-Man, Jason Aronson, Inc., 1993, and "A Half Hour with Dr. A.," in *The Fifty-Eighth Century: A Jewish Renewal Sourcebook,* edited by Shohama Wiener, Jason Aronson, Inc., 1996.

Please note that there is a glossary at the end of the book to help with pronunciation and understanding of words that may not be familiar to you. Also my website, www.mitchellchefitz.com, contains a study guide, resources, and programs that may be useful.

This work is an act of *hutzpah,* an attempt to wrestle out of God a lucid understanding of Creator, creation, and the relationship between. I have surely failed, but I have learned and grown in the attempt. I hope your reading of these stories, and your telling of them, will dissolve yet one more veil from the divine mystery.

—MITCHELL CHEFITZ

. . . I can't wait to tell you my stories. Some you've heard, some you haven't. It took me a while to hear them, and even longer to understand them. I'm not the same as I used to be. I hope that's okay. If I'm messing up, you'll let me know, won't you?

—from The Eighth Telling

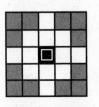
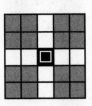

Stephanie Lee considered what she might wear for the seventh cycle of the storytelling. That alone was enough to make her aware that her role in this telling would be of a different order than in any of the previous six.

Whenever Sidney scheduled a course of stories, they left their apartment in the city to make the house in the hills their home for the weekend. Stephanie kept a suitable wardrobe in a section of Rivkah's closet so as not to have to schlep her clothes back and forth across the Bay.

She thought to dress modestly. Not Orthodox modest, but Stephanie modest. Her understanding of Orthodox modest allowed for long knit dresses that hugged and revealed the curves beneath. The material of the Kabbalah was libidinous enough as it was. In the early tellings it mattered little what she wore. She had not been much of a participant, let alone a storyteller, even if she did pass through and intervene from time to time.

So why was this telling different from all the other tellings? She confronted her wardrobe. Simple. This one would be more hers and less Sidney's. Should she wear a hat?

A hat?

Were she Orthodox, a hat would be in order. Or a *sheitel,* a wig, to cover her hair, another expression of modesty. But the wigs the women chose to wear were often so much more seductive than their natural hair.

It wasn't about hats, but the box, the yellow hatbox on the shelf above the dresses. This traveled with her across the Bay. She would not leave her hat in San Francisco, the thought astonishing her, that she could consider a joke at such a moment. But there was truth in the pun. Hat and heart were both in the box.

The box contained a brown hat and, underneath, all the letters she had ever sent her mother. She thought for a moment to reach for it, to open it. There wasn't time. Besides, she knew the contents only too well. At first she had written every month, then every so often, sending the letters through her uncle Al so her father couldn't intercept them. Her mother had kept them all, under her hat.

The box had arrived a month before with a note from her father, written in English. "Your mother died. I found this going through her things. I did not read them." A scrap of paper, taped to the top of the box.

She had known her mother had died. That wasn't news. Her uncle Al had called to tell her. She had not known her mother had saved all the letters, had cherished them. The letters were in bundles, the rubber bands new, not old and brittle.

So her mother had known about the birth of her grandchildren, how each of the girls had blossomed, one playing the violin, the other the piano. The colleges they had attended, the men they had met, the weddings. She had known all of it, never shared it with her husband. Stephanie imagined her at home, when her father was at the store, reading the letters again and again. But her mother never wrote back, never called. Her father had told her not to do that, never to do that, so her mother never did.

This was more important than the dress for the moment. Time or not, she stood on her toes and, with fingertips, slid the box from the shelf, not to open it, but to hold it, a holy object, all that remained of her mother.

Stephanie was more angry than sad, angry her father had stifled her mother so, sad her mother had permitted it. Or perhaps the other way around. She wasn't sure. In underwear Stephanie sat on the bed, hugged the box, and cried, perhaps not because of the box at all. She had found herself crying, unexpectedly, for months. The box was an added incentive.

With determination, even defiance, she placed her mother's remains on the table by the great window, high in the treetops. A shrine, more appropriate than a niche in the closet. She imagined Sidney's complaint. "It's time to let her go." He had never said such a thing, but she imagined it anyway and was angry with him for words he had not spoken. Unfair, she thought, but the anger was there. She noted it as she wiped away her tears before the mirror.

"Whatever," she said aloud.

Ten students had registered for the seventh telling, three of them repeat. Why would anyone choose to take the course again? Were they intending to become practitioners?

Four of the ten were men. There had never been as many as five. Indeed, one of the cycles had been all women.

"This one will be different," Stephanie reaffirmed as she chose a cotton dress, not knit, a batik fabric of blue and white that cloaked rather than hugged her body. The dress gave no hint of what it concealed. She was prepared, she told herself as she turned before the mirror. The work was hers to do, to uncover whatever was necessary, to expose it to herself, if to no one else, to leave it behind and go on.

Not for herself alone, she admitted. She owed this to Sidney. How many years had they been married? Thirty-one? What was the significance of thirty-one? There was no significance she could fathom, and that was the difficulty. There had been no significance to twenty-nine either. Both prime numbers, she recognized, thinking somehow with Sidney's mind instead of her own. That would have been his response: both prime numbers, divisible only by themselves and the number one. Two also was a prime number, the two years between, but they had significance because of Rivkah and Moshe.

Her attire no longer an issue, Stephanie became aware of the sound of furniture shifting about the living room below. Sidney arranged it differently for each of the tellings. Moshe himself had suggested they use the house for this purpose, but, she thought, if he had known the liberties Sidney would take with the living room, he might not have volunteered the space so freely.

For Sidney, the storytelling began with the furniture, how chairs faced each other, the relationship of the sofa to the sliding glass doors. *Feng Shui,* Stephanie thought. For all of his pushing and shoving, Stephanie knew the room would still be a mess, books in piles, magazines stacked on the end tables. That was the most Sidney would do. At least the seating surfaces would be free. She had never known the room to be neat, and that was much of its charm, that and the redwood deck suspended on stilts high in the woods.

Sidney had been excited by Moshe's suggestion to teach, but Stephanie had not. She had no desire to continue with the Kabbalah.

Sidney first attempted to teach the course itself, on Wednesday evenings, much as Moshe had taught at the Institute, but the teaching emerged dry. For all his knowledge, he wasn't much of a teacher. He probably could have recited Moshe's lessons word for word, but he could not charge them with Moshe's energy. Fortunately the students were all members of the Havurah, all somewhat familiar with the material. It was more review than learning from scratch, and the students stayed the course.

"It's not working, you know," Stephanie challenged.

"No," Sidney admitted.

"Why bother? Who benefits?"

"I benefit," Sidney said with certainty.

"What do you gain?"

There he paused, uncertain.

Stephanie had her suspicions and didn't hesitate to express them. "You miss the encounters. You miss the angels. You miss the excitement."

"Maybe," was as much as Sidney was willing to concede. "I'm not sure. But I need to teach. I've lost something, Stephanie. Maybe I teach hoping I will find it."

"But the teaching isn't sharp. The teaching is dull."

Sidney pursed his lips and raised his eyebrows. "How nice of you to remind me. The problem is, I can't teach the way Moshe taught. I can tell stories about how Moshe taught, about Moshe himself, and Rivkah. There's room for you in this. You know stories I don't know. Even the ones I know, some would be better coming from you."

Stephanie considered his invitation, but demurred.

Still, even though she chose not to contribute, she listened in from time to time. She never missed the opportunity to escape the city, or that's the way she expressed it at first. Later it was the thrill of hearing the Kabbalah taught in that house again, even from Sidney. Still later, as the stories developed, the fear Sidney would not get them right, as if there were a right. But there was surely a wrong, and she wanted to be nearby to prevent that.

In the first telling Sidney began with the Institute course. The students were still mostly from the Havurah, experienced and eager to learn. They already knew much of the narrative of Moshe and Rivkah, so even though Sidney was mostly teaching rather than storytelling, they persevered.

In the second telling, Sidney reordered the stories to begin with Moshe's childhood. That was better. Stephanie had more questions than criticisms for Sidney when they were alone together.

In the third telling, Sidney opened with the moment of Moshe's return to the Kabbalah, the fulcrum upon which all the stories were balanced.

Four in the morning, too dark for the morning prayers, Moshe Katan descended to his study. He turned the lights up just enough to delineate pencil marks on white paper and sat opposite the wall of charts. If Rivkah had heard him rise from the bed, she had given no indication of it. It was not unusual for him to rise early, especially when he had a major position open and the exposure was great. In recent weeks he had been trading grains and metals—corn, beans, silver, and gold—but that morning he was neutral in the markets. In the world of commodity futures he had no exposure at all. Still, his sleep had been troubled. . . .

"Better," Stephanie had told him. "Why didn't you begin there before?"

"I didn't know to begin there before."

"It's a good place to begin. But your opening words are so ponderous." Her pronunciation of ponderous mimicked his tone. "Why not just say it was four in the morning when Moshe woke up?"

"I'm not going to begin with some indefinite pronoun. The operative word is four, and that will be the first word."

Sidney was still in charge, so that remained the first word and the last word of the discussion.

It wasn't better, Stephanie realized. Why had she ever said such a thing? He had opened with Moshe the commodities trader. What did that have to do with Rivkah? This was all about Rivkah, not commodities. Was he reducing Rivkah to a commodity? The stories weren't about Moshe's skill in the markets. They were about his skills in the Kabbalah. And there she was, angry with Sidney again, and with herself, for not bringing him up short when the opportunity was at hand.

In the fourth telling Stephanie was enticed enough to remain in the room with the students for extended periods.

"You really should tell some of the stories," Sidney urged her. "Please. You'll learn from them."

She did not respond directly. "How do you know Moshe woke up at four in the morning? Did he tell you that? It might have been three. Or five."

"It was four," Sidney asserted. "When in doubt, the answer is four."

"You're fudging. You're making stuff up."

"I'm teaching the Kabbalah."

He was more than teaching. He was making use of the mystical techniques, encoding within the stories the symbols and processes of the Kabbalah itself to transmit the discipline, and he was doing it well. The stories had begun to stir something within her. She felt a discomfort but could not identify the source.

She remained present throughout the fifth telling. When Sidney began to introduce Rivkah as ". . . a diminutive redhead with square shoulders, hips a bit large . . ." Stephanie silenced him before he could get to the size of her breasts. "It doesn't matter what she looks like. That's not what this is about." From that moment she assumed responsibility for the Rivkah narrative. While the words were her own, the stories were still much as Sidney had told them.

In the sixth telling Stephanie was no longer content to follow Sidney's direction. She said there was something obscured she needed to see. She thought if she surrendered to the stories and let them shape her, rather than attempting to shape them, she might learn more. She told some of Sidney's stories, listened to the rest profoundly, but there was a deeper level to go. She needed to tell not Sidney's stories, but her own.

The seventh telling was soon to begin. Stephanie joined Sidney in the living room. If he noticed her dress, he did not mention it.

"I'd like to move the couches closer," she said. "I want the setting to be more intimate. We won't be going out on the porch tonight." She studied the glass doors. "I wish there were curtains so we could close off the outside. I don't like the way the reflections bounce back."

"What's going on?" Sidney asked.

"I'm not sure," she said.

"Not sure about what?"

"Something in the stories. There are some stories we haven't included yet."

"Which ones are they?"

"How should I know? I haven't found them. This time I'll find them."

Sidney had his back to her, but Stephanie knew he was smiling.

"I'll begin the telling this time," she said. "It's my turn."

Sidney nodded. "Your turn."

Did he know, she wondered, that their marriage was on the line?

CHAPTER 1

They began the seventh cycle of stories at the conclusion of the Sabbath. With experience the cycle had evolved into four sessions, a marathon: Saturday night, Sunday morning, afternoon, and evening, each spanning four sets of stories. Several of the students had made arrangements to stay in the house, either in guest rooms or sleeping bags. Others were commuters or had booked hotel space nearby. Ten students, plus Stephanie and Sidney, gathered in the living room for *havdalah,* the ritual that separated the Sabbath from the ordinary days of the week.

Six women, four men. Each had submitted an application, necessary because the material was so numinous, not fit for the imbalanced. The application requested a reference from clergy, therapist, or physician, and the references were checked. Sidney wasn't prepared for another Emily.

Stephanie had read through the applications. She knew the makeup of the class and attempted to match the person to the clothes. The man who had lost his wife several months before was likely the one in shorts and sandals, a thin white beard, balding. The three repeats, friends, were the middle-aged women in long folksy cotton skirts. Two young men in jeans, a couple. Two young women in jeans, a couple. That was going to be a challenge for Sidney, because the imagery of the Kabbalah was decidedly heterosexual. One man in dress pants, button-down shirt, sleeves rolled up. The executive. He worked on Saturday, something to note. And a woman, also an executive, in the pantsuit, perhaps a Donna Karan. Stephanie looked for and found the jacket draped across a dining-room chair. She also worked on Saturday. They had singled each other out already, though they sat apart. Two engagements had come out of these storytellings. Perhaps this would be another.

So much for judging a class by its clothes.

The three long skirts came to Stephanie for hugs and kisses. They had wept their way through their first course but still had an appetite for more.

Stephanie had no choice but to begin by asking the gathering for the names she would soon forget. Sidney would remember. Sidney was good with names, Stephanie better with experiences. She asked for names and what each hoped to gain from the storytelling. There were no surprises in the responses. "A connection with God; a sense of purpose; a sense of self and my place in the world." No one said, "To surrender unconditionally to an agency beyond my self; to relinquish my beliefs; to risk a transformation of my very being."

Stephanie uttered the standard disclaimer. "There are no guarantees," she said. "We have stories to tell, for you to retell. Each time we do this, the experience is different, different for each of us. You may find what you expect here. You may not. It might be best to have no expectations, to surrender to the stories, and to allow what will happen to happen. That's up to you."

That done, she lowered the lights, lit the braided candle, and began chanting the *havdalah* blessings. She took care to explain each of the symbols—the wine, the spices, the candle itself—for the students who were not Jewish and for those who were. She knew from her own experience that being Jewish did not guarantee familiarity with the symbols of Judaism.

"We let *Shabbat* go gracefully," she said. "As we brought her into the house with wine, we let her go with wine. As she entered a house fragrant with spices, we let her go with fragrant spices. And as we greeted her with the light of candles, we let her go with the light of candles, but you see the candles have become braided into one. That's the grace of *Shabbat*. What was divided in the beginning has become one by the end."

Sidney chanted the blessing separating the Sabbath from the ordinary days of the week. Together they sang *Eliahu Ha-navee,* an incantation intended to bring Elijah the prophet back into space and time.

Stephanie raised the lights, but not to their full intensity. She sat in one of the deep chairs, looked from student to student, and then surprised herself.

She began with Sidney's words.

Four in the Morning

Four in the morning, too dark for the morning prayers, Moshe Katan descended to his study. At the top of the steps he acknowledged his exposure. With each step down, his anxiety grew. He descended into trepidation.

He needed some light, even though he could navigate the room with his toes through the shag rug. He turned the light up only enough to locate the CA125 chart and unpin it from the corkboard, then sat, not in the swivel chair behind his desk, but in a coffee-table chair, his back to the painting. He didn't want to be distracted. Perhaps that's why he would have preferred the lights not on at all.

8

The chart appeared ordinary. He knew it, didn't have to look at it. It could have been mistaken for something as benign as the progress of November beans, but CA125 was a cancer marker, not a commodities contract. Moshe closed his eyes and followed the flow of data with a light that emanated from within. It was there. Subtle, but there. Movement. Only a trader would see it. Rivkah's oncologist was not a trader.

Dr. Dowling had held the chart up to the light as if it were an X ray. "I don't see anything," she had reassured him. "What do you see that alarms you? We've had isolated readings this high before." Her patience barely masked her annoyance.

Moshe retrieved the chart from her, smoothed it on her desk, and traced his forefinger along the path of the most recent entries. "The movement has settled into a new pattern. It wasn't doing this before." He traced the line he could see, and she could not.

"I'm sorry, Rabbi, I still don't see anything."

"I chart things all the time. That's my business. I see things that look like they're not there, but are there. What I am seeing here frightens me."

The doctor looked again, shook her head. "I wouldn't take any action because of this," she said. "There's not enough change to justify it."

"If the marker continues to go up, what would you do?"

"If the marker goes up, we'll worry about it then. We'll do some additional tests. But I don't see anything in this that's cause for alarm, Rabbi. If you will excuse me, please, I have patients to see." She left him alone at her desk, an overprotective husband who saw things that were not there.

Maybe Dr. Dowling was right. Maybe there was nothing to worry about. What could he do anyway? Even if there was something he could do, what would Rivkah allow him to do?

Those were the two questions he asked himself at first. Those were the two questions he pondered as he fell asleep that evening. If they had been the only two, if he had not heard the deeper questions in his sleep, there would be no story to tell. The deeper questions awoke him and drove him to his study.

He had asked first what he might do. Was there indeed anything in his power to do? Surely he would never have been troubled to rise from his bed if there weren't within him a notion of something to do, a vague sense of something distant in the Kabbalah.

Then, what would Rivkah allow him to do? He knew how she felt. Rivkah wanted no involvement with the charts, and she had a disdain for the Kabbalah. She had made both abundantly clear. The charts were a reminder she had

9

been ill. And as for the Kabbalah, throughout their marriage any attempt to share with her his passion for Jewish spiritual discipline had been met with an apathy just short of contempt. He had learned to keep his discipline to himself, and then not even to himself. To do away with it, no longer necessary, an impediment to him and to his marriage.

The third question was the deceptive one. Was there any reason to do anything? Might he respond with no response, by doing nothing at all? The doctor saw no cause for alarm. Who was he to disagree? If he did nothing, who would challenge him, even if it turned out something was there? Who would expect anything from him? The very notion he might be able to intervene in any effective way was in itself presumptuous. So rational, such thoughts would have lulled a lesser man into deeper sleep. But for Moshe, the suggestion of denial was an alarm and gave rise to a fourth question.

If he should do nothing, then who was he? What was there to him if he perceived even a hint of a need and failed to respond to it? That he considered no response even for a moment touched an emptiness within him. His life had become comfortable. Actions that would have sprung from urgency years before were impeded by complacence, satisfaction.

Sitting in his study in the early morning darkness, he held the chart in his left hand and opened his right, staring at it as if something were missing.

He summoned his breath back into control, settled in his chair, and allowed his eyes to survey the room, from the bookcase to the left, across the wall of charts, to his desk, the computer, the globe, the wastebasket. The crumpled letter.

The letter was an invitation for him to teach a course about the Kabbalah at the Metropolitan Institute of Expanding Light. He had not offered such a course in years. The synagogues and Jewish organizations had long since stopped asking. Out of habit he had discarded the letter. Yet he had awakened early in the morning to retrieve it.

Moshe positioned himself more comfortably in his chair. He had an exercise to do. Between any two points in the universe, between any two points in any of the worlds, flows a straight line. He would surrender conscious thought so he might be moved by the most subtle of influences, that his perspective might change. The two points, the cancer marker and the invitation to teach, were still separate. He needed to shift his perception until the line disappeared, until one could be seen within the other. At that point he would know the connection for a certainty.

Monitoring his breathing, he inscribed the Hebrew letters of the Divine

Name on his body. He traced the *YOD, HEY, VAV, HEY* along the path of breath as it entered his nostrils, inside the lids of his closed eyes, across his forehead, around the curve of his ears. Layer after layer of concentration bound him deeper and deeper to the body of God. He descended gracefully, the world above disappearing. Suspended, frictionless, beyond sense, he asked himself the only question he had ever asked at that depth, "From here, where?"

When he rose to the surface and opened his eyes, he could distinguish the outline of the eucalyptus trees against the predawn sky. The time had come for morning prayers. He ascended from his study to the living room, enveloped himself in his *tallit,* the ritual prayer shawl, bound the *tefillin,* the leather cubes containing words of Torah written in the ancient form, to his arm and head, and walked out onto the deck. He wore the uniform for prayer, but prayer did not rise easily from his heart. The flow of words slowed and ceased as images broke through.

He visualized the doctor in her office. She had remembered him as the "Rabbi." The Metropolitan Institute had asked the Rabbi to teach, but the Rabbi had been absent for years. Moshe had exorcised the Rabbi from his system, or so he had thought. The unbidden images were telling him otherwise. Something of the Rabbi needed to return. With a calm acceptance he resumed his prayer and sought comfort under the wings of the Divine Presence.

When the students realized Stephanie's introduction was complete, they began to ask questions. Sidney held up his hand to stop them. "The stories speak for themselves. Rather than ask us questions, ask each other. The stories will be as complete as they need to be. If there are spaces, they are left for you to fill."

Elements of Stephanie's story had taken her by surprise. Moshe's four questions she had never heard before. She realized they had sprung from Moshe's own framework, the Four Worlds.

First a question about what he might do, what action he might take, a question in the World of Action.

Then a question about feelings. Moshe had been angry with Rivkah all those years, angry he had to sacrifice his discipline to preserve his marriage. Was that correct, Stephanie asked herself, or was she projecting her own anger with Sidney onto him? A question in the World of Formation.

And then a question from the world of reason, the World of Creation. Why not just let events take their course? If Rivkah died, she died, and the marriage with it. It wasn't a terrible marriage, but was it so good he should go to any great risk to save it? Again, was that Rivkah and Moshe or herself and Sidney? The question registered. Stephanie didn't pause to ascertain an answer.

And a last question, from the World of Emanation, concerning the very essence of being. If he did nothing, then what was he? And as for her, Stephanie thought, if she did nothing, then what was she?

She wasn't doing nothing. She was telling the stories, and even the first one had nearly overwhelmed her. She needed time to consider before she could continue.

Sidney provided it by changing the venue, doing just what she didn't want him to do. He drew the students outside onto the deck under the vault of the heavens. She had wanted the first session cozy, confined in the textures of the pillows.

She remained curled deep in her chair, still aware of Sidney saying, "This is where much of the work took place." He gestured to indicate the living room the students were leaving as well as the California redwood planks ahead of them. A bench ran about the perimeter, enclosing four primitive chairs and a glass coffee table. Eucalyptus trees grew out of the hill below and towered above the deck. Several of the students reached out to caress the trees, the parchment bark holy in their hands.

Stephanie succumbed to Sidney's lead and sat in the chair the students had left open for her. She saw him close his eyes, as if searching for a new place for his own beginning. He leaned forward and said, "To Moshe Katan, angels often appeared in the form of winged lions. I suspect these lions had their origin early in his childhood. This was long before his name became Moshe Katan. Then he was known as Michael Kayten."

Lions

Young Michael always accompanied his father to *shul* on the Holy Days of *Rosh Hashanah* and *Yom Kippur*. They walked, not because they were religious, but because they lived nearby. Michael carried his father's purple velour *tallis* bag, the rampant lions, embroidered in gold, presented proudly to the world.

Michael and his father sat in the front pew, to the right of the *bimah,* close enough to lean forward and play with the turned dark maple of the railing. When he leaned back against the soft rose cushion, Michael wrapped himself in his father's *tallis* and toyed with the fringes. When he became bored, he needed no permission to leave the service to sit with his friends outside on the steps, but he always returned to his father's side for the auction.

"How much am I bid for this *aliyah*?" In Yiddish the men called out, "Ten dollars, twenty dollars." *Aliyahs* were honors, the privileges of attending to the Torah. Because writing was forbidden on the Holy Days, records of pledges were kept by folding tabs on cards prepared in advance.

Every year, for twenty-five dollars, an amount befitting a dentist, his father bought *hagba,* the honor of raising the Torah scroll when the reading was done. After the Torah was dressed, Michael's father would beckon him to the *bimah,* sit him in a tall chair, and set the Torah scroll in his hands while the *haftarah* was read. The velour of the Torah mantle felt like the velour of his father's *tallis* bag, but the embroidered lions were made of a coarser thread and scratched back when he touched them.

The lions sometimes appeared to young Michael in his dreams. He didn't know them yet as angels. They were not yet threatening. No, they were watching and waiting, at a distance.

Stephanie observed Sidney scanning the room. She knew what he was doing. He was sensing how the students responded to the first mention of angels. He had it down to a science. If they flinched, if their faces were puzzled with lack of comprehension, then the task would be easier. Even one such student provided a foil from which to reflect and intensify the learning.

In past tellings Sidney complained that most of the students came from some spiritual discipline outside of Judaism or from the peculiar Western path known as New Age spirituality. They came to confirm their own agenda, to reaffirm some established belief rather than to open themselves to new perspectives and growth. "There is no greater hindrance to growth than belief," Sidney was fond of saying.

So Stephanie followed Sidney's lead and looked into the faces, hoping for blank slates. There were some. Dress slacks and the Donna Karan seemed lost. All four in jeans seemed apprehensive. On the other hand the long skirts were nodding their knowledge, too full of what they knew already to admit any more. Still this was a good grouping, better than average. Each had paid $180, a donation to the Havurah. Some, Stephanie observed, were likely to get their money's worth.

Sidney paused, leaving room for Stephanie to add or comment. When she had nothing to say, he continued the stories of young Michael.

In Michael's *shul* the women sat in the balcony and the men sat below. Michael noted further divisions. Those men who knew enough Hebrew to be on the correct page he separated from those who did not. Of those who knew the correct page, there were those one could interrupt and ask, "What page are we on?" Michael was proud that his father was in this category. Then there were the very few who were never to be interrupted. They were really praying. He watched them, trying in vain to understand what they experienced.

One man in particular stood apart. Mr. Lieberman came early and secluded himself under his *tallis* in front of the *bimah*. He was the only one who wore sneakers on Yom Kippur so as not to have the hide of an animal under his feet. He stood when others sat, swayed when others were still, scowled when the service was interrupted for any reason or when his concentration was broken by the noise of children scurrying between the pews.

Once Michael found Mr. Lieberman's gaze on him. There was neither censure nor approval in his expression, but an acceptance that both pleased and confused Michael.

Again Sidney paused, leaving room for Stephanie, if she had something to say. He had not done so in any of the previous sessions. She realized he, too, sensed something different about this telling.

What might she say? When she was a little girl her mother had taken her to the *shul* below Fifth Street. They had sat upstairs while the men did whatever it was they did below. The women talked and paid little attention to the prayers. Prayer was a guy thing, she thought, though that's not the way it would have been expressed.

"Men had the obligation to pray," she reminded herself in an internal rabbinic voice she had heard somewhere, not from Moshe. From someone else, years before. "Women were excused from all the obligations fixed in time, except three." The rabbinic voice couldn't recall all three. One was lighting *Shabbos* candles, she remembered. Her mother didn't light candles.

Twice her mother brought her to the *shul*. Only twice, when she was a little girl. She had no interest in it, and neither did her mother, so they never went back.

Sensing that Stephanie had nothing to insert, Sidney continued.

The *shul* had a new Rabbi every year. Michael could not remember the names of any of them except for Rabbi Margolis, who had taken him along with three other children to visit the Israeli destroyer when it came into the harbor.

"Look at this. Look at this!" the Rabbi said over and over with each new wonder. Cannon, anchors, the quarterdeck, the galley, even the sleeping spaces for the crew. "Look at this! Who would have thought we would live to see such a thing! Our own navy!"

When it came time for Michael to prepare for his bar mitzvah, his family joined the Conservative synagogue. There had been no Hebrew school for Michael at the small Orthodox *shul*. His father found a tutor to prepare him to read his portion. The morning of his bar mitzvah, Michael met the Rabbi for the first time. Michael sang his blessings, chanted his *haftarah,* read his speech, and became sick at the party afterward. His uncle Bernie had given him a rye and ginger ale to drink because, after all, Michael was now a man.

Within a year Michael had forgotten his Torah portion, the blessings, the chant of the *haftarah,* and the Rabbi's name.

When Michael was in the ninth grade, his parents were eager for him to be in the company of other Jewish teenagers, so they joined the Reform temple. He attended confirmation class on Monday nights. The boys, except for Michael, did not pay attention. They waited for the class to be over, to light up cigarettes in the bathroom, to joke in the hall and check out the girls.

Michael alone argued with the Rabbi. The Rabbi answered each of Michael's questions with care and patience. The class became a dialogue. The others paid no attention.

"I understand!" Michael proclaimed one evening. "The universe is like a clock, and it was God who wound it up!"

"Aha!" exclaimed the Rabbi. "Yes, but an electric clock, and God is the electricity!"

Michael understood the Rabbi's correction. A wind-up clock once wound no longer had need of the winder. An electric clock was in constant need of electricity.

Several nights later Michael awoke with a question. "But why would electricity need a clock?"

With a start, Stephanie realized she had a story. Before Sidney could continue with Moshe's college career, she raised a finger, just enough for Sidney to notice.

Stephanie had spoken her introduction while seated. She had been much too comfortable seated and had become lost in her own words. This time she rose from her chair. She would not become lost while standing and pacing, not if she kept her eyes open and moving, reading the light reflected back from the eyes of the students. "Moshe was Michael as a child," she explained. "Rivkah was Rebecca. Becky Shapiro."

The Robe

Becky Shapiro was sick in Sunday school, sick to her stomach and upset she was going to have to leave class just when they were about to make Purim masks. Every year they made masks for Purim, the Jewish Mardi Gras. It was just about the only thing in Sunday school she liked. That was the morning she was tired and sick enough so her teacher noticed and sent her down to the Rabbi's office. The office doubled as the infirmary on Sundays.

"Oh dear!" the volunteer said. "What do we have here?"

"I'm sick," Becky confessed. "But don't call my mother. I'll be better soon."

Becky lay down on the sofa in the reception area. She recognized several of the paintings on the walls. They had similar paintings at home. Her father sold paintings. That was his business. Maybe he had sold these to the synagogue. The paintings were orange, red, and purple. She closed her eyes.

When she opened them, the Rabbi was standing above her. "How do you feel?" he asked. He was in a black suit and so tall his head went up to the ceiling, almost to the light fixture in the center of the room. She squinted, trying to make out his face in the brightness. "You're shivering. Are you cold?"

She was either cold or afraid. All the kids were afraid of the Rabbi.

When she did not answer, he retreated, then returned within a few seconds. "This will keep you warm," he said. He spread his robe over her.

She knew that robe. In the synagogue, when the Rabbi raised his arms, the robe hung massive from his shoulders. Three stripes of black velvet were seared into each sleeve. When those arms were raised, the congregation followed suit, rising collectively to its feet. It was impossible to remain seated when those arms were raised. They commanded. They didn't embrace.

16

Becky knew a story of Moses. When the children of Israel were fighting in the valley below, Moses stood on a hill above with his arms raised. As long as he held his arms aloft, the children of Israel succeeded. When his arms tired and sagged, the Israelites did not fare well.

The Rabbi tucked the robe about her. The cotton was smooth and thin, not much warmth to it. Under the robe she trembled even more. Still she had the courage to search out the arms for the stripes of black velvet. As long as she touched them, she thought, she would be all right.

She slept until her mother came to take her home.

There were other stories she suddenly wanted to tell, needed to tell, but this wasn't the place. They were stories about herself, not Rivkah, not Moshe. Stories about Stephanie had no place in this telling, she knew. Sidney's only purpose in these stories was to lay the groundwork for the Kabbalah to follow.

Well, screw Sidney's purpose! There was another story to tell, and she could damn well make it work!

To the students she said, "Rivkah grew up in Baltimore. Me, I grew up in Miami. Rivkah and I met once when we were children. We didn't know that for a long time, but later, when we were talking about our childhoods, we realized we had the same grandmother."

Stephanie almost laughed aloud at the confusion in Sidney's face.

Becky on the Beach

I was born in New York, just before my parents moved to Miami. My parents had come to this country from Poland, left weeks before the war. I was supposed to be a boy so I could be named for my father's brother who died in the Holocaust. Everybody on my father's side died. Everybody.

My father's family had been jewelers. Generations of jewelers. My mother loved to tell me about the house in Poland. It wasn't the biggest house, but it was beautiful, in a nice neighborhood. They had a maid. And china, Rosenthal china. I can't tell you how many times I heard about the Rosenthal china.

It took everything my parents owned to get out of Poland. Everything. They came to New York with nothing, and to Miami with even less. A cousin on my mother's side brought us to Miami. My father started a store on Miami Beach, on Washington Avenue, a small store. He sold Jewish stuff, silver plate *kiddush* cups, *shabbos* candlesticks, *esrog* holders, spice boxes for *havdalah*. Sometimes

17

a sterling piece. Mostly plate. Not old. Nothing really precious. Jewish stuff. His customers were tourists, from the hotels on Collins and Ocean Drive.

My mother crocheted *yarmulkes,* which my father sold. He wore one in the store. It was good for business. As soon as he got home, he took it off. My father was bald. He preferred bald to the *yarmulke.*

We lived two blocks away, in an apartment. I had my own room, but I didn't spend much time in it.

I was raised on Washington Avenue. I knew all the shopkeepers. The butcher, the grocer, Al in the corner store who sold newspapers, magazines, and comic books. This was my family. These were my uncles and aunts.

I had lots of grandparents, too, in the hotels. Some came down only for the winter, but some stayed all year. My favorite grandmother was Ida. Ida stayed all year round. Ida had a favorite chair on the porch of the Regency, and I had a favorite place in her lap.

One day I came to visit with her, and there was another girl in her lap. "This is Becky," she said, "my granddaughter." When she saw the look on my face, she added, "My other granddaughter. Becky is my other granddaughter, from Baltimore."

This was Rivkah. We were about the same age. She was down for winter vacation. She and her parents stayed at the Algiers, one of the new hotels, around 34th Street.

We went to the beach together. That was just one block away. I think her parents must have been with us, because we wouldn't have gone to the beach alone. I was allowed to walk all over Washington Avenue, Collins, and Ocean Drive, but I wasn't supposed to go on the beach. We built a sand castle down by the water. I remember it. A breaker came and took it away.

One night, here in this house, right here on this porch, this deck, Rivkah and I were talking about when we were kids. She told me about her one trip to Miami Beach. When she mentioned the name Ida, I knew she was Becky, and we had the same grandmother.

Ida died that year, and Becky never came back to Miami.

Stephanie didn't look toward Sidney. Rivkah had never visited Miami Beach. Sidney knew that. She and Stephanie had never met as children. But they might have, Stephanie thought. She would have liked that. So why not tell the story? She couldn't wait to let Rivie know they had the same grandmother.

The rest of it was true. Ida was true. Mildred and Sophie and Rose, but Ida was the best of all, because she was there year-round, and she made *tayglach* in her efficiency kitchen, hard balls of dough covered with honey and ginger.

And Al was true. Of all the aunts and uncles, he was the best. Al had the corner news store where she sat and read everything. Everything. First the comics, then the magazines, then the books he would leave for her.

Al also was from Poland. He had known her father there. Al hadn't gotten out in time. Al had blue numbers tattooed on his arm, but he never talked about it. Her father didn't like Al, didn't like that Stephanie spent time in his store. Stephanie went there anyway.

Why didn't she follow her father's wishes? What was it about Al and his store that she liked being there? That her father disapproved of it made it so much more desirable. Why was that? The questions flooded in upon her. How come she had never asked such questions before?

At home Stephanie spoke Yiddish with her parents. In Al's store, they spoke English. He didn't want to talk Yiddish. This was America, they would speak English. He didn't want to be reminded of Poland. Al wanted to be American. Stephanie wanted to be American.

Her father sat all day on the stool behind the counter of his store, never said a word, but Al talked all the time. He talked with everyone who came in, argued politics, always politics, and always a book for Stephanie. *Black Stallion* was among the first. *Mutiny on the Bounty* and the rest of the trilogy. Horatio Hornblower stories, she couldn't remember how many of them.

It was probably because of Al she skipped fourth grade, because her reading was at such a high level, or perhaps because she could argue so well. When she wasn't reading they talked about what she was reading. They talked about what she was doing at school. They talked about everything. Al was the very best uncle.

Harry was also a good uncle. He gave her a pickle whenever she came into the deli. And she had aunts, Sally at the clothes store, and Blanche who worked in the fruit market. But Al was the best.

Acceptance

Sidney continued with a story of the young Moshe.

Throughout his years of high school Michael's grades were no better than necessary to keep him in the company of his friends. He applied to Harvard

19

and Yale. The admissions officers had, at least, been courteous. The interview at MIT had been different.

"Your grades are terrible," the admissions officer began, his gaze on the file before him.

"Yes, sir," Michael agreed.

"Do you know any math?"

"Yes, sir."

The admissions officer flipped through the pages. "Your grades say you don't, but your boards say you do. Which tells the truth?"

"The boards, sir. I know my math."

"Physics, too?"

"Yes, sir."

"Your boards are fine, Michael. Your grades aren't."

"Yes, sir. I've been thinking about that. Grades haven't been important to me. Learning has, but not the grades."

The admissions officer closed the file, the interview all but complete. "Do you have any questions for me?" He leaned back in his chair and checked his watch against the clock on the wall.

"Yes, sir." Michael unfolded a map of the campus. "Where is Building Nine? I took the tour this morning. Building Nine is missing."

"Where do you think it is?" the admissions officer countered as he returned to an upright position.

"Here," Michael said, pointing to the empty space in front of Building Ten. MIT was centered about a courtyard. One entered the odd-numbered buildings from Massachusetts Avenue. Across the courtyard were the even-numbered buildings. Connecting them under the dome was Building Ten.

"Why here?"

"Over on this side is engineering," Michael said, closing his eyes to draw course titles from his memory. As he named each course, he pointed to the appropriate building. "And this side is science." Again he named courses as his finger moved across the map. "If there's a Building Nine, it's here. It would be where the students from all of the different disciplines meet. Science, Humanities, Engineering. They meet here as they walk from class to class."

Michael waited patiently while the admissions officer tapped his pencil on the desktop. "Okay, that's where Building Nine might be," he conceded. "Now what courses might be taught there?" For twenty minutes they explored the imaginary building and the imaginary courses that might be taught in it.

Michael Kayten received early admission to MIT, even though he had not applied for early admission. He was rejected everywhere else.

Illumination

Before exams Michael studied through the night in an empty classroom to avoid the distractions of the dormitory. One such night, shortly before dawn, he returned to the dorm to shower and change. His room was dark. He turned on the light. The window shade was open. Most of the light from the fixture in the ceiling remained in the room, but some escaped through the window. He watched it go and wondered where it went. Out, out the window. Away, away from the earth. Deep, deep into space. Beyond, beyond the solar system to the very edge of the universe.

"Does the universe have an edge?" he asked himself. "If it does, the light bounces back, or it is pulled back. If it doesn't, the light escapes, and more light escapes, and it becomes thinner and thinner out there, and nothing relates to anything anymore. There would be no purpose. No relationships, no interactions, no purpose. The light has to come back."

His thoughts followed the light out the window. How long he followed that light he did not know, but when he returned from his reverie, he was excited. He wanted to share his experience with someone, but with whom? He had not yet studied quantum physics or cosmology and had no notion that others before him had followed that light out to the edge of the universe. With whom could he share such thoughts?

He sat at his desk and wrote a letter to his Rabbi.

Sukkah Building

Stephanie said, "When Michael was beginning college in Cambridge, Rebecca was beginning high school in Baltimore." This wasn't a new story. She had told it twice before.

Every autumn, following *Yom Kippur,* the men of Becky's synagogue erected an immense *sukkah* in the courtyard. The structural poles were fixed and remained in place throughout the year. The men strung cables to connect the top of one pole to the next and spread a latticework of wire between the cables. On three sides they erected plywood walls. The fourth side remained open. They threw leafy branches on top of the wire lattice, enough to create the illusion of a roof and a modicum of shade by day, but not so much as to block the stars at night.

At the beginning of the harvest holiday of *Sukkot,* children brought fruit to hang from the roof. In religious-school classes they made decorations to tack to the walls.

The *sukkah* was wonderful the first day of the weeklong holiday. By the end of the week, the fruit was rotten.

"Let's build our own," Rebecca suggested to her parents. They were content to celebrate the holiday in the synagogue.

"Let's build our own," she suggested to Sharon. Sharon was thirteen and not about to do anything her older sister suggested.

Rebecca begged lumber scraps from a construction site. She carried them home, found nails in the toolbox, and hammered out the frame of a small *sukkah* in the backyard. She tacked old sheets to form three walls. She hauled a saw to a nearby woods, cut and dragged branches and brush to throw onto the roof. The space inside was just large enough for the bridge table and four chairs.

"We eat in our *sukkah* tonight," she proclaimed when her parents returned home.

They rejoiced in their *sukkah*. The weather remained crisp and clear. They ate outside every night, each night more wonderful than the last.

Even Rebecca's poison ivy was not enough to diminish her delight.

A Miracle

Stephanie paused to harvest the smiles. She had one more story to tell.

Summers Rebecca attended Camp Hadera in the Poconos. Camp Hadera was a few acres of ersatz Israel surrounding a mountain lake. The buildings had Hebrew names. The paths and lanes were named after Israeli boulevards and avenues. Rebecca became *Rivkah*.

Friday afternoon the campers swept the asphalt of *Rehov Ben Yehudah* clean. They trimmed the hedges and weeded the flower beds in front of the *Hadar Ohel,* the dining room. In pairs one washed the windows while the other wiped them clean with balled-up newspaper.

Dressed in white shorts and T-shirts, the campers sang all the way from the cabins to the pavilion that served as the *Bayt Knesset,* the synagogue. The *Shabbat* service was led by senior campers. The songs were melodies of their own generation, the words ageless.

Rivkah first attended Camp Hadera for a half session when she was eight. At nine she wanted to stay the entire summer. At ten, she did. At sixteen she was a counselor-in-training, at eighteen a counselor fully trained.

The camp was a miracle.

Rabbis came to teach and talked about the miracles in the Bible—the Red Sea parting, the sun standing still. For Rivkah those were stories, not miracles. The miracle was the camp in the Poconos where people spoke Hebrew. The Hebrew language was a miracle. Israel was a miracle. That after two thousand years Jews had their own land, that an ancient language could be revived to provide a common tongue for people from Iran, Iraq, Morocco, Poland, Germany, Hungary, South Africa, England, and America—those were miracles, the land and the language.

Rivkah had lots of stories about summer camp, the time the boys sneaked over to the girls' side and got caught, the time she and a friend climbed the hill to the highway and the grocery store and brought back ice-cream sandwiches for everyone in the cabin. Those were good stories, but there wasn't any point in telling them.

Stephanie had her own stories, but not about summer camp. She worked summers in Uncle Al's store. It wasn't busy during the summer. She had plenty of time to read. Thomas Mann, Isaac Singer, Henry Miller. Strange stuff, challenging stuff, stuff to talk and argue about. The Henry Miller more than the Isaac Singer. Al didn't like to talk about Isaac Singer.

There was an adult section in the news store where the men went to look at *Playboy* and *Escapade.* She had looked, too. Al never stopped her from looking, only said to ask questions if there was something she didn't understand. There was a lot she didn't understand, and sometimes Al admitted he didn't understand either.

She and Al talked about the boys in high school. There was one she kind of liked. All the girls liked him. He had a motorcycle, not a scooter. A Harley-Davidson, a big motorcycle. Al asked why she liked him. She didn't know how to answer. Most of her friends were on the debate team. He was on the football team.

One afternoon, as he was about to get on his bike, she asked if she could have a ride. He didn't know her name, but he couldn't refuse her a ride. She liked it. A lot. They began to ride together, over the causeway and south through Coconut Grove and Old Cutler.

They weren't a couple. He dated other girls. They were motorcycle buddies. One trip Stephanie asked if she could ride the front seat, if he would show her how to control the bike. He did. Left foot the shift, right foot rear brake. Left hand the clutch, right hand front brake. Roll back the right hand, the throttle. "Roll back slowly," he cautioned.

She sat up front, he sat behind. She rolled back the throttle not slowly enough. The bike lunged forward, the front wheel coming up, dumping him on the asphalt behind. She wrestled the machine into control, slowed, turned, and found him okay, dusting himself off. She couldn't help but laugh. It took him some time to the see the humor.

They made sex that night, not love. She was curious about it. It was his first time as well, a learning experience. It was the only time for sex, but they enjoyed the motorcycle together until she left Miami.

Stephanie wondered what that had to do with anything. She had shared the story with Rivkah. Rivkah had shared her own first experience. Was there a story in that? Yes, but Stephanie couldn't think of any justification in telling it.

Laughing

Sidney said, "When Rivkah was finishing her summer at Camp Hadera and contemplating her freshman year at Brown, Michael was considering what his path might be after college."

"To travel and see the world," Michael would say when his friends asked him why he had joined the Navy. There was nothing else he wanted to do when he had finished MIT. He had no desire for graduate studies, nor were his grades adequate in any case. He needed some other space in which to mark time. The Navy seemed a neutral choice, and safe. He enlisted for the romance of the sea a few weeks before the Gulf of Tonkin incident and the escalation of the war in Vietnam.

The Navy sent its MIT grad to Officer Candidate School in Newport, Rhode Island. The uniforms were blue, the shoes black, the buckles brass, the blankets gray, and the asphalt tiles of the living quarters green. At inspection the uniforms had to be crisp, the creases sharp, the shoes luminous, the buckles molten in their radiance, the bed blankets taut and wrinkle-free, the floor unmarred, a brilliant green. Michael learned to tuck and fold, to polish, buff, and shine. He learned to suspend his intellect, surrender, and submit. He learned to laugh.

His roommate was Chuck Harris, an engineering graduate from Georgia. They sewed creases into their uniforms, walked in socks, slept under the beds, did everything the system required no more than once, if possible. They laughed at the weird world they marched through daily, at every attempt to break their will.

Neither man had to study. Both learned in class at first hearing. During study hours at night they played gin. Moshe won.

"How come you keep winning?" Chuck asked.

"Because it's not important to me," Michael answered.

They played in the drawer of the table they shared as a desk, their books open in front of them. They drilled what they would do should the Officer of the Day enter their room unexpected. They would drop their cards, close the drawer, and pivot toward the books, studious and proper. They played for weeks, every night, and kept a cumulative score. Michael's advantage rose into the thousands.

It had to happen. Michael saw the doorknob turn, dropped his cards, closed the drawer, turned toward the books.

"Attention on deck!" he shouted as the Officer of the Day entered. He sprung to attention, expecting Chuck to do the same.

"Gin," Chuck said, still holding his cards as he came to his feet.

"You're playing cards," the Officer of the Day said.

"Yes, sir," Chuck agreed. "I have gin, sir. I don't often have gin, and I'd rather keep this hand than throw it in."

"You will march, mister," the officer said. "Both of you."

March they did, that weekend, the two of them. No liberty on the town. They marched, and they laughed. Four months of training and they never stopped laughing. Only the laughing made that world bearable.

Ensign Harris wanted to fly. His eyes were such he could not be a pilot. The Navy sent him to learn the second seat of a combat aircraft, to become a Radar Intercept Officer. Ensign Kayten had no notion of what he wanted to do. The navy tested him and found he had a rare ability to see sense in what others saw as a random pattern. They sent him to Combat Information Center training with a specialty in air control.

The navy wasn't stupid. In spite of the folding, tucking, shining, and buffing, it used its talent well.

There was a summer-camp story worth telling, Stephanie realized, and spoke quickly before Sidney could continue. "While Michael was learning the art of war, Rebecca learned to dance."

Above all, Rebecca liked to dance.

She had learned Israeli dance at camp, at age eight. Every camper, every counselor, every staff member danced *Hora Hadera*. At all major assemblies, outside or inside, the entire camp danced, circles within circles within circles.

At age eighteen Rebecca taught dance at camp. She taught counselors and senior campers how to teach new arrivals. At assemblies, Rebecca set the pace in the center of the circles.

Among the factors that brought her to study at Brown University was Israeli dance. The Hillel Jewish Student Center had a weekly program that became the center of her campus life.

Israeli music had evolved far beyond horas, borrowing from all the cultures contained in the state. The rhythms were Yemenite, Arabic, East European, even American. The sequences of steps had become so complex only those with devotion could master them.

Women were the most likely to be so dedicated. Men seemed to have other uses for their time. The few who attended were in much demand for couples dancing. They had their pick of the women. The remainder of the girls paired off, dancing with each other, taking their turns as pretend boys.

A Rabbi's son was the most talented among the men. His father was a Rabbi, even *the* Rabbi in Southern California. Rebecca had not heard of that Rabbi, but his name was known among her fellow dancers. He was the Rabbi to the stars. She was flattered when the Rabbi's son asked her to dance, once, then often, then more often still.

The couples dances became an obligation. She had to know every step, every sequence of steps, the bridges between the sequences. She practiced alone, the music humming in her mind as she counted the rhythm. If she should falter and make a mistake, she feared the Rabbi's son would turn to someone else, reducing her to dancing with pretend boys.

He was the Rabbi's son. She wanted to know what it was to be a Rabbi's child, but there were few words between them beyond the dance. When he invited her to walk outside with him, she was eager to go. When he pulled her to him and imposed a kiss, she was too startled to resist and still afraid to offend. When he reached for her breast, she pushed him away. When he reached for her again, she said, "No. I don't want to do this." When he became forceful, she slapped him with her open hand, catching him not flush on the cheek, but awkwardly, against his nose.

That night she did not sleep. All that time she had practiced so as not to disappoint him. He had not practiced so as not to disappoint her.

She was angry, more with herself than with him. He was what he was, but she had been sacrificing herself trying to please him. Had she been faithful to herself, she could have avoided an awkward moment.

Rivkah returned to the dance, taking her turns along with the other women.

The Gulf

Stephanie had a defiant look about her. Sidney had not heard that story before. She wondered how he might respond.

He made time for himself by chanting a soft *niggun*, a wordless repetitive tune. Moshe had taught them, whenever in doubt about how to continue, chant a little, and that's what Sidney was doing.

In the previous tellings he had mustered Michael quickly out of the Navy. This time he had another Navy story to tell.

A month at a time Lieutenant Kayten's destroyer patrolled a five-mile line between the Communist Chinese island of Hainan to the east and the North Vietnamese city of Haiphong to the west. Two carrier task groups steamed in battle formation two hundred miles to the south.

Lieutenant Kayten's day began with a wake-up call shortly before midnight. Without words he dressed and walked through red-lit passageways up ladders to the Combat Information Center. He sipped coffee as he listened to the briefing of the officer he was about to relieve.

When he sat at the radar console and assumed control of the two F-4 Phantoms circling above, he was fully awake. The safety of the fleet was in his hands.

The carriers launched strikes into North Vietnam day and night. Lieutenant Kayten's task was to be certain that every aircraft that came out of the North to return to the carriers was friendly. Any suspicious contact merited an intercept and an eyeball, if not a missile. There could be no mistakes.

At 0400 his relief appeared. Lieutenant Kayten returned to his quarters, stripped to his underwear, and fell instantly asleep.

At 0615 came a wake-up call. He climbed to the bridge. The quartermaster had the sextant ready. Lieutenant Kayten shot the stars. "Mark," he said, to record the time a particular celestial body was a precise angle above the predawn horizon. Even though the radar painted the mountaintop on Hainan every few seconds, regulations required celestial navigation to fix a ship's position. He worked the tables, drew the lines, recorded the data, ate his breakfast, met with his chief and department head. At 1100 he studied the messages, top secret strike information, how many aircraft, which targets. He ate a sandwich and at noon returned to the Combat Information Center for the afternoon watch, four more hours protecting the fleet.

At 1600 he celebrated the Sabbath.

Seven days a week, a month at a time, the ship steamed that five-mile line. No days off. But one hour a day Lieutenant Kayten separated from the other hours and proclaimed it a Sabbath. He might listen to music or sunbathe on the fantail. The time was holy, inviolate. His division knew not to bother him.

At 1700 the messages came, whatever they were. At 1800 dinner with the captain in the wardroom. At 1845, back on the bridge for the evening stars. Then a few minutes of a movie before going to sleep to be awakened before midnight.

Every day for a month on that five-mile line fatigue was the enemy, more so than any Russian-built MiG.

One day like all the other days Lieutenant Kayten lay on his mat on the fantail soaking up sun. Noise and confusion roused him from his Sabbath. The ship turned and put on steam. "Plane down," a sailor informed him. The recovery team manned its stations. Lieutenant Kayten had no role to play. He remained by the rail in his bathing suit as the ship backed down to coast beside a body dead in the water.

"Oh God," he thought with a sudden dread. "Please, God, don't let it be Chuck. Don't let it be Chuck." The war in that moment became real. Until then all the strikes going into the North had been exercises, no more than training. In that moment the bombs became real. Screams became real. Terror became real. "Please, God, don't let it be Chuck." The Phantoms became real. The airman, dead in the water, real. He was not Chuck, but he was broken, and dead, and ever so real.

The next day, during his Sabbath, he wrote his Rabbi. "I don't know what I'm doing here. Yesterday we fished a dead man out of the sea. The war didn't become real until yesterday. It was only images on a radar screen. I don't know what we're doing here. I don't know anything at all. I don't know what to do. I don't remember the last time I cried. I'm crying now, and I don't know what to do."

At the end of the month Lieutenant Kayten's destroyer steamed into Hong Kong harbor for R&R. The festival of Passover was to begin that evening. One synagogue was listed in the phone book; one call was all he needed. "I am a Jew," he explained, "a United States Navy officer. My ship has just come out of the Gulf of Tonkin. I need a place at a *seder* table this evening. Can you help me?"

"Yes." The answer was immediate and unequivocal.

Before sunset a taxi brought him to the synagogue, an awesome classical edifice. He wore civilian clothes, a jacket and tie, and sat with the men through the service. A word to the Rabbi led to an introduction to a family—father, mother, and college-age daughter. Their home was an apartment high on the Victoria hillside.

His host was American, the manager of Asian operations for a major corporation, his wife French of Moroccan birth, and his daughter a student at Berkeley, home for the holiday. They read the *Haggadah,* the Passover *seder* service, in English and sang the songs in Hebrew. The songs were Ashkenazi, familiar European Jewish melodies Michael remembered. The foods were Moroccan and strange to his palate. But the *matzah,* the flat bread of freedom, and the sweet red wine were the same.

"You've been to Vietnam?" the daughter asked.

"The Gulf of Tonkin. The waters off of Vietnam, not Vietnam itself."

"What do you do there?"

Michael explained.

"You shouldn't be there." The parents looked to quiet her.

Michael didn't ask whether she was referring to him in particular, or to his country.

After dinner they sat in the living room overlooking the harbor. His ship floated at anchor, tiny so far below.

At another time he would have invited the daughter aboard for dinner in the wardroom, but his ship was at war. Even in port his ship was at war, and so was he.

As for the daughter from Berkeley, no relationship was possible. There was a gulf between them. The father drove him to the dock when the time came for him to return to his ship.

"There was a gulf between them."

Stephanie heard the echoes within the words. Sidney knew what was going on. The story was as much for her, for them, as for the students.

Why hadn't Sidney ever told that story before? Perhaps it was her own story of Rivie and the Rabbi's son that opened the way to Moshe and the gulf. Her stories were doing something. They were having an effect. Where they would go, what they might stimulate in Sidney, what they might stimulate in her, she did not know, but she was encouraged by the process.

"Let's return to the living room," she suggested. "We need a different setting for the next collection of stories."

CHAPTER 2

"The Navy had wrung the laughter out of Michael," Sidney said. "He knew what was happening from the outset, but knowledge was not enough to prevent damage. Day after day, week after week, month after month, it wore him down. But it did not kill him. His Sabbath kept a spark alive."

A Name

After leaving the service, Michael went to Israel to experience and to learn. He wanted to experience a Sabbath that would last an entire day. He wanted to learn what was running the clock of the universe. There had to be more than electricity behind it. Electricity provided him little comfort.

The flight from New York had been seventeen hours, including an unscheduled stop in Athens. When he landed in Israel, an exhausted and irritable Michael was shunted aside into a small room for an interview.

"You are Jewish?" the bearded man behind the desk asked.

"I am Jewish," Michael agreed, hearing the question more as a statement of fact.

"Your name is Kayten? What was it originally?"

"My name? My name is Kayten. Michael Kayten."

"But originally, before you changed it. What was it?"

"My name has always been Michael Kayten. I've never changed it."

"But your father, he changed it?"

"My father is Marvin Kayten. He never changed his name."

"Your grandfather then?"

"What is this with my name?" Michael looked about the room for relief. He had expected no such confrontation. Why had they not just stamped his passport and directed him to Tel Aviv?

"You are Jewish?" the man began again, after but the slightest pause. Sweat stained the pits of his short-sleeved white shirt.

"I am Jewish," Michael agreed once more, aware of his own perspiration.

"You were Bar Mitzvah?"

"Of course I was Bar Mitzvah." A ceiling fan circulated above at a ridiculously low speed.

"Do you know what your Jewish name is?"

"Of course I know what it is. *Moshe ben Hershel.*"

"Good." The man paused to write on his forms. Without looking up he asked, "Now, your last name. What was it, do you think? Katzenberg? Katinsky?"

"Kayten!" Michael insisted, sharply enough to draw the man's eyes up from the papers.

"Katan," the man said, pronouncing it ka-*tahn,* with the accent on the last syllable.

"No, *Kay*ten." Michael shifted the accent back to the first syllable.

The bearded man pushed his chair from the desk and adjusted the large black *kipah* to a more prominent place on his head. "Young man, I'm writing here the name by which you will be known in Israel. If I write down *Kay*ten, Ka*tan,* it doesn't matter. Everyone here will pronounce it Ka*tan.*" His attention turned again to his forms. When he finished, he presented Michael with a small blue book. "Welcome home, Mo-*sheh* Ka-*tahn.*"

Moshe Katan left the airport with his new name and ten Israeli *lirot,* a gift from the government in lieu of transportation. He had no idea why the government owed him transportation. He slept through the day at a hotel in Tel Aviv and boarded a bus the next morning for Netanya.

Engagement

The romance stories had been Stephanie's for some time. The words had become comfortable, familiar. Comfortable and familiar no longer suited her purpose. Comfortable and familiar were not conducive to learning or growth.

She paused to consider her stories. In a flash she saw they were filled with angels and archetypes. But what romance wasn't? Even her own, she admitted.

Coleridge was the angel who had brought Stephanie and Sidney together, at a seminar by someone famous whose name she could not remember, at University College London in Bloomsbury. By that time Sidney had shifted his studies to literature, and Stephanie was in her junior year abroad from Tufts. This famous person was giving a boring lecture on Coleridge and his genius. Sidney was sitting next to her. She heard him mutter, "Not so much genius as opium." The lecturer heard him also.

"Would you mind explaining that?" he challenged.

"Opium," Sidney repeated. "I suspect much of his poetry came not from himself, but from some source beyond himself, when he was under the influence of opium. We see it in his visions . . ."

A dialogue had ensued, Sidney holding down the more interesting side of it. Granted, Coleridge used opium, but did that diminish his talent in any way, or enhance it? And if enhance it, should we not all use opium to enhance whatever talent we might have?

Sidney quoted some lines to reinforce a point:

In Xanadu did Kubla Khan a stately pleasure dome decree, where Alph, the sacred river ran . . .

"Hebrew!" Stephanie interjected. "Alph, the sacred river. Alph, from the letter *ALEPH* in Hebrew, the first letter of the Hebrew alphabet."

Sidney stopped to consider Stephanie, seated to his left.

"My point exactly," he said. "Coleridge was unlikely to know Hebrew, and here a Hebrew word, coming out of a trance state, into one of his poems. My question is, where does such material come from? Is the writer responsible, or does it come from beyond the writer?"

Coleridge had been the angel. The seminar done, Sidney turned to Stephanie to ask if she knew Hebrew. "Only the alphabet," she admitted. "*ALEPH* is the first letter."

"It's a beginning," he said. "Would you like to have lunch? A picnic in Hyde Park, perhaps? We can get something on the way."

That way had been an education. They walked to Oxford Street and turned toward the park. At Oxford Circus Stephanie stepped off the curb looking for oncoming traffic to the left instead of the right. Sidney pulled her back. "I'm still not used to it," she said.

"Let's walk through Selfridge's," Sidney suggested. "It will be good for our imagination, if nothing else."

They walked through fragrances, women's accessories, and the men's department.

"Mr. Lee," a man spoke from behind them. "We haven't seen you in some time."

"James," Sidney said. "Forgive me, we're just passing through."

They kept walking. "You buy your clothes here?" Stephanie asked.

"Not recently," Sidney answered.

Behind the men's department were fine foods, the finest. Smoked salmon and caviar in all of their varieties. "For the imagination," Sidney repeated.

"Not for me," Stephanie added, looking at the prices.

They continued through Selfridge's into Marks & Spencer. There were foods there also, fine, but not quite so fine.

"Here," Sidney said, making a collection of day-old delectables. "Marked down, but still delicious."

It was delicious, Stephanie remembered. When she and Sidney returned to London years later, well able to afford the delicacies at Selfridge's, they still collected the day-old delectables at Marks & Spencer for their picnics in Hyde Park.

She began speaking the stories of Rivkah's romance even as she heard her own stories echoing inside.

Rivkah noticed Moshe before he noticed her. She was in the doorway of the *ulpan* and saw him step down from the bus, bags in hand. She wrote of it in a letter to her parents a few weeks later:

"It was clear at the outset he had a mission. He wasn't escaping from anything. Almost everybody else here is leaving behind bad memories, running away from one situation or another. They think by coming to Israel they leave it all behind and can start with a clean slate, but of course, they can't. They think they leave their baggage at home, but it catches up with them later. Moshe was different. When he stepped off the bus, he brought his baggage with him. All of it. He wasn't ashamed of any of it. He wasn't running away. He was running toward something as fast as he could go. He generated excitement. I wanted to meet him, to find out more about him.

"Sharon, of course, will want to know what he looks like. Tell her to think of Robert Redford, but Jewish, shorter and heavier. He has sandy hair, beautiful green eyes. She'd kill to have lashes like his. A mustache, but he's growing a beard to go with it. He wears khaki a lot, maybe things left over from the Navy. So what if he doesn't look like Robert Redford?"

Moshe was certain he had noticed Rivkah first. He thought she was one of the Israeli staff, she was so comfortable in her surroundings.

At dinner he tried to sit next to her without realizing she was trying to sit next to him. They both failed. A woman from Sweden squeezed between them and began talking at once, first to Rivkah, then to Moshe, and back and forth. When she left at last the exasperation both Rivkah and Moshe shared became a ground for immediate intimacy.

In later years they remembered the woman and always mentioned her when they told of that initial meeting, but she was always the "woman from Sweden." Neither one of them could recall her name.

34

When the woman from Sweden had departed leaving the two of them side by side, Moshe looked to Rivkah's finger and saw there a Turkish puzzle ring. "Is that one of those magical rings a woman wears, a puzzle ring, which, if a man solves it, he solves the secret to her heart?"

Of all of the opening lines she had experienced, in her high-school years in Baltimore and in her college years at Brown, none had been so stilted, so dramatic, so honest. "Yes," she said, smiling. "Would you like to try to solve it?"

She removed the ring from her finger. It fell out of its intricate unity into a chain of four interconnected rings. Moshe held the chain between himself and the light, examined the nature of each of the rings, and, with the slightest hesitation, placed circle to circle and wove the rings together into a single entity.

He held her hand, put the ring on her finger.

"That was quick," she said, her heart pounding. "I hadn't expected that. That was very quick."

Words

Moshe's name had been Michael. Rivkah's name had been Rebecca. It was not Michael and Rebecca who met in Israel. It was Moshe and Rivkah.

Rivkah was comfortable in her name. Her family had deep ties to Israel and to Conservative Jewish organizations in Baltimore. Her father had been president of the synagogue, a position that kept him away from home nearly every night for two years. It was important, he said, because of his business. During those years she had been Rebecca at home, but when she escaped to camp, she rejoiced in being Rivkah.

Moshe had no such camping experience. Everything was new to him. His parents in Newton gave money to the United Jewish Appeal, but there was no Israeli art on the walls, no affinity for Israeli culture. Rivkah's parents had visited the land many times. Moshe's parents spoke about visiting Israel but spent their vacations on cruises in the Caribbean.

Rivkah had learned to dislike the synagogue. She thought it a vaulted space suspended on egos. To Rivkah the synagogue was a building. Moshe's experience had been not with the building or the structure that supported it, but with the rabbis, the only source he had for a particular kind of exchange.

Rivkah joked that the word *rabbi* derived from the word *robe*. Moshe understood the joke, but didn't appreciate it. When Moshe wrote to his Rabbi, he didn't envision him wearing a robe.

Rivkah had taken Hebrew classes from early on, Hebrew she learned in the synagogue sharpened by her summer experiences. Moshe had learned as much as he could from tapes and books in the months before the program began. He had started his studies aboard ship and considered ways of convincing the Navy to send him to the language school in Monterey. His fellow officers took to calling him the rabbi some six years before he was ordained.

Moshe and Rivkah sat together for the placement exam. Both placed in the second level. Rivkah was at first upset; she thought she could study in the third level. Moshe was at first upset; he thought he was not ready for the second level. When they discovered they had been assigned to the same class, neither was upset at all.

Moshe and Rivkah spoke Hebrew as much as they could, in the city and with each other. It was torture at first. Rivkah was much more determined than Moshe. For him Hebrew was only a means to an end. For Rivkah the language was an end in itself. She had dreamed of being fluent, of dancing through Israel with the music and the language of the land.

The energy they expended in the learning of Hebrew bound them together. Their inability to express themselves adequately in a new language masked the differences between them.

They walked hand in hand by the Orthodox bathing beach, unaware of the disdainful glances thrown their way for their public show of affection in a religious neighborhood. Their clumsy Hebrew could hardly express the passion in their hearts. Their hands conveyed much more. They fell in love through their fingertips.

If they had been able to speak to each other in clear language, they might not have fallen in love at all.

Again Stephanie kept her head down, not looking at Sidney. In the past the romance of Rivkah and Moshe had been idyllic. That last sentence was new. It had surprised her, and perhaps astonished him, but she did not look to see.

God Language

Moshe was determined to learn the language of the scriptures and the liturgy. He joined the *minyan,* the prayer assembly, at the *ulpan.* They embraced him along with the others who came to learn. They instructed him in the use of *tallit* and *tefillin*. He struggled to wrap his lips around the words of the morning, afternoon, and evening services.

A month into his studies, he presented himself at a nearby *yeshivah* and professed his desire to learn. The *rosh yeshivah* listened politely and paired him with a teenager who was fluent in English. Three nights a week they learned together. Moshe began to understand the idiom of the Talmud. The teenager was curious to learn the idiom of America. The learning ceased at ten o'clock when a student came forward to don a large *tallit* and begin the evening service. It was there Moshe learned the sweetness of the prayer that comes out of study. Already close to God through attachment to Torah, it was but three small steps forward to stand before the Throne of Glory.

Moshe learned also how to learn. The learning in the *yeshivah* was done in pairs. Forty students might be learning, in twenty pairs, speaking, singing, even shouting the text back and forth across a narrow table. Each student had ears only for his partner. There was no rest, no lapse in attention, not when one was being challenged and then becoming the challenger. A teacher patrolled the aisles between the tables, not to scold, but to help with a difficulty when a study pair's argument came to a halt. That technique of learning would eventually serve Moshe as much as the learning itself.

Moshe and Rivkah were in each other's company everywhere, except at the *yeshivah*. Only men argued with each other across the narrow tables. Moshe described his experience to Rivkah with regret that she could not join him there, but Rivkah had no regret. It wasn't for Talmud that she had come to Israel, but for the language, the music, the dance, the culture. The people.

The *minyan* at the *ulpan* was also Orthodox. The women who chose to attend remained in the rear even though there was no *mehitzah*, no physical barrier to separate the men from the women. One afternoon Moshe was the first to arrive in the large room that housed the *minyan*. The big prayer book used by the leader of prayer was open on the podium to the afternoon service. Moshe approached and began to learn from the large type, unaware the rest of the *minyan* had seeped in behind him.

"*Nu,* Moshe?" one of the men said, and added in Hebrew, "are you going to begin, or are you going to keep us waiting all afternoon?"

Moshe led his first service. He read slowly and made many mistakes. No one hurried him. No one expressed the least impatience or displeasure. When he finished, they clapped him on the back, and said, "*Yosher koach.*" He had done as well as he could with the strength and expertise available to him at the moment. No one could have asked for anything more.

Moshe would have liked Rivkah to have been there, in the women's section, to see him lead his first service, but prayer was not a delight for Rivkah as it was for him, and Rivkah had little tolerance for a women's section.

Intimacy

On *Shabbat,* after services, Moshe and Rivkah walked the beach. They carried their lunch with them and ate by the Mediterranean in silence, engulfed in the history of the land. They sensed the tides of Roman legions coming ashore.

Moshe spoke of his prior life, when he was Michael Kayten at MIT. He spoke of math as a language but could not excite her in its fluency. "It is the universal language, more than Esperanto could ever be." Rivkah spoke of Becky Shapiro, dancing at the JCC, eloquent in her Israeli dance, expressing grace in sentences of motion Moshe could not follow.

Lieutenant Michael Kayten had his say. He shared the exhilaration of navigating a ship across the Pacific, of standing on the wing of the bridge of a destroyer alone with a myriad stars and the phosphorescence rippling back from the bow wave. Rebecca Shapiro spoke of a broken heart when she was not offered a part in her high-school play, her fear of rejection when she extended herself in drama at Brown. "I had a small part," she said, "but it was enough."

They traveled together. The *ulpan* sent them for a week on a *kibbutz,* a communal agricultural settlement not far from the Jordanian border. Rivkah worked the fields, picking peppers; Moshe worked on security, digging trenches around the perimeter. In the evening, exhausted, they wrapped themselves in each other and made love under palm trees laden with dates.

They ascended to Jerusalem together, to visit the school where Moshe hoped to study, to eat *hummus* and *felafel* in the farmer's market, to wander the old city in awe, to explore the recesses of the *shuk* in search of bargains. Moshe found for Rivkah amber beads strung with silver bells. Rivkah searched in vain for just the right gift for Moshe. "It's not here," she lamented, but assured him, "I will find it."

In the mystical city of Safed she discovered a large shawl, patterned after a painting of a popular primitive artist, birds and trees in ranks rising from the ends of the fabric toward the clear sky at the center. "It's beautiful," Moshe told her. "You will look beautiful in it."

"No," she shook her head. "It's for you! You will look beautiful in it."

She bought threads to convert the shawl into a *tallit,* and together they tied the *tzitzit,* the intricate ritual macrame, on the four corners. Moshe had a prayer shawl unique to him. Rivkah smiled from the rear of the room when he wrapped himself in his *tallit* for the first time in the *minyan.* "You are a lucky man," they told him, and pounded him on the back, as if the *tallit* needed breaking in.

In Haifa, in the gardens of the Bahai Temple, high on the hill overlooking the sea, Moshe spoke of marriage. He was nervous about it. They had wrapped themselves in a cocoon of common experiences, traveling the land. He spoke of that image in his proposal, expressing his hope a butterfly might emerge from their cocoon. She was patient, listening until he could get his words out right, and then, when his intent became clear, burst out in full color. They embraced fiercely. Tears flowed. They had new worlds to talk about.

"We have to tell our parents," Moshe said.

"Mine already know," Rivkah responded.

They walked together in silence while Moshe digested the implications of that.

In the previous tellings Stephanie had ended the story there. To continue would be difficult.

Marvin and Barbara Kayten were surprised but happy to hear of the engagement. "Let us speak with her," they said. "We can't wait to meet you!" they told her. "We are so happy for you."

When Michael took the phone they said, "You never even told us about her. What is she like? Why didn't you write us about her? We have to call her parents."

"They're excited," Michael apologized to Rivkah afterward. "I was afraid to write home about you. I didn't want them to get their hopes up. If something happened between us and we split up, I didn't want them to be disappointed. They're really excited. When I went into the Navy, they were sure I wasn't going to marry a Jewish girl."

Sam and Gloria Shapiro knew the call was coming. Only the timing was a surprise. "Becky's written us all about you," they said. "We are so eager to meet you. You must be very, very special."

When Rivkah took the phone they said, "We already have tickets. We'll be arriving in Israel next Thursday. Tell him we love him already."

For Stephanie the last words were lip biters.

When she and Sidney had decided to marry, Sidney hadn't called home at all. His family had already cast him aside when he had announced he would study literature instead of business, that he had chosen to go his own way rather than continue the family tradition. Sidney had known what his family would do. It came as no surprise. He had known he would be on his own, without support, and had welcomed it quite consciously.

Stephanie had been so naive. She had no idea.

She had written home, effusive in her descriptions of London and the Tufts program abroad. She had written of Sidney. Her mother had written back to express her father's concern, but she had paid no attention. Sidney wasn't one of their people. He wasn't Jewish. But then how Jewish was she? She had been to synagogue only twice in her life. Her father wore a *yarmulke* in the store, not because he was Jewish, but because it was good for business. They had no Jewish tradition, didn't light *Shabbos* candles, didn't celebrate the Holy Days. What was Jewish about them?

And it wasn't as if Sidney was something else. Sidney had no religious tradition. He wasn't a Catholic or a Protestant. It wasn't as if he was a *goy*, like the *goyim* her father disparaged. It wasn't as if she was marrying a *shaygetz*, like Aunt Sally's daughter did, a Catholic, in a church ceremony her parents refused to attend. Sidney wasn't Jewish, but he wasn't anything else either. He was a wonderful, sensitive, courageous man. That's what she wrote in her letters.

When she called home to tell them she wanted to marry Sidney, her father said, "If you do that, you are dead to me. If you marry him, your mother and I never want to hear from you again. It will be as if you never lived, as if you were never our daughter. If you marry him, he has won."

"*HE* has won." Hitler. Hitler would have won. The name Hitler had never been spoken in their home, but Stephanie knew who *HE* was.

She and Sidney married the following week.

She was twenty years old and married. She had her National Merit scholarship and could work in the library when she returned to Medford, if they returned to Medford. Sidney thought he might continue his graduate studies at Harvard. He had so many languages—Chinese, German, French, Spanish—and such an elegant English, he could make his living anywhere, translating, tutoring, while he pursued his degrees.

Her father's words had pushed her into the marriage, left her no choice. She

40

would have waited to marry, maybe not married at all. There were cultural differences, but in the end, they were alike, both cast off by their families, and that bond overcame all difficulties.

For so many years, Stephanie thought. For so many years.

A month after the wedding she wrote her mother the first letter, a long letter, and waited anxiously for a reply. A month later, she wrote again.

Al wrote back that the letters had been delivered. When her mother came into his store for a magazine, if he had a letter, he slipped it in. Her mother never said a word, not a word. Her husband didn't like Al, didn't want her going to the store.

Stephanie kept writing. After four letters she knew her mother would not respond, could not respond, but Stephanie did not stop writing. She wrote everything she thought her mother might like to know. After a year, she wrote more to herself than to her mother, letting her mother eavesdrop on her thoughts and concerns, but she wished for a response, a dialogue.

She'd had one, Stephanie realized, an internal dialogue. When she had sifted through the letters in the recent weeks, she had detected two voices, her own, and the imagined response of her mother.

It was not always approving.

Jerusalem

Before continuing with the Jerusalem stories, Stephanie cautioned, "You have to hear these stories in a different key. In the last story they were not married. In this story they are married. In the last story they were in Netanya. In this story they are in Jerusalem. There is a change in status and a change in location."

After the wedding in Baltimore and a honeymoon in Bermuda, Rivkah and Moshe returned to Israel, to Jerusalem, for a year of work and study. They found a two-room apartment on a hill overlooking the Hebrew University. They had a small refrigerator, a stove, hot water from a tank on the roof, but no central heat. During the summer and late fall, they lived in luxury, by Israeli standards. During the winter they would have traded all their amenities for some warmth.

Moshe enrolled in the seminary. His Hebrew was sufficient to place him in the highest level, intended for the third-year students who had come to Israel for accelerated training. Moshe struggled to keep pace.

The teachers were intrigued by this stranger who was older than his fellows but new to the work. One took him under his wing and guided him through the grammar of biblical Hebrew. "You are devoting so much of your time to me," Moshe told him. "Let me pay you something."

His teacher responded, "Someday someone will come to you wanting to learn the grammar of the Bible. When you teach him, that will be payment enough for me."

Rivkah worked at the Israel Museum. Her father, an art dealer in Baltimore, was well connected. Connections were everything in Israel. He arranged for her to assist in the development of programs to attract American art collectors and dealers to seminars at the museum. Her work brought her into contact with these Americans on one hand, with the finest artists, artisans, and art historians of Israel on the other.

She would have much preferred to have been hired for her own talent and skill rather than because of her father's influence, but she knew the system. No influence, no job. That's the way it was.

They saw American movies with Hebrew subtitles. They found their favorite restaurants in the old city, others in the Arab neighborhoods. They discovered coffee shops, *felafel* stands, *baklava* bakeries. They felt safe wherever they walked.

One afternoon, in the winter, they reached out from under the blankets to answer the phone. Barbara and Marvin wanted to know if they were all right. "Why shouldn't we be all right?" Had the rocket landed anywhere near them? "What rocket?" A *ketusha* had been fired by a terrorist. It had landed in an open field a mile away. The story made the national news in America, but they heard of it only the next day in Jerusalem. Such events failed to slow the pace of their life. Their illusion of safety was *ketusha*-proof.

Rivkah and Moshe could not see enough, hear enough, smell, taste, or feel enough of Jerusalem. They walked the walls, the roads, the lanes, the alleys, the paths and slopes of the city. They elbowed and pushed their way onto buses to carry them when they tired of walking. They explored and experienced every quarter, every neighborhood, every national and religious enclave. Jewish, Coptic, Catholic, Muslim, Armenian, Persian, Italian, Yemenite, German, Ethiopian, Moroccan—each had its own incense, flavor, color, texture, and sound. Rivkah and Moshe imbibed and absorbed everything Jerusalem had to offer. They became like semipermeable membranes to the compounds of the city. A holy osmosis drew Jerusalem into their souls, and on this heady nourishment the young marriage thrived.

Stephanie struggled for a moment to coordinate the times. Were she and Sidney at Harvard when Rivkah and Moshe were in Jerusalem? Or was that the year they were still in Medford? The order of events had become blurred.

Sidney was waiting for her. She shook her head, no more stories to insert at the moment.

Reb Hayim

Sidney assumed the narrative. It was his prerogative to introduce Reb Hayim and his teachings because he had learned from Reb Hayim and Stephanie had not, but also because he had an affinity for Reb Hayim Stephanie did not share.

During one of the early story cycles Reb Hayim himself, quite unexpectedly, had come to experience a lesson. He had been traveling in the States, called the Havurah to learn what was happening, and asked if he might visit. How could they refuse him? They feared the *rebbe* might be a distraction, but Reb Hayim sat unnoticed, in jeans, sandals, and a sweatshirt. He was not the only one with a beard, even if his was substantially the longest and whitest. The knitted *yarmulke* he had chosen to wear instead of his orthodox black velour was as colorful as those worn by the other men and some of the women. Reb Hayim had asked not to be introduced, and his presence passed unnoticed.

An artist Rivkah had come to know through her work at the museum invited them to join him for a *Shabbat* afternoon in Meah Shearim, the Jewish religious neighborhood, to hear a special teacher. On *Shabbat* one walked in Meah Shearim. No cars moved. No radios sounded. No business was transacted. Rivkah dressed modestly, her hair and shoulders covered, her dress down to her ankles.

Tzvi, the artist, knew the neighborhood well. He had been born into it, then left to pursue his calling. His talent was prodigious, but not to be developed in Meah Shearim. Graphic art and Orthodox religious principles were in conflict. The neighborhood had not cast him out. It was he who had left it, religious still. He followed his talent. When he returned home, he took care not to antagonize the families who had nourished him.

"Reb Hayim is a remarkable teacher," Tzvi told Rivkah. "You and Moshe will feel comfortable learning with him." He led them through the convoluted paths, through doorways into courtyards, up stairs, and into an open room. Reb Hayim Ostracher raised his hands when he saw the artist enter and stood to welcome and embrace him.

"How good to see you, Tzvi," he said, beard to beard in embrace. To the assembly he said, "You know, the work Tzvi does, the work you don't approve of, it does more to hasten the coming of the Messiah than you can possibly imagine. He reaches with his art to the remote corners of the Earth and raises from there sparks no other can touch. I have seen this happen with my own eyes in the fancy galleries of Paris, New York, and San Francisco."

"It's okay, Reb Hayim," Tzvi said softly to his teacher. "I am comfortable here. They know what I do, and they always welcome me back."

"It's good that it's okay, Tzvi. But someone has to tell them of the impact you make in the world. If not me, then who?"

"Reb Hayim, these are my friends," Tzvi presented Rivkah and Moshe. "Rivkah makes my work easier at the museum. Moshe is learning to be a Rabbi."

"Welcome," he said to each of them. He shook Moshe's hand firmly. Rivkah knew to keep her hands at her sides. "Join us please."

He seated Moshe close to the table. Rivkah found a seat behind her husband. Reb Hayim lifted a glass, sipped, and began to chant.

It was the first time Moshe had heard a *niggun,* a repetitive tune that began simply and grew in momentum until it tended to overwhelm. It resonated in his body, heart, and mind. It was awesome, wonderful! Once started, how it could stop was beyond imagining. It might never have stopped, had there not been such a great desire to learn. After the *niggun* came words of Torah.

Rivkah was uncomfortable sitting behind. Only men sat at the table, the few women present back against the walls. She also heard the *niggun* and could not deny its hypnotic power, but only the men sang. The other women did not so much as open their mouths, so she kept hers shut as well.

The teaching was mostly in Yiddish. From time to time Reb Hayim would look toward Moshe and speak in Hebrew. Moshe had no Yiddish, but the Hebrew was enough for him to understand something about Abraham and a World of Creation. The teaching was from a book called *Sefer Yetzirah,* of combinations of letters and numbers, the foundations upon which all worlds were based. Reb Hayim spoke of the Garden of Eden, the expulsion, the generation of Noah and the Tower of Babel. The process of redemption, he said, began with Abraham. *Sefer Yetzirah,* which Abraham had authored,

44

contained the secrets to hasten redemption. Moshe grasped only the barest outline of the discourse. Its pace was fast, the language strange, the concepts without definition.

"I want to speak at your seminary," Reb Hayim told Moshe when he and Rivkah were preparing to leave. "Tzvi can tell you how to reach me. I will be back in Jerusalem the beginning of next month. Arrange it for me, please. I'll teach again what I taught here, but so you can follow it."

Such *hutzpah,* Moshe thought, for Reb Hayim to assume he had not understood the lesson. And some chance, dressed like that, Moshe would invite Reb Hayim to speak at the seminary. Any student who wanted exposure to the likes of Reb Hayim could do what Moshe himself had done: venture through the streets and courtyards, accept the neighborhoods as quaint rather than filthy, and sit for hours listening to a mixture of Yiddish and European-accented Hebrew, absorbing the atmosphere if not the meaning of the words.

The Land

Stephanie knew the land better than Sidney, so this intermezzo fell to her. It reminded her of the many forays she and Sidney had made into New Hampshire and Vermont.

Rivkah and Moshe went on a bus to Sinai. It was an adventure, replete with cans of water, rifles for guard duty, metal screens to put under the drive wheels of the truck should it bog down in sand or mud. They traced the history of the Six Day War rather than the forty-year trek of Moses and the children of Israel through the wilderness. It was a Zionist expedition, not a religious one.

They met with the monks at the base of the mountain, paid a tourist's homage to the bones of centuries grinning at them in the charnel house. Long-unused refectory tables stood in silence like a *minyan* at prayer. These were the real thing, in their intended place, Rivkah knew. She thought it good they should remain untouched, standing where they were in eternal loneliness, but even better if she could a find a way to take one home.

Early in the morning, they climbed Sinai to its summit. Moshe imagined the finger of God cutting the tablets out of the face of the mountain; Rivkah recalled the ultimate moment of Cecil B. DeMille's cinematic theophany. The

45

magic of the trip, the real miracle, came in the waters of the Red Sea, near Eilat, when, with scuba tanks on and a guide to lead them, they parted the seas to dive on reefs teeming with life and color. Underwater the wonder of God's creation washed through them in waves. Undeniable, the presence of God seemed many times more magnified than on the heights of Sinai. Their common experience underwater dissolved for the moment all their differences above.

This expedition encouraged them to broaden the scope of their explorations. They climbed the cliffs of Ein Gedi and penetrated the caves where the Dead Sea community lived its monastic life. Mountain goats grazed near them unperturbed, almost in touching distance. They floated on the surface of the Dead Sea. Rivkah coated herself with Dead Sea mud supposed to have magical powers for healing. Moshe was not a man for mud or magic. They trekked through wadis and visited Bedouin tents in the desert near Beer Sheva. On a Thursday morning, at the Bedouin market, they bargained with good-natured spirits and bought primitive eye shadow and a Bedouin dress for Rivkah.

Even as Stephanie spoke she was reliving hikes through the gorges and mountains of New England, trekking across the bridges that covered the profound differences between herself and Sidney. How hard they had worked to build a foundation of shared experiences! Then she got pregnant. The hiking, the trekking became less important. They had something to share, undeniably and uniquely theirs.

Creation

Sidney continued the story of Tzvi and Reb Hayim.

Passover came and was gone. Rivkah cajoled Moshe to join her for an evening in Tel Aviv.

"I don't like the city," he complained. "Every time I go, I come back depressed."

"Please, Moshe. For Tzvi. You've never seen his work, and this is an important opening. He wanted it to be in Tel Aviv."

He knew his grumbling would be fruitless. It was a given he would accompany her. Tel Aviv suffered from an American blight that was spreading and threatening to overwhelm the emerging Israeli culture. Moshe preferred to keep his distance.

The *sherut* left them off by the gallery and continued on its way with its other passengers. Moshe wore a white shirt, open at the collar, formal wear for the State of Israel. Rivkah wore pants and a blouse. They were properly dressed and mingled easily with the restrained mélange of art aficionados who wandered between trays of cheese and wine to ponder paintings and trade poignant remarks.

"It's like a different world," Moshe commented.

"It's like being back home," Rivkah agreed.

Moshe turned his attention from the people to the paintings and knew the trip had been worth the descent from Jerusalem. The paintings were constructed of the bodies of Hebrew letters writhing in ecstasy in their desire and urgency to fulfill the will of their Creator.

Moshe searched for and found Tzvi, besieged in a corner, defending his humility from a bombardment of praise. He wanted to thank him for revealing the letters, for opening doors into the work of creation, but did not want to pester him with words or abuse combinations of letters in banal remarks. The intimacy he had discovered, the secrets he suspected in the portrayal of the letters, he accepted in trust. He caught the artist's eye, raised his palms in a gesture of awe, respect, appreciation. The artist nodded and resumed his defense.

"They're wonderful, aren't they?" Rivkah said as she held his arm.

Moshe roused himself from his reverie enough to nod.

A heavy hand fell on his shoulder and snapped him to attention.

"So, it's Moshe and his Rivkaleh!"

They spun around to see Reb Hayim looming in black, an amulet on a silver chain around his neck, a smile on his face and a challenge in his eyes. He looked not like a *rebbe* in Meah Shearim, but a hippie from the Haight-Ashbury in San Francisco.

"You owe me an invitation, you two. I'm very serious. I want an opportunity to speak at your seminary. I know they don't want to hear from me. I want to speak there anyway. Moshe, arrange it, please. Rivkah, make him do it."

"I can't make him do anything," Rivkah protested.

Reb Hayim laughed. "I'll be away for two weeks. I'm going to Moscow and Vienna. When I come back, please. Any opportunity at all. I will be grateful."

He turned to leave, then turned back with a question for Moshe. "You understand why Tzvi chose to show these paintings in Tel Aviv rather than Jerusalem?"

In the *sherut,* on the way home, Rivkah asked, "So what did Reb Hayim mean when he asked you about why Tzvi chose Tel Aviv over Jerusalem?"

"I'm not sure," Moshe answered. "I think it's that Jerusalem has its own holiness. It doesn't need the paintings. Tel Aviv needs them."

The Story of Creation

Moshe managed an invitation for Reb Hayim to speak on a Sunday after morning prayers. He expected the hippie from San Francisco, but Reb Hayim arrived in Hasidic garb: black hat, long black coat, white shirt without tie, black pants, white stockings. He enveloped himself in his huge *tallit* and bound himself in his *tefillin.* This was going to be more difficult than Moshe thought.

A student led the service. Reb Hayim paid no attention, *davening* to his own inner rhythm, bits of strangely accented words and discordant tunes escaping from his mouth. A Mr. Lieberman, Moshe realized, remembering the pious old man in the *shul* in Newton who prayed not so much with the congregation, but within it.

At the conclusion of the service Reb Hayim leaned over to feel the texture of Moshe's *tallit,* the one Rivkah had given him, the birds rising up from the edges. He fingered the fringes, the *tzitzit,* and nodded in approval. "Now this," he said, "is a *tallis* to be buried in."

Moshe introduced Rabbi Hayim Ostracher to the assembly of faculty and students. There had been no great eagerness in the school to invite this man to speak. Reb Hayim didn't make it any easier for Moshe with his opening words.

"I want to thank my friend Moshe for giving me this opportunity," he began.

Not a friend, Moshe thought, just an opportunity for the students to hear something new, something from a different perspective.

Reb Hayim continued, "I remember the political battles when you were trying to build this institution in Jerusalem. I must tell you, I was in favor of it. It cost me no little amount of political capital. So you owe me. I've come to collect."

He paused for reaction. When there was none, he continued. "Why was I in favor of it? Because if you had stayed only in New York, you might have had no exposure to the likes of me. Your students might never have come to *daven* in the *shuls* I *daven* in. If you do not do these things, if you do not have these experiences, then there is no real reason for you to be here in Jerusalem. You might as well have stayed in New York.

"I had promised my friend Moshe I would come and teach what I had taught on a *Shabbos* afternoon in Meah Shearim. This is what I taught, if not exactly as I taught it.

"Do you know the four creation stories? You know how God created the world in six days and rested on the seventh? That's the 'P' fragment. I think that's how you call it, you who are masters of the documentary theory."

He could have said nothing to cause greater surprise. To hear that he had supported the building of their institution in Jerusalem was astonishing. The Orthodox community had been adamant, at times militant, in opposition. To hear from the mouth of a *Hasid* any reference to the documentary theory of the authorship of the Torah was beyond astonishing. The documentary theory attributed the Torah to four different writers, in four different periods, and undermined every notion of divine revelation, a notion central to Orthodoxy.

"That," he continued, "is the first creation story. Then you have your 'J' account, Adam and Eve in the Garden of Eden. Creation story number two. You can be sure I didn't teach it like this in Meah Shearim."

Laughter broke the tension. Reb Hayim was speaking their language. Resistance disappeared in spite of his dress.

"Now there are two more creation stories. I know you don't often think of them as such. But there is the story of the generation of Noah, and then the generation of the Tower of Babel. Four creation stories altogether.

"In the first God creates our world of nature, puts Adam into it, and gives him the power to give names. That's a sharing with Adam of divine power, an investment in Adam of a divine attribute. God takes some of His stuff and puts it into exile, into space and time in the form of Adam. What does this Adam do? He complains. He says, 'It's not working for me out here. I'm lonely. Take me back.' God doesn't want to take him back. He puts him to sleep, divides him into two, and sets him back into the garden. The first rebellion against the exile from God is Adam's complaint. It fails, because God has a solution for him. A partner. The original Adam, who was male and female combined, is now separated further from God. No longer a oneness. Adam becomes a twoness. For me this is the end of the first creation story."

49

Reb Hayim paused and examined the face of each student for questions. When there were none, he continued. "Creation story number two, the rebellion of Eve. Eve sees how far she and Adam have been put into exile, how far they are away from God. She wants to get back. How does she do it? She tries to eat her way back. She eats the fruit of the tree of knowledge, gives Adam some to eat. What does God do? God puts them further into exile. He doesn't want them back so quick. He boots them out of the Garden of Eden before they can eat from the Tree of Life and cancel out creation. He puts an angel with a sword at the gate to make sure they can't get back.

"Why doesn't He want them back?"

It was not clear if the question was rhetorical or an answer was expected. Reb Hayim paused, closed his eyes, and swayed gently in his chair. "Imagine this. Imagine you had just built a building for a million dollars and had it fully leased. It was intended to provide income for you and your family for the next fifty years. What if someone came to you the day after it was built and said he'd like to buy the building from you. He'd give you a million and one dollars. Do you want to sell it to him? Look, you'd make a dollar profit! But that's not what you want out of it. You chase him away and say, come back in fifty years when the building has lived up to the purpose I created it for.

"So God has a big investment in this universe. He's not looking for a dollar profit. Adam complains. God finds a solution. He doesn't let him back home. Eve rebels. God kicks them out. God says to the man and woman, 'Do some work. Go out there and continue my work of creation.'

"Ten generations pass. The generation of Noah is an evil generation. Why are they evil? What are they doing? They are having sex with angels, that's what they're doing. Adam and Eve tried to eat their way back. The generation of Noah was trying to fornicate their way back. And God drowned their rebellion. The way you'd throw a bucket of water on some fornicating dogs, God threw a bucket of water on a fornicating generation. He saved Noah and his family and sent them further into exile."

The image was strong enough to create a stir among the students.

"And then the generation of the Tower of Babel. What were they trying to do? It wasn't that they were building a tower to climb back to heaven. Read it closely. They were creating a name for themselves. A *shem* to get back to *she-mayim*. *Shem* means name. *Shemayim,* which means heaven, may be derived from the word *shem*. It's the place of the Divine Name. So what does God do? God confuses their language and puts them further into exile, further away.

"And that was the state of the world when our father Abraham came on

50

the scene. Creation had been pushed away from God, through Adam, through Eve, through the generation of Noah, through the generation of the Tower of Babel.

"Now, what was Abraham's greatness?"

No one dared answer, but Reb Hayim heard the unspoken response.

"No, he wasn't the first to recognize there was one God. Do you think Adam didn't know there was one God? That Noah didn't know? Abraham's greatness was that he was the first to begin the process of redemption. He went out to the corners of the desert, set up his tent, and began to bring in strangers. We human beings had grown so far apart from each other, we had forgotten how to talk with each other. He begins the process of the return to God.

"It's as if God says that creation has gotten far enough away to do what it has to do. It's okay now to begin to return. So Abraham begins to develop a discipline of return. We're still developing that discipline today, trying to get it right.

"That's why it's important you have this school here in Jerusalem. You reach sparks we can't reach. You present a challenge to those in Meah Shearim. Those in Meah Shearim are a challenge to you. Some of them think they know everything and don't need to learn from anyone else how we go about this business of return. Some of you think you know everything. But some of you and some of them aren't as polarized as you might think. Some sharing can go on. We can refine each other, sharpen each other.

"So this then, I hope, is a beginning. I know the teachers with whom you can learn, who will be curious about you. I'll send you their names. Go learn with them. They may not be as willing as I am to come here. But you can go there. You will find yourselves welcome. Suspend disbelief for a while. It will be worth your expense of time and energy."

The students stirred and ventured polite questions Reb Hayim answered in kind. At the appointed time, Moshe thanked the Rabbi for visiting and sharing words of Torah and accompanied him out of the building.

On the steps Moshe stopped. "May I ask a question? I didn't want to raise it in the group."

"Surely." Reb Hayim looked up to the sun, then back to Moshe.

It was hot on the white steps, and Reb Hayim was dressed in black. "When I heard you speak the first time, you mentioned a book, *Sefer Yetzirah*. You didn't mention it here."

Reb Hayim nodded. "This wasn't the time to mention it. *Sefer Yetzirah* isn't the kind of book you study here. Have you ever heard of it before? No. But you've seen it in Tzvi's paintings. Tzvi's letters are from *Sefer Yetzirah*. The ecstasy Tzvi puts into his paintings is some of the ecstasy that our father Abraham put into *Sefer Yetzirah*."

"What's it about?"

Reb Hayim laughed. "It isn't a novel that's about something. It's one of the first texts of the Kabbalah. It describes the fabric of creation."

Moshe had another question to ask. "Did Abraham really write it?" That wasn't the question, but it served to temporize until the real question might rise to the surface.

Reb Hayim shrugged. "What do I know? Someone said he wrote it. Who am I to argue? Does it hurt anyone if I say Abraham wrote it?"

They walked down a few steps. Across the street was a kiosk where a Moroccan Jew sold *mitz eshkoliot,* cold grapefruit juice. Moshe considered buying a bottle for Reb Hayim, but wasn't sure the juice would be kosher enough. "May I ask another question?"

Reb Hayim nodded patiently.

"In the Garden of Eden, if God didn't want Adam and Eve to eat from the Tree of Life, why not just cut it down? Why leave it there and go through all the trouble of kicking them out and putting an angel at the gate to guard the way back?"

Reb Hayim stopped and looked at Moshe with respect. "Now that's a substantial question. Now that you've asked it, the answer is obvious, no?"

Moshe listened to his own question and offered an answer. "God wants us to eat from the Tree of Life. Otherwise, He would have cut it down. There is a way back."

"In due time. All in due time. Moshe, now I have a question for you. Do you like your name?"

"Which name?"

"What names do you have?"

"Michael Kayten." Moshe pronounced his English name with an American accent. "My Hebrew name is Moshe ben Hershel."

"Michael." Reb Hayim pronounced it *mee-ki-ayl*. "'One who is like God.' No, you're a little more like Moses. *Moshe.* Moshe *Katan.* A little Moses. That's you. *Moshe Katan,* my little Moses, my *Moshileh.* It's a *hutzpadik* name, but a good name for you, Moshe Katan. You know the story of Zusya? When Zusya was dying?"

"No." Now Moshe was sweating. Surely Reb Hayim must be soaking in his black coat.

"Well," Reb Hayim said, drawing out the word, in no hurry and no apparent discomfort, "Zusya was dying. He was a great saint, and his students had gathered around his bed. They saw him trembling and asked why he should tremble. Wasn't he like Moses in their generation? What did he have to fear? Zusya said to them when he would stand before the Throne of Glory, God would not ask him why he had not been more like Moses. God would ask him why he had not been more like Zusya!

"So, *Moshileh,* your name is Moshe Katan, little Moses. When you stand before the Throne of Glory, what is God going to ask you?"

In his last three weeks before leaving Jerusalem, Moshe Katan was too busy with final exams and preparations for the return to New York to give any thought at all to what God might ask him.

CHAPTER 3

The Calendar

Stephanie said, "Tradition teaches that the person who knows the Jewish calendar knows all of Judaism. The key to the Jewish calendar is *Shabbat*. The week pulses out from *Shabbat* to Wednesday and then back toward *Shabbat,* to Friday evening and Saturday. Six days we work in the world of polarity. Then we take a breath. Our souls are refreshed. We reserve a single day in the week to rest, to become one again before dividing ourselves in our work. Jews throughout the world do this.

"Except Rabbis."

The school found them a one-bedroom apartment in Riverdale. They lived in a three-story building. Many of their neighbors were Jewish. At least they had *mezzuzot* on their doorposts. The neighbors were, for the most part, older. The couple who lived next door expressed relief when they learned the Katans did not have any children, no pets either, not that pets were permitted in the building anyway.

Moshe and Rivkah awoke at 6:20 every weekday morning. Tuesdays, Wednesdays, and Thursdays he took the car to school. Tuesday nights he lectured in Queens. Wednesday and Thursday nights he taught in Westchester. Monday afternoons he served as a resource person at a Hebrew school in the city, not far from the seminary. Fridays Moshe returned early from his midmorning class. Friday afternoon he and Rivkah traveled to New Jersey together, Rabbi and Rebbitzen for the weekend. Moshe led the evening service. The congregation praised his sermons. Together they taught in the religious school on Saturday morning. Early Sunday they returned to Riverdale. Some Sundays Moshe needed to catch up with his work, though he managed to complete most of his assignments in school.

As for Rivkah, she decorated the apartment. Occasionally they stayed in New Jersey through Sunday afternoon to drive through the small antiquey towns and hunt for furniture. Rivkah had a good eye, bargained well, and the apartment in Riverdale showed the results.

Their life was so full that within a few months their marriage was courting disaster.

Paretzky

Sidney said, "Moshe had a reputation in New York that followed him from Jerusalem. He was the only student in the school on the GI Bill. One might think in a school that had become a refuge for those seeking deferrals from the Vietnam conflict, the faculty and students would shun him. Rather, it was quite the opposite. This was a man of experience and accomplishment, an officer and a gentleman, and both his peers and his teachers treated him with respect.

"Except Paretzky."

Moshe was learning Torah in the library, aware of Dr. Paretzky's presence nearby. Paretzky was Distinguished Professor of Bible, chairperson of the Translation Committee, author of several books still in print. The word was that learning Bible with Paretzky was agony. His assignments were on the order of, "Copy the book of Isaiah, all sixty-six chapters, with vowels." Moshe had managed to avoid Paretzky's courses his first semester in New York.

Paretzky paced behind him, his belly protruding between his suspenders. "Katan!"

"Yes, Dr. Paretzky."

"Do you know who *I* am?"

"Yes sir, Dr. Paretzky."

"I know who *you* are. Let's see if you're as smart as they say. Tell me, Katan, how do you spell PHARAOH?"

"PEH RESH AYIN HEY," Katan responded instantly in Hebrew.

"In *English,* Katan. In *English.* How do you spell PHARAOH in *English?"* Paretzky's voice filled the small library. When students looked up, his scowl turned them back to their books. Paretzky was on the prowl, had cornered his prey. Better Katan than themselves.

Moshe considered for a moment. "P-H-A-R-O-A-H."

"Wrong!" Paretzky shouted. "Katan, you don't know *bupkis*! It's damn well time you took a course with me!"

Moshe found the correct response at once. "I'm not ready yet, Dr. Paretzky. Next year I'll be ready." There was truth in that. He was at that time fully engaged with Hinderman.

"Pharaoh," Sidney said. "A-O-H. Not O-A-H. The word is transliterated from the Hebrew. The A is for the *AYIN.*" The blank look on the faces of the students indicated none of them were familiar with Hebrew grammar or the conventions of transliteration.

Wallpaper

Stephanie said, "The first overt sign of difficulty was the wallpaper in the kitchen."

"I can't stand it anymore," Rivkah said. "Look at it. It's coming apart up there. It's covered with grease."

Moshe made a quick calculation. "It's not a very big kitchen. We could put up new paper, if you like."

They found a light blue contact paper with a nonrepetitive pattern. "It won't matter if we make mistakes," Moshe said. "The pattern has no beginning and no ending, so it doesn't matter where we start and where we finish."

They began on a Sunday afternoon. The Giants lost to the Eagles, and the Jets defeated the Patriots before it was done.

"I still don't like it," Rivkah said, hands on hips. "I don't like the answer you gave Nate Gellman either." The non sequitur left him nonplussed. "What you told him when he asked how prayer worked. It was bullshit. I knew it was bullshit. He knew it, too, but he was too polite to say anything."

"Rivie, I don't remember what I told him."

"Well, it was bullshit."

"It was during an Ask-the-Rabbi session after services. I didn't have time to give a complete essay with footnotes. I did the best I could."

"If you couldn't answer him properly, you should have said so. That would have been better than a bullshit answer."

"I did what I could, Rivie."

"It's all a bunch of crap. You don't know how prayer works. You stand up and mouth a lot of words and call it prayer. It doesn't do anything. I don't like this paper."

She began to tear it down.

"Moshe had a great need to know," Sidney said. "He didn't know what it was he needed to know, but he knew he needed to know something. Because he didn't know where to find it, he approached each of his classes earnestly, hoping that whatever it might be, he would find it there."

Dr. Hinderman was among the last to leave Germany, rescued from the Holocaust by the seminary. He was revered worldwide for his scholarship in both Talmud and philosophy. It was Hinderman who had been trapped in the elevator during the blackout of 1965 and remained there for hours on end until power was restored.

"What did you do in the elevator during the blackout, Dr. Hinderman?" his students had asked. "Did you sit down?"

"Sit down?" Dr. Hinderman had responded. "How could I sit down? There was not a chair!"

As he ascended in that same elevator, Moshe thought of Dr. Hinderman. Where had he been trapped? Was it here between the fourth floor, Rabbinics, and the fifth floor, Bible? Or was it between second floor, Hebrew Literature and third floor, Theology?

Moshe thought of himself during the blackout. Where had he been? Mr. Kayten had been on the other side of the world during the blackout, on a destroyer in the Gulf of Tonkin. Lieutenant Michael Kayten had been trapped between a cause he didn't believe in and being without a cause.

Dr. Hinderman spoke softly and sprayed when he talked. The trick was to arrive early and sit close enough to hear but not so close as to get wet.

Moshe was in awe of Dr. Hinderman. Other students gently ridiculed the accent and the spray. Moshe wished earnestly only to understand. Dr. Hinderman taught as if no one was listening, as if no one was there to hear. Indeed, in his mind, no one was there to hear. No one at the seminary was prepared to learn philosophy as Dr. Hinderman was prepared to teach it. If that was true for philosophy, how much the more so for Talmud! Still Moshe was eager to learn. He strained to learn, suspecting there was a knowledge hidden from him that could be found nowhere else.

The time came for Moshe Katan to present in Dr. Hinderman's seminar. Moshe had labored in earnest. He had strained and pushed at the envelope of his understanding to grasp and contain the logic, the arguments, the essentials of the lesson. He spoke for forty minutes without interruption. There was silence when he was done. No student dared a question. They were, for the moment, in awe of him. They would not be the first to speak. Dr. Hinderman busied himself, cleaning his glasses.

"Katan," he said at last. "You are an *am ha-aretz*,"

A gasp erupted from around the table. *Am ha-aretz* was the Hebrew idiom for ignoramus. What had Dr. Hinderman said? "Katan, you are an ignoramus!?" After such a presentation!

"Don't be upset, Katan," Dr. Hinderman continued. "*Am ha-aretz* is a *madraygah*." Dr. Hinderman stood and left the room.

For some time the students did not move. *Madraygah* meant rank. Katan, in Dr. Hinderman's estimation was an ignoramus, but that, at least, was a rank. It was on the scale. The rest of the students weren't even on the scale.

The ignoramus sat there, his fellow students not knowing whether to congratulate him or console him.

Stephanie had heard that story from Moshe himself. It was a school story, either apocryphal or about some nameless student who had studied with Hinderman years before. Sidney from the first had transformed it into a story about Moshe.

"It is a story about Moshe," Sidney insisted when challenged.

"But Moshe told it about someone else, not about himself."

"If the story fits, wear it. The story fits Moshe, so he gets to wear it."

The story did fit, even if Sidney's logic seemed strange on first hearing. Moshe had sharpened his intellect, much as the student in the story. Such intellectual sharpening was as necessary for spiritual discipline as the sensitizing of the imagination. The story served its purpose, even if Moshe had not been the original subject. It was an exercise of Sidney's intellect and imagination to bring the story and Moshe together.

Stephanie considered her own story of Becky on the beach and Grandma Ida. That had been so much more daring, to invent a story out of whole cloth. But what did it bring together? What principle did it teach? What foundation did it lay for the Kabbalah to follow?

Those were Sidney's criteria. How did her story of Becky on the beach fit into Sidney's rules?

In this storytelling Sidney no longer made the rules. If he could assign new forms to old stories, she could bring new stories to light. It was only a matter of courage, the courage to tell those stories she knew but had not yet told, and the courage to descend deeply enough to discover those she didn't yet know.

Her own rules would come, later.

"You will learn soon that there are four worlds of experience," Stephanie told the students. "The physical, emotional, intellectual, and spiritual. To extend oneself in balance through the four worlds is to experience growth. To fold one-self into any one of the worlds to the exclusion of the others is to invite tragedy."

On a Thursday evening in December, Moshe returned to the apartment in Riverdale from teaching the confirmation class in Chappaqua and found Rivkah crying. The breakfast dishes were still on the table. He did not know what to do to comfort her. She couldn't tell him why she was crying. She did not know.

Moshe was shaken. He called Sam and Gloria and explained the situation. He had class the next day and needed to be in New Jersey Friday night. He didn't know what to do.

Gloria arrived at two in the morning. Rivkah was in bed sleeping. Moshe had stayed awake, confused and agitated, waiting for Gloria to arrive from Baltimore. Gloria's demeanor agitated him still further. Not that she wasn't polite, but there wasn't any warmth in her greeting. "We'll see how she is in the morning," she told him.

He tried to sleep but could not. He felt himself a stranger in his own bed.

Rivkah was free that year to do whatever she pleased. She went some nights to the JCC to dance and participated in a Hebrew group. She never said she wasn't happy. Moshe could not understand why she was crying, and he told Gloria so.

"I don't understand it. She's free to do whatever she wants. I wish I had more time to be with her, but I have to study and work."

"You really don't understand it," Gloria responded icily.

"Do you understand what's happening?"

"All I know is that my daughter is very unhappy. She needs help."

Moshe's wrestling with Rivkah's depression was compounded. His father suffered a mild heart attack. Moshe was drawn and quartered by compelling needs to be in Newton with his father, to study, to teach, to care for his wife. The harsh winter made it difficult to get anywhere.

"Moshe never took a course with Dr. Kantor," Sidney said. "Still the advice he received from him was the best, the most honest advice Moshe ever received. He knew it later, if not at the time."

Moshe had asked for an appointment with his advisor. Dr. Kantor walked at an astonishing pace. "Faster," he encouraged Moshe, "A young man like you. Let's move. I have to be back before one." Moshe jogged a few steps occasionally, just to keep up. "So, Katan, what's on your mind?"

Moshe shared his difficulties. They gushed out. Difficulties with his learning, with his parents, with his marriage, financial problems.

At McDonald's Rabbi Kantor ordered a fish filet sandwich, said a blessing, and ate as he listened. All the way back Moshe continued, a litany of problems. At the entrance of the school he asked, "So, what do I do?"

What answer did he expect? Turn here for financial aid, there for tutoring, there for counseling?

"Study Torah," Rabbi Kantor advised him. "Study Torah," he said again, and raced up the steps toward class, leaving Moshe behind, confused and angry.

What kind of advice was that? "Study Torah?" His problems were real. What kind of advice was that?

Moshe became angry with everything and everyone in turn.

In class his remarks became sharp. He had no patience for the ignorance and laziness of his fellow students. His anger seeped out in his sermons and left his congregants confused. They asked each other why their Rabbi was angry with them. He was upset with his father. How could he not have exercised properly? How could he not have known enough to lose weight and take care of himself? How could he have been so stupid?

He became defensive with Rivkah. "All I wanted was to take care of you, like my father has taken care of my mother. Why do you think I work all these nights? I don't understand anything anymore! I don't know why you're angry with me all the time!"

Rivkah became angrier still.

Stephanie told a story of the Baal Shem Tov.

"The Baal Shem Tov was a spiritual master, the founder of Hasidism. A student of the Baal Shem had worked hard to learn the hidden intentions behind each sound of the *shofar*, the ram's horn. Each sound was a key to open the gates of heaven on Rosh Hashanah. The intentions he distilled into prompts, and the prompts he wrote on a piece of paper he tucked away into his garment on the holy day. When it came time to find the paper, it was gone. In despair, with a broken heart, he sounded the *shofar*, all the prompts and intentions forgotten.

"Later the Baal Shem Tov said to him, 'Done properly, each of those sounds would have been a key to one of the doors of heaven. But a broken heart is more powerful than any key. It is an ax, and to such an implement all of the doors fall open.'"

Moshe was numb when he hung up the phone. "My father died," he said blankly. "He had another heart attack. He died."

He had been lying in bed beside Rivkah, close to sleep when the phone rang. At that time of night it could have been only bad news. Rivkah sat beside him on the edge of the bed and held his hand.

"My father died," he said, feeling the strange words in his mouth, words that had difficulty registering in his mind. He turned to Rivkah. "What do I do?" he asked without knowing what he meant by the question. "Rivkah, what do I do? I am so alone." The last word broke his heart. The sobs began in his shoulders. His back bent, his head drooped, and convulsions of loneliness and grief shook him.

"Moshe!" Rivkah grabbed him. Her arms went around him. She helped him to the floor. She embraced him, wrapped her legs around him, rocked him, held him while the tears poured from him. Her nightgown became soaked in his tears. She did not let him go.

Moshe learned from Rabbi Kane how a funeral was done.

Rabbi Kane visited the house and sat with Moshe and Rivkah, with his mother and his aunts. They sat in the living room. Rabbi Kane mumbled a word or two of comfort, then held his peace. Barbara told him how Marvin had died. He had gone to the kitchen, opened the refrigerator door, suffered another heart attack, and fallen to the floor. It had been that fast. She heard the thump, ran to the kitchen, called 911. The rescue squad came. It was too late. She did not say, "If I had only . . ."

"That's a good sign," Rabbi Kane told Moshe later. "Your mother will do well. I'll stay in touch with her and keep you posted."

But that was later. At the house, Rabbi Kane said hardly a word. He listened.

Moshe spoke of the last time he saw his father. Rivkah described the wedding and the toast he had made. Marvin's sisters praised their older brother. They spoke of childhood experiences and more recent encounters. Soon the remarks the family had prepared in anticipation of the Rabbi's visit were exhausted. They began to talk to each other, as if the Rabbi were not present.

"Do you remember when . . ." The conversation moved rapidly around the room. They smiled, even laughed. At poignant memories, they stopped and reflected.

Rabbi Kane moved in his chair and cleared his throat. "I don't mean to interrupt," he said. "Please go on, but I have to leave. I'll see you tomorrow at the chapel. I'll be there a few minutes early. If there's anything more we have to do, we can do it there. Of course, if you need to call me at any time, please do so. My office can always reach me, wherever I am."

"Have we told you enough, Rabbi? We didn't have a chance to answer any of your questions."

The Rabbi took his hat and coat, mumbled good-bye, and left. Moshe realized the Rabbi hadn't asked any questions. That surprised him. What surprised him even more was the Rabbi hadn't taken any notes.

At the funeral service in the chapel the Rabbi apologized that, while he knew Marvin Hershel Kayten as a congregant, he had learned the details of his life only in the last day. He spoke of Marvin when he was a child, as his sisters remembered him. He recalled a time when the sisters were out on the lake in a rowboat and had lost the oars, how Marvin had jumped into the water and rescued them. He recalled how Barbara and Marvin had met, that Barbara could have had any man she wanted, but chose Marvin because of some wonderful qualities. Rabbi Kane remembered every one of the qualities. He spoke of the trip Michael and his father had taken to New York after Michael's bar mitzvah. For four days and three nights, father and son did together whatever it was Michael wanted. Rabbi Kane remembered everything. He remembered the pet name Marvin had for his daughter-in-law, how proud he was his son was studying for the rabbinate. Moshe had Rivkah on one side of him, his mother on the other, and no hand free to tend to his tears.

In the limousine, on the way to the cemetery, they spoke of the eulogy. "It was as if he had known Marvin all of his life," the aunts said. "He remembered every word we told him."

Moshe realized Rabbi Kane had done even better than that. They had told him very little; they had told each other a great deal. What the Rabbi had done was to remember every word he had overheard. He had overheard what they had been sharing with each other. Even in his pain, the observer within Moshe was admiring a colleague's superb technique. The preparation of the eulogy, the eulogy itself, could not have been any better.

At the cemetery Rabbi Kane offered Moshe the opportunity to read some of the service. Moshe summoned his professional reserve and read the prayers without hesitation. Those who chose to do so shoveled dirt into the grave. For the first time Moshe said *kaddish,* the orphan's prayer, for himself, not as the leader of a congregation. That was more difficult for him than reading the committal prayers. His voice broke momentarily. He was supported by the responses of the assembly. The immediate family passed through a corridor of comforters back to the limousine, then to the family home in Newton.

The only thing wrong with the funeral was that afterward everyone talked about the Rabbi, how wonderful the eulogy had been. The eulogy *had* been wonderful. Moshe said so himself. Still there was something wrong that everyone talked about the Rabbi. He couldn't quite articulate what that something wrong was.

Moshe learned that a broken heart was not selective. All of the chambers broke at once. The void where his father had been was palpable, but then so also was his distance from Rivkah, his testiness at school and in the congregation. Did his father have to die so that his heart should break? Would the distance from Rivkah have been enough, with a little more time? Would his colleagues have taken him aside, eventually, or the leadership of the congregation, to do some heart surgery and put him back on course? He would never know. The very thought he should benefit from the death of his father was a source of pain.

Moshe's tears eased Rivkah's recovery. Because she had better access to him, she had better access to herself as well. They made rapid progress together. Moshe accompanied her to therapy, and the therapist gave them homework, reading assignments and sharing assignments.

They learned the difference between freedom *from* and freedom *to*. They came to realize Rivkah had been imprisoned by her freedom from obligations because it was a freedom without direction or purpose. Only her husband had purpose, and the purpose of her husband was not enough for her. She had been cast into the role of the Rabbi's wife. A cast is for something broken, she told Moshe in therapy, where angry words erupted to the surface in relative safety. She resented she was not being defined for herself but bent into the definition of her Rabbi husband. "The man I married," she complained, "was Moshe, not Rabbi Katan." Still Moshe wanted to be a Rabbi. How could he be a Rabbi and Rivkah not be a Rabbi's wife? "A rabbi's wife is okay," she said. "The Rabbi's wife is not!"

The Elevator

"Moshe's emotional life began its *tikkun*—its repair—after his father's death," Sidney said. "Perhaps that opened the door for the integration of his intellectual life as well."

Moshe ascended in the school elevator.

Each floor held a different department. He rode through Theology and Liturgy and Bible and Rabbinics. The elevator was the connection. Moshe was in the elevator; then, suddenly, the elevator was in Moshe. The connection had been made. Theology was Liturgy. Liturgy was Bible. Bible was Rabbinics. History, Talmud, Human Relations, Speech. It was all the same in the elevator. The door opened; Moshe didn't know which floor it was, but it didn't really matter. The elevator in the seminary was Building Nine at MIT. It was the place where all courses met. All floors were the same.

"What do I do with this?" he asked Paretzky.

On the table Moshe had placed two volumes, one of history and the other, the scholarship of liturgy. The first denigrated an early school of mystics; the second attributed to them much of the liturgy that constituted the *siddur,* the Jewish prayer book. Both authors were eminent in their fields.

"We can't have it both ways."

"What do you propose to do?" Paretzky countered.

"When this history was written, a lot of the documents we have today weren't available. What I would like to do is to study those documents, immerse myself in the period, and see if I can learn something of the inner life of that community. Maybe I can learn how they came to create such liturgy."

"It's a thesis," Paretzky said. "But you can't do it with me. I'm Bible. You need Liturgy."

"You know Liturgy."

"Hah. I know everything! But I'm still Bible."

"I want to do it with you anyway."

Paretzky considered. "Ezekiel then. You base your thesis on the first chapter of Ezekiel. Then we're in the Bible, and I can be your advisor."

"Why Ezekiel?"

"These mystics you want to explore, they based their speculations on the first chapter of Ezekiel. You'll see when you get into it."

"You know their writings?"

"I know everything."

Transition

"Rivkah knew what she wanted," Stephanie said. "She wanted Moshe and something else. She wanted their life together and her life apart."

Rivkah and Moshe made substantial decisions. They would live in the city. Rivkah would go back to school.

Moshe's father had left him an insurance policy. They chose not to use that money, but to set it aside and let it grow toward a time when they would need it for a house and for children.

They found a fourth-floor walkup they could afford and a parking place they could not. It was a hard decision, but in the end they chose to surrender the car rather than invade their savings. Rivkah was accepted into the graduate program in social work at Columbia. Sam and Gloria contributed to her tuition.

Moshe studied more and worked less. Rivkah devoted herself to her learning with a direction and intensity that awed him. She quickly made a name for herself in her program. Her friends from Columbia mingled with Moshe's fellows from the seminary. The Katan home became a social center on the upper West Side. Marriages were made out of the mingling.

When Moshe took the bus out to New Jersey for weekends, he mostly went by himself. When Rivkah accompanied him, he tried valiantly to allow the congregation to see her in her own light. He thought if they could have friends in the congregation, other couples who would relate to them as Moshe and Rivkah rather than as Rabbi and Rebbitzen, it might be easier, but they found no such friends. When he shared this with the president of the congregation, the president told him, "We're paying you to be Rabbi and Rebbitzen, not to be Moshe and Rivkah." Moshe filed that remark, true as it was, in the same compartment of his mind that held the discomfort he'd experienced in Rabbi Kane's excellent eulogy.

Moshe and Rivkah studied at home on the dining-room table. Learning together, even if it was not with each other, provided a symbiotic energy. Rivkah shared with him points of interest from her courses in psychology and sociology. Moshe shared with her his gleanings from Jewish history and literature, but the arguments of the Talmud and his fascination with liturgy did not involve her.

They found time to explore the lower East Side, Chinatown, and Little Italy. They visited the Statue of Liberty, became tourists and climbed to the top. Lincoln Center was a walk away. They stood in line at the opera and found affordable seats more often than not. They chose a neighborhood, any four square blocks, and dived into it like divers on a reef, sampling the tastes of the diverse restaurants, a course in each place. Their love was restored, stronger than before.

Rivkah graduated a year before Moshe. Sam and Gloria hosted a party in her honor at a small Middle-Eastern restaurant on Columbus. Barbara came in from Newton, Rivkah's sister, Sharon, from Johns Hopkins. Friends started a hora. The family joined in the circle, and ultimately all of the other guests in the restaurant as well. The following week Rivkah began an internship at a large general hospital on the Upper West Side.

Surrender

Sidney said, "The color of insight is black-and-blue. Bang your head against the wall long enough and then give up. That's when insight comes."

Moshe became desperate. Six months he had been attacking the text without results. He took a break now and then to venture between the lions on the steps of the library downtown and learn some Freud and Jung, hoping that might help, then returned to the text.

The text was *Hechalot Rabbati,* the great work concerning the temples, seven temples corresponding to seven heavens. One descended through them, always a descent. That made no sense, no sense at all.

The long lists of angelic names were, at first, incomprehensible. Paretzky helped.

"Gabriel," Paretzky wrote on the board. "*Gibbur* and *El*. Might and God. The might of God. Rafael. The healing power of God. Michael. *Mi-ki-el*. One who is like God. Angel names are on one side an abstraction and the other a God name, each conveying some aspect of the divine."

But the names were not often so simple.

"*Tzurtak*." Moshe mentioned a name from the text.

"An abbreviation," Paretzky said. "*Tzurat ha-kodesh*—the form of the holy."

"*Totarossia*."

"From the Greek. *Tetra,* four. *Totarossia,* the four letter elements of the name of God."

"*Azbogah*." Moshe presented yet another name.

"Look, Katan, I have to leave something for you to do."

Moshe tried his best to do it. Deep into many nights he reviewed the text, again and again, attempting to make sense out of nonsense. "How many crowns fit on the head of an angel?" he asked himself. "And who cares?"

One night he read aloud softly from the Hebrew. After several repetitions, without being aware of it, he was chanting. "When the Angel of the Presence enters the throne room to prepare the Throne of Glory for the Mighty One of Jacob, a thousand thousand crowns are fixed to the *Ofanim* of Majesty for each and every one of them on its head, a thousand thousand times each bows and falls and prostrates itself before each and every one of them. Two thousands of crowns are fixed to *Heruvim* of Glory for each and every one of them on its head, and two thousands of times each bows and falls and prostrates itself before each and every one of them. Three thousands of crowns are fixed to the *Hayot Ha-kodesh,* the Holy Living Beings, for each and every one of them on its head . . ." And on and on, from one class of angel to the next. Without thinking he followed the progression of images, an ever-increasing number of crowns, until one became lost in the thousands of thousands of myriads of myriads . . .

Until Moshe became lost one night in the thousands of thousands of myriads of myriads . . .

Lost.

In the corners of his imagination he saw lions but was afraid to look directly at them because they were not imagined lions. They had come from somewhere else, and he knew it. He closed his eyes tightly to make them go away. Still the breath of lions filled his nose; their panting filled his ears.

Summoning courage from some source he had never known, he allowed himself to see. They prowled, eyes fierce and penetrating.

What if in his trembling he had flinched? What if in his fear he had bolted?

Tendrils of thoughts, images of Daniel and his lions, tapped at his consciousness. He denied them entrance. His concern was with lions of his own, how to continue breathing in their presence. Breathing became suddenly important. He was alarmed his breathing had stopped and started it again, in a steady rhythm. As his breathing settled, so did they, four lions, two on each side.

They contemplated him contemplating them for some endless time.

A muscle cramp brought Moshe slowly to the surface. His clothes were soaked. Where the lions had been, only questions remained. What had happened to him? He had been lost somewhere beyond, in the thousands of thousands of myriads of myriads. He had been lost among the images of the angels with crowns and crowns upon their heads. Lions had issued forth to meet him, to greet him, to keep him at bay. The imposition of his body had chased them away, and finally reason returned to lock them in their den.

Only the text remained in his hands, and it made no sense. That no longer troubled him. The text was not meant to make sense. It was a vehicle. It was a chariot meant to carry one beyond sense, to the place where angels sang before the Throne of Glory and lions emerged to sniff and growl and keep one at a distance.

Those who heard the angels sing returned to space and time to transcribe those songs. Those were the songs that became the liturgy. Moshe knew how the mystics did what they did. A chill pressed him to the very bone. He knew, but would he be able to share his knowledge? Would his thesis ever be expressed in writing? How, in this modern world, did one write of angels and receive credit?

Moshe studied alone in his last year. He became absorbed in text, lost in worlds within worlds. The first time Rivkah came home from a late shift at the hospital and found her husband in a trance, she was alarmed. "What happened to you?" she asked.

Moshe explained the nature of the *merkavah* texts. He read some aloud to her, and while she recognized the profound effect they had upon Moshe, they did not move her at all. He did not speak of the lions. That was his journey to make alone.

Whatever it was he was doing, wherever it was he went, it did not detract from their life together. They still found time to explore the city, to discover new neighborhoods, and to rediscover each other. If anything, his learning was making him more perceptive, more responsive, more loving.

Moshe brought Jung with him from the library to testify on his behalf before Paretzky.

"Quaternity," wrote Jung. "The mind bends into figures of fourness," Moshe explained. "From one culture to the next, each mind that penetrates to the collective unconscious finds figures of four.

"*YOD HEY VAV HEY*-ness," Moshe continued. "The name of God-ness. The quintessential four upon which the rest of consciousness is patterned."

He opened the Hebrew text and traced a path through the temples. "The mystic descends to the gate of the first temple. It is an awesome gate, protected by angels. Four angels. He works his way through the angels and finds inside the first temple a second temple greater than the first, and at the gate of this second temple, more angels, in multiples of four. Always in multiples of four. Temple after temple after temple, ever-increasing numbers of angels, in multiples and powers of four."

"Seven temples," said Paretzky, slicing without hesitation to the salient flaw in the presentation. "Seven temples, seven heavens. Not eight. Not a multiple of four."

"*Azbogah,*" countered Moshe.

"*Azbogah?*"

"You told me to do some work on my own. *Azbogah,* a key element of the seal of the seventh temple. The experiences these mystics were having were spontaneous. They would descend into the collective unconscious, and the symbols would leap out at them. The names of the angels were the keys to the experience, the keys to the gates. By chanting the names of the angels they could bring themselves to a particular entrance. *Azbogah* is the last name chanted." Moshe spelled the name. "*ALEF ZION BAYT VAV GIMMEL HEY.* The numerical value of *ALEF* is one and of *ZION,* seven. Together, eight. The value of *BAYT* is two, *VAV,* six, together making eight. *GIMMEL,* three, *HEY,* five, together, eight. The name *Azbogah* is the key to the eighth temple. There has to be an eighth. Experience demands it. But its existence was a secret. They hid it. The experience of it was so deep it was not to be mentioned except in hints."

Moshe trembled as he waited for Paretzky to respond. Paretzky seemed lost. Moshe was in no hurry. He knew what it was to be lost.

When Paretzky returned, he said, "I did not know that."

The rest was academic. That Moshe had found something Paretzky had not known was enough to guarantee acceptance of his thesis. Moshe found some other references to an eighth temple, an eighth heaven, spiced his text with ample footnotes, and included a chapter on Ezekiel. He was set for ordination.

The terror he had experienced in his confrontation with the lions he did not include in the thesis.

Heroic Measures

Stephanie said, "When Moshe traveled to his congregation for weekends, Rivkah was busy at the hospital. She claimed what she did at the hospital was no more a violation of Shabbat than what Moshe did in the pulpit."

Rivkah was assigned to an ethics subcommittee. Such a subcommittee consisted of a physician, a nurse, a social worker, and, sometimes, a clergyman.

Nine times out of ten the work of the subcommittee was to convince a reluctant family to remove a patient from life support, or to write a DNR order so heroic and expensive measures need not be taken should a patient fail.

The subcommittee worked mostly with indigent patients, those who could not afford to pay for services rendered. Those who could afford to remain alive and suffer were allowed to do so without protest. That was what Rivkah thought at her most cynical, though she understood the reality of the situation as well. Families that could afford to keep a loved one alive could also afford a family physician, a trusted friend who offered good advice. Because of the trust the advice was taken without any recourse to a subcommittee. Difficulties arose when families had no trust.

Mrs. Rabinowitz's breast cancer had metastasized to the bone and brain. She also suffered from emphysema, cardiac problems, and only God knew what else. What the physicians knew and were certain of was enough for them to encourage the family to write a *No Code,* a DNR, so that Mrs. Rabinowitz would not be placed on a respirator and consume an expensive ICU bed needlessly for days.

The family had resisted all such suggestions.

Exasperated, the physician and the nurse, who were of a single mind, summoned Rivkah to complete a subcommittee. The family did not want a clergyman. They did not trust rabbis, or physicians, or nurses, for that matter. Rivkah's task was to build a bridge of trust.

"Mrs. Rabinowitz," Rivkah said in an attempt to arouse her. "Mrs. Rabinowitz, my name is Rivkah Katan. I've come to see how you are doing."

"She hasn't responded in days," one daughter said.

"She hears everything, though," said the other. "She understands everything we say." To prove it she turned toward her mother and said something in Yiddish. The mother responded no more to the Yiddish than she had to the English, but the daughter smiled. "You see? She hears us. She hears everything we say."

Rivkah invited the daughters to come with her to the family room so they might talk, but the daughters would not leave the bedside. "Whatever you want to talk about, we can talk about right here. We're not leaving. Mama has a right to hear everything you have to say."

Rivkah looked toward Mama, considered whether to address her or her daughters. She chose the daughters. "Your mother may get better," she began. "She may wake up and be able to go home. But there is also a chance something else will happen. Her heart may give out, or something like that. Then the doctors and nurses will have to rush in and put tubes into your mother. They will hook her up to machines. She may suffer terribly. She won't get better after that. She will only suffer. What the doctor wants is to write an order so that if something bad happens to your mother, they won't put her on the machines. They will do everything they can to help her get better. But they won't prolong her suffering, if it comes to that."

Even as Rivkah spoke, she knew her words were having no effect. The daughters had already heard and absorbed all such arguments.

"Do you want your mother to suffer?" Rivkah pressed.

"Our mother won't suffer," the second daughter said.

"How can you be sure of that?"

"Our mother has already come through worse than this."

"Birkenau," the first daughter explained. "It was worse than this."

"Four years," the second daughter added. "Four years. This she has had for only three."

"Whatever it takes, she gets every chance," the first daughter said. "She survived before when the chances were a million to one. She knows how to do it. She survived Hitler. If she wants to survive this, she will survive this."

"It is her suffering that is the concern here," Rivkah tried again, "not her survival. There's no reason for her to endure pain needlessly."

71

The daughters looked to each other as if they had heard the greatest folly and were not certain what to do about it.

"What does pain have to do with suffering?" the first daughter asked.

"Our mother has endured great pain without suffering," the second added.

"Who ever said that pain is suffering? Do you have to be in pain to suffer?"

"Pain is inevitable. Everyone has pain."

"Pain is inevitable. Suffering is optional."

"Suffering is optional. Our mother isn't suffering. As long as she is alive, she won't suffer."

"Every moment of her life is a triumph, a victory."

"She gets every moment."

"Every moment."

They went on like that long enough to make Rivkah dizzy. When they finished, she repeated the essence of their message. "Every moment. She gets every moment." So she told the physician and the nurse. "Mrs. Rabinowitz is not suffering," she explained. "Even if she should awake and find herself on the machines, she would not be suffering. A long time ago Mrs. Rabinowitz made a decision not to suffer. I don't know how she did that, but it is precious. Every moment of her life is precious. We can't write a DNR, not for Mrs. Rabinowitz."

They did not write the DNR. Mrs. Rabinowitz died a few days later, in her sleep, without any heroic measures necessary. Rivkah was called to the room when she died.

"She was a hero," the daughters said through their tears.

They buried their mother the next day. At the graveside the daughters spoke of their mother to Rivkah. There wasn't anyone else to hear.

The daughters returned to their homes in California. Rivkah returned to the hospital.

She had told Moshe of Mrs. Rabinowitz. He had asked if he might come by to visit, but Rivkah had said that was not necessary. The family did not need a rabbi.

"No," Moshe had agreed. "They have you."

Stephanie had told that story before without crying. This time something in the story she had not heard before moved her to tears. Something to do with her mother, perhaps. Mrs. Rabinowitz and her mother. Or something to do with Birkenau. Uncle Al and Birkenau.

Could it have been Birkenau?

She thought she might repeat the story to hear it more closely. There were stories within that story. She opened her mouth to begin, but before she could utter a sound, Sidney announced the story of the rabbi.

She was thankful rather than annoyed. Her new stories weren't far away, but she was in no hurry to find them.

Rabbi

"Moshe Katan was ordained a rabbi," Sidney said. "His intentions were good."

They invited Dr. Paretzky for dinner after the thesis was done. "He's going to ruin his life by becoming a Rabbi, you know that, don't you?" he asked Rivkah. Rivkah knew better than to answer. "They wanted to make me a Rabbi. They offered me *smichah* once, and I turned it down flat. What good would it do me? It would make me an object of scorn and ridicule. It would have detracted from any serious scholarship I hoped to do. Why don't you talk some sense into him? Let him go on for a Ph.D. You're an MSW now. You can support him for another four years or so."

Rivkah served a chocolate dessert. Moshe shifted the conversation to the New York Mets, after Bible translation and chocolate, Paretzky's greatest passion.

The seminary provided a dinner for the graduating class and their families on the eve of ordination. Moshe received three of the four major academic awards and was asked to speak on behalf of his class. He spoke of titles. He spoke of how he had felt when he had received his commission as ensign in the Navy, what it meant to put on the stripe and to return the salutes of the enlisted men. When he left the service, he resigned his commission. He did not continue in the reserves. The title, he felt, would inhibit his growth.

Other titles inhibited growth as well, he said, and spoke about the title "Mrs." If "Mrs." was used to define a woman in terms of her husband, it limited growth and impaired a marriage. Gloria passed Rivkah a handkerchief, but Rivkah had one in hand already.

Lastly he spoke of the title Rabbi. He said Rabbi could be spelled two ways, with a lower case *r* and an uppercase *R*. In the lowercase it was a mission. In the uppercase it was a coffin.

"A *coffin*?" The exclamation burst unspoken from his audience.

"Yes, a coffin," he repeated. "In the lowercase, the mission of the rabbi is unlimited, undefined. He can grow to his full extent. He can define and redefine his role in the community. He has flexibility to interpret his role and his relationships. But with the uppercase R, his role is defined for him. He is put into a coffin and doesn't know it, until the praises of his community swell him so he fills the confined area. His growth becomes restricted, his attitude warped. Ultimately he dies there.

"I know each of you," he addressed his classmates. "You are all wonderful, every one of you. We have over the years developed a love of Torah and a love of God. We all know the kind of uppercase Rabbis I just described. We make fun of them. But I bet when they were sitting here at their ordination dinner, they were full of wonder also, with a love of Torah and a love of God. Then they went out into their congregations and got put into their coffins and were confined there until the love was wrung out of them. Is that going to happen to us? How will we keep it from happening?

"It's dangerous out there. I remember when I was in the Navy, before going to Vietnam, we were told how dangerous it was, what to look out for, what precautions to take. It occurs to me, we haven't been given the warnings. We don't know what we need to know."

Moshe finished with a prayer. "May the one who blessed our fathers Abraham, Isaac, and Jacob also bless us and protect us, enable us to remain focused in our work and at the same time refrain from definition, that we may expand and grow to our full potential, that we may be happy and fulfilled in our profession, that we may learn much Torah and accomplish many deeds."

All responded, "Amen." The mood was subdued.

The next morning, a robed Moshe stood before the president of the seminary. The president said some words to him, but Moshe trembled too much to hear them. He felt the weight of the president's hands upon his shoulders, and with that he was ordained.

Barbara had all of the guests to a luncheon at the Hotel Pierre. Rabbi Katan smiled and thanked each of them for their support over the years. He felt the burden of his title and wondered how long, if ever, it would take him to feel comfortable carrying it.

Stephanie completed the third series of stories, aware of how gracefully they had flowed, back and forth between herself and Sidney, stories of Rivkah and Moshe. She and Sidney worked together so well.

Why would she consider leaving him?

The next day Moshe met Rivkah midafternoon at a coffee shop near the hospital. He wasn't thirsty but ordered coffee, so his hands would be busy with something while she ate.

"They'll fly both of us in for the interview, and they'll set up appointments for you to look at the hospitals, if you like. They pay all the moving expenses. We won't have to pack anything we don't take with us in the car."

She considered that. "You're trying to sell me on it? Do you think it's a good place?"

"It's the best place available. We'll be able to watch the sun set behind the Golden Gate Bridge."

She turned her attention back to her lunch, some generic fish and mashed potatoes. "You didn't answer my question. I wasn't talking about the neighborhood."

"Yes, it's a good place. He's a good man, Rivkah. Congregations don't get any better than this one. They have a day school, a beautiful library, playing fields. It's like a campus."

"Are you excited about it?"

"A little, maybe." The waiter came by to ask if they needed anything. He added coffee to Moshe's cup.

"They have cheesecake," Rivkah suggested. "It's good."

Moshe acquiesced to the cheesecake, though he didn't need it. He had gained weight in New York.

"Is there anything else you'd rather do?" Rivkah asked.

"I don't know of anything else to do. Do you? How many times have we been through this?"

"One more won't hurt."

Moshe looked about the restaurant as if for help. Posters of Greek islands adorned the walls. Were there any congregations there in need of a rabbi?

In past years, wherever they had traveled, small towns in Massachusetts or Maryland, Moshe had always asked the question, "What would it be like to

75

be a rabbi here?" They formulated lists of desirable qualities in a place to live. The East Coast figured in all of them. California had never crossed their minds, so far away from their families.

"I think he would be a good man to work with," Moshe said. "He saw I was having difficulty making the decision and said something very smart. He said my decision only had to be acceptable. It doesn't have to be perfect. This isn't going to be for a lifetime. Two years, maybe three. The position is certainly acceptable. More than acceptable. We might as well try it and see what it's like. We'll find out if we can do it."

"Okay."

Moshe waited for the end of her sentence. He knew too well that Rivkah's "Okay" was a negotiating tool. It was almost always followed by a "but." He waited, but there was no "but."

"It's really okay?" Moshe asked, to be sure he had not missed something.

"It's okay," she said. And then with emphasis, "It's okay, Moshe."

That was two okays. Moshe became alert. If one okay was a negotiating tool, two was staking out a firm position. "What's going on?"

"I'm off birth control," Rivkah said. "The doctor said I should stop taking the pill for a while and do something else. I thought we might do something else." Moshe finished his coffee and looked intently into the cup. "I want a baby," she continued. "I was thinking this might be a good time. So what do you think, Moshe? We want a baby. Wouldn't this be a good time to do it?"

Moshe looked about. "The waiter's not around," he said.

She paused to catch his meaning, and when she did, kicked him under the table. "When we get home, you fool!"

Two decisions were made that afternoon.

CHAPTER 4

Uncertainty

"Stretch," Stephanie suggested to the students, setting an example by reaching on tiptoes toward the ceiling fan. "We have one more series, a long one, before we break for the night."

She remained standing to begin the California stories.

The packers had come to their apartment on the West Side and boxed everything not already in the hand-me-down Buick, a gift from Rivkah's parents. "This is too easy," Rivkah said. "There has to be a catch somewhere." The congregation paid for their moving expenses and for their travel. The first night out, Rivkah and Moshe checked into a Motel 6, out of habit. The second night it was a Holiday Inn. In Kearney, Nebraska, they talked of a Hilton but were road-weary and settled into a Best Western. They were boiling when they reached Rock Springs, Wyoming, and chose the first clean place with a swimming pool. In Reno they arrived early enough to tour the town. They surrendered to the neon and became tourists for the night.

Rivkah pumped a roll of quarters into a slot machine. Moshe won $200 at blackjack.

"Maybe it's a sign we made the right decision," he said.

"Then how come I didn't win?" Rivkah asked.

Milton

The campus of Temple Shalom was overrun by the summer camp. Moshe had nothing to do with the camp. In truth, he had nothing much to do. Adult Jewish life came nearly to a stop in August.

"My secretary gave me my calendar," he told Rivkah. "She's in charge. Tuesdays and Fridays mornings I go to the hospitals to visit congregants. Maybe we can arrange to have lunch together. Wednesday afternoons I have Bar Mitzvah kids. Thursday's my day off."

"What did you do today?"

"I unpacked my books. I wrote a press release for my sermon Friday night. I had one appointment, Milton Kramer, an eighty-year-old who doesn't like Rabbis and came to tell me so. I was told he does that to each of the new assistants."

"Why doesn't he like Rabbis?"

"Because both of his daughters married non-Jews. Milton blamed the Rabbis for not educating them properly. When he couldn't find a Rabbi who would officiate at the marriage of his first daughter, he became angrier. Then when he did find a Rabbi who would officiate at the marriage of his second daughter, he became angrier still. He couldn't understand how a Rabbi could have so little respect for the tradition."

"You like Milton," Rivkah said.

Moshe nodded. "He was testing me. Wanted to see how defensive I would get."

"How defensive did you get?"

"I laughed. I told him I wasn't concerned whether he liked Rabbis or not, so long as he liked me. I asked him what he really wanted, why he had really come. Then we had a good time. He's an old doc, retired out here a dozen years ago. His wife died. His kids are back in Chicago. He'd been reflecting on the purpose of his life, of life in general. What he wanted was someone to learn with."

"What will you learn?"

"Kabbalah," Moshe said. "We'll learn some Kabbalah together, Milton and Moshe, not Milton and the Rabbi. He was happy about that."

"You, too," Rivkah said.

The Rabbi's Wife

"Rivkah didn't accompany her husband to his first service," Stephanie said. "She stayed in the hospital late that Friday night. A twelve-year-old child had been struck by a truck. She was brain-dead. Rivkah worked with the family, helping them come to a decision, to harvest organs or not."

Tawanda Thomas was dead, though the machines kept her heart beating and chest breathing. She was beyond knowing, feeling. She would never ride her bike again. She had ridden it only the once, that afternoon, after her twelfth birthday party. She had been struck by a delivery truck hurrying out of a neighbor's driveway.

Tawanda looked remarkably good for a dead girl. Her ginger cheeks were suffused with rose. She had a bandage on her head. Underneath the sheet some bones may have been broken. They were of no importance. The head trauma had killed her. There was nothing more to do, except make a decision.

Rivkah had been called to the emergency room that Friday afternoon when it was certain Tawanda was dying. Mr. Thomas paced, talking mostly to himself, words of guilt and anger. Mrs. Thomas was afloat in her tears, curled up in a corner on the floor, her two older daughters holding her, providing ballast. A young son, maybe ten years old, sat by himself, watching his father pace.

Rivkah sat with each of them in turn. Nurses came and went. Doctors spoke a few words with compassion. When there was no more to be done, Rivkah accompanied the family behind the curtain to see Tawanda. She was a little girl in a large white bed surrounded by machines, some with screens, yellow lines that peaked and subsided, and one with a diaphragm, breathing in and out.

The young boy bolted to leave and ran directly into Rivkah. She held him, reassured him. "The machines won't hurt her," she said. "They won't hurt you. Don't be afraid of them. They're only here to help."

The mother was oblivious to that exchange. She saw only her daughter in the bed. "She's okay," her mother said. "She looks fine."

"The machines keep her that way," Rivkah said. "When they stop, she will stop. It's hard to imagine that."

The machines were living, the girl was dead.

"Why don't they just do it, then?" the father asked. "Do it and be done with it!"

"Because there is a decision to be made," Rivkah said. "Tawanda is already gone, but she can still give life to others." There was much to explain. The procedure was new. A national organ donor network was still in the early stages.

Rivkah walked with them, sat with them, talked with them, cried with them well into the night. When they had questions she could not answer, she summoned one of the transplant surgeons.

During one such break, she retreated to the cafeteria, extracted her dinner from vending machines. Rivkah attempted to withdraw into *Shabbat,* away from the urgency of the situation, but the family sought her out and surrounded her table.

"What would you do?" Mrs. Thomas asked.

"Why is it important what I would do?" Rivkah defended herself.

"If it was your child?" Mrs. Thomas continued.

"I don't have any children."

"If you did have children, what would you do?"

"Why do you ask me?" Rivkah pressed again. "Why is it important what I would do?"

"Because you're a Rabbi's wife," Mrs. Thomas said. "They told us you're a Rabbi's wife." The Thomases did not know the word *rebbitzen,* but they knew how to translate it.

"I can't answer you as the Rabbi's wife," Rivkah replied, sidestepping the unintended attack on her integrity. "I can only answer for me." She reached out for the mother's hand, hoping a gentle touch might soften the words she had to say. "It's everything I can do not to collapse in tears when I look at Tawanda. I very much want a child myself, and here you are losing one. If I'm confused, I can only imagine how impossible this is for you. She looks like she is alive, but she isn't. She can give life to others, and you lose her. You lose her anyway. You've lost her anyway. It's how much you can bear. That's what it comes down to. How much can you carry? Does it lighten the load to know she may give life to others? Or does the thought of donating her organs make the burden heavier? I can't decide that for you. She's not my child. I didn't have the joy of bringing her into this world, and I don't have the pain of watching her leave it. Which way is lighter? Feel it. Weigh it. I know both sides are heavy, but one is lighter. Which one? Whichever one makes you lighter is the way to go."

When the students saw that Stephanie had finished her story, they wanted to know what happened, whether the organs were harvested or not.

"It's not important," Stephanie said.

The Rebbitzen

The second Friday Rivkah put on her *Rebbitzen* outfit, a blue suit with large white buttons, and sat in the front row of theater-style chairs. A robed

Rabbi Katan led the procession of officiants and officers onto the mauve carpeted *bimah*. Rivkah strained her neck to look up at him. She followed the service dutifully, standing when he raised his hands to stand, sitting when he lowered his hands to sit, mouthing when he advised the congregation to read along with him. He read well, his voice steady, deep, polished from hours of practice in speech class.

The sanctuary was nearly filled, unheard of for a *Shabbat* the second week in August. The newspaper had made the sermon the lead story in the local section and the word had spread. The new Rabbi was to speak about teenage sex. Parents came and dragged in their wake whatever teenagers they had in town.

Rabbi Katan paused to ponder the expanse of the congregation before he spoke. "There are a lot of people here tonight," he began. "I have the feeling it wasn't the *Shabbat* service that brought you out, but the sermon topic, maybe a chance to see the new Rabbi in town. And you're wondering what he's going to say about teenage sex, as if somehow whatever he had to say was very important.

"Well, here it is. Some teenagers will have sex when they're teenagers, and some won't. Some who have sex will be responsible about it. Some won't. Some will make mistakes and pay for them. *But . . .*"

"It is a wonderful conjunction, that *but,*" Stephanie said, interrupting her story. "Moshe taught us that it is a pivotal word between two prayers in the early morning service.

"'Sovereign of all worlds,' the first prayer begins, 'not because of our righteousness do we come before you with our supplications, rather because of your great compassion. After all, what are we? What is the extent of our lives, our kindness, our merit, our strength? What can we say before You? Aren't even the heroes like nothing before You? The famous as if they didn't even exist? The wise as if they had no knowledge? The perceptive as if they had no understanding? Most of what we do has no worth, the days of our life amount to nothing before You, the advantage we have over a beast is hardly measurable . . .'

"If it were not for the *but* that follows," Stephanie said, "we would be lost. It is the *but* that draws us back from the edge of oblivion. 'But we are Your people, the descendants of Your covenant with Abraham! We extend back through the generations to the very beginning. We stretch forward through our own progeny and our own creativity, creating ripples which extend to the very edges of space and time.' The *but* is the pivotal word that moves us from insignificance to consequence."

". . . *but,*" Moshe repeated, "the mistakes teenagers might make generally don't destroy families. It's mistakes their parents make that destroy families. If I had titled this evening's sermon *Commit Adultery and Watch Your Family Explode,* hardly any of you would be here, and you certainly wouldn't have brought your children."

Moshe waited for the silence to deepen before continuing. "I'm going to speak this evening about responsibility in sexual relationships, teenage relationships, and adult relationships when adults begin acting like teenagers." They listened. His words were straightforward, supported by text and tradition.

Afterward he and Rivkah stationed themselves side by side in the social hall. The receiving line queued back around the tea and pastry table. He was praised by adults and teenagers alike. Rivkah stood by him. The praises were meant for her husband, the afterthoughts for her. After-thoughts were attached by the conjunction *and.* They amounted to, "*And* it's such a pleasure to have you, too, Mrs. Katan, in our community. *And* I'm sure you'll also have a great deal to contribute during your stay with us."

"You spoke well, Moshe," she said in the car on the way home.

"It was okay. I kept them entertained. I surprised them enough so they couldn't fall asleep."

"No, you were really good. You touched some of the people. I could feel it. Your words made a difference."

"How are you? They left you out to dry." When she didn't respond, he added, "Perhaps if we did away with the receiving line?"

"And the robes? And the steps up to the pulpit? I literally have a pain in my neck from having to look up to you!"

"You mean you don't look up to me?" he joked.

"I always look up to you. But next time I'll sit in the tenth row."

"You mean there'll be a next time?"

She sighed. "What are we going to do, Moshe? We can't let this become another New Jersey."

He slowed the car to stop at a light. Turning to her he asked, "What do you suggest?"

"I don't know. We need something, Moshe. I'm not going to put on white gloves and smile at everything everyone says."

The light turned green and Moshe's attention shifted to the road. "Let me think on it, Rivie. Let me think on it."

They were quiet the rest of the way home.

Stephanie recalled her many discussions with Rivkah about that pain in the neck.

What was so different, Stephanie had wanted to know, between what Rivkah was called upon to do for Moshe, and what she used to do for Sidney? Didn't she have to entertain and attend corporate functions where her husband was the star, to smile graciously to people she didn't give a damn for and play the requisite game? Whether in Boston, London, New York, or San Francisco, she had done the corporate-wife things demanded of her, with appropriate grumbling, to be sure. Sidney grumbled himself. But that wasn't the essence of their lives. It wasn't central to Sidney's work, only ancillary, and she had her own work, whether she was teaching, or tutoring, or volunteering. She always had her own sense of worth, and surely Rivie did, too. The work Rivie did at the hospital was substantial, vital. She was appreciated by staff and patients alike. So what was the problem? Why did she have such a pain in the neck?

"This was week in and week out," Rivkah had said. "Yours was only occasional."

"It's not a matter of frequency, is it?" Stephanie asked.

"What was the purpose of the things you did?" Rivie changed the direction of the dialogue.

"To support my husband. If it was in-house, mostly just to be present. If it was to close a deal, then, I guess, I had to be charming. Why would it have been so different for you. In-house on a Friday evening, charming with members of the board who had a say in your husband's contract? It's the way of the world. I admit, it's a pain in the ass, but not a pain in the neck."

"It's not frequency," Rivkah admitted. "It's the product. What was Sidney producing?"

"Different things at different times. Industrial machinery. Electronics . . ."

"Real things," Rivkah interrupted. "It's a matter of product. Sidney was producing things that supported the economy. Moshe was producing hot air to hold up the roof of a building that was mostly empty."

Stephanie understood. It was a matter of respect. And now it had come home to rest. She had the same problem in her relationship with Sidney. In the years since he had left Freeman March, he had produced only hot air, and not much of that. He was collapsing on himself. There was less and less of him to relate to, and she seemed powerless to reverse the flow.

The Maimonidean Diet

Sidney said, "It's one thing to teach text, and it's quite another to make a text out of yourself. Moshe did that inadvertently and paid a price for it."

Moshe had developed a bad habit in the seminary, a taste for pastry while he studied. Bear claws and apple turnovers were his favorites. He studied a lot, so he ate a lot. During his four years in New York he gained forty pounds.

After he arrived in California he continued to study as a matter of discipline. He learned the *Mishneh Torah* of Maimonides, a twelfth-century code of law, a few pages each day, and discovered a diet. The text made an impression on him. He followed it and lost the forty pounds in twenty weeks.

On a Monday morning the Temple office asked him for his sermon topic for the coming Friday evening service. He hadn't given it any consideration. They needed a press release quickly, so he wrote: "The Rabbi's Diet: How to Lose 40 Pounds in 20 Weeks and Keep It Off. Rabbi Moshe Katan will reveal secrets learned from the text of an ancient Jewish physician and philosopher, Moses Maimonides . . ." He thought it was funny.

Friday night the synagogue was like *Rosh Hashanah*. The custodians had to open the doors in the back of the sanctuary and set up hundreds of extra chairs. The service was delayed twenty minutes to accommodate the traffic.

The *Oakland Tribune* and the *San Francisco Chronicle* wrote stories about Rabbi Katan and his miraculous diet. They mentioned Maimonides, too. The *National Enquirer* picked up the story and ran it on the front page. "Rabbi Discovers Age-Old Diet: Eat All You Want and Still Lose Weight!"

Moshe still thought it was funny, until the phone calls started, calls from all over the country.

"Rabbi, you're my last hope."

He didn't know what it meant to be a hope.

"Rabbi, I've tried everything. I have to have your diet! If I don't have it, I'll die!"

He explained the diet wasn't his. It was written in Hebrew by a Jewish scholar over seven hundred years ago. Even if he translated it into English, it wouldn't help. For the diet to work a person would need to understand the framework within which it was written.

He couldn't hang up on members of his own congregation. He scheduled a course on the diet. No single classroom could hold it, so he taught it in two sections. He translated the diet into English and taught the framework of rabbinic literature. He was such a good teacher the students stayed and learned, even though no one lost any weight.

He had four letters of inquiry about a book on the diet, three from publishers and one from an agent. They remained on his desk for a month before he threw them away unanswered.

It wasn't all bad, he told Rivkah. If it hadn't been for the diet, he wouldn't have been able to teach so many students about Maimonides.

"Did they come to learn about Maimonides, or about you?" she asked.

"Me," he admitted, "but they got Maimonides."

"And you got your picture in the *National Enquirer*."

"The good news about being in the *National Enquirer* is that nobody can admit that they've seen it."

With the exception of Ethel Kaplan and Frank Nusbaum, that was pretty much true.

Scientific American

Stephanie had suggested to Sidney that he invite Frank to tell his own part of the story, how he and Moshe had met. Frank tried it once, but it became clear that he was a scientific American. He had the dates and details, but couldn't remember anything of substance. Thereafter, Sidney told the story himself.

"It was from Frank that Moshe first learned about the Havurah," Sidney said. "*Havurah* is Hebrew for fellowship."

Moshe leafed through a year-old copy of *Scientific American* in Dr. Nusbaum's waiting room. It had been over a decade since he had so much as looked into one. He found it fascinating. Some of the language was beyond him. He promised himself to get a subscription, to catch up with the edge of expanding scientific knowledge. Four years in the Navy, six years of rabbinic training, and nearly three years in the congregation had dropped him a generation behind.

"Rabbi Katan?" the nurse asked.

Moshe was alone in the waiting room. He was bearded, wearing a *kipah*. He looked around, back to the nurse, and answered, "I guess so."

She was not amused. Clearly it had been a long day, and she was ready for it to be over. "Dr. Nusbaum will see you now."

Dr. Nusbaum had a good reputation. Other doctors used him as their primary physician. This Moshe had learned while visiting congregational members in the hospital. He ate his lunch with doctor friends in the staff dining room, and Frank Nusbaum's name was mentioned favorably from time to time.

Moshe's last physical examination had been while he was in the Navy. He reasoned it was time to have another one, to establish a base line. His father had died of heart failure, and beyond that, there was a personal matter he needed to discuss.

"Rabbi Katan," Dr. Nusbaum came from behind his desk to greet him. His shirtsleeves were rolled up, his tie loosened at the neck. "I'm pleased to meet you. I've heard good things about you." A solid, callused hand reached out toward Moshe. The grip spoke of a muscular frame. Moshe imagined the doctor rowing on the Charles River.

"I've heard good things about you, too, Doctor."

"What can I do for you?" Dr. Nusbaum motioned him toward a chair. "Not a diet I presume. The article in the *Enquirer* was surprisingly good." He began to take a history, a patient and thorough history, even at the end of a long day. In the treatment room, he tapped and listened and peered into orifices. "Everything seems fine. I'll have my nurse come in to do an EKG and draw blood. If you would be kind enough to give us a urine sample." He handed Moshe a plastic cup. "Anything else?" he asked as he rose to leave.

Moshe raised his concern. "My wife and I have been trying to have children. No luck."

"How long have you been trying? How old is your wife?"

"Rivkah is thirty-one, and we've been trying for nearly three years."

"That's not very long and not very old. The clock still has a lot of time left on it."

"I was just thinking if there was a way of telling if there's a problem somewhere. Maybe with me. That my sperm count is low, or I'm not fertile, or something."

Dr. Nusbaum weighed his patient's concern against the demands on his time and returned to his stool. "In cases of infertility, usually the difficulty is with the woman. Ninety percent of the time. But we're not sure that there's any difficulty yet. It's only been a couple of years, and your wife is only thirty-one. Still, if you're really concerned, I can send you to somebody. Fertility isn't my thing. There's a good team here in town, if you think that's what you want to do."

Moshe cleared his throat, and asked, "Isn't there a simple way just to make sure I'm not infertile?"

"Sure," Dr. Nusbaum said and handed him another plastic cup. "Give me two samples."

"Just like that?"

"Do you know of some other way? Is it a matter of *halachah* that bothers you? *Hashatat zera,* destruction of the seed? I know Jewish law forbids masturbation, but I think since the intent here is to produce life, we could make this an exception. Don't you?"

Moshe was astonished. "Where did you learn *halachah*?"

"A *yeshivah* in Brooklyn. Where did you learn?"

Moshe gave him a brief summary of his Jewish learning.

Dr. Nusbaum responded, "Your learning came late. Mine came early. I had a traditional home with traditional values. *Yeshivah* all the way up to Harvard."

"What congregation do you belong to?" Moshe asked.

"None."

"You've stopped being observant?"

"We haven't exactly stopped, not that you could consider us Orthodox in the traditional sense. We keep a kosher home, but I drive on *Shabbos* and work when it's my turn to be on call for a weekend. My wife and I aren't members of any congregation."

"Why not?"

"Let me ask you a question first. If you weren't employed by your congregation, would you be a member there? Would that satisfy your Jewish needs?"

"No," Moshe answered without hesitation.

"So where would you be a member?"

"I don't know."

"Could you go to a place where they told you when to stand up and when to sit down? Where the praying was all lip service and no God service? Where the Rabbi always read from the Torah and no one dared correct his mistakes?"

"No," Moshe admitted.

"Well then, how about Young Israel, or some other Orthodox *shul*. Would you belong there?"

"No."

"Why not?"

"Because my wife couldn't participate there the way I could."

"Mine neither," said Dr. Nusbaum.

"So what do you do? Nothing?"

"We *daven* with the Havurah."

"Which *havurah?*"

"We just call it *the* Havurah. There are eleven couples and three singles. We get together every other *Shabbat* morning, and once a month on Friday night for a potluck *Shabbat* dinner. Some of us are synagogue members for our kids. Some not."

"How come I never heard of this?"

"We don't go around telling everybody." He looked at his watch. "I don't want to keep Vickie any later than we have to. Let her come in and give you the EKG. When you're done, drop the samples by my office. I'll take a quick look at your sperm count, nothing very scientific mind you, just a quick look, and I'll call and let you know if there's any reason to be concerned."

Moshe had difficulty urinating, let alone providing the other sample.

Uppercase I

Before Sidney could continue with Ethel Kaplan, Stephanie had a new story to add about Rivkah and the relationship.

Moshe followed his diet sermon with a series that Rivkah referred to as the *Why I* sermons. *Why I Say Morning Prayers, Why I Keep Kosher, Why I Study Torah.* She didn't like them. "Who cares why you do anything?" she asked.

A lot of people cared. Moshe's Friday night sermons drew large numbers, not that those people were interested in morning prayer, keeping kosher, or studying Torah. Moshe had developed a casual, light style of delivery that challenged and entertained. They were interested in Moshe.

Friday evenings Rivkah felt obliged to accompany her husband to the Temple, even after she learned of the Havurah. Though she found the service stifling, she fulfilled her obligation.

She was introduced to the Havurah by Frank Nusbaum. He and his wife, Debbie, had become regular guests in the Katan home. They encouraged her to attend the Havurah *minyan,* the quorum for prayer, which met Saturday mornings in the vestry of the Unitarian church. The service began at nine-thirty. She learned to arrive at eleven, as the prayer service was ending. She came for the hour of Torah study and discussion. The prayer, even as energetic as the Havurah service was, did not involve her, but the Torah discussion was often electric.

Rivkah became comfortable around the tables of the Havurah. Moshe, in spite of his original good intentions, was on his way to becoming a Rabbi, not only with an uppercase R, but also an uppercase I.

Sidney had done that too, Stephanie thought, making an uppercase I of himself, to stand out from the others while he was pursuing his MBA at Harvard. It wasn't bad. Sidney came home with his stories. She had delighted in them. But then she had her own stories. Allison was in day care, and that had allowed her to return to her teaching position at Belmont Hill.

They lived in a student furnished second-floor apartment in Arlington. Little money, but they had everything. They had Harvard Square and Boston Common, sailboats on the Charles River and swan boats in the Public Gardens.

And her mother had a granddaughter and knew it. Allison, for Uncle Al. If her father had known who his granddaughter was named after, he would have turned purple. But her father didn't know. He had two granddaughters, and didn't know about either of them, she thought, with some satisfaction.

Ethel Kaplan

"Three things are required for the pursuit of mystical discipline," Sidney said. "Refinement of the intellect, development of the imagination, and freedom for the pursuit. Paretzky was Moshe's coach for the intellect. Reb Hayim worked with the imagination. Ethel Kaplan was his freedom teacher. Don't think for a moment she was any less of a master than the other two because she worked with money rather than Torah."

Moshe was well aware of what was happening to him in the synagogue. The Havurah would have been a welcome relief, but it was not available. He could not move the Sabbath to a different day to attend services with the Havurah, and the Havurah wasn't about to move its services to Thursday, his day off. He knew he needed to grow. If the synagogue was constricting him, he needed to engage in something expansive outside of the synagogue. But what?

"Something new," Rivkah said. "Something you've never done before. Something as far away from the Temple as you can get."

The next Thursday morning Moshe drove the old Buick across the bridge into the city, parked in the World Trade Center, took the elevator to the top floor, and presented himself to the receptionist at Ferrell Bower. She was a woman in her sixties who, judging from the papers on her desk, did more than smile and channel phone calls.

Moshe began, "Good morning. My name is Moshe Katan. I know nothing about the markets. I have every Thursday available to learn about them. Is there someone here I might learn with?" He winced at the tone of his words, his awkwardness, his affectation.

The receptionist looked up at him blankly over her reading glasses, through a cloud of cigarette smoke.

"I want to learn," he started again. "I have some time free, so I thought I might learn something, if there's someone here who might teach me." That did not seem much better to him.

"What do you want to learn?" she asked at last. "Are you interested in working here or doing business here?"

The question startled him. "Working? No. My interest is only in learning. I'm a clergyman. I have Thursdays free. I thought that I might learn something new. What I would do with it, I can't say."

She leaned back in her chair, as if to take in more of him. "I'm sorry. I still don't understand. What is it you want to learn about?" she asked again.

"Whatever can be learned here. Something about the markets. About business. What money is. The different ways people think about it. How you do business. What brokers do."

"Did you have any particular market in mind? The stock market, bonds, commodities?"

"I have a lot of Thursdays, Miss . . ." Moshe looked about for a name plate.

90

"Kaplan," the receptionist completed the sentence. "Ethel. And you are Rabbi Katan. That was a good story in the *Enquirer*. I tried it, but I can't say I lost any weight. What can I do for you, Rabbi?"

"Call me Moshe, please. I'm not at my office."

"Well, I am at my office, so call me Ethel. And Rabbi . . . excuse me. Moshe. You can begin learning with me. There's a library of sorts around that corner. Go find a book and begin reading. I'm free at twelve-forty-five for lunch. We can talk about what you've been reading then."

So Moshe began to learn with Ethel Kaplan, who had once been the receptionist in that office of Ferrell Bower, who still sat in occasionally when the current receptionist was away from her desk.

In the cafeteria Ethel advised Moshe lunch would be his treat. "It's your treat as long as you're here only to learn," Ethel told him. "If you start doing business, then your broker will be taking you to lunch. Lunch is very important. That's the first thing to learn. There are all kinds of lunches."

"I'm mostly a vegetarian," Moshe said.

"Lunch is not what you eat."

"I gathered that."

He followed Ethel down the food line, selecting salad and a yogurt for himself. He noticed the seamed stockings below her gray herringbone gabardine skirt. The seams were straight. That also seemed important. He was conscious of his corduroy pants and sport coat and resolved the next time, should there be a next time, to wear a suit.

"Well, what did you read this morning?" she asked when they were seated.

Moshe withdrew four volumes from his case and put them on the table. They were all best-sellers of years past.

"Which one . . ." Ethel stopped in mid-question. "You read all four, didn't you?" Moshe nodded. "Well, what did you learn from them?"

"They are all the same," he said. "Someone had a run of luck in the markets and, after the fact, wrote down a bunch of principles he may or may not have followed. They don't prove anything."

"My smoking won't bother you?" Ethel lit up before Moshe had any chance to object. "All four of these authors not only did very well in the market, but they continue to do very well. They all make a lot of money. How do you account for that?"

He had no response.

"They use opium," Ethel continued. "O.P.M. Other people's money. My husband used to say that. He said it's a narcotic. At first they get high on their own funds, at their own risk. Maybe they're good. Maybe they're lucky. They write a book. They make a name. They attract a lot of O.P.M. and make a percentage. Some years they may earn a good return, some years not so good. They find nimble traders to do the work while they write a sequel to their book to attract more O.P.M. So they continue to make a lot of money.

"Would you like to do that? You could, you know. With a little luck, maybe some skill, the Rabbi makes a killing in the market. Being a Rabbi, it doesn't have to be a killing. A little mayhem will do. The word gets out. Everybody will trust a Rabbi. You set up a fund or partnership with other people's money. You begin to deal in opium. You could do that. You're quick. It's possible. Does it appeal to you?"

"I don't think so." Moshe answered, then paused to reconsider. "It's not why I came here."

"So why did you come?"

"I have Thursdays free."

"*Nu?*"

Moshe sighed. "Not really free. My wife works. My idea of freedom is being with her and going to the lake and doing nothing. Or walking in the city. Or seeing a movie. I can't do any of those things without her. So I thought I would learn something I know nothing about."

"So why not astrophysics?"

"I already know astrophysics. I went to MIT."

Ethel raised her eyebrows.

"I'm sorry," Moshe continued. He held up his hand by way of apology. "I don't really know much about astrophysics, but I don't know what good learning more about astrophysics would do for me. I don't have any place to use it. But I do have some money, and I don't know what money is. I've been thinking a lot about that. I know it's important, but I don't understand it. I want to learn more."

Ethel started another cigarette.

Moshe found the silence burdensome. "I'm sorry," he said. "I'm anxious. This is all new to me. I don't mean to be talking so much."

Ethel leaned forward on her elbows. "Moshe," she said, "you needn't be so anxious. I figure anyone who can not only read all four of those books in one morning but also see through them has earned the benefit of the doubt. So tell me, what have you been thinking about money?"

Reassured, Moshe continued. "I think excess money, money you have beyond what you need for survival, is either bondage or freedom. You can use it to buy things which keep you in bondage, servicing them, or you can use it for freedom, to do those things that lead to experience and growth.

"Between my salary and my wife's salary we have more money than we need for survival, and some funds besides that we've inherited, so there are all sorts of reasons for me to learn about money, both practical and philosophical. I have my Thursdays away from the Temple, and this is what I thought I might do with them. I am free to learn something I know very little about. That's good in itself. If in the process I can learn how to move toward financial freedom, that would be good, too."

Ethel finished her cigarette in silence.

"So," she said at last, "you probably give good sermons. Maybe I'll come hear one sometime." She pointed to the books on the table. "Enough with this. It's time to go learn something substantial."

Together they returned to the office and the library.

Appreciation

"Intellect may be measured by IQ, or pages of Talmud mastered," Sidney said. "Imagination? How do you measure that? Through poetry, artwork? A sense of humor? As for freedom, that's simple. Freedom can be measured in dollars.

"Moshe was in the pursuit of freedom, though he may not have understood why. He learned quickly that freedom is gained only at considerable risk."

After ten Thursdays Moshe began to appreciate money.

He had not made a trade, had not opened an account, had not changed the nature of his saving or spending, but his concept of money, his understanding, his regard for it had grown and deepened.

One evening a month he and Rivkah sat at the kitchen counter and reviewed the family finances over coffee. So much had come from salaries, so much from honoraria for funerals and weddings, so much from interest. So much was delegated to this account, so much to that. This amount was set aside for long-term savings, this for a trip to Israel. This for the children's education, should they be so fortunate as to have children. Funds were corralled into discreet categories.

After ten weeks the rails between the corrals in Moshe's mind began to come apart. While they continued to exist in the ledger, for Moshe the columns began to fade. "We can separate our funds on paper into various categories. We can think of it as this fund and that fund. But the truth is, it's all one pool. The money all flows together. We can't lock it up somewhere and think it's safe. All of it is subject to the forces of the market. Leaving it in CDs is no protection. A surge in inflation could wipe out the value of our reserves in a few years."

Rivkah was frightened when he spoke like that. She took comfort in the separate funds, the columns on the ledger page. She was happy when they could add a hundred dollars to the children's account or to long-term reserves. "So what should we do?"

"I don't know yet, but we're not thinking about this right. What are we doing here?" He pointed to the ledger. "We don't even have a real budget. We spend what we think we have to spend, and we call that our budget. What's left over we put into one of these columns. I don't know what we should do. But it shouldn't be like this." He closed the ledger. "One thing I've learned is money is always at risk. There is no safety. Safety is only an illusion. If you let it sit in the bank, taxes and inflation erode it away. There's no such thing as safety."

Rivkah drew her coffee cup closer to her. "I'm frightened, Moshe."

"I'm a little frightened, too."

The exposure had always been there. Neither of them had been aware of it before.

Gains and Loss

Stephanie had a similar story to tell, but from the perspective of a different world. "When Rivie and Moshe sat together to review family finances, Rivie kept accounts not only of the income and expenses, but also of important happenings of the previous month and hopes for the next one. She understood balances not only in terms of dollars, but also in terms of experiences."

The Katan family ledgers assumed a new form. "Here's our capital," Moshe explained to Rivkah. "On this side of the page is a lot of volatility. That means the markets move very fast over here. Like water rushing through a narrow channel. On this side of the page, it's like a flat lake. The markets hardly move at all. What we do is decide how to spread our capital over the page, how much volatility we want to live with. Remember, even over here on the calm lake a storm can come through from time to time. There isn't any safety anywhere. In some ways, the lake is more precarious than the rapids. You know the rapids are dangerous. You take precautions. But over here on the lake you can be lulled to sleep, and a storm can take you by surprise. What I'd like to do is to spread our assets out like this. Most over here toward the lake side. Checking account, CDs, triple-A bonds. Here in the middle, some in mutual funds. Over here in the rapids, some to speculate with."

"Do you understand what you're doing?" Rivkah asked him.

"I think so."

"Do you understand why you're doing it?"

He put off her question with another. "Do you know how much it costs to put a kid through college today? Figure by the time our kids are old enough, a hundred thousand dollars each. Even with your salary and my salary together, we won't have that much."

"Is that why you're doing it, really? How many children are you planning for?"

"How about two hundred thousand dollars for starters?"

"What if we have triplets?"

"Okay, three hundred thousand, but after that they go to state schools. No more private colleges."

"Moshe, I don't understand this." She pointed at the ledger. "I think you're doing it because you're excited about it. It's a guy thing. You're going out to play football with the guys. It's not my thing. I don't want to know about it. If you think it's worth trying, go ahead and try."

So he moved into a place she did not care or dare to be. He took some of their life together with him. She mourned for her lost columns and categories, for the fantasies they shared each month as they allotted dollars to their appointed niche, even as he showed her the markets he planned to explore, the charts and the measures of volatility. She had no more interest in them than in a *draw play* or a *wideout*. It was his excitement, not hers. "All success," she wished him. "Write home when you score a touchdown, or whatever it is you do."

He was so excited with his new venture, he was unaware he had left her behind.

"Draw plays and wideouts are football plays," Stephanie added by way of commentary.

A Regular Guest

"Ethel was first Moshe's teacher," Stephanie said, "then Rivkah's friend."

Ethel became a regular Friday evening guest at the Katan table. Moshe and Rivkah often had guests for *Shabbat* dinner. Some arrived with bottles of wine, some with flowers. Ethel arrived with a cigarette, which she finished at the front door before entering the house and the Sabbath it contained.

Within a few weeks Ethel insisted on clearing the dishes. "My contribution," she said. "You sit." The dishes were china, the glasses crystal, all wedding presents. Rivkah protested. Ethel was adamant. A few weeks more, with nothing broken, Rivkah relaxed, and Ethel had her way without opposition.

One Friday evening, over coffee, Rivkah asked Ethel about her smoking. "Would you like to stop? Have you tried before?"

"After Phil died, I tried. The worst three weeks of my life."

"Forty days would have been better," Moshe suggested.

"Why forty?" Ethel asked.

"Everything of lasting duration is forty. Forty days and nights it rained in Noah's generation. Forty days Moses was at the top of Sinai getting the commandments. Forty years the children of Israel wandered in the desert. Forty. That's what it takes. Maybe you didn't stop smoking long enough for it to become natural. Would you like to try again, for forty days?" Ethel hesitated. "I'll help you. But it has to be for forty days. I won't help you for less than that. I'll teach you how to pray for help when your appetite is strong. You don't have to do it all by yourself. Think about it."

"What do you mean, pray for help?" Ethel asked.

"Just that. I'll teach you how to use prayer to curb your appetite."

Ethel looked to Rivkah to see if Moshe was serious. Rivkah did not look up from her coffee.

"Prayer isn't Rivkah's thing," Moshe explained. "She says it's an affirmation, or some kind of positive reinforcement. But I see it as an appeal for help from God, and God helps."

"Is he serious, Rivkah?" Ethel asked.

"He's serious," she said. "We have this little disagreement about vocabulary. It's not that I don't appreciate prayer, but for me prayer is a cultural thing. It can be beautiful, even meaningful. But it's a performance. It's not something that works. At its best it entertains and makes you feel good."

Without further comment she began singing the grace after meals. The grace was a rhythmic recitative punctuated with cascades of folk melody. She sang, "May the merciful one bless all those who are dining here," and Moshe responded, "Amen." She continued, "May the merciful one not only bless us, but bless us as Abraham and Sarah, Isaac and Rebecca, Jacob, Rachel, and Leah were blessed." "Amen." "Up in the heights may they intercede for us and use their influence to provide for us an abiding peace. May blessings and salvation descend from God upon us so that we may find grace and wisdom and goodness in the eyes of both God and our fellow people." "Amen."

The grace concluded, Rivkah poured more wine into the *kiddush* cup, said the blessing, drank, and passed the cup around the table, as Moshe had done earlier to initiate the meal. *"Shabbat Shalom,"* she said.

"Good *Shabbos,"* Ethel answered. "Tell me what you were doing. I'm curious about this. You weren't praying when you were singing that?"

"I was singing," Rivkah said. "The words are beautiful. The music is beautiful."

Ethel turned to Moshe. "And what were you doing when you were saying 'Amen'?"

He smiled. "I was praying."

"I'm confused," she admitted.

"It's not so bad," Moshe reassured her. "Rivie and I have this little difference. Other than that, we get along just fine."

"But where does that leave me?"

"What do you mean?" Moshe asked her.

"I want to stop smoking," Ethel said. She withdrew two packs of cigarettes from her bag, one pack open, the other closed, and put them on the table. "Forty days, on a song and a prayer. And God help me."

Referral

Sidney said Moshe was ready for a visit from Reb Hayim. Moshe needed a visit from Reb Hayim. Stephanie commented that it seemed that Reb Hayim was an angel come to earth. He made appearances as needed.

Sidney seemed surprised. "I thought you didn't care for Reb Hayim."

"I don't care for Reb Hayim," she insisted. "I care for angels even less. They frighten me."

Reb Hayim was dressed in a blue-striped business suit. "*Baruch ha-ba!*" Moshe greeted him. "Welcome!"

"So this is where a famous Rabbi works," Reb Hayim said as he entered Moshe's study. "This is very impressive. This whole establishment is very impressive. What goes on here, Moshileh?"

Moshe laughed. "Nothing goes on here. Nothing at all. I was happy to get your call. How did you find me? Why did you find me?"

"Paretzky." The one word explained everything. "He sent me your thesis, Moshileh. It's a very nice piece of work. I came to hear the rest of it, the part you didn't write."

"Will you come and have dinner with us tonight?"

Reb Hayim shook his head. "I'm sorry. I'm really just passing through. I had one meeting this morning, and my plane leaves in three hours."

"Do you live anywhere? I've never met you except when you're going someplace."

Reb Hayim laughed. "My mail goes to New York. My family is in Jerusalem. I live wherever I am at the moment. Where do *you* live, Moshileh. Where are *you* going? Are they two separate places?"

Moshe let out a long sigh and sat in one of the chairs by the coffee table across from Reb Hayim. Moshe shared his history in the congregation, his uncertainties and frustrations. "So what do I do, *rebbe*? What do I do?"

He knew what the answer would be. Rabbi Kantor had said, "Study Torah." Surely Reb Hayim would say the same. Studying Torah was fine. No problem there. He was just lonely, studying Torah.

"Start a *havurah*," Reb Hayim said.

"But the *havurah* is a reaction against the synagogue," Moshe protested. "I can't start something like that inside the Temple."

"Start two *havurot*. Start ten," Reb Hayim continued, as if he had not heard Moshe at all. "People are hungry to be Jewish, Moshileh. They're really hungry. The better you are at being Jewish, the worse it is for them. The better you speak, the more space you fill, the less room there is for them. Give them a chance. Empower them. Get them together in each other's homes. Teach them how to celebrate *Shabbos*, how to prepare for *Pesach*, how to build a *sukkah*."

"I know these people. If I bring them together, they won't do *Shabbat, Pesach,* or *Sukkot.* They'll play bridge, canasta, gin rummy."

Reb Hayim shrugged. "You won't know until you try. And as long as it's Jewish it's better than what you had before. Let them learn from their own mistakes." He reached out and touched Moshe's knee. "I've heard you are a wonderful teacher, Moshileh, but you're not as good a teacher as their own mistakes." He consulted a worn pocket diary and scribbled a note on a pad. "Here. Arlene Turkletaub. Program director of Beth Israel in Philadelphia. She's started a *havurah* program there. Give her a call. It'll work for you. You know how to do it. Trust yourself. It'll make your job easier.

"Now, tell me, Moshileh. Your thesis was very short. I'm astonished they accepted anything so short. I thought you had to write a long thesis to be a big important Rabbi. What was it that you didn't write?"

"I wrote no more than I had to."

"You wrote no more than you dared to! Tell me, Moshileh. Tell me about the angels. What did you see?"

Moshe leaned back in his chair. "How much time do you have?"

"For this, if I have to, I'll miss my plane. What did you see?"

Moshe began speaking about the texts he had learned in the apartment on the West Side. As he recalled the discipline he had impressed upon himself, he yielded to it, and the words began to flow. He touched upon the combinations of meditations he had intuited after his first experience of losing time while chanting the progressive mantra from the *hechalot* literature.

One night his meditation had started with the forty-two-letter name of God.

"You know the forty-two-letter name?" Reb Hayim challenged.

"No," Moshe admitted. That name had been lost centuries before. The early kabbalists had used it to invoke the creative aspect of God, but it was so secret that there no longer remained any certainty as to its composition. But there was a reference to it in the liturgy. "I chanted *Ana v'Koach,*" he said. "I think I was afraid even to chant it in Hebrew, so I chanted it in English."

"I've never heard English for *Ana v'Koach,*" Reb Hayim said. "Can you chant it for me?"

Moshe closed his eyes and monitored his breathing. In a low voice he intoned: *Please now with might, with the strength of your right, untie the bound . . .* Three measures filled with words, and then a fourth, to rest and inhale. He began the second verse: *Accept our song, strengthen us, purify in awe . . .* Then the third: *Awesome in grace, we who see you as One, guard from harm . . .* He required an extra breath before continuing: *Cleanse us and bless, mix mercy with justice, and always redeem . . . Holy power, in your great goodness, guide your people . . . Exalted unique, turn to us, who recall your holiness . . . Receive our cry, hear our plea, you know what is hidden. . . .* That completed the hymn, but tradition demanded the chanting of an additional verse to seal the experience, as a letter of great importance was once sealed by wax and a signet ring: *Blessed is the name, glorious your kingdom, throughout space and time. . . .*

"Very nice," Reb Hayim said, but Moshe no longer heard. He relived his experience, bringing bits and pieces of it to the surface so Reb Hayim might follow.

He had chanted the hymn, breathing his way through it so that he descended deeply into a meditation on the four-letter name of God, etching the image of the letter *HEY* (ה) before his eyes. The *HEY* was the last letter of the four-letter name. He enlarged it and adjusted it about him until it became comfortable, like a doorway. Through the doorway the letter *VAV* (ו) was suspended, a stick-shaped letter, the same size as his spine. He allowed it into him, adjusted his position to accommodate it, imaged a second letter *HEY* in the distance, and breathed himself still deeper. Yearning toward the second letter *HEY,* he pulled himself away from the *VAV,* leaving his body behind. Old familiar images rushed forward to greet him and block him. Glistening white, winged lions approached from the four quadrants, not threatening, but determined. They smiled and showed their teeth. If he moved forward, they joined in a wall before him. If he moved back, they retreated to the corners. The *HEY* was kept from him. He could see it from the distance. He could not approach.

"What do you want?" he mouthed to the winged lions. They answered with rumbles and roars. He breathed and descended deeper than he had dared before, curious about these images. "What do you need?" he asked from the deeper place.

In unison they rolled onto their backs, flying through space upside down, waving their wings and tails, an invitation for him to follow. They brought him down through darkness, through a passageway he remembered but dimly, before a locked door. A large door. A bolted door. A barred door.

He looked up at the four wood-grained panels. "Let me in," he demanded. The winged lions laughed at him.

Moshe recalled his anger, flinched at the memory, and withdrew from the re-experienced vision to find Reb Hayim seated opposite, waiting for him.

"What happened after that?" Reb Hayim asked.

"They wouldn't leave me alone. Wherever I went, they were there. I'd lose concentration in the middle of a class, and there they were on the blackboard, laughing at me. I'd see them at intersections when I was stopped for a red light, during dinner with Rivie."

"Did you tell her about them?"

"No. I've never told anyone about them. I'm not sure why I'm telling you. Maybe I figure *you're* crazy enough to know *I'm* not crazy. But my purpose was to write a thesis and get ordained, not to waste time sharing my visions."

"So what happened with the flying lions?"

"I went back. It was easy to go back. Two or three breaths and I was through the *HEY,* and bang, there were the lions, flapping their wings, laughing at me, wondering what I would do next. I went deep with them, and deeper still. The door wasn't wood this time. It was steel, with diagonal rows of rivets running across the panels. The door was so heavy it sank through the floor, and I sank along with it until the pressure seemed unbearable. When I stopped sinking, I realized two of the lions had gone. Another turned to leave, and only one stayed behind, watching me. He wasn't laughing. He was waiting. I asked him what he was waiting for. He didn't say anything. The rivets had disappeared. What was left was an old rusty door, falling apart. I could see motion on the other side of it. I was curious, so I peeked through.

"A wave of heat nearly overwhelmed me. I felt for sure I had been burned, that my skin was blistering. I tried to step back, but it was too late. There was no escaping the heat. It pounded against me. Sweat poured over my forehead into my eyes. Even though they were closed, my eyes stung. It made no difference whether I had them opened or closed, so I opened them. I saw a man and a woman on a bed, having sex. That's all. That's all there was. It was a faceless man and a faceless woman having sex. They didn't see me. They weren't aware of me. I was just a little boy. This wasn't for me to see. I knew who they were, but I kept the faces off of them. I didn't want to see their faces. Then I realized I wasn't a little boy any longer. It wasn't terrifying anymore. It was all right. I could see their faces and live. The heat became bearable. I think it was my father and my mother. I think once, when I was a little kid, I must have walked in on my father and mother having sex. I ran away. I think that's what happened, but I'm not sure. I turned back to look again. I became aware of my breathing. I was gasping for breath, trying to settle myself down. It seemed like forever to get my breathing down to something reasonable. I was more aware of my breathing than what I was seeing. It wasn't clear anymore, something at a distance.

"I looked around for the lion. He was waiting for me. I turned back one more time and the whole scene was gone. The lion seemed impatient, as if he needed permission to leave, so I gave him permission. He turned all the colors of the rainbow and flew away. All that was left was darkness."

In repeating the stages of the vision, Moshe had fallen back into the experience. He heard Reb Hayim's voice coming as if from a great distance. "How did you get back?"

"I looked upward. There was a dot of light way up above me. I relaxed and floated toward it. The closer I got, the brighter it was, all colors, just like the lion. It was the most beautiful, awesome experience, floating upward like that, back to the surface."

Moshe floated back to the surface, opened his eyes, and focused again upon Reb Hayim. "So we both know I wasn't crazy. But I wasn't about to share that experience with anyone. Not even with Rivkah. It was done, over, finished. The lions didn't come back. I wasn't about to go that deep again." Moshe reached for a handkerchief and in doing so found his shirt was soaked through. He withdrew the handkerchief, made a cursory wipe at his forehead, held the cloth in his hand for fear he might need it again.

"How were things different for you after that?"

Moshe shrugged. "Nothing cataclysmic. Something had changed, but I couldn't say what. My work advanced more gracefully. I went back over my writing and added more material, new insights. The important thing was the lions didn't come back. I was thankful for that, but at the same time, I missed them."

"Had you really walked in on your father and mother when they were having sex?"

"I don't know. Maybe it was my father and mother, or maybe it was Adam and Eve or something archetypal. It doesn't matter. The experience of the vision was real."

"That's right. The experience of the vision was real. Tell me, Moshileh, what do you know about the *Zohar*? What do you know about the *sefirot*? Have you read anything of the holy Ari? Ever studied *Likutai Moharan*? Anything of Shneur Zalman of Liadi?"

To each question Moshe nodded his head in the negative.

"Do you know anything about Sufi stuff? Ever done TM? Studied Zen?"

Moshe said, "No. Nothing."

Reb Hayim's eyes widened. "And you did that all by yourself, a descent with the *Hayot Ha-Kodesh*? You are lucky to be alive, my friend. *Hayot Ha-Kodesh* are the deepest most dangerous of all the angels. You could have been consumed from the inside out. You know the story of the four . . ."

Moshe interrupted him with a raised hand, "Who descended into Paradise."

Reb Hayim paused and sat back from the edge of his chair. With annoyance he said, "I didn't ask if you had read it. Of course you have read it. I asked if you *knew* it. Four of the great rabbis descended to Paradise. Ben Azzai died. Ben Zoma went crazy. Aher broke away from the tradition. Only Akiva returned safely. Why did Ben Azzai die, Moshe? What happened to him?"

The tone was that of Paretzky, a rhetorical question. Moshe knew better than to interrupt.

Reb Hayim waited for all of Moshe's attention. "Do you know the story of the young man who was learning in his master's house? The book was open to Ezekiel. He read the first chapter. The *hashmal,* the energy, came and consumed him from the inside out. He died. Do you know that story? Why did that boy die, Moshe? Why did Ben Azzai die? You think we're talking bullshit here? That they made up these stories? They died. Why did they die?

"The child died because he was too young," Reb Hayim said, "too young to have any protection from the insight. Ben Azzai died, and the others were damaged, because they pushed themselves beyond limits. They pushed themselves beyond safety.

"Ben Azzai was consumed. Imagine a fire like heartburn in your belly, Moshe, except it isn't heartburn. It curdles the stomach and broils the liver. It steams the kidneys and cooks you from the inside out, because you have no defenses against the heat, because you pushed yourself too deep too fast.

"Ben Azzai needed to push himself. All four needed to push themselves. They needed to know how to direct the Jewish people after the destruction of the Temple. They were the spiritual leaders of their generation. They needed to know where to go, and it was worth risking their lives for that. They knew they were putting their lives in danger. They were heroes, great heroes. Only Akiva remained unimpaired, but the insights he gained saved us as a people. Ezekiel before him. And Akiva. How many do you think there were in the generation of Ezekiel who tried and died? We don't have their stories because they didn't live to tell them.

"And you, Moshe? What great need drove you to such depths? What was pushing you? Why did you put your life on the line?"

Reb Hayim left an opening for Moshe to speak.

"I had to get my thesis done." His words were so weak. "I didn't have anything to write. I had to get my thesis done. If I didn't get my thesis done, I wasn't going to be ordained."

"So you pushed yourself to the very limits. You read the warnings but didn't pay attention to them. You put your life at risk to get your thesis done."

"To get my thesis done," Moshe confirmed.

"*Mazal tov,*" Reb Hayim said flatly. "Now that you have your thesis done, what should we do with you?" He leaned forward and pulled Moshe toward him with his eyes. "You are a receiver, Moshileh. A *mikubal,* a kabbalist, and you are learning from the downside up. The rest of us are all upside down. You see, I was raised on *hasidus.* I knew the stories of Reb Nachman before I could speak. After *hasidus* I went back and learned the systems of the holy Ari and Cordovero. And then the *Zohar* and Abulafia. I know some of the texts you speak of, but I haven't learned them. Not really. They don't yield to me the way they yield to you, because I have been colored by everything I learned before. You see them fresh. You came to them a virgin, a spiritual virgin. And you survived."

The eyes broke away.

Reb Hayim rose from his chair, his attention turning to the room. At the wall of books his fingers ran across the spines of the volumes. "You have a gift," he said, his back turned. "What do you intend to do with it?"

Moshe stood, uncomfortable to remain seated while Reb Hayim was standing. He shrugged. "I have no idea."

Reb Hayim reached into his pocket, extracted a notebook crammed with slips of paper, wrote down a name, tore it off, and handed it to Moshe. "Teddy Porter. He's not far from here. You get in touch with him. You have some work to do."

"A kabbalist?" Moshe asked.

"A priest. A Jungian analyst. A surprise for you, Moshe. You don't have to be Jewish to be a *mikubal.* He's a man of great sensitivity and power. I'll call him and tell him what to expect. I wish you safe and fruitful journeys, my friend. When you're ready, let me know, and I'll steer you to where you can learn the rest of the stuff. But let me tell you, it's only commentary. Where you're going is the deepest place. The deepest of the deep."

Reb Hayim embraced him. "Safe and fruitful journeys, my friend," he repeated.

"How many of you have ever done anything with the Havurah?" Sidney asked.

None of the students raised their hands. All of the members of the Havurah who had been inclined to learn the course had attended one of the earlier cycles.

Moshe called Arlene Turkletaub. She had indeed begun a *havurah* program within her synagogue. He learned from her how it was done and explained the concept to the senior Rabbi. "It's like the couples clubs we used to have," he said. "Sure go ahead. As long as everything else is covered, any constructive use of your time is all right with me."

Moshe explained the concept from the pulpit in a sermon, to the brotherhood at their sports day breakfast, to the sisterhood at their fashion show, to the parent teacher association in the day school. *Havurah* was Hebrew for fellowship, a group of individuals and families willing to assume some substantial responsibility for their own Jewish lives. The plural of *havurah* was *havurot*. The members of a *havurah* were *haverim*. *Haverim* would meet in each other's homes. The staff would provide programs for them, from which they could learn without having a Rabbi or a teacher present.

Enough members volunteered to form two groups, one of young couples, with young children, the other of older members, empty nesters. In both he introduced the *yeshivah* style of learning, what it meant to sit across from a study partner and argue texts. It took some time to convince them they knew enough to argue with each other, but once that threshold was crossed, they could not be restrained.

Moshe instituted a regular Wednesday night class on *havurah* dynamics. It was called the *bayt midrash,* the house of study, a place where one could come once or whenever and learn how to learn. Every week the text was different. From this class, and from the excitement generated by the two existing *havurot,* additional groups were formed. Soon there were five *havurot,* two family-based and three constituted of older adults.

The members of the family *havurot* celebrated Hanukkah together in the social hall. They planted a tree for *T"U b'Shvat,* the holiday that celebrated the new year of the trees. On Purim adult and child alike came in costume to the Temple Purim service. They stamped their feet, pounded on pots and pans, waved *graggers* in the air, and elevated what would otherwise have been a sedate service into a traditional outburst of levity and joy.

A column in the weekly Temple letter was devoted to *havurah* activity. *Havurat Emet,* the Fellowship of Truth, wrote about its study of Maimonides' *Mishneh Torah,* and compared the twelfth-century rabbi's understanding of nutrition with modern standards. They accomplished more learning with each other than Moshe had been able to teach in all of his classes. *Havurah Gimmel,* Fellowship #3, wrote about its potluck Shabbat dinners. *Havurat Ha-mishpacha,* the Family Fellowship, wrote about the *haggadah* it was preparing for Passover. They were willing to share it with any other *havurah* that would like to use it.

One Sunday in May was designated Havurah Day. Each of the nine *havurot,* even the new ones, gathered on the playing field around its banner. They held games, races, contests, and ultimately a parade of the *havurot.* The synagogue leadership stood in the center of the field to watch several hundred Temple members march in a huge circle, carrying banners, singing for no apparent purpose whatsoever.

The rabbi in Moshe was contesting with the Rabbi. Moshe was aware of it. Rivkah too. She prayed the rabbi would win.

Present Tense

Stephanie said Moshe described his first trade as something like jumping into the North Atlantic Ocean in the middle of a winter storm.

He had chosen the commodity markets. "All free markets are the same," he ventured. "Some are slow, some are fast. I could speculate in bonds and wait a decade to see a full cycle. Stocks, maybe in a few years. Commodity futures, a couple of months. Let me get my experience quickly."

Six months after Moshe first appeared at Ferrell Bower, he sat at Ethel's desk, completed the forms to open a margin account, and funded it with $25,000. Based on his analysis of the fundamental data and technical trends he bought one contract of November beans. That night he could not sleep. He was shaken, the seas were heaving so. He was long one contract, 5,000 bushels of soybeans for November delivery, at the price of $6.25 per bushel. Each penny of movement represented a $50 gain or loss. Twenty cents would be $1,000: $1,000! That could happen overnight! "Do you know how long it takes me to earn $1,000?" Moshe protested as he tossed in bed that night. "How many funerals, weddings, bar mitzvahs? Do you know what I could do with $1,000? I could be $1,000 poorer in the morning with just a twenty-cent move in soybeans, and I've never even seen a soybean. I don't know whether they move or not!"

The following morning, on the opening, he sold his contract of beans for $6.29 a bushel. After commissions he had a profit of a little more than $100, before taxes.

"What happened?" he asked himself. Whatever it was, it wasn't worth $100, even after taxes. There was a difference, he realized, between holding oneself above the ocean while observing the waves, and jumping in and getting wet. Above the waves was objective; in the waves, subjective. The first allowed him to see the whole picture: the tides, the currents, the winds, the storms. The other subjected him to the winds, the waves, the fear of the depths below, and the sharks in the sea. He could see no farther than the reach of his arms.

"That's why day traders do what they do," Ethel reminded him. "Every afternoon they even off all of their positions. They sweat during the day and sleep at night."

Moshe began to day trade on Thursdays. He arrived at Ferrell Bower before the opening and positioned himself at an empty desk. Ethel made a computer terminal available to him. He watched the flow of the markets, sensed when the tide was turning, and bought and sold soybeans and soybean meal and soybean oil. Corn and wheat. Cattle and even hogs and pork bellies, so long, he said, as he never had to take delivery. Occasionally he would buy and sell orange juice, cocoa, and coffee, though he thought those markets were controlled by big users. With experience he became accustomed to larger positions. When the markets opened, at first he would buy or sell one, two, maybe three contracts. Within a few months he was doing five, maybe ten, adding to his position during the day. He did not go to lunch when he was trading. Each Thursday was a marathon. He wrestled with the markets. He felt the strain. He sweated. He lost weight.

During the day he did not keep score. Stop orders protected him from major losses. He had no preference between buying or selling. He was as likely to be short as to be long. One day, at the conclusion of trading, he found Ethel and several of the brokers in the office standing behind him. He had caught most of a limit move on soybeans with twenty contracts long and had made a profit of $14,800. The guys pounded him on the back. "Way to go!" they said.

"Nicely done," Ethel added. "Next week, Moshe, you take the day off, and I'll take you to lunch."

Moshe had learned about lunches. There was lunch downstairs in the cafeteria, lunch at the Orchid Room of the Intercontinental Hotel and lunch at the members-only Beacon Club. The lunch Ethel took him to, and paid for, was new to him. It was a lunch at Emily's Grill, a noisy place a block outside of the financial district. She and Moshe completed a table for eight.

"So this is your miracle-working Rabbi, Ethel," said the balding man in suspenders.

"This is he," Ethel confirmed. She introduced Moshe to six of the leading commodity brokers from various firms. They were all men, none older than forty-five.

"We heard you caught the big move in beans last week," one remarked.

Moshe confirmed it. "I was fortunate."

"Fortune helps," said another.

Soon conversation left the subject of Moshe and floated from experience to experience. They were content to settle on a historic move in the silver market. Silver had jumped from $5 an ounce up toward $50 and fallen back again. Fortunes had been made and lost on both sides of the move. "I was thinking . . ." one of them began, and they joined together in a fantasy of how best to play such a market. "If I started with five contracts and then added five more . . ."

Moshe withdrew his attention from the conversation. This was not a broker's lunch with a client. This was where the professionals came to dream.

Walking back to the office, Ethel asked, "What did you make of that?"

"Interesting."

"Interesting indeed!" she exclaimed. "What a nice word when you don't want to say anything bad about someone. So what was so interesting?"

"They sell futures and live in the past."

Ethel found this insight funny and laughed so hard she had to stop walking. She began to cough and couldn't stop coughing.

"Are you all right?" Moshe was alarmed. "Ethel, are you okay?"

She waved him away, concentrated to catch her breath, and nodded. "Okay. I'm okay. That was very funny. They sell futures and live in the past. So what do you do, Rabbi Katan. What is it you do on your Thursdays?"

Moshe waited to be certain she was all right. "I trade in the present," he answered finally. "I'm informed by the past, but I trade in the present."

"Yes, that's what you do," Ethel agreed. "You don't even know when people are behind you watching, do you? I didn't tell those brokers about you. Some of the men in the office did. The brokers were curious. They called me. They wanted to meet you. To see if you were for real. Moshe, there aren't many people in this world who trade in the present."

Moshe went home that night and reviewed his trades. In the last month he had made a profit of $35,000. That was more than his annual salary. In the six months he had been trading, the original $25,000 account had grown to $87,000.

He shared with Rivkah that they could afford to send .87 children through a private college.

Stephanie reflected that while Moshe was making money at Ferrell Bower, Sidney was making money at Freeman March. With his language skills, Sidney was a natural. The firm moved the family from Arlington back to London. In short order, Sidney was supervising European operations. Ada was born in London, Ada for Ida. Allison and Ada. They had a flat, not an apartment, with more rooms than they needed, and help for the children. Stephanie could teach again. Life was still good.

Very good, Stephanie corrected. It was in London she bought her first motorcycle, a Triumph. Sidney wouldn't ride on it. There were any number of reasons she shouldn't ride a motorcycle. They were so apparent he didn't bother mentioning them more than once.

She wrote her mother about it, what it was like to ride through the British countryside. She had no idea if her mother could relate to that, but she enjoyed writing about it. She had never shared her earlier experience, riding on the Harley in high school. Her parents knew nothing of that.

They hadn't known much, she realized. When she was awarded the National Merit scholarship, they were surprised. When she announced she wanted to go to school in New England, they were more surprised still.

Uncle Al had told her about Harvard and Tufts. His nephew had gone to Tufts undergraduate and then Harvard medical school. His nephew was very smart, so these had to be the two best schools in the country. He provided the bus fare. She traveled to visit the schools during winter vacation, shivered through her interviews. She didn't have enough warm clothes.

Both accepted her. She chose Tufts because of the working-class neighborhood. Harvard Square frightened her, it was so neat and prosperous. The porches in Medford and Somerville reminded her of home.

"Moshe had implemented the *havurah* portion of Reb Hayim's advice," Sidney said. "He had chosen to forget the second part of that advice until one Thursday morning at Ferrell Bower. As he sat in front of his terminal, lost in the markets, a white, taloned claw swept across the screen in front of him. It sliced four neat lines diagonally, top right to bottom left, its path littered with broken letters and numbers. Moshe tried to blink the vision away, but he was not able to do so. He closed out his positions for the day, shut down his terminal, and went home. He sat alone in the kitchen and waited away the hours until Rivkah returned from the hospital."

Rivkah made herself a cup of tea and joined Moshe at the table.

"I'm considering analysis," he began.

"Five times a week on the couch?" she asked, astonished.

"I don't know. Reb Hayim gave me the name of someone to work with, and I thought I would at least go see him and find out what's involved."

"Is there a problem, Moshe?" Her cup remained suspended between the table and her lips. "Are you having some kind of difficulty? How could I not know about it?"

"It isn't a problem, Rivie. It's something I want to explore." He shared with her his descent with the lions. "It really scared me," he concluded. "I didn't want to tell anybody about it at the time. I just wanted to get my thesis done. But since Reb Hayim asked me to tell him what had happened, it's become real again. I'm scared again."

"Why didn't you share this with me? I didn't know you were so terrified. I got used to coming home and seeing you spaced out, but I had no idea what you were doing. Now I'm scared."

"I didn't share it with anybody. I think I was afraid talking about it would make it real, as if somehow it wasn't real if I kept my mouth shut. I stopped doing it. Once the thesis was secure, there was no more reason to continue."

"But now you want to do it again."

"I may not have any choice." He told her about the incident that morning. "Anytime I allow an opening, it's likely to happen again. I can either stay on the surface and live my life there, or find some protected environment in which to go deep, experiment, and work through whatever it is I need to work through. Maybe I can do it with this fellow. I'd like to find out."

She lowered both the coffee cup and her eyes to the table. "Can we afford it, Moshe? Analysis is expensive."

"We're doing well in the markets. If it's all right with you, we can use some of those funds. Our kids don't have to go to Ivy League schools."

On the wall behind the desk a wooden Jesus was draped on a Lucite cross. Father Porter rose to greet Moshe. He had but the slightest crescent of gray hair about each of the ears that stuck out from his head not quite at right angles. His smile was wider than his collar. Humpty Dumpty, Moshe thought.

"Rabbi, thank you for coming." He indicated a comfortable chair underneath a modern triptych, three different perspectives of the crucifixion. "Please sit down," he said with an expansive gesture. "Can I get you anything? Coffee, a Coke?"

"No thank you, Father."

Father Porter sat opposite. "How is Rabbi Ostracher? I met him only once, really. He was a speaker at an institute I was attending in Switzerland. We sat and talked together after his presentation. He is quite remarkable."

"Reb Hayim is well, thank you. He thought it would be good for me to come and learn with you. You are a Jungian analyst?"

"Yes. I don't practice anymore, but I am an analyst."

"Are you familiar with the Kabbalah?"

"I have some knowledge. I know what it is."

Moshe gave him a brief report of his own introduction to the Kabbalah and his experience with the winged lions. "This has been on my mind ever since Reb Hayim's visit. It isn't so much that I want to do more. I have to do more. I can't do it by myself. Not safely, anyway. Would you be willing to guide me?"

Father Porter reached for a pipe. "Would this bother you?" he asked, and proceeded to fill it with a practiced care. "Would you tell me a little about yourself. Are you married?"

"I'm married. I have a beard. But I'm not forty yet."

Father Porter smiled. "I know the requirements, thank you. Between us we average forty. And then some. If we choose to do this work together, that will have to suffice. Where were you born? How were you raised?" Moshe gave him a history. "Do you have children?"

"We're trying. Nothing yet."

"How much time do you think we would need, if we did this together? You're not talking about an analysis, I don't think. At least not in conventional terms."

111

"I was thinking perhaps we could begin with one session a week, but a long session, an hour and a half, maybe two hours."

Father Porter consulted a round gold watch from his pocket. Gold links attached it to his belt. "Tuesday mornings," he said. "Would that be all right? Tuesday mornings? Early? Starting at six o'clock?"

Moshe looked at Father Porter's watch, puzzled, but did not ask about it. "I can do that," he said. "Thank you."

"Beginning next week, then. Come in through the side door. The front doors of the church won't be open that early." Father Porter returned the gold watch to his pocket.

Moshe understood it was time to leave. "Can I pay you for your time?" he asked.

"I'm not an analyst anymore, Rabbi. But I am curious to see what comes out of this. Let the satisfaction of my curiosity be payment enough."

"Allow me to make a contribution then." Moshe wrote a check for $100 to the Church of the Immaculate Conception and placed it facedown on Father Porter's desk, a procedure he would follow after every meeting. Every time he wrote the name of the church into his checkbook, he wondered what the IRS would make of it, should he ever be audited.

Opium

The stories had titles. The titles changed from telling to telling. This story Sidney had titled "Opium" from the outset.

Opium was a positive word for Stephanie. It was the word that had brought them together. But even when Sidney had used the word in the Coleridge seminar, it had an underlying meaning for him. There were elements of his life he had never fully shared with her. She knew little of his family's business. He didn't like to talk about it. She knew it extended throughout four continents, from Asia, through the Americas, into Europe, and dealt in all manner of commodities and manufactured goods, especially electronics. He had hinted that, in previous generations, opium had been among the commodities. For all he knew, his family was still involved in the opium trade, but he had left his family before the deepest secrets had been revealed to him.

Rabbi Katan had eleven bar mitzvah students in his office singing the *haftarah* blessings when the phone rang.

"I'm sorry, Rabbi," his secretary said. "It's an Ethel Kaplan. I told her you were busy, but she said it's an emergency."

Moshe punched the flashing button on the phone. "What's happening, Ethel?"

"I'm sorry, Moshe. Harold Bower is in town. He would like you to come and have dinner with him tonight. Can you make it? Please?"

"This is an emergency?"

"It's an emergency for me. You don't know the name? Harold Bower? Bower, as in Ferrell Bower? He's in for the day from New York. He's heard of you and would like to meet you. I've been asked to arrange it."

"When and where, and do I bring Rivkah if she wants to come?"

"Seven-thirty at the Beacon Club and yes. Thank you. If I didn't already owe you big, I would owe you big."

Moshe loved to watch Rivkah dress for a night out. It was a fashion show. She settled for a beige outfit that flattered her figure but was still suitable for a Rosh Hashanah service. "You look beautiful," he told her. "It doesn't matter what you wear. But this outfit is especially nice. All it needs is something to dress it up a bit."

She caught on at once. Her eyes became eagerly suspicious. "Like what?"

"Maybe something like this." Moshe retrieved a box from his dresser, opened it, and presented her with a gold necklace, an intricate braid, like a continuous *hallah,* the braided Shabbat bread.

Her mouth agape, he stepped behind her and held it to her throat. She looked first at it and then at him in the mirror. "Moshe? What for? What's the occasion?"

"You. You're the occasion."

On the way to the Beacon Club she wanted to know, "Was it expensive?"

"I don't know. What's expensive? Would you say a twenty-cent move in soybeans is expensive? How about forty cents? Well, I'll tell you the truth. It was less than sixty cents. I got a good deal."

Ethel Kaplan and Harold Bower were waiting for them at the table. Mr. Bower was pleased to meet Rabbi Katan, but all of his attention during dinner was on Rivkah. He had questions about her work and her ambitions. He never once asked her what it was like to be the wife of a Rabbi.

After dinner, over coffee, Mr. Bower turned to Moshe. "I've heard extraordinary things about you," he began. "You are highly regarded in the community. I know Solomon Karnoff well, and he has only praises for you." Solomon Karnoff was the president of the congregation. "I've also heard, of course, that you are a remarkable trader. Are you aware how rare such a talent is? Have you considered the various ways you might make use of it?"

"I'm making use of it now." Moshe smiled at his wife and her new necklace.

"There are ways of doing more than you are doing now. I'm not talking about trading two days a week instead of one. Or of leaving the rabbinate. But if you chose to use your one day not only to trade for your own account, but to trade for a partnership, you would benefit not only from your own profits, but from a percentage of the profits of the partnership as well. Twenty percent is not unusual. And while you may be trading five, ten, or twenty contracts now, with a partnership you might be trading one hundred, two hundred, maybe three hundred or more. The work doesn't have to be any greater."

Moshe looked to Ethel who, by reflex, was searching her pocketbook for a cigarette that was no longer there.

"And, of course," Mr. Bower added, "there would be a management fee whether you made a profit or not. The management fee alone would offset whatever personal losses you would be likely to take in your own account. So in a way you would be able, almost, to trade risk-free."

"How would I find such a partnership?"

"As I said, you have a good name in the community. People like you. They trust you. They are right to like you and trust you." Mr. Bower withdrew a folder from his briefcase. "Here is a prospectus I would like you to look over. It's for a partnership pretty much like the one I'm describing. It earned a net return of forty percent for its partners last year. The partnership began the year with $8 million, made a profit of 3.2 million. The managing partner received as his percentage of the profits $640,000, plus a management fee of about $240,000. So gross proceeds to the managing partner were $880,000, less about $100,000 in operating expenses leaves a net profit of about $780,000 for the year. It would not require much more from you than one day a week, once the partnership was established."

"And how do I establish it?"

"I expect you know people yourself, and we have clients who would like to participate in the commodities markets. It can be done, Rabbi."

"I would work for Ferrell Bower?"

"Oh no. Not at all. You would have your own partnership. It would be completely independent of Ferrell Bower, though we hope you would continue to exercise your trades with us. We will do everything in our power to provide you the support you need so our relationship continues to be profitable."

With that, Mr. Bower's attention returned to Rivkah, and a short time later he excused himself, leaving Moshe and Rivkah with Ethel.

Ethel broke the long silence. "Opium," she said. "Three-quarters of a million dollars a year. Seductive, isn't it?"

Neither Rivkah nor Moshe had anything to say in the nearly empty parking garage. Most of the few cars left were those of the Beacon Club members. Jaguars, Mercedes, Cadillacs. One Ferrari. The old Buick was incongruous.

After some time on the freeway, Rivkah broke the silence. "They think a lot of you. What you've done must be extraordinary."

He had no response.

"Are you tempted, Moshe? That's a lot of money they're talking about."

"Are you tempted?" he turned the question back on his wife. She fingered her new gold necklace. "It's not as easy as he says it is," he continued when she did not respond. "It's not one day a week. It's all the meetings with the prospective partners. Sales meetings. I'm selling myself. Making charts of my trading. Inventing theories of market performance that I don't really have. Keeping the partners happy. More research. A separate office. A manager. Tax forms. All sorts of federal forms. CPAs. Attorneys. Lawsuits if something goes wrong. I don't know of any commodity broker who isn't subjected to a lawsuit sooner or later. I don't know if that goes for managing partners in a partnership, but I can't imagine otherwise. Brokers have their firms to cover their asses. I'd be out in the cold.

"And the return wouldn't be what he said it was either. Forty percent is a huge gain to maintain year after year. The larger number of contracts would make my trading more difficult. I'm in and out with five, ten, twenty. I operate with a scalpel. If I'm operating in the hundreds of contracts, it's like operating with a hammer and chisel. The only one assured of a large profit is Ferrell Bower. Commissions.

"It's a lot more than one day a week. It's pressure on all the other days, too. I couldn't continue running such a partnership and do what I'm doing." His silence extended through a stop light.

"How much money do you think you'd really make?" Rivkah asked when the light turned green.

"To begin with, a hundred thousand a year. Maybe two. Within a few years, a half million. Maybe a million."

"A million dollars a year?"

"Why not? If I do well. If I'm lucky. He's right, you know. They would trust me. Karnoff and his friends would put up a couple of hundred thousand each to see how I would do, and if I did well, let's say even twenty percent, millions of dollars would follow. They have the dollars, and commodities is the place to be. We could do a million dollars a year, to us, for some time. Until something moved against us and we crashed. We'd take our profits and move them offshore somewhere where they couldn't be reached.

"I'd travel a lot. Ferrell Bower would set up speaking engagements all over the country. I'd go and preach the commodity markets, attract new partners. The big ones we'd invite for dinner. We'd need a bigger house, better neighborhood."

"It's a lot to consider," she said.

They remained quiet the rest of the way home.

That's where Sidney finished the story. Apparently it was all he knew.

"That's not where the story ends," Stephanie said. "There's more."

When they were ready for bed, Rivkah said, "I'm exhausted."

"Me too," her husband agreed.

"The necklace is so beautiful. I was feeling so sexy earlier."

"Me too."

"I'm churned up. I don't think I can sleep."

"Me neither. So, what do you want to do?"

"Talk."

Rivkah talked about what it felt like to have a thousand people in the congregation discuss what she was wearing on Rosh Hashanah.

Moshe spoke of what it was like to choreograph a service for a thousand people and try to pray at the same time. He recalled Marjorie Schwartz, the rebellious confirmation student, who challenged him one night after class, claiming no one in the congregation really prayed. "I pray," he pushed forward a pawn in his defense.

"You don't count," she argued. "You get paid for it." The queen had taken the bishop's pawn. Check.

"I used to pray without being paid for it," Moshe mused afterward. "Would I still pray if I didn't get paid for it?"

"It would be nice to enjoy *Shabbat* after dinner," Rivkah said. "I don't like leaving the house. I'd like to stay home with our guests rather than go to the service."

"I keep telling you you don't have to come to the service. You can stay home anytime you want."

116

"And I keep telling you I don't want to be home without you on *Shabbat*."

"We're not talking about money," Moshe said. "We're not talking about money at all. Is a big house important to you?"

"No. Is a Porsche important to you?" She knew his fantasies well.

"No. Do you like your necklace?" She nodded. "Would you like it better with diamonds?"

"No. The necklace is just right."

They were quiet long enough to come to a decision. "We're not going to do it, are we?" Rivkah asked, more statement than question.

"No, we're not."

"We're going to pass on a million dollars a year."

"We're going to pass."

"We must be very rich if we're going to pass on a million dollars a year."

"We must be very something, that's for certain."

Rivkah wore her necklace to bed that night. She felt rich and desirable. How many women had a million-dollar necklace?

Analysis

"Analysis," Sidney said, announcing the next story.

The word transported Stephanie back to a couch on Park Avenue in New York. She lived so close she could walk to her appointment five times a week. She knew Sidney's story, didn't need to hear it again. She had her own analysis to consider. It was at a time when everything was going so well. Sidney was a senior vice president at the New York headquarters. Allison was deep into violin, so profoundly she had been moved to a master class. Ada had lost her English accent and had started piano. Everything was so good, there was no reason for Stephanie to feel so miserable. She could afford herself the luxury of five times a week on the couch.

She didn't pursue the discipline long, only a few months. One strong image remained from the experience, the metal screen, the accordion security gate in front of her father's shop. When he left for the day, he closed and locked it with a huge padlock. A rusty, dirty fence. When he opened in the morning, he removed the lock, but never opened the grate all the way. He could have pushed it back flush against the wall, but never did. Even though it covered part of the display window, he left it ready to deploy, as if he might have to rush and slam it shut in an instant.

A screen, a gate, a fence, a grate. That was the image, nearly every day for months.

Analysis had been good for Moshe, not so good for her.

Tuesday mornings at six o'clock sharp Father Porter greeted Moshe without a word. Moshe took his place in the chair under the triptych on the wall. Father Porter removed the gold watch from his pocket and held it in his hand. Moshe began the process of descent, explaining what he was doing, each step of the way. Father Porter spoke rarely, making interventions ever so carefully. Moshe usually terminated the sessions himself, having reached the point of exhaustion before the two hours were finished. On rare occasions, Father Porter would say, "We have only a few minutes left." The urgency would hasten Moshe's process so he could reach the surface before the time expired. Rarer still, Moshe found more than two hours had passed, on one occasion more than three. At the end of each session, Father Porter accompanied Moshe to the side door, again without words. It was not quite a bow they gave to each other on parting, but a nod, a physical acknowledgment of the work they had shared.

Within a few months Moshe had penetrated through encounters with the symbols of the personal unconscious into prolonged engagements with the archetypes of the collective unconscious. That was Father Porter's terminology. Moshe understood his process differently. He had left behind the World of Formation with its angels and was gaining experience of the archangels of the World of Creation.

As he became more and more focused from the work, he wrote to Reb Hayim and received back suggestions for further study. He learned how to translate the dimensions of space, time, and soul through the four worlds. He learned the secrets of the permutations and combinations of the Hebrew letters. He learned of the uses and misuses of arcane systems of numerology. He sharpened his Hebrew to study the passages of Isaac Luria, the holy Ari, and advanced to the teachings of the Hasidic masters.

Months passed. Moshe became more adept at descent. He had names for the angels or archetypes he encountered and learned to summon them by chanting the names in rhythmic cadence. He had the illusion he controlled the angels by manipulation of their names. In one cataclysmic encounter they taught him otherwise.

He was drawn deep much too fast, so fast he was not able to report so much as a syllable to Father Porter. His lips were drawn back as if by a wind blasting against his face. He accelerated like an express train through gates and passages that had required hours of negotiation in previous descents.

The angels delivered him into a vision of blue, gray, and mauve. A female figure stood nude, her back to him, her long hair swaying, her body pulsing. She turned to face him, walked toward him. Breasts engulfed his cheeks, taut nipples brushed against his lips. She reached down for him, drew him out, tongued him to a hardness that was painful, straddled him, drew him into her, and demanded his release.

He could not release. He knew that. He resisted release with reserves of strength that were fast diminishing.

Mow-sheh . . .

Two long sounds, *mow . . . sheh,* resonated through him. It took forever for him to recognize his name. His name had power. He drew upon it and found resistance. The vision faded.

Moshe had slipped from his chair to the floor. Father Porter held him, rocked him as he chanted his name. "Mow . . . sheh. Mow-sheh. Mow-she. Mo-she. Moshe," until Moshe relaxed, unwound, and opened his eyes. His hands went to his groin. He had not soiled himself. He began to cry.

Father Porter sat on the floor with him, held him close, a frightened child, or a lover in embrace, until Moshe had the strength to return to his chair.

"I'm sorry," Moshe said. "It happened so quickly I couldn't speak."

"I saw you were in difficulty. I brought you back."

"I'm not sure what it was. What she was," he corrected. Unabashedly he looked Father Porter in the eye and said, "I almost came. I was that close. An orgasm. Autoerotic. It was the most intensely sexual experience, the most commanding sexual experience."

"A succubus?" Father Porter asked. "An attempt to draw seed out of you to make demons?"

"No, I don't think so. Once, maybe, it would have been understood that way, at a time when it was defiling to masturbate or release seed involuntarily. Then it would have been a profane seduction, demonic. Mix a sexual experience like that with guilt, and you get demons. No, I don't think it was demonic. It was some insight into the process of creation. Creation by its very nature is sexual, orgasmic."

"Why not have the orgasm, then? If it wasn't demonic, what was the danger?"

"I liked it too much, Father. She was so fucking beautiful, I might have stayed there."

119

Moshe chose to wait for Rivkah to come home from work. Any number of times he raised the phone to bring her home early, and then thought how absurd that was.

"Wow," she said when she found him waiting for her. "What happened to you?" She had never seen him smile like that.

"Wow," she said again, several times that night.

Cute, thought Stephanie. Sidney had not ended the story that way before.

She and Rivkah had shared with each other, through laughter and tears, the satisfactions and frustrations of their sex lives. Rivkah knew of the sexy aspects of Moshe's analysis. She had joked that if the analyst were a nun rather than a priest, she might have been jealous, and suspecting the sexual orientation of the priest, perhaps she should have been jealous anyway.

The students wanted to know more of the process with Father Porter. "So did I," Sidney said. "I pressed Moshe to share more with me. It wasn't that he was unwilling, it was that he couldn't. The process was experienced in symbolic form. Symbols expressed in words lose not only their power, but their sense. When he tried to explain his experience, it was nonsense.

"There was only one other session he could convey to me, the three-hour session. I had asked him about that one, what was so special that it lasted so long. He said it was too long. They did that once and never again."

Sidney turned his attention away from the students and back to the story.

Once at MIT, in a bio lab, Moshe was watching some amoeba-like things through a microscope. He watched them for the longest time, bent over the eyepiece. He didn't even know enough at the time to bend the eyepiece back so he could be more comfortable. The specimen was suspended in a solution, caught between the slide and a cover. What did he hope to see? Maybe binary fission. He wanted to experience something miraculous. When his body was cramping from the imposition, when he thought he couldn't look anymore, to his amazement, he saw the cell borders of the amoeba beginning to change. They started to break down. Something was happening! The boundaries of the cell disappeared completely. Then the inclusions within the cell began to change. They became brown. Then, ash.

The strong light of the microscope had boiled away all of the solution. What he had witnessed was the death of the amoeba.

He wasn't disappointed. It wasn't reproduction. It wasn't binary fission. It was death, the end of a life, and that, too, was miraculous.

In that one long session with Father Porter he removed himself from himself and sat back to watch what would happen to himself. When he saw his boundaries begin to disappear, he knew what was happening and came back.

He learned how tenuous his life was. He learned how frail the boundaries were. It was an awesome experience, one he never dared to repeat.

Sidney said, "In those experiences with Father Porter he pushed the envelope beyond the place of words, even to the point of stretching it very thin. Sex and death. He must have trusted Father Porter very much to have taken such risks."

This was also new to Stephanie. Moshe had shared some of his erogenous experience in analysis without inhibition, but never anything like this. Perhaps he was afraid. Sex was one thing; death quite another. If Rivkah knew the risks he was taking, she might have intervened and insisted that the process stop.

Dragon

Stephanie had never met Milton Kramer. He was gone before she had come on the scene, but she liked him. She liked that he had a close relationship with his daughters even after they had married out of the faith. His daughters were lucky to have such a father.

To the students she said, "Milton Kramer was Moshe's study partner from his first week at the Temple. Moshe began with texts from his thesis, explaining every word so that Milton could follow. The benefit to Moshe was that he learned from his own words more deeply than he had ever learned from the text. Milton was an exacting student.

"When Reb Hayim suggested new texts, Moshe learned them with Milton. Some were in translation. Milton followed the English and Moshe the Hebrew. Some Moshe had to translate word for word, a difficult process. Milton questioned and challenged everything. That was his nature. Whether he learned with Moshe one-on-one, or participated in a class, Milton challenged him. Moshe accepted this as blessing rather than a curse."

One afternoon Milton Kramer came to visit Moshe at his home. They had always met before at the Temple. "My youngest grandson will celebrate his bar mitzvah next month," Milton began after he had settled his large frame comfortably into an oversize chair.

"*Mazal tov,*" Moshe responded.

"In Chicago."

"It sounds like that's a problem."

"Five years ago, when his brother was bar-mitzvahed, it wasn't a problem. I was still driving. But I can't do that anymore. Moshe, I'm afraid to fly. I've never been on a plane in my life. If I can't get over my fear of flying, I'm afraid I will miss my grandson's bar mitzvah. I can't let that happen."

"The airlines have programs . . ."

"Programs shmograms. I don't have time for them. I know there's something keeping me from getting on the plane. Help me get through it, will you?" He held up his hand to ward off interruption. "I know I give you a rough time. If I didn't, somebody else would. So you owe me. Let's do it, eh? Either the stuff we've been studying works, or its full of shit. Let's find out. Give me some of your mumbo jumbo and get me on that damn plane."

That was how the euphemism of traveling became associated with Moshe's *merkavah* system of descent. Milton spoke of it later to anyone who would listen, how he and Moshe had traveled together through the inner worlds so he could travel through the outer world to Chicago for his grandson's bar mitzvah.

Moshe asked Milton to find a comfortable position, to observe his own breathing, almost as an outsider looking in, how the stomach rose and fell. Moshe began a guided meditation, a variation upon the descent through the four-letter name of God. He asked Milton to imagine himself on a road, a straight road that vanished at the horizon. Only the road was important, the edge to the left, the edge to the right, two lines that came together at the vanishing point. And a dotted line down the middle. The Hebrew letter *HEY* (ה) stood on the road like a doorway.

"If you like, stand in it," Moshe suggested. "Look at the road underneath your feet. See the detail. The cracks. The gravel. The sand.

"Look down the road. Even a few feet ahead, you can no longer see the cracks. Everything blends in. You have the feeling of the road, not the details. Image the letter *VAV* (ו) there, and if you like, walk into the letter *VAV*. Adjust your position so that it is comfortable in you.

"Then look farther down the road. Deep down the road. Where you can see only the edge of the road. Another *HEY* there, if you like. Something to yearn toward. And through that *HEY* you can see the vanishing point. But no matter how far you go, you can never get to the vanishing point."

Slowly they penetrated the divine letters and left behind the higher realms of the empirical world. The two traveled together. Milton reported the images he experienced. To some degree, Moshe experienced them as well, and guided Milton to the more salient, energized areas. They found the fear of not being present at the grandson's bar mitzvah. Entrance to the bar mitzvah was guarded by an angel in the appearance of a fire-breathing dragon. Moshe withdrew slightly and checked Milton's vital signs. His breathing rate had increased, no doubt his pulse rate also. He was sweating profusely, his muscles tense.

"What does the dragon want?" Moshe asked.

"To keep me away. The dragon wants to keep me away."

"Away from what?"

"From Chicago."

"Can you see Chicago?"

"No, the dragon is in the way."

"Can you move so that you can see Chicago?"

"No. It breathes fire. It keeps me away."

"Describe the dragon."

"It breathes fire. It's green. It has red eyes and red nostrils. Fire comes from its nostrils. And from its eyes! It's very scary, Moshe! It wants me to stay away."

"Milt, if you can, stay where you are but monitor your breathing. Slow your breathing. Focus on the letters of the divine name, on the stages of the breathing cycle. Stay where you are by the dragon, but allow your body to slow down, if you can."

Moshe watched and waited. Milton's breathing came under control.

"Is the dragon still there?"

"Still there. Waiting."

"Waiting for what?"

"Waiting for me to try to get to Chicago again."

"Are you willing to try?"

"I have to. I have to get to Chicago."

"Focus on the face of the dragon. Two eyes, two nostrils, fire coming from all four. Focus in the center. Let the fire come out around you, on all sides of you. Focus on the center. Be mindful of your breathing.

"Again, now, what does the dragon want?"

Milton's voice was slower, softer. Moshe had to lean forward to hear it. "To keep me from seeing Chicago."

"Not to keep you from getting to Chicago? To keep you from even seeing it?"

"Seeing it."

"Deeper still, Milt. If you are willing, focus on the nose of the dragon. Right in the middle of the eyes and the nostrils."

"Like a window," Milt reported. "Like a cloudy window. Cloudy." Milton became agitated. "Cloudy? Not cloudy. Steamed!" The image went through him like lightning. Milton jerked upright. His breath came in gasps. "Steamed," he murmured. "Steamed. Steamed. A kettle. Steam kettle. Chicago. Sound. Whistling."

Moshe was alarmed. "Breathing. Do the breathing. Breathe through the letters. *HEY, VAV, HEY, YOD* . . . Milt, do it!"

"It's okay. I'm okay. I see Chicago. It's a steam kettle. It burned me. It burned me. I'd forgotten. Why is Chicago a steam kettle?"

"Where's the dragon, Milt? What happened to the dragon?"

"It's there. No fire anymore."

"What does the dragon want?"

"To keep me from seeing. To keep me from seeing Chicago. To keep me from seeing the kettle. I got burned. I was screaming. I got burned. They were screaming. Everyone was screaming. I remember."

"The dragon was there to keep you from remembering?"

"I couldn't sleep afterward. The burns. The fear of the burns."

Back and forth Milton went through the steamed window. Forth and back and forth and back until the transition became easier and the vision clear.

"The dragon came to keep you from the memories," Moshe suggested. "What does the dragon want now?"

"The dragon wants to leave, Moshe."

"Is that okay, for the dragon to leave?"

"Yes."

"Would you like to thank the dragon? It protected you for many years."

"Yes."

Milton was crying. Tears fell from his cheeks.

"Don't be concerned for the tears," Moshe said. "Where is the dragon?"

"The dragon is gone."

"What do you see?"

"The kitchen, the old house. My mother and my father, comforting me. My grandmother screaming."

"That's all right?"

"It's all right. The burns weren't that bad. The screaming was bad. The screaming. I had forgotten the screaming. I had forgotten everything."

"The dragon came to protect you from the memories. You don't need the protection anymore. You confronted the dragon. You endured the pressure of confronting the dragon. So it's as if the dragon says, 'If he can handle that kind of pressure, I'm not needed here anymore. I don't need to protect him any longer.' So the dragon is gone. Milt, bring up the image of an airplane, if you can. What does it look like."

Milt smiled. "A dragon."

"It's big and it breathes fire. Do you need anything to master this dragon?"

"It's not as difficult as the dragon I just faced."

"Is there anything more we need to do here?"

"No. I don't think so. I'm tired."

Moshe helped Milton breathe his way back to the surface. "How long do you think that took?" he asked.

"Twenty minutes?" Milt suggested. "A half hour."

"Look at your watch." Two hours had passed.

"Something happens to time when you experience it deep in the worlds. Twenty minutes in *yetzirah* is two hours in *asi-ah*." Moshe used the kabbalistic Hebrew terminology for the various worlds of experience. "Imagine how long a few minutes might be in *bri-ah* or *atzilut*. Do you think you'll be able to fly to Chicago now?"

"I can try."

The week of his grandson's bar mitzvah, two members of Milton's *havurah* helped him to his seat on the plane. He reported afterward he had kept his cane at hand, a sword if necessary to slay a dragon, but he didn't need to use it.

Sidney said, "Moshe asked Father Porter if and how his experience with Milton differed from analysis."

"You did that in one session," Father Porter said.

"But we had some years of studying kabbalistic texts together."

"That's how it differs," was the priest's response.

Sidney said, "Moshe taught me that the text of a contract was the portrait of an angel. Such angels, properly drawn, could serve to perfect the world, and improperly drawn, could tear the world apart. A contract rendered through co-ercion was a demon, exacting punishment even beyond its term."

Moshe worked hard at the congregation in his third year. Six days a week he worked. He taught the Bar Mitzvah class, the Confirmation class, served as a resource to the religious school, supervised adult education and the basic Ju-daism classes, did his share of pulpit work and counseling, visited the ill in the hospital and in homes, motivated the youth groups, and did whatever else the senior Rabbi requested of him.

Midway through his third year he sat with two members of the board of trustees to negotiate an extension of his contract. One was a partner in a pres-tigious law firm, the other the owner of a chain of carpet and tile stores. They offered Moshe a compensation package of $37,800, plus pension, health in-surance, disability insurance, and a travel allowance for conventions. "We're very pleased with the work you've done for the congregation," the lawyer said. "This represents a salary increase of $3,000, plus an increase in the ben-efits. That's more than we've ever offered an assistant before. We hope you and Rivkah will stay with us for two more years."

Moshe read through the letter. There were only three paragraphs, the first describing his duties, the second his compensation, the third a statement he would not seek to renew his employment with the congregation at the con-clusion of the extension, nor would he remain in the region either to work at another congregation or to form one of his own.

Moshe looked to the lawyer, to the businessman, back again to the lawyer. He was surprised to find himself angry.

Was he angry with these men? They were the best negotiating team the board could assemble to represent the congregation. They were doing their job. Why should he be angry with them?

Was the money too little? What did a few thousand dollars mean to him?

Was it the mention of his wife? His wife was not an employee of the Temple.

Was it the exclusionary paragraph, the third paragraph that was intended to force him out of town, because the congregation would not want him around, a loose cannon, to become a competitor?

"Thank you," Moshe began. "You are very kind. I would like very much to continue with the congregation, and I know Rivkah would like to remain here. She's very happy with her work at the hospital. Now, as for this letter . . ."

In a flash Moshe understood what kindled his anger. The board had sent two of them, two men well practiced in the art of negotiating, to one clergyman, alone, without representation. They intended to overwhelm him. For them this was a little thing, to be presented and done within a moment. These men had better things to do and were eager to return to them. For the Rabbi, it was two years of his life and a trip out of town afterward.

". . . the second paragraph. Compensation. The increase in salary you offer is really no more than a cost of living increase. There's nothing there for merit. I would like a salary increase of $6,000, plus the appropriate increase in benefits, and an additional $500 in my travel allowance."

The two men were plainly startled, but they recovered quickly. It required no more than five minutes to reach an agreement at $5,000, with benefits, and the additional $500 for travel.

"Now the third paragraph. I have no idea what I will be doing in two years, but I do not want my choices limited. This is not acceptable."

"But Rabbi," the lawyer responded, "this is the way of the world. Junior Rabbis work in one community, then leave to work in another. I think we've been very generous here." He pointed to the second paragraph. "I really think that this is the best arrangement you can get. I earnestly suggest you sign."

Earnestly, Moshe thought. A powerful word. It rankled him. Or perhaps it was the word *junior.*

"I have no intention of hurting or damaging the congregation in any way," he said aloud. "But I don't like the paragraph. It feels to me like I'm being hounded out of town. If I wanted to open a congregation of my own, I could do it this year. This year, next year, it doesn't make any difference, really. I don't like the paragraph."

"Is it your intent to hold us up for more money?" asked the businessman. "The board will not be bullied, young man!"

"The money is all right," Moshe responded. "I don't like this third paragraph. I don't like the way it feels. I won't sign the letter with this paragraph included."

"I'm sorry, Rabbi Katan. This is the way it is. This is the way these things are written."

"Let me consider it overnight. I think I'd like to share it with my attorney and see what she has to say."

"We'd like to get this done right now," the businessman said adamantly. "I for one would prefer not to have another meeting." He looked at his watch, turned to the lawyer. "I know Rabbi Katan, Bill. I don't think he intends anybody any harm, do you? Let's take him at his word, cross out this paragraph, and get this thing finished."

So it was done.

Rabbi Katan signed on for another two years, at more money than the board expected and without an exclusionary cause.

"We have the extension," he told Rivkah that evening when she returned from work. He reviewed the negotiating process, sharing with her his feelings of anger.

"You're still angry about it," she said.

"I don't know why."

"The money wasn't important to you. Why did you argue for it?"

"Because I was being badgered. Because I was imagining other guys sitting there who need the extra dollars and don't know how to ask for them because they're being overwhelmed by two high-powered professionals. And I really didn't like that third paragraph. I didn't like it at all."

"Were they angry with you because you held out?"

"No."

"Were they proud of you because you stood up to them?"

"No."

"So, what?"

"So they couldn't have cared less, one way or the other. I wasn't important to them. I was an inconvenience in the middle of a busy day."

"No wonder you're angry."

"Moshe's anger was not a good sign," Sidney said. "Moshe later taught there is no anger that doesn't emanate from pride. At the root of all anger is the question, 'How could this happen to me?'

"The battle in Moshe's life was not over a few thousand dollars and a clause in a contract. It was between the rabbi and the Rabbi.

"That contract had been written for a Rabbi."

Thursdays he continued his trading at Ferrell Bower. He and Ethel were among the first to arrive, long before the markets opened. Together they had breakfast and reviewed the technical and fundamental information of the week. Moshe asked questions without looking up from the charts and text. Ethel had answers, or went to find them. By the time breakfast was done, he had decided which markets were likely to have the volatility to warrant attention that day, what his opening position would be. Only then, business put aside, did they relax over coffee and talk about more important matters.

"I wonder what I would do if we had enough money so I didn't have to work in a congregation?" he asked, surprised that he was asking. Some part of him was suggesting that a congregation might not be the best place to be. The question began as hypothetical. Underlying it was, "How much money is enough money?"

"So how much do you have already?" Ethel asked, though she knew the answer.

"About half a million."

"That's about $50,000 a year income for you, before taxes. Is it enough? How much would be enough?"

"A hundred thousand," he suggested. "After taxes."

"Ooo, after taxes, he says. A hundred thousand after taxes, that's two million dollars you need, Rabbi Katan. When do you need it by?"

"No hurry. It's only hypothetical."

"How would you do it? Would you start a partnership?"

"Why don't I like the idea of a partnership, Ethel? Why don't you like the idea? You don't, do you? You haven't said a word about it. You'd stand to make a lot more in commissions, but you don't want me to do it. How come?"

Ethel shrugged. "I've seen what it does to people. Maybe I'd rather not make the commissions and not have to see what it does to you."

"I love you, too, Ethel."

Ethel pushed her chair back from her desk. "Moshe, what do you think I would do if I had enough money so I didn't have to work here?"

"I don't know."

"I do. I know exactly what I'd do. I'm doing it. I'd work here. I have enough money, Moshe. Phil left me with a lot of money. I work here because I like it. I don't like to travel, but I do like to see the world, and I can do that right from here. I like to meet people. I'm curious about people, about why

129

they do what they do. Did you know that a person's wallet is an opening into his soul? I can learn more about a person the first time he opens his wallet than most shrinks learn about their patients in a year. I've seen what happens to successful traders when they begin to think they really know what they're doing, when they go the opium route and start hustling other people's money. I don't need the extra commissions I'd make from your partnership, Moshe. I like you just the way you are. It's fun to see the world through your eyes.

"Now, do you really intend to try to run your half million to two million? How do you imagine to do that?"

"I don't know, Ethel."

"Yes you do. You're just afraid to admit it."

That night Moshe took the commodities market home with him from the office.

"What's all this?" Rivkah asked. Charts were spread over the dining table.

"Last week's charts. This is soybeans, that's live cattle, and this is orange juice. These are the markets I'm interested in this week. You can see the volatility. See all these spikes? I need volatility for what I do. This book is a history of spreads going back to the beginning of the markets. It doesn't tell me what's going to happen, but it gives me ideas about the kinds of things that can happen. It helps me know where to be."

"What are you going to do now that you haven't been doing before?"

"Nothing new for a while. Nothing at all until I see something. Until I think I see something. Maybe a hint of something. Then I'll do it big and hold on until I'm blown out one way or the other."

Fairness

The phone rang during bar mitzvah class.

"It's your wife, Rabbi. She says it's in an emergency."

"Ethel is in the hospital," Rivkah told him. "I'm here with her. Could you come as soon as you can?"

"Is she all right? I mean, what's wrong?"

"They don't know yet. Not for sure. She was coughing, Moshe, and she began to cough up blood."

"Oh shit," Moshe said. The bar mitzvah kids were startled. To Rivkah he said, "I'll be there within the hour." To the kids he said, "I'm sorry. I just found out that someone I like very much may be very sick." He caught his

130

breath. "Where were we? The blessing after the *haftarah*. No. We'll do something else. I'll teach you this instead. It's the shortest prayer I know. Miriam has leprosy and Moses prays to God. He says, 'God, please, heal, please, her.' The Hebrew is, '*El na rafa na la.*' That's all there is to it. And here's a way to sing it."

They sang the prayer until the class ended.

"But she stopped smoking," Moshe protested in the hospital corridor outside Ethel's room.

"It's probably been there a long time," Rivkah said.

"It's not fair, damn it. She stopped smoking." Tears welled up in him.

Rivkah hugged him, and they cried together.

Terminal

Moshe thought long and hard before his first platform dive into the market seas. Each night he had pondered the technical data, perused the fundamental information that poured out of weather services and crop reports. Shuffling his papers together, he came to the decision that it was the right time to buy orange juice. He established a substantial position, with plans to add to it in incremental stages if the market moved with him in the following weeks. He trembled and gained weight. The market did not move with him. He lost $31,000.

The loss numbed him. He told himself it was only six percent of his capital. But he also told himself it was a year's worth of college tuition, room and board for a prospective child. Or, a Porsche. He had lost a Porsche in two weeks of trading.

"I lost a Porsche," he confessed.

Ethel was not alarmed. She removed the oxygen mask, and asked, "How did you decide when to buy and sell?"

Moshe sat in the chair beside her hospital bed. The television cantilevered from the wall was muted.

"I did my homework, Ethel. I really did."

"I'm sure of it. How did you make your decisions?"

"I wrote all of the positive factors in one column, all the negative in another. When the positive outbalanced the negative this much, I bought. When it moved the other way, I sold."

"Is this the way you used to do your day trading on Thursdays?"

131

"I didn't have time to do that on Thursdays. You know that. Everything happened so fast."

"So how did you make your buy and sell decisions on Thursdays?"

Moshe did not know how to respond. At last he asked, "How much is eight times nine?"

"Seventy-two. What does seventy-two have to do with anything?"

"How did you arrive at seventy-two?"

"I just know it."

"That's how I traded on Thursdays. I just knew."

"How come you just knew, Moshe? How did you get to the place where you just knew?"

Moshe closed his eyes, put himself back at the desk behind the terminal, and imagined the electronic information flow across the screen. He watched and absorbed the market until the market absorbed him, and he became the market.

"Moshe," Ethel interrupted him, "you remember what you told me? You trade in the present. You stopped doing that. There isn't any difference between day trading and keeping a position open overnight, except for the exposure. The exposure is greater." She paused for a while to inhale some oxygen.

"Listen. Imagine a tightrope walker on a wire two feet above the ground. That's a day trader. Now imagine him two hundred feet up in the air. It's the same wire. Only the exposure has changed. If the tightrope walker starts thinking the wind is such and such, and the clouds are moving this way, and the birds are flying that way, he's going to fall. But if he does just what he always does when he's two feet above the ground, he gets safely to the other side."

That was a long speech for her. She was exhausted. Moshe held her hand until she fell asleep.

Watch

Nearly a year and a half into the process, Father Porter deviated from their parting ritual. "Rabbi," he said, "are you in a hurry this morning? Could we take a few more minutes, please?" Moshe sat back in his chair. "I have some news I have to share with you. I'm being called away in two months to go to the Vatican. It's a good opportunity for me. I'll have a chance to study and to teach. But there is something I would like to do before I go. If we could reverse roles occasionally? If you would be kind enough to guide me?"

"It would be a privilege, Father."

In the next two months Moshe learned the techniques of guiding, how to descend with the traveler, to experience what he was experiencing while retaining a firm anchor in the World of Action, to suggest gentle interventions to drive the traveler deeper, to assist the traveler in raising redemptive, transformational words to the surface.

When the two months were done, they sat in their chairs opposite each other and looked into each other's eyes. Both of them understood eyes to be windows into the soul.

"Thank you, Moshe," Father Porter said.

"Thank you, Teddy," Moshe replied.

Father Porter fumbled at his belt to detach the gold watch. "This is for you, Moshe." He held out the gift.

"How can I take that from you?" Moshe protested. "It must be precious to you."

"Please, Moshe. Please. I'm going to the Vatican. I won't be back. I want you to have this. It will help you to understand Tuesday." Teddy smiled.

Puzzled, Moshe accepted it. The two men embraced and parted.

That day was a Tuesday. They had always met on a Tuesday. Father Porter had consulted his watch so many months before when they had set Tuesday as their day of meeting. How could a watch determine a Tuesday?

At his car, Moshe withdrew the watch from his pocket, opened it, and saw inside instead of a timepiece a representation of the breastplate of the High Priest in Jerusalem from the days when the Temple was standing. The breastplate was in gold on a black background. Twelve gems represented the twelve tribes of Israel. "Urim and Thumim," Moshe said aloud. "He was consulting an oracle!" As he held the artifact in his hand, light reflected from first one stone and then another. "How would he know which stone was Tuesday?" he wondered. As he moved the watch, one stone shone brighter than all the others. "So that one is Tuesday," he said, but without conviction. That was enough for the moment. He returned the watch to his pocket and went home.

Stephanie had heard this story many times. Early on she had asked Sidney what it meant. Why should one stone shine brighter than any other? Was it divine intervention? Did God direct the sun's rays to illuminate a particular stone?

Sidney confessed he didn't understand the story himself. He thought if he kept telling it, allowing it to change from telling to telling, his understanding would grow. There was a continuation to the story, but the continuation was more unsettling than the story itself.

"Well, what is it?" Stephanie had asked, annoyed she had to insert the question into his inscrutable silence. "You can't tell me you know something without telling me what you know."

It was late in their learning, Sidney shared, when Moshe had opened the gold case containing the Urim and Thumim. It was a pocket watch with the works removed. Inserted under the glass was crushed black velvet, and fixed on the fabric a representation of the High Priest's breastplate, twelve stones of different colors in a rectangle, four high, three across. Perhaps the stones were precious. More likely it was a cheap souvenir inserted into an old watch case. The symbol had become precious to Father Porter, so whatever the nature of the stones, gems or plastic, the gift was precious to Moshe.

Moshe suggested that Father Porter didn't need it anymore. When Father Porter had returned from a deep descent during the last few weeks of their time together, he had found droplets of blood on the palms of his hands. That was a profound moment for him. Perhaps the realization of his internal faith was such that he no longer needed external representations.

Sidney had asked Moshe if such a thing was really possible.

"The envelope of the body is very thin," Moshe reminded him. "It doesn't take much to break it down."

Sidney had asked Moshe if he could do that too.

Moshe smiled at that. "Me? Stigmata? I'm Jewish, Sidney. I don't do hands."

As if to belie his words, he extended his arms Christlike, draping them across the back of his chair. He closed his eyes, monitored his breathing, and, within a few seconds, produced a rivulet of blood—from his nose!

"I don't want to make this part of the story," Sidney had told Stephanie. "It disturbs me. In some way it was funny. Maybe Moshe meant it to be funny. But it was imbalanced, more terrifying than funny. Moshe was being stretched dangerously thin."

Stephanie respected Sidney's discomfort and hadn't questioned him any further.

Stephanie said, "Ethel did not spend much time in the hospital. She had medication to manage her discomfort. She didn't miss many days of work.

"Ethel and Moshe had their Thursdays together, and many evenings as well. Rivkah prepared the guest room. During her last months Ethel spent more time with Moshe and Rivkah than at her own home."

"It's the young who suffer from exposure," Ethel told Moshe, as if that somehow explained her balance in the face of her impending death. "I'm old enough so it's not so terribly frightening. I don't have so much to lose." This she shared with him as they studied charts of live cattle futures on the dining table.

Moshe knew her well enough to keep his silence.

"It's not live cattle. Pork bellies," she said. "That's where the volatility is. You don't pay much attention to hogs or pork bellies. Is it because they're not kosher?"

Moshe only smiled.

"*Nu?* That's a question I asked you. I want an answer."

"It's no problem," Moshe said, "so long as I don't take delivery."

"Pork bellies then." She flipped the book of charts ahead to the current month of pork bellies. "What do you see?"

Moshe looked at the activity on the chart. He covered it with his hand. "What I see is your talent, Ethel. You can't hide it from me."

His response caught her by surprise. She recovered quickly. "It's your talent," she said, "your ability to remain objective, above the markets. It's your discipline that makes for success, Moshe."

He shook his head. "It's your talent that draws the discipline out of me. You did it from the very first day, bringing me along, step by step. You knew just what you were doing, how much exposure I could stand."

"It's very rare, what you do, Moshe."

"It's very rare, what you do, Ethel. You do it so well, hardly anyone has an idea. Your talent is to bring out potential and make it kinetic. That's a rare talent, and the price one pays for such talent, for any talent, is praise. You have to pay the price. Admit it. You're good at what you do."

"Okay," Ethel said at last. "I admit it. Thank you. Now, what do you see in the chart?"

Moshe lifted his hand and looked from the chart to Ethel. "What I see here," he said, "is your love for me. Thank you, Ethel. I love you, too."

Stephanie said, "It wasn't in pork bellies that Moshe made his first really big hit. It was in sugar. And his success, sweet as it was, almost derailed him."

Sugar was at record highs, impossible highs. It was only a matter of time.

Moshe began selling short even before the peak, adding to his position as it began to fall. By the time the price fell below the trend line he was ahead $80,000, and when he sold as it bounced off the bottom his profit surged to $290,000.

He was numb, more so as a winner than a loser.

"I did it!" the pride proclaimed and struggled to rise within him.

"I did *bupkis,*" he responded. "I rode the markets. I was lucky as hell."

"No, I did it! I really did it!"

"So tell me what you did, wise guy."

"I . . . I . . ."

"See. You can't tell me. That's because the 'I' wasn't there, you shmuck. I thought I got rid of you, and all it takes is a little success, and there you are bragging again. 'I, I, I.' That's all you ever think about. 'I.' It wasn't the 'I' that did it. It was the absence of 'I' that did it."

So Moshe Katan struggled with himself to keep his balance in the face of success.

An Opening

"Moshe was uncertain of his direction," Sidney said. "His success in the markets had given him some freedom from financial worry. He didn't have his two million, but he had reached one. Freedom from, he had already learned, was only half a freedom. There also had to be a freedom to. As his contract with the Temple neared its end, nothing attracted him.

"Nothing is not such a bad thing. There's a lot worse."

The senior Rabbi called Moshe into his study. "What are your plans for next year, Moshe? What positions are you looking at? Can I be of any help?"

"I have nothing specific in mind," he answered. "I'm thinking of taking a year off to do some studying. After that I might begin to look at a congregation somewhere."

The senior Rabbi toyed with a paper clip, moving it rapidly between his fingers. "It's not a good thing professionally to take a year off, Moshe. Your time here has been a good stepping-stone into a medium-sized congregation. All of my assistants have placed well. You never can be sure of what goes on in the placement process, but I think you have a good chance to get most any job you want. You are on a good career track. A year off at this point will be a major setback."

"Rivkah is happy in her job, Rabbi. We have the financial freedom to take some risks."

The senior Rabbi arranged his desk top before responding. "The board is concerned you might be thinking of starting a new congregation in this area. Is that what you're thinking? Be honest, now, Moshe."

"No, sir. I assure you I'm not thinking of a new congregation."

The senior Rabbi allowed the silence to extend uncomfortably. "I have something to share with you, Moshe. I'm going to retire this year, leave the pulpit. I haven't told anybody that. You're the first.

"My wife isn't well. Nothing serious, but we've made a decision. It's enough. We're going to retire and move to San Diego. This pulpit will be open next year. I'm telling you first because I want you to consider carefully your response when the news becomes public.

"You are much liked. You have a following, and you deserve it. You're a good person, and a good Rabbi. You have a great future ahead of you. Someday, if you like, you will have a congregation like this, whatever it is that you want to build. But there is another step or two before that.

"According to the rules you don't have the seniority for this position. I'm not saying you couldn't handle it. I'm saying you don't have the seniority. The Rabbinic Placement Committee won't even consider putting you on the panel of Rabbis to be interviewed. If you disregard the rules, you jeopardize your career, and you may very well tear this congregation apart.

"As soon as I announce my retirement a lot of people are going to ask you to apply for the position. That's why I'm telling you first, so you can think it through ahead of time and be responsible in your answer."

To his credit Rabbi Katan had never before imagined himself at the helm of that congregation.

Stephanie said, "Moshe's decision to apply for the position of senior Rabbi might have been influenced by the impending loss of Ethel."

Ethel was mostly at home. Occasionally she returned to the hospital, but for short stays, just long enough to control the pain. Moshe and Rivkah visited often, at home and at the hospital. Rivkah brought soup. Moshe brought reports of his trading activity.

"What's happening?" Ethel asked when he told her about his loss in soybeans. It wasn't the loss that disturbed her, but the nature of it. He had averaged down, buying contracts of beans as the value fell. His custom had always been to average up, building a position, allowing profits to run. Moshe had taken a loss of $70,000 but did not seem disturbed by it.

"The potential in this congregation is huge," he said. "I could expand the *havurot,* create alternative services, ongoing study sessions, real learning, real Jewish experience."

"Would you still have Thursdays off?"

"Why not?"

"Would you still trade?"

Moshe didn't respond. He had taken the loss in beans by violating most of the rules he had written for himself. Ethel had not been there to scold him. He hadn't made any trades since. Trading without Ethel wasn't as much fun and surely not as profitable. Ethel was asking him, "Will you trade after I'm gone?"

"I don't know," he answered at last. "I expect the congregation will keep me busy enough."

"Can you buy a Porsche if you're a big-time Rabbi in a big-time congregation?" She had never mentioned a Porsche before.

Moshe laughed. "I don't know. Not right away. Certainly not until I get the job."

It was Ethel's turn to be quiet. "What else couldn't you do, Moshe?"

"I don't think about it that way. I think about what I could do, about the possibilities."

She coughed, her pain evident. Moshe helped her settle back into the pillows. "Possibilities on one hand," she said, "and limitations on the other. At the moment you see the possibilities because you have few limitations." She turned toward him to be certain she had his full attention. "Your soul is un-

138

fettered, Moshe. But once you experience the limitations, you might not be able to see the possibilities."

She paused for him to digest her words, then added, "How come you didn't anticipate the weakness in beans?"

The rule of the congregation was that the Rabbis were not to officiate at funerals of nonmembers. Moshe spoke to the president, explained that this was for a close friend.

Ethel had touched many lives. The funeral chapel was filled to overflowing. Moshe spoke of Ethel's ability to travel through other people's eyes. Heads nodded in agreement. She could see into a soul, he said, and acknowledged her as one of his spiritual teachers.

After the funeral the congregation congratulated the Rabbi on a service well-done. "She was my friend," he said over and over. "I wasn't her Rabbi. I was her friend."

"It was a good service," Rivkah told him.

"I wonder what Ethel would have said about it."

"She would have said, 'Good service, Moshe. Now remember not to forget the Porsche.'"

Sidney said, "The senior Rabbi had prophesied well. Events transpired as he had forecast. Moshe submitted his name to the Rabbinic Placement Committee and was turned down, politely but firmly. He wasn't senior enough. His supporters in the congregation rallied to nominate him for the position directly, bypassing the committee. The committee sent a certified letter to Rabbi Katan. If he allowed his name to be placed in nomination, he would be expelled from the rabbinic union. Rabbi Katan allowed it.

"The congregation became bitterly divided. Moshe had not expected that. He had his supporters, the members of the *havurot,* those who had studied with him, those who enjoyed his informal, personal sermons. He was surprised to learn he had many detractors, those who disliked his informality, his approach to the tradition, his emphasis on spirituality. There were parlor meetings for and parlor meetings against.

"In the end Moshe's future came down to a congregational vote at the annual meeting. By only ten votes the members decided against calling Rabbi Katan to the pulpit of Temple Shalom.

"Moshe had lost."

"Moshe had won," Stephanie inserted. "He just didn't know it at the time."

139

"Moshe had lost," Sidney repeated. "He was devastated. It had never occurred to him he might lose. Not only was he not going to be the senior Rabbi of Temple Shalom, he was barred from placement in any other congregation. Suddenly he was looking at the rest of his life without any clear sense of what he might do."

Sidney continued, "That's where we end for the night. Tomorrow morning we'll learn how it was that Moshe became a kabbalist, stopped being a kabbalist. How he became one again. Then the lessons.

"Then the lessons," he repeated.

The members of the class seemed subdued as they retreated to their lodgings, some to their homes, some to rooms in the house, others to a nearby hotel. Sidney and Stephanie withdrew to the bedroom upstairs.

"The real work comes tomorrow," Stephanie said.

"Tomorrow," Sidney agreed.

He stopped to ponder the yellow hatbox on the table before the window but said nothing.

He knew how much was at risk, Stephanie realized. She suspected he was afraid to say anything. There was too much open, too many places to fall in. Open trenches. It was best left to the structure of the stories. They provided a framework for risk taking.

They kissed as they had most every night for thirty-one years and rolled away from each other in the king-size bed. The silence was numbing. There could be no sleep without some words. Sidney was the first to speak. "You've told me about your uncle Al," he said into the tree-filtered moonlight that played about the room. "The grandmother story is new."

"Yes," Stephanie admitted. "I think there are other new stories. They may not fit into the course. I squeezed that one in. You don't mind, do you? It's so cute."

"I don't mind. It's a most beautiful story, Steffie. I'm still thinking about it."

"I wish I had written my mother that story. I've been going through the letters. There are some stories there, but not enough of them. I think I have others. Maybe a new collection, to share with Rivie."

"You'll share them with me, too?"

Stephanie paused. "Yes."

"Please?"

"Yes, I'll share them with you, too."

That was adequate for Sidney. She felt him slide into sleep beside her, but she was still agitated.

Mostly she thought about her daughters, Allison and Ada. They knew who they were named for, but that was the extent of their knowledge of family. She had told them little of her life before Sidney. Sidney had shared even less. It was as if he had sliced his childhood away surgically. His life began at a Coleridge seminar in London. Their life, Stephanie corrected. That's all the children knew. They had no other family. No grandparents, no aunts, no uncles, no cousins.

She and Sidney were no better than Al, she realized. They each had their stories, but they were too painful to tell. They had buried them in silence and, in doing so, deprived their children of a family.

Her father's last words echoed through the decades. "You are dead to me." With those words he had killed not so much Stephanie as himself, and his wife. He had orphaned his grandchildren as well as his daughter.

With his own words he had killed himself.

No, Stephanie thought, he was already dead by the time they arrived in Miami. Something had killed him, killed them.

She fell asleep not knowing what.

CHAPTER 5

Early Sunday morning Sidney sliced bagels and Stephanie brewed coffee. Some students meditated on the deck, others walked in the hills. At nine they gathered in the living room. Stephanie noticed that Mister Dress Pants and the Donna Karan had changed into jeans. They sat together. The white beard in shorts was in the same shorts, same shirt. She wondered if he had slept in them. The male couple wore matching T-shirts bearing the slogan "Benefit of the Doubt." What a good way to remain a couple, Stephanie thought, to give each other the benefit of the doubt. Would she be so generous to Sidney?

Sidney began the morning session with a teaching.

"Moshe taught that the bedtime prayers conclude with the words, 'Into Your hands I commit my *Ruach,* my spirit,' spirit being the second lowest of the four orders of soul. When you wake up, the first words you utter are supposed to be, 'I acknowledge before you, living and existing King, that you have returned my *Neshamah* to me.' *Neshamah,* soul-breath, is above *Ruach* in the order of soul. Moshe wondered how it was when we go to sleep we give God a *Ruach,* and when we wake up we get back a *Neshamah*. It's like giving someone a twenty and getting two fifties in change.

"Moshe taught that after a day full of work our souls can be scuffed up, like shoes. Shoes, after all, have soles. What happens at a great hotel? You put your scuffed shoes outside for the night, and an agency you do not know or see comes and shines them for you.

"So it is with your soul. When you sleep, your soul is put out for the night. You put out a *Ruach,* and an agency you cannot know or see comes and shines it for you. When you wake, you have a bright, shiny *Neshamah*.

"I hope your *Neshamahs* are bright and shiny this morning. We have a long day ahead of us."

Stephanie said, "Moshe was a lame-duck rabbi for several months. After he lost the election, his supporters grumbled and spoke of a breakaway synagogue, but Moshe quashed that idea. It would damage the Temple, and I suspect he knew it would damage him. Everyone asked what he would do. He would study, he told them. That had always been his intent, to study for a year. Now he would have the opportunity.

142

"Not everyone was upset he had lost. Rivkah wasn't upset. She didn't tell him that. She told him not to worry, it would work out for the best. Milton wasn't upset. He was delighted Moshe would be out of the rabbinate and told him so. 'It wasn't good for you,' he said.

"It was a long time before Moshe was able to see it that way."

The Diet Book

Sidney said, "We'll begin our learning for the day with a text.

"When Moshe left the Temple, his first project was to expand his sermon on the Maimonidean diet into a book. He began by translating the diet from the Hebrew. The text is from that translation.

"The way you learn a text is much the way you tell a story. You need a partner. One speaks. The other listens. Back and forth. But a text you question and challenge. The questions are more important than the answers.

"This is a good one to begin with. There will be a lot more before the day is done."

Sidney distributed the text.

"No," he said when the partners fell into comfortable pairs. "As much as possible, learn with someone new." The two young couples split and paired with each other, the man in shorts with one of the long skirts, the remaining long skirts with each of the executives.

Good pairings, Stephanie thought. Enough variety, enough challenge to keep a text alive.

> Since a body must be healthy in order to follow the proper path, since it is impossible to divine any understanding of the Creator if you are ill, it is therefore necessary to remove yourself as far as possible from those things which damage the body and to conduct yourself in such a way as to remain healthy, and this is the proper way. You should never eat unless you are hungry and never drink unless you are thirsty and should never delay going to the bathroom; rather, when the need arises, you should go to the bathroom at once.
>
> You should never eat to the point that your stomach is completely full. Rather, you should stop one-fourth short of being full. You should never drink water during the course of a meal except for

143

small amounts, and wine should be diluted. After the meal begins to digest in your intestines, then you can drink whatever is necessary, but you should not drink too much water even after the food has begun to digest. You should not begin eating unless you examine yourself carefully; perhaps it is necessary to go to the bathroom. You should not eat until after you have had some exercise, until after your body has begun to heat up a little bit, or until after you have done some work or exercise. Here is the rule: you should exercise every morning until you warm up, then you should rest a while and settle down and then eat. If you should wash in a hot bath after exercise, that is good. Afterward, rest a while and then eat.

If you choose to eat chicken and beef together, eat the chicken first. So it is with eggs and chicken, eat the eggs first; and for lean meat and fat meat, eat the lean meat first. This is the rule: always eat first what is easy to digest and save what is difficult to digest for later.

Sidney allowed the students ten minutes to read and discuss. Then he said, "It took Moshe maybe two hours to translate the entire diet. The entire diet, not just what you have here. For the next two weeks he tried to write the commentary. He wrote and erased, typed and deleted. After two weeks the translation still stood naked. He couldn't add anything to it. He gave up writing the book.

"In the Temple he had given a sermon and taught a class. If you remember, no one lost any weight. Why not? Because the students were learning a diet without the motivation for the diet. The whole diet is in the opening lines. The reason a person is to keep his or her body healthy is to follow the proper path and gain some understanding of the Creator. The purpose of the diet is to intensify one's relationship with the Divine, not to lose weight. When Moshe taught the diet in the Temple, he said that he had lost forty pounds in twenty weeks. He had. But that had been a by-product of his learning, not the purpose of it. When he came to teach Maimonides, he taught the diet. The relationship with God was secondary. With Maimonides, God is never secondary.

"After two weeks, there was no commentary. Moshe was depressed. The Rabbi can leave the Temple, just like that." Sidney snapped his fingers. "But the Temple doesn't leave the Rabbi that quickly.

"There is no story associated with the diet, at least not from that time. Later I heard Moshe teach that text. He had learned how. But then, after two weeks, the story was a blank piece of paper."

Stephanie said, "It was more like two months before Moshe began to turn around. It was not an easy turning. Rivkah waited that long for an opening to remind him again not to forget to buy the Porsche."

Moshe flew to Denver and bought a used Porsche 911 that had belonged to a customer of a broker at Ferrell Bower. He saved $12,000 by flying to Colorado. While there, he stopped by a race-driving school to learn how to use his new toy.

On the way home, Moshe drove into the mountains.

The Porsche surged upward, the engine roaring at high revs out of each turn. "Damn!" he said out loud, downshifting to second and breaking the rear wheels free just a bit from the road, sliding, catching, and expressing resentment, anger, fury upward. "Damn damn damn damn!"

"Hey," the Porsche said back to him, "what the fuck ya' doin'? Don't take it out on me!"

"Who the fuck asked you?" He accelerated smoothly through the next curve, lifted the machine into third up a straightaway, and sped on to the next turn.

He was high, he knew, and getting higher. He risked a glance over the rail, looked out over the valley below and was astonished to the very root of his being. The beauty of the day, the expanse of green and blue, penetrated numbly through his anger. "God it's beautiful," he heard a part of himself say aloud. "It's so fucking beautiful."

The Porsche screamed again in second gear. All of Moshe's energy was back on the road, projecting ahead to the apex of a turn. "It's glorious," is how the feeling registered within him. The car drifted through gravel and began to slide toward the rail. He was aware of the exposure. The awe slipped into fear. The Porsche skidded and fear snapped into terror. "Do it right!" he screamed silently to himself in the words of his driving-school teachers. "Do it right! Stay with it. Don't panic. The car will do more than you ever imagined. Stay with it!" The Porsche recovered from terror into fear, downshifted from fear to awe, firmly on the road, planted steadily, and aimed at the next turn.

"Damn it all!" Moshe said aloud, braking into an overview, stopping to gaze out over a panorama of glorious grandeur. "Damn it! It's so fucking beautiful!"

"Five years of growing apart can't be reversed all at once," Stephanie said. "Still the first step is the most vital. The rest can follow after that."

Rivkah and Moshe packed the Porsche for a long weekend. Even in August the weather was cool. They rode south on the Pacific Coast Highway, the heat on, the top down, into the Big Sur. At Nepenthe they stopped for lunch and watched a single surfer brave the breakers far below.

Few words were spoken.

On the tabletop Moshe explored Rivkah's fingers, rediscovering them. About her wrist she had tied a single strand of crimson twine, the latest expression of her desire to be pregnant. It was a charm a friend had given her to ward off the infertility demons. She did not believe in charms or demons, but she did believe in friends. It was a small price to pay for friendship, and as for the charm? Let it work, she thought. Her own suspicion was that the tension of rabbinic life had somehow been the problem.

They backtracked to Carmel and walked hand in hand through the galleries, Moshe's desire more than hers. They argued the difference between fine art and the commercial. "Like professional warmth," Moshe said, referring to a clergyman's solicitous concern for the welfare of his congregants. Clergy became so smooth in the expression of concern, even when sincere it was difficult to distinguish the genuine from the professional. So in Carmel, where the commercial was so manifest, one became inured to what was truly fine, suspicious of everything.

"There is one piece of fine art here," Moshe said. "Let's find it."

The search was on. The art became the medium for open expression of feelings and ideas. They talked through the past five years.

Late at night behind the pool, in the hot tub, Moshe switched the floodlights off but left the bubbles on. Suits no longer necessary, their bodies met and joined. One piece of fine art, Rivkah thought, sure the result would be a boy.

"Why a boy?" the students asked.

Stephanie chose to answer. "Jewish tradition teaches that if a woman has her pleasure before the man in intercourse, the reward for the man's generosity is that the child, if one results, will be a boy.

"No matter. It was a healing for Moshe and Rivkah, but no pregnancy."

146

No pregnancy for herself, either, Stephanie thought. She had two, Allison and Ada. Allison was preparing for Julliard. Ada couldn't match in piano what her sister was accomplishing with violin. Ada announced she was going to be a doctor, a surgeon, so she could cut off pieces of her sister when her sister became ill.

They were so cute. They were enough, Sidney had said, and she agreed. Two active daughters and the relationship between them were quite enough.

The Havurah

Sidney said, "Moshe had his Porsche. He had Saturday mornings as well as Friday nights with Rivkah, the Havurah for learning, ample time to deepen his discipline in Kabbalah. Within a few months he understood how much he had been blessed."

Other than Rivkah, who never said so in as many words, no one was as delighted as Milton Kramer that Moshe had lost his bid to become senior Rabbi. Rivkah didn't have to say it in words. Milton relished every opportunity.

Milton no longer drove. Moshe came to him Wednesday afternoons to study. Monday nights Moshe learned with Frank. Frank had Hebrew. They learned *Likutai Moharan* together, the teachings of Reb Nachman. Frank thought it uncanny the way Moshe anticipated Reb Nachman's direction. "You looked at this ahead of time," he accused.

Moshe protested he had not prepared in advance. "I feel where he's going. That's all. It's as if we've visited the same places. I have an idea of what he's seeing."

Frank accepted that at face value without pretending to understand, and Moshe did not trouble himself to explain it further.

After several months he told Frank he would like to teach a class. Perhaps on Wednesday nights. He would open his house to the members of the Havurah and whoever else would like to attend. He would teach the framework of the Kabbalah at some depth, share some texts.

"I don't see any problem with that," Frank said.

"Think about it, Frank. If I open the class to the Havurah and the public both, the public will become aware of the Havurah. They might want to *daven* with us on a Saturday morning. What would we do then?"

"Oh." He thought for a moment. "Paradise lost?"

"Or paradise gained. If the *minyan* doesn't attract new people, it will die. We need the infusion of new people, a steady flow, or it's going to become stagnant."

"You might be right. Before you came it was already getting a little stale."

"So what will the other members of the Havurah say about the study sessions?"

"I don't know, Moshe. It's your house. It doesn't have to be a Havurah activity."

Rivkah and Moshe opened their home for learning. In the second month, Milton arrived by taxi to make sure his young friend wasn't developing rabbinic pretensions. The first session he sat in the back and said nothing. The next week he was familiar with the text and challenged Moshe's interpretations. Moshe responded evenly, accepting each challenge as an opportunity to deepen the learning. Soon it was apparent Milton was enjoying the exchange. Milton became a regular, and the dialogue, which at first the other students had considered an irritant, became a featured attraction. At times Milton argued Moshe to a tie. More often Moshe countered deftly, anticipating Milton's challenge. Whenever Milton found himself cornered, his response was a loud guffaw of amazement tempered with delight, much as a father might react to a son who had mated him at chess. Milton was accepted as a member of the Havurah. Other members picked him up and drove him home. He no longer needed a taxi.

In time Moshe served the Havurah as a rabbi.

That had never been his intent, but the growing community came to rely on him. The larger Havurah had outgrown the original fellowship to such a degree a council had been formed to provide the services of a board of trustees, over Milton's objection. "Too much like a synagogue," he snorted. But it was not like a synagogue. The council was not an elected body but a constituent organization with representatives from the *Shabbat* morning *minyan,* the family study program, the Wednesday night *bayt midrash,* and the eight small *havurot,* independent fellowships, each with its own direction.

Frank raised the question of Moshe's role within the Havurah. "He's giving us twenty hours a week now, and it's likely to become more. He's our representative to the larger community. He's the one we come to for scholarship and advice. He's our rabbi, and we should recognize that."

Milton opposed the very notion. "I thought the whole point of the Havurah was that you wouldn't have to put up with a Rabbi," he insisted again and again. Ultimately, knowing his resistance to be futile, he chaired the committee that developed the definition of *rabbi* as it was to be understood within the Havurah. He was terrified that what had happened to his friend once might happen again:

1. *The title* rabbi *is to be spelled with a lowercase* r *when it stands by itself;*
2. *The word* rabbi *in the Havurah means coach, not minister, preacher, priest, or even teacher;*
3. *The Havurah* rabbi *serves as a coach to the members of the Havurah, encouraging them as much as possible to assume full responsibility for their Jewish lives, with the full recognition that if he or she does his or her job well enough, he or she will be out of a job.*

Moshe accepted the position under those conditions. He said that he looked forward to the time when he might be unemployed.

Exposure

"Do you remember the story of Moshe in the Porsche?" Sidney asked. "When you see the mountains from a distance, you might say they are lovely. When you are up high enough, and close enough, then the mountains are not so much lovely as they are awesome, and you are not so much seeing them as you are experiencing them. If you are driving so fast that you think you might not make it safely around the next turn, then your experience moves beyond awe to fear, and if you skid and slide toward the rail, then the fear becomes terror.

"It's all a matter of exposure.

"Sometimes you don't have much choice. A bus comes around the turn. You steer to avoid, and there you are, just like that, hovering over the edge."

In the previous cycle Stephanie had told this sequence of stories, but the exposure proved too great for her. If she held her feelings in check, she did not tell the stories well. If she succumbed to her feelings, her very words carried her over the edge, and she could not finish. Sidney had to finish for her. So she surrendered the stories to him.

He told them, but not to her liking. What could she do? She listened and held her peace.

Once again Moshe was in Frank Nusbaum's waiting room. Moshe had his own subscription to *Scientific American,* so to keep himself occupied, he scanned through his date book and saw he had a wedding, the sister of a member of the Havurah marrying the son of a member of the Temple, and realized with alarm the wedding was scheduled for the Saturday night of the weekend he had invited Reb Hayim to share a *Shabbat* with the Havurah. The hotel was forty minutes away. An hour to do the wedding, he thought, another forty minutes to get home. He would miss nearly two and a half hours of Reb Hayim's Saturday evening. "How the hell did I manage to do that?" he asked aloud, then looked about the waiting room to be certain he was still alone. He closed the date book in disgust.

The nurse opened the door. "Dr. Nusbaum will see you now."

Frank remained behind his desk and looked up at him over his reading glasses. "You've taken your time getting back here, rabbi." He looked again to the file open in his hands.

"How often should I be coming back?"

Dr. Nusbaum looked at the record. "Given your age, and your father died young of heart disease, even two years is too long, Moshe. Maybe come by here now every year. Besides, it gives us another chance to get together."

Frank did the appropriate poking and listening and gave him a cup for the urine sample. "Just one cup today, Moshe? How are you doing with the other cup?"

"It's frustrating, Frank. It's the only thing that's not going well. We're thinking it's time to be a little more proactive."

Frank wrote out the name of the fertility clinic. Moshe looked at it. "It's the same one Rivkah's doctor mentioned. It must be the right one."

The first appointment available was the Friday morning of the *shabbaton* with Reb Hayim. Once they had made the decision, the urgency to begin was so great they could not postpone it for a moment. Together they had studied the materials from the clinic as if they were the deepest of texts. They had each completed long, intricate medical histories, the like of which neither had ever seen before. They were as ready, as earnest as they could be.

Dr. Matthews welcomed them into his office. "Rabbi, Mrs. Katan. Please." He gestured them to a comfortable sofa. "I'm sure you've done your home-work and know everything I'm going to tell you, but I'm going to tell you anyway." For the next half hour he reviewed the process and procedures, the testing that would be done in the office, the hormone levels that would be checked, the measurements they themselves would take at home throughout the menstrual cycle.

Dr. Matthews's office was a comfortable sitting room. The desk was not obtrusive. As Moshe listened to the litany of technical information, he silently thanked the doctor for doing what he could to keep the process within the realm of the human. He found himself nervous anyway.

"What we'll do right now," the doctor concluded, "is a brief physical exam. Rabbi, you stay with me, and Mrs. Katan, if you would go with my assistant. We're going to do an ultrasound just to have a quick look inside and see how your reproductive system is laid out. Have you ever had an ultrasound? It's not invasive at all. You'll be able to watch everything on the screen as we do it."

An assistant entered and led Rivkah away. Dr. Matthews presented Moshe with a cup and said, "I suspect you know what this is for. The bathroom is this way. If you would be so kind."

Moshe noted that Dr. Matthews's bathroom was better equipped than Frank's. Dr. Matthews provided visual aids.

Afterward Moshe fidgeted in the waiting room. He leafed through *The New Yorker* magazines looking only for the cartoons. He flipped from cartoon to cartoon, couldn't find one that was funny. He had been waiting too long. His unease slipped into anxiety.

Dr. Matthews himself came to get him. "Rabbi, would you come in please."

Moshe took one look at Rivkah on the sofa. Fear rose so high in his throat he had difficulty phrasing the question. "What's wrong?"

"Please, sit down," the doctor said.

Moshe rushed to her. "Rivie, what is it?"

Rivkah was shaking, too terrified to answer. Moshe put his arm around her and held her close.

"We found an abnormality on the left ovary," the doctor said. He pointed to a shadow on a photograph. "This is the ovary. And this is a growth on the ovary. This is not good news."

"What is it?" Moshe asked. He felt himself retreat into reason, away from feeling. The feeling was too overwhelming to touch. This was war. That gray area in the photograph was a sudden enemy.

"It's a tumor."

"Malignant or benign?" He needed to know more about the enemy.

"We can't tell from the ultrasound. We'll know only after the surgery."

"Surgery? When?"

"As soon as possible."

"Oh God," Rivie said. "Oh God oh God oh God oh God oh God." She began to heave in sobs, huge convulsive sobs.

Moshe held her and rocked her. "We'll be okay. We'll be okay. We'll fight it. We'll fight it."

The doctor waited until they had settled, until Rivkah's chest stopped heaving. "I know this is frightening for you." He spoke slowly, softly. "But let me give you the good side of this bad news. We've found it early. It's only three to four centimeters. Whatever it is, it's in the early stages. Even if it is malignant, we may well have found it in time to stop the progress of the disease."

Moshe looked around the office, as if for a weapon. Nothing came immediately to hand. "We have some calls to make," he said. "We have to find the best surgeon, the best place."

They returned home to marshal their forces for battle. Frank came over at once. After many calls they had narrowed the list of surgeons to two names. "Either one," Frank said. "Toss a coin. It doesn't make any difference. They're both tops." But only one of them could see Rivkah the next morning.

"Reb Hayim will be with us tonight," Rivkah protested. "We have to get the house ready. Tomorrow's *Shabbat*. I don't want to go tomorrow. Can't it wait until Monday?"

Moshe looked to Frank, who shook his head. "Don't wait," he said.

"This is silly." Rivkah waved her hands as if to push the whole matter aside. "This thing has probably been growing inside me for a year, maybe more. What difference will two days make?" Her calmness was disturbing to the men.

"I don't know," Frank said. "Just don't wait."

They made the appointment for eight o'clock. "At least we'll get back in time for the Torah discussion," Rivkah said.

"We shouldn't tell anybody about this yet," Moshe suggested "We have the Havurah coming to be with Reb Hayim. If we told them, it would ruin the weekend. So we won't say anything about this yet, okay?"

"I won't say anything, but what will the *minyan* think when you're not there for the morning service?" Frank asked.

"I don't know." Moshe was angry he had not thought of that. He turned to Frank. "Tell them we had a doctor's appointment. Just don't tell them why."

"Whatever you want. You guys just let me know what I can do to help."

Rivkah was already in motion. Reb Hayim was to stay with them, so the house had to be prepared to receive an Orthodox guest for *Shabbat*. The Havurah was to gather in the church vestry for the learning Friday night and Saturday morning, but the Saturday evening program was to be back in their home.

Rivkah gave instructions. Frank went to buy four loaves of hallah. Moshe made the house ready. He taped the light switches in the refrigerator so the lights would not come on if Reb Hayim opened the refrigerator door. The doorbell and phone were disabled. He and Rivkah moved folding chairs from the garage to the living room. "Don't," he said. "Let me." But she would have none of it and did her share of the lifting. Together they set the table with their *Shabbat* china.

Frank returned with the loaves of hallah and a bunch of flowers. The three of them sat in the living room, surrounded by empty chairs. There was nothing to say. A knock on the door signaled the arrival of Reb Hayim.

They went to greet him. He looked first to his Moshileh, then to Rivie, to Frank, and back to Rivie.

"What's wrong with Rivie?" he asked.

Rivkah burst into tears. Moshe caught her before she could fall.

Dislocation in Time

Most of the students had never experienced an Orthodox *Shabbat*. The questions they asked about *Shabbat* Sidney and Stephanie answered. Other questions had to do with personalities. They wanted to know more about Reb Hayim, or why Rivkah behaved in such a fashion. Those they did not answer. "What's in the story is in the story," Sidney reminded them. "If we give you every detail, every feeling, every motivation, you won't do any work. We're not here to entertain you. We're here to encourage you to work."

Stephanie was not satisfied with Sidney's response. That was the kind of thing he would say to divert attention from his own ignorance. There was a great deal that could have been said about Rivkah and her feelings at that time, but she would have to be the one to say it. How much could Sidney know? Did he have any sense of how it felt to be out of control? To have events rushed like that by Moshe and Frank? It was Rivie's body, not theirs, but they were making the decisions so rapidly, so forcefully, she could not resist.

Stephanie was angry with herself she did not have the courage to tell these stories. She was angry with Moshe and Frank for having subjected Rivkah to such pressure, with Sidney by association, because he rushed into the stories and did not leave room for her. She felt so much anger, it surprised her. She wasn't certain of its target, or its source.

On the way to Dr. Fowler's office, Moshe and Rivkah sang the *niggun* Reb Hayim had taught them. "It will calm you," he said. "If you are relaxed, good things can get in. You don't want to be uptight and keep good things out. When in doubt, sing a *niggun*."

They did not have to wait at all. Dr. Fowler came out to meet them in his white coat. "Good. I'm happy you're early. You two must be very special people. Not only did Dr. Matthews call me, but his nurse called my nurse. That's special." They passed through a maze of treatment rooms. "You wait in here, Rabbi. We won't be long."

Moshe waited in the doctor's office, wondering how Matthews knew they had chosen Fowler, then realized with a start Rivkah must have called Matthews to send over her records. Rivkah had made the call, not Moshe. Moshe's control was only illusion.

Rivkah returned, adjusting her dress. He rose to embrace her and led her to a chair. There was no sofa. He sat on the arm of the chair to be close to her. The doctor sat behind his desk. "There's a mass," he began.

Frank had warned them. They were using Fowler because he was among the best surgeons, not for his bedside manner.

"It's very, very unusual to catch an ovarian tumor this size. There aren't any symptoms, you see. Usually it's as big as a grapefruit, and the first hint we have of it is when it's pressing against organs and the patient complains of the pain. By then it's probably spread throughout the abdomen, and we have a real mess. This is most likely contained. You're very, very lucky."

They looked at each other, neither of them feeling lucky. Moshe asked, "Can you tell if it's malignant?"

"Can I tell? No, I can't tell until we get in and look at it and take a section. If I had to guess, I'd say sixty-forty it's benign. Considering its size and shape, eighty-twenty."

"What will the surgery be like?" Rivkah asked.

"We could do a bikini opening. This way." The surgeon moved his hand horizontally across his lower belly. "No ugly scar. Of course, if we found something wrong, we might have to open you up wider. But the odds are we can do everything we have to through the bikini incision. Then we make decisions. Best-case scenario, maybe we can dissect the tumor away from the ovary. Most likely not. Most likely we take the ovary and tube. That's what I would expect."

"What's the worst-case scenario?" Moshe asked, and regretted his question at once.

"Worst case, it's malignant and spread through the abdomen and up into the diaphragm. But that's most, most unlikely, considering the size of this mass. Like I said, it's extremely unusual to catch an ovarian tumor at this stage. You are very, very lucky."

Rivkah was to enter the hospital Sunday. The surgery would be on Monday. A few days, perhaps a week in the hospital, then home for another week or two of recovery. That's all there was to it. Eighty-twenty the tumor was benign.

They forced a *niggun* on the way to the *minyan,* arrived in time to join in the Torah service.

When he woke from his *Shabbat* afternoon rest, Reb Hayim sat with them in the living room. "*Nu,* Rivie. What can we do?"

"I'd like it just to go away. Can you do that, make it go away?"

Reb Hayim shook his head. "No, I can't do that. I can't make it go away."

"Why not? What's the good of prayer if you can't make miracles happen? What's the good of it?" She left the room angrily.

Moshe rose to follow her, stopped at a motion from Reb Hayim. "Let her go. She needs to be angry for a while. You sit with me. We'll talk about the best possible thing that we can do tonight."

When the Havurah assembled, Shabbat was just ending. Reb Hayim began with a *niggun,* calming the various energies. He sat at a table in the living room. Some of the *haverim* sat at the table with him. Concentric circles of chairs emanated out to standing room at the perimeter.

"I'll talk a little about prayer and about a great principle, the principle of all things being equal. When all things are equal, that's when prayer works.

"We have a story. A man returns home from a journey, comes over the hill, and sees his town in the valley below. A house is on fire. The rabbis ask, can the man pray that it's not his house?

"They reason like this. It's either his house that's on fire, or it isn't. If it is his house on fire, the fire has started already. Can we pray we should go back in time and avert the catastrophe completely? Can we pray the fire should somehow transfer magically from one location to another? They conclude it's too much to ask for. You can't pray for this. Or if you do pray for it, it's too much to expect to happen."

Reb Hayim paused to sip his tea. As he sipped, he looked over the rim into the eyes of those circled around him, gauging the effect of his words, asking himself if another example would be necessary.

"Mashal li'ma ha-divar domeh," he resumed in Hebrew. "I'll give you a different parable. You work for a company as a salesman. You're out in the country selling widgets. You have a client who would like ten thousand yellow widgets. When you look into the catalog, you see that there aren't any yellow widgets listed. So what do you do? You call back to the main office and see if they can fill your order for yellow widgets. If they can do it, you make your sale. That's what the business is for, after all, to sell widgets. Your prayer is answered.

"But what if the main office says they would have to shut down the factory and retool before they could fill your order? They would tell you they were sorry, they couldn't do that. They would like to fill your order, but they couldn't shut down the factory just to make yellow. In this case you prayed for ten thousand yellow widgets, but the prayer wasn't filled.

"So we go back to our house on fire. We can pray it's not our house, but this order can't be filled. The main office tells you it is your house. You're going to find out pretty soon anyway. To change it from your house to another, or to go back in time and do things differently, means shutting down the factory, destroying worlds, and as much as the main office would like to fill your order, it can't.

"So what can you do? First of all, you put in the order anyway. It isn't for you to determine what can be filled and what can't be filled. Only the main office determines that.

"So what else can you do? You put yourself into the place where all things are equal. While you wait for your prayer to be considered, you suspend yourself so you are not dependent on the answer. The main office is always considerate. If you are not fixed on a single response to your prayer, you might find there are other responses. The main office might come back and say they can't make yellow, but they can make green and red, and those aren't in the catalog either. Go back to the client and ask if either green or red will do. But if you're fixed only on yellow, you never get a chance to find out if you can sell the green or red.

156

"Don't fix yourself to a single answer to your prayer. If you put yourself into the place where all things are equal, if you suspend yourself, an answer might come from some unexpected direction. You don't know. You can't determine that in advance."

Reb Hayim sipped again from his tea. He lowered the cup gently, closed his eyes, and began a sweet *niggun*. It was the same *niggun* Rivkah and Moshe had sung on the way to the doctor's office that morning.

When he stopped singing and the attention in the room was again focused on him, he began, "*Haverim,* do you know the story of the students who came to Reb Elimelech and asked him how you love God on a bad day? I see some of you know it. I'll tell it again anyway.

"Elimelech and Zusya were brothers. Elimelech lived in luxury, Zusya in poverty. You might ask why Elimelech allowed his brother to live in poverty. Whenever Elimelech shared his wealth with Zusya, Zusya would find someone poorer than he was and Zusya would be poor again. It was the nature of Elimelech to be wealthy, the nature of Zusya to be poor. One day students came to ask him about the commandment to love God. It says, 'You shall love the Lord your God with all your heart.' They told him they knew how to love God when things were going well. How were you supposed to love God when things were going badly? Reb Elimelech said, 'You will learn this lesson better from my brother than you would learn it from me.' It was a cold day, so they knew they would find Reb Zusya sleeping behind the stove in the synagogue to stay warm. They waited for him to wake, then asked him how you love God when you're having a bad day. Zusya looked up at them from his rags and said he didn't know. He had never had a bad day.

"So what does Zusya mean, he never had a bad day? It means that in whatever situation he finds himself, comfortable or uncomfortable, there is always work for him to do on his soul. Wherever he is, from that place, too, he can see God."

Reb Hayim returned to the *niggun*. It allowed time for the story to set, and it provided a buffer between teachings.

"Let me ask you," he resumed. "Are there any bad squares on a chessboard? Are there any bad Torah portions? Some may seem better than others to you, but unless you stand on each square, unless you read all of the Torah portions, you never get an opportunity to polish, to refine, to work on every corner of your soul.

"Let's say you are a queen standing on a square of a chessboard, King's Knight Four, and you pray to move to King's Knight Five. It so happens one

157

of your own pieces is already on King's Knight Five. You can't move there. What do you do, sulk? It's the rules of the game. We can't ask to suspend the rules of the game. But if you suspend yourself instead, if you put yourself into the place where all things are equal, your prayer may be answered differently. The insight may be granted to move to Queen's Bishop Five, check. But if you are focused only on the one move you have in mind, you never get the message about the other."

Frank Nusbaum tapped Moshe on the shoulder. Moshe was lost following the thread of the stories and teachings. Frank tapped him again. "I can't get the phone to work. My service beeped me, but your phone is dead."

"We disabled it for *Shabbat,*" Moshe whispered. "It's off the hook in the bedroom."

"The rule is this," Reb Hayim continued. "Pray for whatever you think is the best thing for you. The act of prayer itself is what is important, not the result you hope for. Then suspend yourself, go to the place where all things are equal. Prayers never go unanswered. Sometimes the answer may be, 'No,' but that's an answer."

He stopped for a moment, then began a new *niggun.* The melody was strong, the energy began to build.

Frank tapped Moshe on the shoulder again. "There's a call for you. Stanley Halberg."

"Who?" Moshe asked as he left his chair, annoyed. "This is Moshe Katan," he said into the phone in the bedroom.

"Rabbi? Are you all right?"

"Yes, I'm all right. Who is this, please?"

"You haven't had an accident or anything?"

"No. Who is this?"

"This is Stanley Halberg. You were supposed to marry my sister tonight, but you never showed up, and your phone has been busy."

"What do you mean, marry your sister?"

"You were supposed to do her wedding, at the Sheraton."

"Wedding? My God. Tonight?"

"Yes. At seven o'clock. You haven't had an accident or anything?"

"No." Moshe looked to his watch and saw that it was nearly nine-thirty. "My God. I don't know how this happened. What's going on? What have you done?"

"We've done what we had to do. We had a judge who was one of the guests. He did the ceremony. We waited as long as we could. We tried to reach you by phone. Your line was busy. The operator said it was off the hook."

"We had an Orthodox rabbi with us, so we had the phones turned off. I don't know what to say."

"I don't know that there is anything to say, Rabbi. My father is not very happy about this. He's not happy about this at all." Stanley Halberg broke the connection without saying good-bye.

Moshe had barely enough energy to return to the living room. He found Rivkah and shared with her what had happened.

It was her turn to hold him, to comfort him. "What can you do?"

"I don't know. I can't do anything. The damage is done. I can't believe what I've done to them. I see them pacing the floor, waiting for me to come, and I never came. I can't believe what I've put them through." He doubled up in pain. Rivkah held him while he trembled and cried.

Stephanie had heard it too many times before, the fire in the house and the yellow widgets. Who gave a damn about pieces on a chessboard? And on top of it all, he was telling the wrong Zusya story!

No, it was the right story for the students, but the wrong one for her. What was the right one?

There were a thousand Zusya stories, no end to them. But there was a right one, and she knew which one, but not why.

Zusya and the jeweler.

Sidney told his story to the students. Stephanie told her story to herself, and heard it differently, more a story about the jeweler than Zusya.

There was a rich man in the town, the jeweler. The jeweler had a beautiful home. He had everything, even Rosenthal china.

There was to be a wedding. In those days there were no invitations, but rather a list of guests posted on the synagogue door. Zusya read the list, and to his astonishment found his name at the bottom of the second page. He was so excited to be invited to the wedding, he was up early in the morning. Because he was up early in the morning, he had a good place near the *hupah,* the wedding canopy. He got to see everything, how the groom beamed and the bride radiated. And then, when the refreshments were served, he was at the head of the line, and oh, did he eat! What delicacies!

After the wedding, he was walking home when the jeweler's carriage came up behind him. "Get in, Al," the jeweler said. "I'm going by your shop. You might as well ride."

Zusya was happy for the ride and thanked the jeweler, at the same time noting the rich man's dour mood. "I understand how you're feeling," he said.

"What would you know?"

"It's not difficult. When I went to the synagogue to read the names of the honored guests, such guests were on the list! And there was your name, at the bottom of the first page. I knew you wouldn't be happy about that, to be so low on the list. Me, I was at the bottom of the second page, but I was happy even to be included. Who would ever have expected they would remember me?

"So, I can imagine you thought you wouldn't attend the wedding. But when you heard all the commotion outside, at the last moment you decided to go. And since you went at the last moment, you were way in the back and didn't get to see anything. When it came time to eat, you were at the end of the line, so there probably wasn't much left.

"See, I understand how you're feeling."

All the jeweler could do was grumble. He didn't say a word.

"Do you know the difference between you and me?" Al continued. "You expect everything, and no matter what you get, it's like nothing. Me, I expect nothing, and if I get anything at all, it's like everything."

Stephanie was crying. No problem, she thought. They will think it's because of Moshe. They won't know why.

The story was incomplete. There was no more about the jeweler. What happened to the jeweler? Did he change, or did he sit and grumble the rest of his life because he found himself at the bottom when he should have been at the top?

You don't get to choose what page you're on, Stephanie realized. The blessing was being on any page at all. Zusya was blessed. He took delight in telling us so. Did the jeweler remain always cursed? Was there no hope for him? End of story?

No, she was wrong. Zusya wasn't Al. The jeweler might have been her father, but Zusya wasn't Al, because there were a thousand Zusya stories. Al had no stories. Al had kept all of his stories to himself, and so had the jeweler.

And Zusya wasn't much of a *rebbe*, either, because all the stories were about Zusya. There was only one story about the jeweler. And that wasn't even the right story.

But it was a start.

160

Reb Hayim said good-bye on Sunday morning shortly before Rivkah and Moshe were due to leave for the hospital.

To Rivkah he said, "May the one who blessed our mothers, Sarah, Rebecca, Rachel, and Leah, bless you. May you be open in complete faith to all the healing that pervades the universe which the Holy One created in this world so we could exist and grow within it. May you relax into that healing, so you do not resist it in any of the worlds, so it should pervade your very being, settle your questions, calm your feelings, and restore your body, so you should be restored soon to complete health." He hugged her, kissed her cheek, and let her go.

To Moshe he said, "May the one who blessed our fathers, Abraham, Isaac, and Jacob, also bless you, and give you that equanimity of soul, that deep-rooted balance to stand securely even in the strongest of winds, to weather the vagaries of your failings and successes, to see clearly from one end of the universe to the other, from the beginning of time to the end." He hugged Moshe also and kissed him.

He brought the two of them together, and hugging both, said, "May the one who blessed our fathers and our mothers bless the angel that presides over the two of you together, that your union should be strong enough to withstand whatever pressures you might encounter in your descent into this tight place. May you emerge from it stronger and wiser for the experience. May you convert whatever difficulties you encounter into blessings."

The three of them embraced. Rivie and Moshileh accompanied Reb Hayim to his car. They watched him drive away, held hands, and walked back into the house.

"I'm so scared, Moshe," Rivkah said without looking up from the overnight bag into which she was packing her toiletries. "I'm so scared."

"I'm scared too, Rivie."

"We may never have children, Moshe. Never."

"It's one ovary, Rivie. There's still the other."

As if she had not heard him her fear continued to flow from her. "All this time we've been trying, I've never let myself think we would never have children. It's always been under the surface, that thought, but I never let it come up. We've always assumed it was just something we'd get through. I'm scared, Moshe. I'm so scared we won't ever have any children. What will we do?"

"It's one ovary, Rivie. We don't have to give up hope yet. Maybe they can even dissect the tumor away from the ovary. Maybe they can open whatever might be closed. Maybe we'll have a better chance of having children."

"What if it's malignant?"

"Eighty-twenty, Fowler said. Eighty-twenty it's not malignant."

"You'll pray for me that it will be okay?"

"Of course I'll pray for you. I'll pray for you every moment."

Decision

As Sidney began the next segment, Stephanie shuddered. She didn't want to hear it. She didn't want to hear Sidney tell it. She thought to go to the kitchen for a cup of tea, to excuse herself to go to the bathroom. She did neither. She sat, sympathetic cramps developing in her abdomen, and endured.

Moshe was not alone in the waiting room. He had his book of psalms and a steady stream of social workers and physician friends who came by as they were able.

Frank Nusbaum opened the door. "No word? I'll stay with you for a while, okay?" He sat.

Moshe paced. He could not sit. He tried, but bounced up almost immediately. When he was agitated, he opened at random to a psalm and read the Hebrew in a whisper. That calmed him momentarily.

"It's taking too long, Frank. We should have heard something by now."

"These things take a long time, Moshe. We don't want to hurry him, just to put us at ease. Do you want me to go into the operating room and see what's happening?"

"No. I'll wait." He opened his book and whispered another psalm. Adonai, *what are we that you should take notice of us? What are we that you should think of us?*

Frank looked at his watch. "I have to go," he said. "You'll let me know as soon as you can? I'll be in the hospital. This is my beeper number."

Two social workers entered as he was leaving.

"Nothing," Moshe said to their unvoiced question. "No news."

"Is there anything we can do?"

Moshe shook his head and continued his pacing. He was absorbed in a psalm, unaware when Dr. Fowler entered the room. "Rabbi?" Moshe looked up to see the doctor still in his green gown, a cap on his head, a mask suspended from his neck.

"How's my wife? Is everything all right?" He knew from the doctor's demeanor, even before he finished the question, that everything was not all right.

Dr. Fowler looked at the two social workers sitting nearby. "Can we talk alone for a moment?"

"We'll leave," the social workers said.

"No, please. Stay," Moshe said.

He walked with the doctor into the passageway outside. A janitor guided a rotary floor polisher back and forth across the linoleum. They moved away from its incessant buzz. "What's going on? What's happening with Rivkah?" Moshe asked.

"We found the tumor, as we expected," Fowler said. "The good news is it's encapsulated. The bad news is it's malignant."

"What does that mean?"

"It means it's cancer."

"I know malignant is cancer," Moshe said, not able to keep the annoyance out of his voice. "What does that mean for Rivie?"

Dr. Fowler sighed. "First of all, you should know it is very unusual to catch an ovarian tumor this size. It's a 1A, maybe a 1B. No metastasis at all we can see." The doctor paused, waiting for questions.

Moshe didn't have any. "Go on," he said.

An IV bag swinging behind a gurney passing through the corridor nearly caught Moshe on the head. He moved closer to the wall to avoid the traffic.

"I wanted to come and tell you what I plan to do," Fowler continued.

"What you plan to do? You mean the surgery isn't over yet?" Moshe paled at the thought of Rivie still open on the table, her surgeon absent from the room.

"She's all right. My assistant is watching her, and I'll be back there in just a moment. I wanted to speak with you first. All of us were astonished to find a malignancy. But that's the pathology. There's no doubt of that. I took some of the surrounding tissues. We won't have the pathology back on those for several days. Are you with me? Do you need to sit down?"

Moshe leaned back against the wall. Its coolness fortified him. "Go on, please."

"This is the situation. The tumor was attached to the left ovary, and I've already taken the ovary and the tube. That was even before I knew it was malignant. There was no way of dissecting the tumor away from the ovary, so that ovary had to be taken whether it was malignant or benign. You're all right? You're following me?"

"I'm all right."

"Now this kind of cancer is terribly pernicious. It's a very, very dangerous cancer. If we had caught it some months from now in a more advanced stage, your wife's life expectancy might have been a year, maybe a year and a half. But we caught it early. It's very unusual . . ."

Moshe interrupted him. "I know it's unusual. Please go on." The wall behind him was cold. His forehead was hot. He dug into his pocket for a handkerchief.

"You understand how dangerous this cancer is?"

"I understand what you're telling me."

"All right, then. I think I have it all. I didn't see anything else suspicious. The pathology we won't have back for a few days. But this thing is so dangerous, I would not take any chances here. I would go ahead right now and take everything. I wanted to let you know first."

"What do you mean, take everything?"

"The other ovary and tube and the uterus. A complete hysterectomy."

Moshe wiped his forehead and realized he was hyperventilating. By an exercise of will he slowed his breathing.

"Why would you do that if there's nothing suspicious?"

"Because this cancer is so dangerous."

"This is what you would do in this situation?"

"Yes."

"Then why haven't you done it? Why do you come to ask me?"

Dr. Fowler was confused. "Because you're a Rabbi."

"What does my being a Rabbi have to do with your surgical decision?" Moshe felt his anger rising.

"I didn't know if there would be any religious objection or not. I didn't want to . . ." Dr. Fowler moistened his lips. "I have a pediatrician friend who did a circumcision once without knowing the child was Jewish. The parents were very upset. I didn't want to do this if there was a religious objection."

Moshe held his peace for the moment necessary to reflect on the situation. Rivkah was open on the table. One ovary was gone. A decision to take everything else was pending. The doctor was an idiot. No, he wasn't an idiot. There was a commandment to be fruitful and multiply. One of the 248 positive commandments was to be fruitful and multiply. The commandment rested on him, the man, not on his wife. It was the man's responsibility to be fruitful and multiply. Did this have anything to do with anything? Even if it rested on her, would he . . . Could he even for an instant consider putting Rivkah in danger so he could fulfill the commandment to be fruitful and multiply? That he even thought about it, he realized, meant he could consider it, and he was embarrassed.

"Doctor, these are my instructions." Moshe spoke as if from the bridge of a destroyer. "I understand my wife's life is in danger. You do everything within your power to save her. You use your very best judgment. That's what my religion demands. Do you understand?"

"I understand." Dr. Fowler returned to the operating room.

"I understand!" The words echoed within Stephanie. They were Fowler's words in Sidney's mouth. Sidney pronounced them with such authority. Sidney understood? What did Sidney understand?

When they were in New York Sidney understood he did not want more children. They had two daughters. It was enough. He had convinced Stephanie she also wanted no more children.

When he discovered she had become lax in the use of her diaphragm, he picked himself up, went to a urologist, and had a vasectomy. She had not accompanied him and had not comforted him when he returned home in pain.

He had taken away her future children.

She did not know it then, why she was angry, or even that she was angry. A dozen years later she was surprised when the resentment simmered to the surface.

Pathology

"I understand," Stephanie said. Sidney was surprised by her words. "I understand. I'll tell this next story."

She had not told this story before.

Rivkah's morale was fine until the pathology report.

There were two beds in her room. The hospital staff played with the admissions computer and kept the other bed free for Moshe. He stayed with her, among the flowers, and catered to her needs. They had her up quickly, walking through her grimaces. In bed she kept a pillow pressed over her abdomen. "It's because of the gas," the nurses told him. He had a fleeting image of a grotesque mock pregnancy. "The pressure of the pillow helps. It's normal after a hysterectomy."

The pathology showed no malignancy other than the tumor itself, fully encapsulated. None of the other tissues showed any sign of cancer. It was as positive a report as they could have prayed for, Fowler told them, smiling.

It was then Rivkah became angry.

She saved most of her anger for Moshe.

"It was his decision," she told her sister.

"Then it was the right one," Sharon defended him.

"You have two children," Rivkah snapped back. "For you it might have been the right one!"

"Men have no idea what it means," she told her parents when they arrived from Israel bleary-eyed from time shock. "For them it's just plumbing."

"Honey, we're just happy you're alive."

"They didn't have to scoop me out like that. They had the tumor. They had all of it. They scooped the rest of me out like a melon."

"I'm sure my son did what was best, Rivkah," Barbara said. On hearing the tumor was malignant, she had come right away. "How could he have done anything else? How could he have taken a chance with your life?"

Moshe protested in vain. "It wasn't my decision," he said. "It wasn't. The doctor asked me only if there was some religious reason not to do it. It was his decision all along. Rivie, how could I put your life at risk? Don't you think I wanted children, too? But given a chance for children and a chance to keep you alive, there wasn't any choice."

"So you did make the decision," she said flatly.

"The doctor made the decision. I chose to go with his best judgment."

"You used the past tense," she accused him.

"What do you mean?"

"You said you wanted children. Past tense. I still want them, Moshe, and I had no part in the decision to give them up. It's so damned easy for you! It's not so easy for me!" She made a motion as if to throw the pillow at him, but the pain prevented her. She returned it to her belly and pressed in on her emptiness.

Rivkah recovered quickly, especially after they put a sign on the door limiting visitors. Everyone on staff wanted to come by, and everyone in the Havurah.

Dr. Dowling, the oncologist, came to the hospital room. "It's your choice whether to have the course of chemotherapy or not," she told them. "On one

166

hand it looks like they got it all. On the other hand there may be some of it in hiding. I wish I could tell you that it's an exact science. All we can do is follow the path of best probability."

"So what's the best probability in this case, Doctor?" Moshe asked.

The doctor shrugged. "There is no best probability. We don't have a significant amount of information on this class of ovarian cancer at this early stage."

"I've made my decision." They were Rivkah's first words during the consultation. "I want the chemotherapy."

Two weeks out of the hospital, Rivkah and her mother went to shop for wigs. "Would you like to be a blonde?" her mother asked. "Moshe might like a blonde."

"I don't give a damn what Moshe might like," she snapped. She chose two wigs as close to her own color as she could find.

Moshe went to Gloria for advice. "Give her time," she advised him. "What else can I say?"

Rivkah's hair came out in clumps. "I didn't know it would happen this fast," she said. Within a few days she had lost all of her body hair. She was transfixed by her image in the mirror. "Is that me? I look like a little girl. A baby." She thought she might cry. She thought she might laugh. She did neither.

Moshe came home with irises, purple and voluptuous. He found her sitting naked on the bed.

"Rivie?" he sat beside her, flowers in hand. "Rivie, what can I do for you?"

"I had to have the chemotherapy," she told him. "I had to do it." She looked down at her juvenile nakedness, then up to his eyes. "I had to do it. It was the only choice. They took everything because I was sick. If I was sick, then I had to have the chemotherapy. If I didn't have the chemotherapy, that would mean I wasn't sick. If I wasn't sick, they shouldn't have taken everything. Does this make any sense, Moshe? You're the logical one. Does this make any sense?"

She curled up and cried in his arms.

Stephanie made no attempt to wipe her tears away. She wore them defiantly. When she finished her story, she curled up in her chair. The tears were contagious. Several of the students were also crying. The long skirts gathered about her, to comfort her and each other.

Anger a dozen years old coursed through Stephanie as she told the story of Rivkah's despair. The anger had been braided together with strands of reason.

167

Sidney's vasectomy was reasonable. It had been for the best. She didn't want another child any more than Sidney. She knew that, even at the time. But in which world did she not want another child? Her reasoning carried little weight in the balance of her feelings. Had reason masked her anger and resentment all these years?

As she sat, seething, another source of resentment tugged at her, what she had learned of Jewish tradition concerning birth control. Vasectomies were not permitted because the surgery resulted in destruction of the seed. No form of male birth control was permitted because of destruction of the seed.

The holy fucking male seed!

Only the bodies of women were considered in the arguments about birth control, and only the Rabbis had a voice in the arguments about what women might be permitted to do with their bodies. Women had no voice.

Somehow this, too, was braided into her resentment. That this should be part of the resentment aimed at Sidney made no sense whatsoever, for he had chosen to have the vasectomy. He hadn't insisted that she have her tubes tied. He had made the decision about his body. That should have been a relief, but in all these years she had never felt any relief.

It had been his decision, she realized. She had had no part in it. Even though he had done it to himself, to his body, she had been excluded from the argument, like all Jewish women since the birth of time. She had been excluded.

She hoped her realization would extinguish her anger, but in a moment it flared up again. The vasectomy was so final. What if she should change her mind and want another child? The window of opportunity was still open, just barely, but open nonetheless. She could change her mind.

God forbid, she thought, something terrible should happen to their children and they should want another child.

God forbid.

Such irrational thoughts. Such agitation. She made an unsuccessful effort to quell them, but one strand of resentment became intertwined with a host of others.

To be fruitful and multiply was the first among the commandments, so powerful that if a man had not fulfilled it in his lifetime, the *Zohar* declared he would be reincarnated to satisfy his obligation.

And what about the woman?

Stephanie bristled at the arrogance of the *Zohar,* a mystical commentary to Torah written only by men for men. What of the woman who died childless?

Would she, too, be reincarnated to fulfill her obligation? What did the *Zohar* have to say about that? Not a word. Not one fucking word!

To be fruitful and multiply was for the men, as if they could actually do such a thing. If a man died childless it was such a tragedy, no son to follow and continue his name. Nothing of the woman who died childless. No, it was only the man who was of any concern.

If a man died childless, it was written that his brother had the obligation to lie with the widow, with his sister-in-law, to produce a child to continue his dead brother's name. Stephanie had been dumbfounded when she learned of that. The sister-in-law had no choice. The *hutzpah* of it all!

Such were Stephanie's thoughts and feelings as she sat curled up in her chair. She would have liked to weave them all into a story, but they had nothing to do with Rivkah and Moshe. This was a Sidney and Stephanie story that had yet to be told. Still subliminal, she had no notion yet of how to express it.

Sidney offered a handkerchief. Stephanie hesitated before she took it, but she took it, and used it.

Detachment and Attachment

There was one more story concerning Rivkah's illness. Sidney told it.

Their relationship improved to the point Moshe made a joke about buying platinum futures. Platinum was the poison they pumped into Rivkah's veins each month. That sparked Rivkah's fury and prompted Moshe's apology. It was a bad joke, but a good apology, and that made for better understanding.

Rivkah was sick for one week, worked the other three. Her office kept her away from the oncology floor and away from pediatrics, until she noticed. "Don't you dare," she challenged them. "Don't you dare." She gravitated toward the difficult cases, pediatric oncology. They let her have her way.

At the end of the course of treatment, they were told to go about their lives with the assumption the cure was one hundred percent.

"With a more advanced tumor," the doctor added, "we might recommend going back in for a second look, to make sure everything was clean. But that isn't warranted. All we need is for you to come by every month so we can take a blood sample and monitor your CA125."

Moshe heard the clash of the two expressions, *one hundred percent* and *blood sample*. If there was a blood sample every month, there was no one hundred percent. Rivkah had heard it also. He could tell from her sudden stiffness.

She spoke up. "That means every month I give you some blood and wait to see if there's a death sentence? I don't think I can live like that. If I'm cured, I'm cured. That's all there is to it. I don't want any blood tests."

Moshe squeezed her hand. "Let me ask some questions."

She turned to him with a defiant attitude. "I'm not going to live like that. I'm cured. That's all there is to it. If it comes back, there isn't a damn thing anyone can do about it anyway."

"There may not be much we can do right now," the doctor protested, "but there may be something we could do in the future. The treatment five years from now will be very different from the treatment today. The prognosis might be much better."

Moshe reached out for Rivkah's hand, to comfort her, but also to keep her from bolting for the door. "Rivie, what if there should be an effective treatment. Would you have the blood tests then?"

"There isn't any effective treatment."

"But what if? What if there should be one in a few years. Would you have the tests?"

"If there is one, but not until then."

Moshe turned to Dr. Dowling. "Would it be beneficial, if there is an effective treatment some years down the line, to have a record from past years?"

"Yes, it would."

"All right, damn it!" Rivkah was out of her chair. "I'll have the lousy blood tests! But I don't want to know the results. You look at them if you like," she said to Moshe. "Just don't tell me about them!"

So Rivie shut the book on her illness.

Rivie's friends made a party to celebrate her complete cure. Colleagues from the hospital mingled with members of the Havurah. They had their love for Rivkah in common, and that was enough to make them all good friends.

Coming home from the party Rivkah asked, "Moshe, how much money do we have?"

"Altogether? Something less than a million. Why?"

"What should we do with it?"

"I don't know. What did you have in mind?"

"I'd like to build a house."

"What would the house be like?"

"It would be in the woods. Walking into it would be like walking into a forest, but as you moved through the forest, suddenly you'd find yourself inside a house. The entrance hall would open into a big room with a wall full of windows that would open onto a deck running back into the woods. We'd have a fireplace open on two sides, one side in the kitchen and the other in the living room. The room would be big enough for the Havurah, or a small chamber orchestra. A library. Lots of books. A bedroom upstairs with no curtains on the windows, up in the tops of the trees."

Moshe kept his eyes on the road ahead and gripped the steering wheel tightly. "Is there room in this house for me?" he asked.

"Oh. I didn't mention your study. Two walls full of books and a fine rosewood desk. The biggest computer in the world and a globe for you to spin. A carpet so thick you'd never want to wear shoes. You could sit and read and wriggle your toes. What do you think?"

"Let's build it."

The house was Rivkah's baby. She nurtured it from conception through completion. She consulted Moshe from time to time, more about money than materials. Whenever a decision had to be made, she opted for the more expensive path. As the house developed from concept to plan, from structure to domicile, she became more and more engaged. In consultations with architects and designers she quivered with possibilities. The professionals could barely keep up with her. Moshe tried at first to rein her in, but her imagination ran unbridled. He retreated to the sidelines, watching with admiration and apprehension. The house became glorious. The demands on the family resources became onerous.

"So make more money," Rivkah responded flatly when her husband spoke of the financial pressure.

"Rivie, my success in the markets has come, I think, because I'm not under pressure to make any certain amount. I float in the markets. I become one with the markets. I'm afraid if I have to produce just to hold on to what we have, I will sink in the markets."

"So do something else."

"I don't know what else to do."

171

"Moshe became a kabbalist," Stephanie said. "It wasn't his intent to do so. It just happened, bit by bit. He was drawn to it the way a magnet is drawn to the north by an agency outside itself."

Milton Kramer continued to give Moshe a difficult time in classes until his short-term memory began to fade. After repeating the same retort a third time during a study session, he guessed what was happening from the concern of his fellow students. "I'm repeating myself, aren't I? I said that already. How many times did I say it? I'm sorry," he apologized. "I'm leaving this world. I'm leaving it behind." He said it with acceptance and a touch of wonder.

Milton withdrew into the realm of angels and archangels, symbols and archetypes. When he could no longer care for himself, his children, Sarah and Beth, recognized it was in his best interest not to take him back to Chicago but to leave him in his familiar community with the Havurah. They moved him from his home on the second floor of the ACLF to the third floor, where he could receive more intensive care. The Havurah established a visiting rotation so Milton was not without company on any day.

Moshe visited once a week. Milton sat in his recliner by the window. Moshe drew up a chair to sit beside him. He spoke as if Milton were fully available, guiding his friend though a meditation, beginning with the breathing, invoking variations of the letters of the divine name. Sometimes he was able to penetrate to Milton's world, draw him back a little, hear murmured reports, disjointed nouns and verbs describing the barest hints of visions. Sometimes Milton remained silent, so Moshe descended. Anchored by the presence of his friend, Moshe reported his own experience as he floated among the worlds. Sometimes Milton did not speak and Moshe did not descend but stayed on the surface holding his friend's hand, wondering how time passed for him. Milton was so deep. Minutes at that depth might be days on the surface. Milton's life was speeding away as his body was slowing down.

Sarah and Beth came from Chicago to be with their father in his last days. Moshe came to comfort them and be comforted by them. "He used to tell us of the work you two did together," they said. "Can you do some of that now and bring him back for us so we can say good-bye?"

It had been some months since Moshe had elicited any response, but he did not hesitate. He sat by Milton's bed, held his hands, and talked to him as he always did, as if he were present and aware. He verbalized the process, more for the children's benefit than Milton's, the breathing, the descent. If Milton could not describe what he was seeing, Moshe could at least describe his own experience. He descended beyond petty thoughts, beyond emotional concerns of the day and the week, into the process of creation, the colors, the letters, found angels to guide him and bound his soul to Milton's soul.

"Moshe!" Milt said, as if surprised to see him. The word was weak, but it rose to the surface. "Moshe! What are you doing here?"

The children seized the opening. "It's me, Dad! Beth and I are here with you! Dad? Dad? Can you hear us? Rabbi, can he hear us?"

Moshe did not, could not respond. He was so deep. It would have taken so much energy to raise a word.

"Sarah," Milton said after an eternity. "Don't be afraid for me. Don't be afraid."

Moshe felt Milton drop to a depth he could not follow and let him go. He did not hurry to bring himself back to the surface. He rose gently, through no effort of his own. When at last he opened his eyes, he found the children crying.

"Thank you," they said. "Thank you."

Milton died that night. He was eighty-eight years old, and it was enough.

From time to time therapists who had come to experience *merkavah* descent with him suggested he open a practice.

"I'm not a therapist," he objected.

"So don't do therapy," they responded. "Our work is with conflict in the world of emotions. Your work is with conflict in the spiritual worlds. There has to be a name for a person who does that." Moshe knew the name. The name was *rebbe,* but he resisted the notion of becoming a *rebbe.* He was afraid of it. He was afraid of the isolation, the loneliness of being a *rebbe.* Nor did he think he had the knowledge, the foundation, the stability to be a *rebbe.*

"I can't do that," he told them.

They sent him clients anyway. They sent him clients with addictive and dissociative disorders, the most difficult, complex cases. Some of the clients were Jewish, some not. He worked with the therapists in partnership. His livelihood from his counseling practice became of consequence, if not substantial. As he refined his techniques in practice, he returned to the primitive texts and penetrated them still further, divining still more of the framework of the early mystics who had transformed the very essence of Jewish tradition.

173

In vain he searched for an arena in which to share what he had learned. The seminary had academic symposia, inviting scholars from university departments of Jewish studies to present papers reflecting the expanding frontier of Jewish academe. Moshe heard presentations about the history of the Kabbalah, but none concerning current practice. He gained from learning of new texts and manuscripts, but any attempt he made to share his practical work with others met with disbelief at best, hostility at the worst. The mindset of the scholar relegated the practice of the Kabbalah to the past. In the past it was history and worthy of study. In the present any practice of the Kabbalah smacked of magic, and the practice of magic was not considered career-enhancing.

Magic was openly discussed at Jewish New Age institutes, but it was difficult to distinguish the shamans from the charlatans. The effusiveness that bubbled incessantly came from the fringes rather than from the foundation of Jewish life. At these gatherings the center of Judaism, Torah and text, was too often lost. Moshe was not willing to leave the center behind.

Rivkah accompanied him occasionally on his expeditions into academe and the New Age, but did not venture with him into the worlds of the Kabbalah. What he did with his clients in his study she understood within the frameworks of conventional therapies. What she did with her patients at the hospital Moshe understood within the framework of Jewish tradition. They rarely argued the boundaries of their disciplines, sensing such arguments would put distance between them. They needed all of their closeness to be able to comfort each other, she to soothe him when he rubbed against his isolation, he to console her when she sobbed in empathy with the family of a dying patient.

Still, there were times when Moshe's work brought him into Rivkah's domain.

Aunt Doris

Stephanie continued quickly, before Sidney could begin with Aunt Doris. There wasn't any particular reason she had to tell this story, only that she wanted to keep talking. Something was tugging at her, reaching for the surface. If she kept talking, she wouldn't have to wrestle with it. Talking required less energy than wrestling.

174

"Had it not been for Aunt Doris," Stephanie said, "we would not be here now telling these stories."

Frank called to tell him his aunt Doris was dying and his uncle Ted had questions about the funeral. Would it be all right for Ted to call? Moshe knew what Frank was asking. Frank was knowledgeable enough to answer any question about a funeral himself, but his uncle was driving him nuts. Could Moshe help?

"We met you once at Frank's birthday party? Do you remember?" Ted asked. Moshe remembered Doris, a lively lady whose smile was genuine. "I need to know if you will do the funeral. How to go about it."

"How is Doris?" Moshe asked.

"Doris is dying. They say a day or two. Do I call over and make preparations now?"

"Where is Doris?"

"At the hospital. We have cemetery plots. But I haven't made any funeral arrangements. I don't know the first thing about picking out a casket."

"Is she in any pain? Is she awake and aware? Is she frightened?"

Ted had still more questions about the funeral. "Ted, Doris isn't dead yet," Moshe interrupted. "It won't make any difference if you go to the funeral director now or later. The real question is what can we do for Doris. Would you like me to visit her? Would it alarm her if I walked into her room? What do you think?" Ted thought that it would be nice if he could visit Doris, but he shouldn't make a special trip.

Moshe found her alone in a two-bed room. "Hi, Doris," he began, "I was in the hospital and heard you were here, so I thought I would come by and say hello." That was true enough, he thought. He was in the hospital, and he had heard she was there, if not in that order. "I'm Moshe Katan. Do you remember me?"

Doris looked up at him through uncertain eyes. One tube of the oxygen hose had slipped out of a nostril. "Here, let me help you with this." Moshe bent over to adjust the hose.

Doris opened her eyes fully. "Rabbi," she managed to say.

"Yes." He slid a chair close enough to the bed so he could sit and hold her hand. "How are you doing?" She did not have the strength to answer, but she looked at him steadily. "Are you in pain?" Her eyes rolled up to the IV drip. That gesture told him the medication was adequate. "You don't have to say

175

If it's all right with you, I'll sit here for a while. Is that all right?" A
[...] him it was all right.

[...] es were open to him. He saw no fear in them. He read there some
[...] ory. She knew where Ted had gone. It wasn't the first time he had
buried her. There was no denial concerning her situation, but no acceptance
either. Only resignation.

His eyes were open to her. She saw in them a reflection of her situation.
She looked deep into pools of concern and compassion. She knew he had
made a special trip to see her.

"Would you like me to pray for you?" Moshe asked her, still holding her
hand.

Her surprise was evident. She had never prayed before in her life. The notion someone else should pray for her seemed doubly strange. Her surprise was
she wanted him to say a prayer. She sincerely wanted it. Her desire warred with
her notion of hypocrisy. It was a battle between worlds. She felt the desire and
at the same time knew it to be hypocritical. All her life she had denied the
power of prayer. Now that she was dying, she welcomed it. For the moment she
held herself in suspense between her desire and her disbelief. Her desire won
out. More than anything else in the world, at that moment, she wanted a prayer.
"Yes," she said, "I would like that."

"What do you want me to pray for?" Moshe asked, knowing full well the
impact his words would have.

He felt the shock through her hand. It flashed across her face. She knew
for a certainty the gates of prayer were open. She had two choices. She could
pray to die. She could pray to live. She had known she could die. She had not
known she could live.

Moshe read the argument in her eyes. She had a good reason to die. Could
she find a good reason to live? He saw and felt the shift in her aspect when she
had found it. He didn't know what the reason was, but she had found it.

"I want to live," she said.

"Would you say it again, please?" Moshe asked, though he had heard it
clearly the first time.

"I want to live," she repeated.

In that instant her prayer transcended all the worlds. Moshe sealed it with
a *mishebayrach*. He said, "May the one who blessed our fathers, Abraham,
Isaac, and Jacob, and our mothers, Sarah, Rebecca, Rachel, and Leah, bless
Doris, who is ill. May she be open to the healing that pervades this universe,
so that she can continue to function in this world, to work in partnership with

divine purpose." The words were nice enough, he knew, but he also knew they were superfluous. The real prayer had burst from Doris's heart. His words were necessary only for aesthetics.

He squeezed her hand. "I'm going to leave now. I hope to see you again soon." She smiled in response.

Doris recovered. The doctors called it a remarkable spontaneous remission. She lived another six months during which she healed a rift with a son from whom she had been estranged for years. The next time she came to die, the son was present to hold her hand. Moshe presided at the funeral.

He had shared with Rivkah his encounter with Doris. "It was just a spontaneous remission," Rivkah said. "No one knows why such things happen. We see them now and then."

"But I saw this one. I mean, I literally saw it. I saw the moment it happened. I felt it. I had asked her if she wanted me to pray for her, and when she said yes, I asked her what it was she wanted me to pray for, and in that moment, it happened." ʼ

"You're telling me your prayer caused the remission?"

"Not my prayer. Her prayer."

"But you had something to do with it?"

"I enabled it. I showed her the possibility of prayer. I don't think she had ever prayed before in her life. It took her by surprise."

"How long were you with her?"

"I don't know. Not long. Five, ten minutes."

"In those ten minutes she learned how to pray? You were able to teach her?"

"Something happened in those ten minutes." Moshe accepted Rivkah's skepticism not as a criticism but as an opportunity to review the events once again. "I came into the room, introduced myself. She recognized me. She looked like she might die any second. One of the oxygen tubes had fallen out. I put it back in for her. I moved up a chair, sat down beside her, held her hand, and told her she didn't have to say anything. We just looked at each other." He closed his eyes.

"That's not right. We didn't *just* look at each other. We *really* looked at each other. Into each other. Her eyes were wide-open. She wasn't hiding anything from me. I could see everything through her eyes. That's how I could see it happen. When I asked her if she wanted me to say a prayer for her, I asked at the deepest place, where it could really make a difference. When I asked her what I should pray for, that shifted something. I felt the shift. It was as if she could choose between life and death and shifted her choice from death to life. I saw it happen."

"Why do you call it a prayer, then?" Rivkah challenged him. "It was her choice. What did prayer have to do with it?"

"I don't know. But it was a prayer. That's all I know. Prayer had something to do with it."

"If you could bottle it, you could make a fortune."

He ignored the remark. "There was access," he said. "She was open. All the barriers were down. She had no resistance. Almost no resistance. The suggestion of prayer broke through what little resistance was left, then the question became the prayer itself."

Rivkah could not accept that. "The question provided her with a choice. She was able to switch her energies to focus on life. Maybe that had something to do with the remission. Moshe, I'm not saying what you did wasn't a good thing. I'm just saying prayer didn't have anything to do with it."

"I've been thinking about Ethel." Moshe changed the course of the dialogue.

"You're guilty now you didn't cure Ethel, too?" Rivkah pursued him.

"I've always felt there was more I could have done, but I didn't know how to do it."

"Do you imagine if you knew the magic words, Ethel wouldn't have died? Aren't you carrying this a little too far, Moshe?"

"I didn't even try, Rivie. I never asked her if she wanted to pray. I don't even remember if I mentioned her in my prayers. We were never taught how to pray. Do you realize that? All those years at the seminary, and we were never taught how to pray. How to read the prayers, sure. How to pronounce them properly, how to tell the congregation when to rise and when to sit. But to actually pray for someone? They never taught us that. They never even suggested it was possible."

Rivkah withdrew behind a stern aspect, and said with certainty, "Ethel was a smoker. She had lung cancer. She died. That's all there is to it. I think you did very well with Ethel. You kept her working right to the end. That's what she loved to do. I remember coming into her room and finding the two of you arguing about soybean futures."

"Maybe I could have done better by her with prayer than with soybean futures."

From time to time Moshe returned to the topic of Doris and her remission, but Rivkah's resistance ultimately wore him down. They stopped talking of Doris. They stopped talking of prayer.

He shared his thoughts with Frank, trying to find the right words to describe his encounter with his aunt Doris. "It's like a surgery," he told him, "a very simple surgery in a difficult place to reach. So much work has to go into the dissection, laying the heart bare, but once it's open, the correction is so easy to make. With Doris, the opening was already there. I came into the room, and it was like she was open on the table. All I had to do was . . ."

"Was what?" Frank asked.

"I don't know. That's the problem. I know something happened. I can feel just what happened, I can't find the right words to express it."

Without the right words, Frank soon stopped listening. "It was a spontaneous remission," he said. "We don't know why these things happen. They just happen."

"Spontaneous remission is a cop-out, Frank, words you attach to something when you don't know what the something is. Because you have an expression for it, you think you have explained it. But you haven't explained anything. You hide behind the words."

Moshe stopped trying to explore his experience with Frank, because he could not find the right words. Words were the medium for his learning with Frank.

Had Teddy Porter not been so far away, Moshe might have pursued the matter with him in the worlds of symbols and archetypes, but Teddy was far away. The experience with Doris faded from his concern.

Princeton

Stephanie continued, leaving no interval for Sidney. "Ultimately it wasn't for lack of colleagues to share with but because of what happened at Princeton that Moshe withdrew from the Kabbalah."

The Princeton Institute excited him. He shared the brochure with Rivkah and tried to share his excitement as well. "This one looks interesting," he said. "Reb Hayim will be there."

"Will you teach?"

"I'm invited. Reb Hayim wants me to teach the *merkavah*."

179

"Maybe this will be the right mix of text and experience," she encouraged him. "It's surely in the right setting."

"Can you come with me?"

She shook her head. Ronnie and Danny and Mario and Jeanne were the names of the children who, at that moment, kept her tied to the hospital. They were too many to leave behind. He went alone.

The driver of a small car came to Newark Airport to take him to Princeton. "Rabbi Katan?" the driver asked. "We have to wait for one more person." The trunk was half-full with uncrated books, magazines, and newspapers. Only one of his bags would fit. The other went into the backseat.

"I'm taking your seminar," the driver said. They sat in the car, the windows open. "Reb Hayim told us a little about the *merkavah,* but he wouldn't teach us how it was done. We're waiting for Jaime. Jaime is videotaping the conference. He's doing a documentary on New Age spirituality. I really want to know about the *merkavah*. Reb Hayim says it's something like shamanism. I learned about shamanism when I was in New Mexico last summer. Jaime is coming from Montreal. He's not from Montreal. He's from Costa Rica."

"Do you have air-conditioning?" Moshe asked. "Perhaps we could close the windows and put on the air?"

"It's not working."

Moshe struggled in the front seat to remove his jacket. The driver did nothing to help.

"Jaime should be here any moment. They had a shaman at the Locus in New Mexico. I didn't understand him very well. Native American. It's the one thing in the Kabbalah I know nothing about at all."

"You know the rest of it?" Moshe asked, and regretted asking even before the question was complete.

"I don't know all of it, of course. But every summer I go to . . ."

Moshe tuned out the driver and waited, sweating, for Jaime.

Jaime appeared in shorts and an undershirt. He pulled a collapsible hand truck behind him, overburdened with three suitcases, camera bags, a tripod. For all to fit in the car, one sizable bag rested on Moshe's lap. They sweated the entire trip to Princeton. Moshe envied Jaime his undershirt. At registration they parted to stand in separate lines.

The dormitory was old and intricate, a fireplace in each suite, the bathrooms in the cellar below. The windows, wide-open and screenless, allowed the bugs in with the heat. Moshe was the first to arrive in his fourth-floor room. He chose the lower bunk. He had his bed half-made when Jaime arrived with a load of equipment.

"We are together!" he exclaimed. "How nice. In the car I did not know who you are. You are the kabbalist, yes?"

"Moshe." Moshe held out his hand.

"Jaime," the cameraman answered. "I heard of you. I was told to look you up."

"That's very kind."

"I hear what you do."

"Then maybe you'll tell me. I don't know what I do."

"We get my stuff."

The statement allowed for no demurral. Moshe followed Jaime down the stairs and lugged gear back to the room.

"I sleep," Jaime announced without so much as a thank-you. He scrambled into the unmade upper bunk.

Moshe, still breathless from the burden he had lugged up the stairs, turned from his astonishment at his roommate to his own bed. Rather than lie in it, he finished making it and ventured out onto the campus in search of Reb Hayim.

This was his first visit to Princeton. He had not known New Jersey contained such a lovely community. The venerable campus reassured him in a way the driver and Jaime had not. Perhaps Reb Hayim could reassure him still more.

The *rebbe,* dressed in Hasidic garb, held court before a dozen students in a small clearing deep in the campus. He was teaching about trees. Reb Hayim spoke in code, a simple message for the uninitiated, a deeper message for those who were familiar with the vocabulary. Moshe deciphered some of the words and understood allusions to the Tree of Life and the Lurianic Kabbalah. When their eyes met, Reb Hayim interrupted his discourse.

"Moshileh!" he exclaimed. "My little Moshe. I am so happy to see you. I will be done in a moment." All eyes turned toward Moshe Katan.

Reb Hayim's moment stretched to thirty minutes, but for Reb Hayim thirty minutes was truly no more than a moment. Moshe guessed the beginning of the discourse from its end and filed it away whole for later consideration.

The lesson done, teacher and student embraced. "How is my Rivkah?" Reb Hayim asked. "She is all right, yes?" he said without waiting for a response. "I can feel it in the way you hug me. I am happy she is all right. Now then, you have a concern. What is it?"

"Connection, Reb Hayim. I need to connect."

"How so?"

They walked through the campus as they talked, oblivious to the glances they drew. "I feel estranged from my colleagues. My pursuit is a spiritual one. Theirs is political. I try to share my work with them. It's foreign to the way they see things.

"In the Havurah I have a few people to learn with, mostly text. The one who was closest to me, the one who first learned the *merkavah* with me, has died. And Rivie, we share so much, but this she will not share. She walls herself away from it. When Teddy Porter was still in California . . ."

"Teddy is *niftar*," Reb Hayim interrupted, using the Hebrew for passed away. "Last month, in his sleep, in the Vatican."

Moshe stopped as if he had collided with an unseen obstacle. "*Dayan ha-emet*." He said the words of blessing one says upon hearing of a death, praising God whose natural law remains constant. "I did not know. We have not been in touch. I feel the loss. Still one more loss."

They resumed their walk in silence. Reb Hayim was the first to continue the theme. "So you are looking for a connection."

"So I come to these gatherings hoping to find souls to share with, and what I find is astrologers and shamans and idolaters . . ."

"Idolaters?" Reb Hayim asked in alarm. "Really? Idolaters?"

"Women with goddess figures, pronouncing goddess names . . ."

Reb Hayim interrupted with a wave of his hand. "Not idolatry," he said. "An overreaction, a temporary correction. A searching, a groping to learn how a woman is to relate to a God who has been in the province of the man for the last two thousand years."

"Astrology then. Shamanism."

"Not everyone is like you, Moshe. They found these traditions first and are coming to Jewish spirituality second. And something else for you to understand." Reb Hayim stopped walking to command all of Moshe's attention. "The medium is not the message. The message is the message, and it can come through most any medium, whether the medium is true in your eyes or not. You think that because the pre-Copernicans considered the earth to be the center of the universe there is no wisdom to be learned from them? Are you prepared to dismiss the Talmud because of that? How about Maimonides? Or Aristotle? Give the newcomers time. Have patience. Let them learn from you how deep our tradition can be. Pull out your stops. Take the chance. Share from the very depths. The very deepest place. This is what they expect from you, you know."

"How do they know what to expect from me?"

Reb Hayim shrugged. "I've told them. And not only me. You have more students than you know. They spread the word. You are known. They expect you to take chances with them, not to hold anything back. No risk, no gain, I think is what you say."

"Not every risk yields gain, Reb Hayim. Some fail. That's why it's called risk."

"So, Moshileh. Do you have a choice?"

"No," Moshe admitted. "No, I don't."

Reb Hayim and Moshe stopped walking at the same instant, sensing a presence behind them. They turned to find Jaime, in shorts and undershirt, following with a video camera on his shoulder. "Pretty," he said as he lowered the camera. "Very pretty. Good. Thank you."

"I thought you were asleep, Jaime," Moshe registered his surprise.

Jaime shrugged. "So I wake."

In the second session of his seminar Moshe suggested an exercise, a chant of a *merkavah* hymn, an alphabetic acrostic. In the first session he had stretched out the framework of the *merkavah* and provided the warnings appropriate before any descent. The eighteen students were ready, eager to go, to experience the unknown. They sat in the round and sounded and resounded the chant. They descended through their awareness of space and time. The chant filled them and thrilled them. Their very souls vibrated to the communal energy.

Their awe for all of its intensity had in it elements of regret. Full surrender to the experience was hindered by the anticipation of separation from it. When they opened their eyes after twenty minutes, still entranced, they apprehended Jaime in his undershirt, squatting in the middle of the room, his camera on his shoulder, parrotlike, leveled and circling. "Awesome," he whispered. "Awesome. Never. Maybe the monks in Tibet. Thank you. *Gracias*. Thank you." The students looked one to the next, smiling. They had more than memory now. They had a record. Was it conceivable that mere magnetic tape could contain the flow of such an ineffable energy?

The next morning, abashedly, Jaime approached Moshe.

"Moshe, please. Yesterday, the chanting . . . I do not understand. The camera. It did not work. I don't remember ever before. Tell me, that chant, could you do it again?"

Moshe laughed. "I wish," he answered. "I wish I could do it again. Truly I wish it, but I think that class was a one-time event, Jaime. Never again." But Moshe was wrong.

That night after dinner Reb Hayim asked him to lead the grace after meals. The dining room was buzzing with a myriad conversations. Moshe approached the microphone, could not make it work. There seemed no way to bring the assembly to order to give thanks to God for the food that had been provided. In frustration, Moshe began to chant the *niggun* he had introduced in the seminar. Men and women looked up askance at the bearded one who walked and sang. One soul from the class heard the tune and stood to sing with him, then another and another. The *niggun* was contagious. Within minutes the room came alive with a pulsing trail of chanting souls. The *niggun* throbbed. It assaulted the ears, the walls, the ceiling. A hundred strong, two hundred, three hundred, the room resonated and roared. Those who remained at tables pounded with their fists. An ecstatic Jaime leaped on a table, his camera turning on the pulsing room.

Forty minutes later someone shouted. "Outside! Take it outside!" The trail of chanters exited the room and the energy dissipated into the vault of the heavens.

Moshe found himself outside. Reb Hayim stood beside him. "I never said the blessings," Moshe confessed.

Reb Hayim laughed. "No, no you didn't. Perhaps God will be satisfied with the energy instead of the words."

The Princeton class was extraordinary, the most adept and responsive students Moshe had ever taught. All of them came with spiritual discipline, even if few had any true knowledge of the Kabbalah. All were eager for the experience. What had started as a simple exercise the day before had become, spontaneously, profound, and the class burned for more.

Moshe described the process of descent, encounter, reconciliation, and transformation. He pressed to stay within the intellectual; the students pressed for the experiential. They would not be denied. They learned the breathing, the visualizations, each one eager for the transforming moment.

The silent depth of a meditation toward the end of the fourth session was interrupted by the thud of a falling body.

When Moshe was able to open his eyes, he saw that Jaime had slumped to the floor, his body wracked with convulsions, blood gushing from a gash in his head. Moshe stared, helpless, not comprehending, as others rose from the depths around him.

"My God!" a woman screamed. "My God! What's happening? What's happening?"

"Don't move him!"

"Lift his legs!"

"He's possessed! He's possessed!" A woman made the sign of the cross.

"Get something into his mouth!"

Commands flew, hands groped, blood flowed. The alarm went out to campus security. Students barged into nearby classrooms pleading for a doctor. A large bearded man in overalls produced an amulet, waved his arms, and pronounced incantations to ward off evil spirits.

Moshe stood outside of the circle that gathered to help Jaime. "Don't move him," he pleaded feebly. "Don't move him. Wait for help." He had an image of the Sheraton Hotel, of a wedding party, a family pacing up and down, waiting for help that never came. "Wait for help."

"I've got a doctor!" someone said.

She knelt by Jaime on the floor. "Call 911," she said to no one in particular. "Tell them we need an ambulance. Be careful, please. Don't move his head. What happened here?"

"I don't know," Moshe ventured into the silence that waited for the answer. "We were in a deep meditation. I heard him fall."

The paramedics came, strapped Jaime to a board, his head immobilized, and carried him away. The time allotted for the learning had expired. Several students remained to see if Moshe might bring them back to order, but he waved them away. He was in the Sheraton Hotel, sliding down the wall with Rivkah's malignancy, on the floor after hearing of his father's death, severed from the world in disappointment, unconnected, with an overlay of a large man in overalls warding off evil spirits and a witch making the sign of the cross. It was too much for him, far too much.

Jaime remained unconscious into the night. Moshe made a couch of two chairs in the waiting room. Near midnight Reb Hayim came and sat beside him. "Something overwhelmed him," Moshe explained. "I don't know what it was. Everyone was so eager. I gave the warnings. No one listened."

"So what are you doing now?" Reb Hayim asked

"Psalms. Prayers. Whatever seeps into my mind."

"That's good," Reb Hayim said. "A good thing to do."

"It's good for me. Will it be good for him?"

"Can you imagine anything better?"

Moshe returned to his psalms, opening the book at random. *Protect me, God, for I seek refuge in You.* He closed the book. Psalm 16, a psalm he had used for funeral services. Eyes closed, he rested and imagined Jaime sneaking out of ICU in his shorts, undershirt, and sneakers to listen in on the conversation and concerns of master and disciple. Jaime would do that, if he could, bemoaning the lack of camera and recorder. The image became so real Moshe stirred and looked about, hoping to find Jaime lurking behind them. The room was empty other than for Reb Hayim, who had put his head back against a pillow. His mouth open, he snored gently.

Again Moshe turned to the Book of Psalms, his eyes falling upon the conclusion of Psalm 121. *He will guard your soul. God will guard your goings and comings from now until forever.* Another funeral psalm, it brought him no comfort. Moshe closed the book and his eyes. He imagined a nurse in green asking, "Which one of you is Rabbi Katan? Jaime wants to see you."

Jaime lay flat on the bed, his head bandaged, an IV running into his arm.

"I wake," he would say, in his flat tone. "I wake. Something happened, Moshe. Something important, but I don't remember. Do you think you could do that again?"

Moshe winced and squeezed his eyes more tightly shut.

"Rabbi," she said. He felt himself jostled by a hand on his shoulder. "Rabbi."

Moshe awoke to find a nurse in green standing before him.

"Rabbi, he died a few minutes ago. He never woke up. He never regained consciousness."

Moshe was not certain if the nurse was real or imagined. He preferred imagined, feared she was real. He found confirmation in the torment that creased Reb Hayim's face. Jaime was dead. *Never again,* were the first words that came to Moshe. Reb Hayim shook his head, too late to keep the words from being spoken. "Never again," Moshe said aloud. Lips tight, he closed his eyes and shook his head for emphasis. "Never again."

Service and Celebration

"Never again," Stephanie repeated, aloud but to herself, not knowing what she meant by it.

To the students she said, "I asked Rivkah why she and Moshe hadn't adopted children. I didn't think that would be a difficult question to answer, but it was.

186

In the end, she said, they were willing to adopt, but by then their lives were full, and they were already older. If they had been that willing ten years before, perhaps they would have.

"I asked her why they weren't willing before that. She said early on they had talked about it, but neither of them was serious. The second time they talked, Moshe would have pursued it, but she had chosen not to. The third time she realized that talking about adoption brought back the anger she had felt after the surgery. The anger was still there. The next time Moshe had raised the question she told him she already had her children and didn't need any more."

Rivkah stood at the door of the Blue Room to hand out roses. Veterans of the service took a bunch. Newcomers took only one.

The Blue Room in the basement of the hospital derived its name from the color of its asphalt tiles. They had been polished to a high shine. That made it easier to slide chairs into concentric circles. The room was set much like the Unitarian meeting house when the Havurah assembled on Rosh Hashanah, even to the round table in the center.

On Rosh Hashanah the meeting house filled with smiles and greetings. The noise level rose to that of a small waterfall as streams of people who hadn't seen each other since the last year came together and mingled. In the Blue Room, families entered the service in silence. They sat mute, each newcomer holding a single rose, veterans holding several.

The Rosh Hashanah service always began late. The hospice service began on time. Rivkah started with words of welcome and purpose, noting that the work of the hospice did not cease when the life of a patient came to an end. The family was the client, not only the patient. A member of a family may die, but the family does not come to an end.

The service was divided into three lists of names, each to be crowned by an offering of words by a clergyman, Father Patrick McGuire of St. Theresa's, the Reverend Philip Black of the Church by the Bay, and Rabbi Harry Schwartz of Temple Adat Israel.

The congregation rose to recite the 23rd Psalm. *The Lord is my shepherd, I shall not want . . . the valley of the shadow of death, I shall fear no . . .*

The names were in the program in random order. Neither alphabet nor chronology ruled. Staff members attended the podium to read the names, a pause after each, so family members and friends could contribute a rose to the memorial on the center table.

Newcomers learned quickly why the veterans had bunches. They heard names of those they had come to know, friends they had made from other families. Each memory, whether from their own family or another, was marked by an additional offering. The staff had anticipated this and provided boxes of flowers in each of the quadrants.

Rivkah had her own roses in hand, one for each of the children she had lost. Lonnie who had died of leukemia. Michelle, a brain tumor. Ernesto, lymphoma . . . The list went on.

Some names were mourned in silence, some with a sob or a cry. The roses covered the white table, became a mound of green and red, then a mountain.

The priest stood to speak of souls welcomed into the embrace of the Virgin Mary. No brotherhood service this, where the clergymen marshaled their words to fit on some common inoffensive ground. The priest reached for his most powerful spiritual vocabulary, as did the reverend who bathed both souls and mourners in the love of Jesus. The rabbi, a veteran of such services, was unfazed by the Christology. He invoked the Merciful One to shelter the souls of the dead under the wings of the Divine Presence and to comfort all who mourned along with all the others who mourned in the community of Israel. Each message, unique to its tradition, was spoken so intensely from the heart that the words combined into a single utterance of love and beauty.

A staff member closed the service with "Amazing Grace."

Rivkah was the last to leave, alone for a minute with the memories before ascending to the pediatric floor. She had reworked the calendar so the hospice memorial service and the annual reunion of survivors would take place on the same day. She visited her office to place her single remaining rose in a bud vase and proceeded to harvest the smiles and hugs waiting for her in the common room.

The chairs and tables of the common room had been cleared to the perimeter. Only a round table remained in the center. On the table, a large birthday cake with the inscription, "To Life."

The cancer survivors had gathered, children who had grown to be ten years old, fifteen, twenty, thirty—all survivors who returned once a year to celebrate their lives. Some Rivkah knew from her own experience—Michael, Jeanne, Annie, Troy, all fresh in recovery. They rushed to hug her. Others, long-term survivors, Rivkah knew only from the reunions. Mothers and fathers circulated on the perimeter. This celebration was for the children, but the joy of the parents radiated inward toward the center of the room and contributed to the warmth.

Children read poems, shared memories. Tears mingled with laughter. When the time came to cut the cake, patients streamed from the rooms to join in the celebration with the precious alumni. Smiles became contagious.

Retirement

Moshe's counseling practice and livelihood from it declined. His hours of immersion in the markets diminished. He became fearful of exposure.

Friends from the Havurah noticed his depression and offered their assistance.

"Moshe," said one of the *haverim* who was a professor at the university, "we're looking for someone to do a course on the poetry of the Golden Age of Jewry in Spain."

"Moshe," said another, "we need someone to teach an introduction to rabbinic texts in the program for Jewish studies."

Even Ferrell Bower had a suggestion. "Moshe," they told him, "the business school needs someone to teach a course in the futures markets."

Moshe taught three courses at the university, and he took three. He reasoned if he had to expend so much energy to find a parking space, he might as well make the most of it. He would teach, and he would study.

He taught Judah Ha-Levi and Solomon ibn Gabirol, and he attended a seminar on Walt Whitman. One course colored and energized the other. Leaves of grass grew through the images of the Spanish Jews and were fertilized in turn by a spiritual soil deepened and enriched by thirty centuries of wrestling with God.

He taught the theory, history, and practice of the futures markets while studying the philosophy of money, a course taught by a Nobel laureate in economics. Moshe's poem "On Currents and Currency" was published simultaneously in the journal of the Business School and the literary magazine with two commentaries, one from each discipline.

He taught the introductory course in rabbinic texts and sought something of interest in the Jewish studies program to learn, but found nothing that challenged him. He chose to sit in the back of a class in modern art. He chose it because it was offered at the right time and in a convenient location. There he had nothing to offer. He could only receive. There he found solace for his soul.

Toward the end of the year of his teaching and learning, Tzvi came to visit. They had not seen him since their days in Jerusalem. A showing of his work was opening at a gallery in the city. Tzvi's eyes went wide in wonder at the Katan home. "It is glorious!" he said expansively, raising his hands high in slow motion, like a movie Moses. "The most wonderful things must happen here! Such drama, Rivie! Such excitement! What a glorious domain!"

Moshe shared with Tzvi his newfound passion for art. As they leafed together through a coffee-table book, Tzvi pointed to a painting by Max Ernst. "That one's available," he said.

"What do you mean, available? It's in a museum."

"No. It's in a private collection. I know it's available."

"You mean it's for sale? I could buy it?" The notion of owning a work of art so highly prized as to be found in a coffee-table book had never occurred to him.

"All it takes is the willingness and the money, Moshe."

"We could really own something like that?"

Tzvi laughed. "Own it? You will find that a work like this will own you as much as you will own it. This is not a simple matter of possession." He gestured at the expanse of the living room. "Do you own your house, Moshe? Or does your house own you?"

Moshe pressed on. "How would I go about negotiating for something like an Ernst, or"—he turned the pages—"a Braque, or a Miro?"

"You know, you could ask your father-in-law. After all, he is in the business."

Sam Shapiro had supplied most of the art that hung in the house. They were all prints, some numbered and signed by the artists. They were nice on the wall. They caught the eye. They contributed to the ambience. None of them had a significant presence.

"But Sam represents current artists," Moshe protested.

"Sam sells art. If you have something in mind, let him know. If he doesn't know himself, he'll know who will know."

Moshe considered that in silence.

Rivkah and Moshe accompanied Tzvi to his opening. Tzvi had moved beyond his exercises with the Hebrew letters. His sculpture and paintings were raw portrayals of birth and death, side by side.

Tzvi came up between them and draped his arms over their shoulders. "What do you think of this?" They were before a sculpture some six feet high, burned books impaled on a cross of rusted iron railroad tracks, Kristallnacht and Auschwitz compressed together along with all of the crusades and atrocities that had befallen the Jewish people over the centuries.

Rivkah spoke first. "It's almost too much to comprehend. I see a piece of it at a time. It's hard to accept all at once."

"What about the form of it? Is it pleasing to the eye?"

"Yes," Moshe said, removing himself from the meaning of the piece. "The message is one thing, the form another, and the form is pleasing."

"You know, this is hard to sell. Who is going to buy it? Everyone who comes through comments on it, but this and the coffin over there"—he pointed with his head toward another Holocaust piece, a nail-studded coffin-shaped box that opened to reveal a coil of wire and a rusted egg, "not many will buy these. There are not many who are willing to live with them in their homes, who are willing to live with such a constant reminder. Only a rare person, now and then. But all the reviewers write about the power and the presence of these pieces. I always bring a few to each new show. No one may buy them, but they know they should buy them. So they are more inclined to buy my other work, and that finances what I really want to do. The truth is that these are the pieces that will survive. These are the survivors. In another year, maybe two, I will have enough of these survivors to present a show that will remind the world. In another few years all those who were at Auschwitz will be gone, but these pieces will live on.

"I have a proposal for you, my friends. This is the last stop on the tour. The big pieces go into storage. What if I park one of these with you, and you hold it for me for a few months until I go on the road again?" He stepped back and held up his hands to prevent any quick response. "Talk about it please. See if you really want to do it. Think it over." He left in search of champagne.

Tzvi himself supervised the installation of the Kristallnacht Crucifix. Rivkah had thought to put it in one corner of the living room, but upon seeing it, realized that it needed to be on the other side, in an open area, so one could walk about it and experience it from all sides. Together they moved furniture to accommodate the sculpture.

"It is good, here," Tzvi said. "She has a good home now for a few months."

As he was leaving, Tzvi said to them, "Write to me please, and let me know how you are getting along." Moshe and Rivkah were confused at first, then understood the artist's intent.

191

Moshe rose early the next day to greet his guest in the morning light. He became accustomed to her presence from different perspectives. He found that she had a unique odor. The burned books smelled burned. Rivkah thought she could smell the raw iron of the tracks as well. They wrote to Tzvi about their experience. They grew with her, and wondered if she grew as a result of her involvement with them. When Tzvi at last sent for her, it was with some sadness that they let her go.

Rivkah and Moshe became restless in the days following. The house seemed empty. "Let's do something about it," he said. Together they began the search for a new piece to bring life into the house.

Moshe was revitalized. His trading activity increased. His creativity found its expression through new courses and seminars in the Havurah.

Paintings and sculpture enriched their life together. Each work was a blessing.

Reordination

The Katans invited the entire Havurah to the resignation party. The night was warm, the doors to the deck open. Traffic moved freely from the house out onto the deck into the woods. The food and music were Middle Eastern. Two hundred souls wove around sculptures, pondered the work of young artists, celebrated in the glory of the night.

The tinkling of a fork against a champagne glass brought the room to order. Moshe, standing on a stool poised between the living room and the deck, spoke his words and monitored the energy that reflected back to him. The words flowed gracefully. He was comfortable with their substance.

"In my years as rabbi in this Havurah, I have endeavored to be faithful to my contract, encouraging as many of us as possible to have primary Jewish experiences, so that those of you who have come knowing how to teach and lead prayer have, from the outset, taught and led prayer. Many of you who had not the slightest indication you had such abilities have developed those abilities. Whenever we assemble now, who knows who will step forward? Who knows from where the learning will come, whose words and spirit will lead us closer to God?

"More and more you have taken the risks of primary responsibility for your own Jewish lives. It is with the satisfaction of a coach I have retreated to the sidelines and watched you step forward, often into difficult situations, and find the words, either your own or those of our sages, to bring out comfort, direction, solace—whatever was needed. Together we have so many skills within our community, so much wealth of experience, I feel the time has come for me to fulfill the last term of my contract. We have become a Havurah that no longer needs a rabbi."

Into the confusion and consternation that filled the room Moshe interjected, "I'm not going anywhere. I'm not leaving for another community. All I'm doing is what I was asked to do, get out of the way when being in the way would impair our growth. We don't need a rabbi. As long as I am the rabbi, you will continue to defer to me. You don't need to do that. The rabbi is getting out of the way. Moshe is still here, just as you are still there. If you can provide something I need, I will not hesitate to go to you. If you need something I can provide, I have every expectation you will come to me. Moshe is still here, I assure you. Only the rabbi has departed. I hereby release the title." His hands had been clenched. He opened them as if scattering an invisible substance into the air.

"I thank you all for your love and tolerance while I have been the rabbi these last years. I hope your love and tolerance will continue now that the rabbi is gone."

Just like that Moshe stepped down from the stool. The community did what it had been long accustomed to do when confronted by a perplexing question or situation. It divided into small groups and began to argue. The question was, "Is it possible for a rabbi to resign from the rabbinate, or is it a lifetime commission?"

The argument became heated, in some places angry. Moshe, as was his custom, moved from group to group, listening to the tone and intensity of the words. A consensus was building. One small group merged with another, then another, until the community came together as a whole. Moshe knew the response before it was spoken.

"Once a rabbi, always a rabbi. It's a commission you cannot surrender."

So came the decree from the highest court, the community of friends that constituted the Havurah.

"But what if I don't want to be a rabbi anymore?" Moshe asked. "What if I find the title an impediment to my work?"

"We don't find it an impediment," the community answered.

"You don't, but others do. I've done as much as I can as a rabbi. Now the title gets in the way. I don't accept your answer. You have to help me with this. Go back to work please, and find me another answer."

Again the community divided, into twos, threes, fours. The tone of the argument was different this time. They were not arguing a principle. They were attempting to solve a problem for a friend.

"Point of information!" one of the *haverim* said loud enough to be heard above the din. "You want to give up the title, yes?" Moshe nodded. "But not the responsibility? You will still be with us when we need you?"

"Yes," Moshe said, "as you will still be with me when I need you."

"Then there is a way." The community waited, attentive. "You used to be an officer in the Navy?"

"Yes."

"What was your rank?"

"When I left, a lieutenant. Why?"

"What were you when you began?"

"An ensign."

"When you were a lieutenant, did anyone ever refer to you again as an ensign?"

"No."

"Then that's all there is to it. We have to find Moshe a title higher than rabbi, confer it upon him, and he will no longer be a rabbi."

The argument became interesting. Moshe heard ancient titles, *raban, rabanan,* raised and dismissed. The *haverim* congregated around those who knew modern Hebrew. Variants of the word *amen* were discussed. *Ma-aman, mi-uman, mo-aman*—one who teaches faith or discipline. This generated excitement.

One small group became silent.

Silence was the loudest voice of all. Soon even those most excited about the *amen* variants settled into silence also.

"We have it," the speaker from the silent group said. He uttered but one word in Hebrew and all understood.

The community pushed the furniture back in the living room so the Havurah could form a circle. Moshe Katan was brought to the center of it. Those who had known him the longest put their hands on him, and all in turn reached out to touch those closest to the center.

"We designate you our *haver,*" one said. "You are our friend. Friend is the highest title we can give you, higher even than rabbi. So from now on you are our *haver,* and we continue to call you as we always have, Moshe. Moshe our *haver,* our friend."

So Moshe Katan ceased to be a rabbi within his community. He sang, danced, and rejoiced with his friends well into the night.

The next week Mr. and Mrs. Moshe Katan rested by the pool of their hotel on the big island of Hawaii.

"Is it different?" Rivie asked.

"It's too soon to know," he answered without looking up from his book. "The real test won't be here. It will be back home."

A few minutes later, again without looking up from his book, he said, "It's different. Even here."

His mother noticed it when she came to visit. "It's like a burden has been lifted," Barbara said. "You're lighter."

"Should I feel guilty now I'm not carrying the burden?" he asked.

"I don't know how you should feel," she answered. "It's not like you were a rabbi anyway."

He caught the intimation and chose to follow it. "What do you tell your friends, Mom? What do you tell them when they ask what your son does?"

"Even when you were a rabbi it was difficult telling them what you did."

"Do you tell them that I'm no longer a rabbi, just a regular guy, a *haver?*"

"Nobody's asked me," she demurred.

Moshe himself could not easily define what it was he did. Still active at Ferrell Bower, he played those markets like a musical instrument, more often in tune than not. His profits there spilled over into the world of art. At the university he taught courses as a barrel overflows, the joy of learning and sharing bubbling out of him.

In the Havurah he had his share of services to lead, along with the other skilled members. He assisted in arranging weddings and facilitating funerals. His life became simply Jewish. He visited the sick as a Jew. He led services as a Jew. He learned Torah as a Jew. Sometimes his voice was heard above the others, sometimes not. The rabbi in him was released over the months, a long sigh dissipating into the world. He checked himself from time to time, to see what of the rabbi remained, where he was still bloated with a sense of authority.

Rivkah watched the release, but kept her peace. When he would ask, "Is this all right, what I'm doing?" her response was always the same.

"You seem to be happy."

That was true, he knew, but he also knew she was saying she was happy. She was being cautious not to say more for fear the process might stop. The bloat of the rabbi, even the lowercase rabbi, had kept them apart. As the rabbi flowed out of him, he folded more into her, collapsing into the curves of her. It was more than the closeness they had shared in Jerusalem, deeper, broader, more enveloping.

Rivkah's case load, not his calendar, determined when they could travel. On short notice they might fly to Hawaii, or across the continent to Cayman or Andros. On weekends they might venture into the mountains, hiking through the meadows high in Yosemite, or they might take the Porsche up to wine country or down to Santa Barbara. They explored galleries and studios, underwater caves and straw markets, mountain lakes and trails.

Ultimately Rivkah asked him to participate in the hospice memorial service. He read what was designated for the rabbi. In Hebrew and English he pronounced a powerful blessing for the memories of the deceased. Afterward Rivkah led him upstairs to the reunion and shared her children with him.

That night they spoke again about adoption. They found they were willing but didn't have the need. If they had come to that place ten years before, perhaps, but they weren't there ten years before. They had no regrets.

Moshe became comfortable with his life and their life together until he woke early one morning to descend to his study and ponder the chart of the CA125 marker, to tremble in fear and consider what courses of action were available to him.

A Laid Table

Stephanie had been talking for a long time. She didn't have strength left to finish the session. Sidney did.

"Moshe reasoned something like this," Sidney said. "He had it all thought out.

"If the doctor wasn't apprehensive, he surely wasn't going to make Rivkah apprehensive. He could not tell her of his fears.

"Either there was a recurrence of the cancer, or there wasn't. He had to proceed on the assumption there was.

"What could he do about it? He had a history to draw upon. Ethel Kaplan, Milton Kramer, Aunt Doris, Father Porter, even Jaime at Princeton.

"For Ethel he had done nothing. It had never occurred to him that there was anything to do. She had died in her own pain. For Milton he had been able to provide comfort. As for Aunt Doris, he had helped her find a way back to life. A temporary return, but then what life wasn't temporary?

"From his experience with Aunt Doris he had learned that choice was possible. Her choice had been spontaneous, not a result of discipline. From his experience with Milton, he knew the benefit of discipline. It allowed for communication in the deepest of worlds. If there had been a choice for Milton, he was convinced that together he and Milton would have found it.

"As for Father Porter, together they had practiced descending into the very fabric of life. Moshe had explored the flow of soul into space and time and learned secrets concerning the attachment of life to the body. His meditations had taken him nearly to the connection, the point of no return.

"In the class at Princeton he had learned too well the danger of descent without discipline. Discipline was the key. If an intervention should ever be necessary with Rivkah, she would need to know the discipline, and so would he. He hadn't practiced it in years. Before he could teach her, he would have to learn himself.

"But even if he could recover his skill, how could he ever share it with her? Throughout their history together she had an aversion to prayer, the Kabbalah, anything that smacked of the spiritual. How might he convince her to learn, without alarming her?

"That was the question he asked himself in the study that night."

Stephanie held up her hand. It wasn't enough to hear just Moshe's side. "Rivkah knew there was something happening that morning. When she found the table set for breakfast and coffee ready in the thermos, she knew something was in the air, but she didn't know what.

"Moshe was ready. There was a lot he wanted Rivie to learn before she figured out what he was doing. He wanted to teach her the fundamentals of the Kabbalah. She had to be proficient in the operating system.

"He had it all calculated. It was a trade-off. She would learn, then she would be angry when she discovered she had been manipulated into learning. That was a price he was willing to pay."

Stephanie paused before beginning the story. She understood it all. It made sense. Perhaps it was the right thing for Moshe to do.

"Such arrogance!" she added, surprised she had pronounced the words aloud.

"You've been up a long time," Rivkah began, half statement, half question.

"I've been up for a while. I didn't wake you, did I?" Moshe responded.

"What got you up?" she asked, evading the question as she pressed some coffee into her cup from the thermos.

"This." He showed her the letter from the Metropolitan Institute.

She read through it quickly. "You're kidding. You haven't taught anything like this in years."

"Nobody's asked me in years."

"Why are you even thinking about it?"

The answer to that question had kept Moshe occupied since four in the morning. "I've gotten into a rut. I've lost my edge. I look at the charts, and I don't know what to do. I need to sharpen myself a bit. This might be a good opportunity."

"So study with Frank," Rivkah suggested.

Moshe shook his head. "It won't work. It's like the king and the musician," he said, referring to the Hasidic story of the royal musician who played only for the king. After some years the music lost its edge. Only when the king had guests, a fresh audience, did the musician play with restored verve.

Rivkah considered the permutations. "You're telling me you're the musician, Frank is the king, and you need a new audience?"

"Something like that."

"I still don't understand why this woke you up at four in the morning."

"So I did wake you!"

"It's okay. I went back to sleep. What really got you up?"

"I was afraid." Moshe spoke the truth without hesitation.

"Afraid of what?"

"Afraid of teaching again." Concentrating on the half-truth, he kept the flow of words steady. "I don't know if I can still do it. I'm afraid if I can, if I do, it will put some distance between us. I like what we have."

Rivkah examined the letter. "All they're asking for is four weeks."

"I know, but I'm afraid, Rivie. The last time I taught was at Princeton. I'd have to do it differently this time. I'd need someone to help me, to watch the class. Would you help?"

"What could I do?"

"Be a social worker."

Rivkah laughed. "I work with kids with cancer. I'm not a therapist."

"Eyes and ears," Moshe said. "Be there for me with your eyes and ears."

CHAPTER 6

The Turtleneck

Sidney led the students out onto the deck to hear the stories of the first lesson. "It's at this point Stephanie and I become personally involved," he said. "Friends had seen the course advertised in the paper and suggested we might be interested. I was. I had heard the name Moshe Katan in other circles, but by the time we had arrived in the area, he was no longer teaching. This would be my first opportunity to learn from him. I convinced Stephanie to come along."

"Our friends, the Plotkins, convinced me to come along," Stephanie interrupted. "I wasn't all that eager."

Sidney continued, "The space at the Institute was surprisingly large. Square. There were ample chairs for all of the students, but several chose to sit on the plush rose carpet, some in lotus position, some leaning against the wall under huge, voluptuous watercolor blossoms. The paintings were for sale. The Metropolitan Institute of Expanding Light drew income not only from its classes but from its bookstore and art gallery as well.

"Moshe arrived on time. He was wearing jeans, a gray turtleneck, tennis shoes, and a knitted *kipah*. While Rivkah distributed copies of the text, he dragged a table from its place against the wall so that it was positioned between the class and the portable chalkboard. He did much of his teaching perched on that table, his legs swinging below. His legs moved to some inner rhythm, pacing and propelling the words of the learning. He may not have been conscious of it, but it occurred to me perhaps he was, that he swung his legs back and forth the way a hypnotist uses a pendulum, or as a casual gesture to put us at ease. You see, none of us knew quite what to expect. Each of us had arrived somewhat tense. On the other hand he seemed so relaxed, so comfortable. Perhaps he was trying to reassure us, to transmit some of his comfort to us."

"He was anything but comfortable," Stephanie added. "He had his doubts from the outset, not certain he was doing the right thing, but it was too late for him to withdraw. His concern was manifest even in the clothes he was wearing."

She continued with the story of the turtleneck.

The Metropolitan Institute of Expanding Light occupied a large space on the top floor of a low-rise office complex. Moshe and Rivkah ascended together, alone in the elevator.

"What?" Moshe asked. Rivkah had been looking at him curiously.

"I think your shirt is on backwards," she answered.

Moshe looked down at himself, at the gray mock turtleneck. "I think you're right."

The elevator stopped at the fourth floor. Rivkah visited the registration desk to let them know Moshe had arrived. He went off in search of a bathroom. He had not thought he was anxious, but his shirt told him otherwise.

In his student pulpit in New Jersey there were no elevators. The only elevation separating him from the congregation was the two steps up to the *bimah,* but those two steps were a significant barrier to Janet, the organist, who was large, suffered from multiple sclerosis, and had difficulty walking. There was no need ever for Janet to climb those steps. The organ was installed downstairs, but Janet rose from her seat, raised her massive body first up one step, then the next. Moshe came to meet her.

"Yes, Janet?" he asked when she stood as a barricade before him.

"Rabbi," she whispered, catching her breath. "Your fly is open."

"Thank you, Janet."

She remained standing, shielding him while he zipped his fly. As patiently as she had ascended, she returned to the organ and the beginning of the Friday evening service.

Alone in the bathroom of the Metropolitan Institute, Moshe stripped off his shirt before the mirror. He looked into his image, to see how much of that Rabbi was left. His beard had grayed, his forehead was higher, the glasses steel-rimmed. From above the bifocal line, he peered at himself from a distance. "I look like a Rabbi," he said aloud. He pulled his shirt down over his head, front to the front, tucked it in, and zipped up his fly. "Let's go and learn," he said to the Rabbi in the mirror. "Let's go and learn." He left the bathroom, fit, in uniform, ready for his event, denying whatever discomfort there might have been in him.

"If I could teach the course Moshe taught I would," Sidney said, "but I can't. I can't sit on a table, swing my legs, and teach. It isn't the way I teach, and that was an important part of each lesson. I can't teach like Moshe. But I can relay the stories I heard, and tell you the stories I saw."

Stephanie said, "Months later I asked Moshe how many were present for that first class. I was curious. I wanted to know if he had counted heads. He hadn't. He said there were a lot, too many. Rivkah overheard my question, and answered, 'Forty-eight including us.'

"'That's right,' I said. "So you counted the class, too."

"No," she said. "Moshe had prepared fifty copies of the text. After I distributed them, I had two left."

Sidney had copies for the students on the deck and passed them left and right. Stephanie was surprised by what she saw. "I thought Moshe began with the story of the four who descended into Paradise," she whispered her confusion to Sidney.

"For this telling I thought I would start with this and end with that," Sidney responded, also in a whisper. The students were already immersed in the text, albeit individually.

> Matters of Sexuality may not be expounded before (more than) three persons, nor the Work of Creation before (more than) two, nor the (Work of the) Chariot before (more than) one, unless that one is wise and has insight. Anyone who looks into four things, it would have been better if that one had never come into the world: what is above, what is below, what came before, and what comes after.
> —*Mishnah Hagigah*

Sidney spoke just loudly enough to draw the eyes back to him. "Remember how we learned the diet text," he said. "Moshe insisted that we study in pairs or small groups, not by ourselves. He encouraged us to read aloud. There were forty-eight people in that room. Bit by bit the noise level rose. He walked among the groups and listened in, but he made no comments. When we were fully involved, he returned to his desk, and began talking about Reb Nachman. Some time passed before all of us were aware his lecture had begun. When we were all attentive, he started from the beginning again."

"Reb Nachman was a *rebbe,*" Moshe said. "Reb Nachman was a holy teacher who lived in Europe at the time of Napoleon. He used to say when one speaks about God to another, it's as if he's shining direct light on the other person. There's no way for him to know how much light is getting in, but some of the light reflects off that person back toward the teacher. The teacher himself learns from the reflected light. So even as I am talking, I am aware of my own words. I have to weigh each of them and measure each for the truth contained. My words bounce off of you and back to me. The more I weigh each word, the more I learn. If only one of you had come tonight, it would have been enough. I could learn. But since we have more than one, that makes this teaching more complex."

Moshe lifted himself from the table and paced the width of the room. "It isn't fair I should be the only one to do some learning here. You have to have a buddy, just like summer camp before you went into the lake. Have a buddy, someone who will be responsible for you, someone you will be responsible for. From time to time I'll stop and ask you to explain to each other what I have been teaching. If you can't articulate it, you don't know it. It's your job not just to learn it, but to be able to teach it to your buddy. So when you do the teaching, you will be putting out the direct light and instructing yourself from the reflected light that comes back.

"Find yourself a new buddy now, someone you don't know. Introduce yourself, and then study the handout one more time. Read it aloud, question it, argue it, talk it through."

"I don't remember who it was I learned with," Sidney added. "Most of us followed Moshe's request and introduced ourselves to someone new, but as soon as we were able, we returned to sit in the safety of friends. The exposure was too great to stay in the company of strangers.

"Sometime later Moshe told me one of the Hebrew words for learning comes from the word *to sharpen.* Learning and sharpening is the same thing. A person who learns alone is like one who attempts to sharpen his sword by waving it in the wind, but when a sword strikes a sword, they sharpen each other. So it is with an intellect. An intellect that learns alone is like a sword waving in the wind. You can imagine all sorts of wonderful accomplishments, none of them real. But when an intellect strikes another intellect, they are both sharpened in the process.

"All of you have read the text," Sidney said to the students on the deck. "Now take a few moments and study it again in pairs. See if the learning becomes sharper as a result."

Other Reflected Light

Stephanie was perplexed, uncertain.

She was perplexed because Sidney had altered the order of the texts. In all of the previous tellings, the first text had been of the four who descended to Paradise, followed by the warnings that startled and commanded attention. Even Moshe, in his course at the Institute, had begun with the four who descended to Paradise. The story was powerful, a good beginning. The *Mishnah* on sexuality was complex, difficult. Why the change?

She was uncertain because she did not know what came next. Sidney had continued with the Reb Nachman introduction to *hevrusa* learning, study in pairs. By rights the story of the teenagers who had come to proselytize should follow, but she had no idea what Sidney had in mind.

Did Sidney want the story of the teenagers here?

She wasn't sure. This was to be her telling, not Sidney's. How dare he change the order! What was she to do now? She had no idea how the lessons were to flow from this new beginning.

If Sidney wanted the story about the teenagers, he could damn well tell it himself.

No sooner had she completed the thought, Sidney began the story. He said, "I once watched Moshe teach Reb Nachman to some evangelists who had come by to proselytize."

He was telling her story, Stephanie thought, resentful, and then amused by her own resentment. It was her story, because it was she who had observed the incident, but it was she who had chosen not to tell it. Sidney was merely filling the vacuum.

With a start she realized she was following a family tradition. Uncle Al had not told his stories. Her father had not. And now she wouldn't either.

Screw them all. She was angry and knew it, but not quite why. Sidney, because he had started with the wrong text. Her father, because he never said anything, just sat on his stool hour after hour. And Al. Al was more at fault than her father. Her father was silent, but Al talked all the time. He talked politics with

203

everyone who came into the store, talked with Stephanie about every experience under the sun. Except his own. She knew not a single story about Al's life in Poland.

Well, that was his choice, wasn't it, she thought. He had his reasons. It wasn't for her to question them. She owed him so much. Without him she would have rusted behind a screen, behind a gate. A fence. A grate. He had unlocked the world for her. She had no right to question him.

But she was angry anyway.

Al and her father had known each other in Poland. There had been tension between them, a tension that carried over to Miami Beach. She had no right to question, but she still wanted to know. Why had Al never talked about it?

Why had Sidney started with the *Mishnah* on sexuality? What were Al's stories? Why was her father so silent?

What was going on?

Moshe opened the door of his home to find two teenagers, scripture in hand, and two adults behind them. The teenagers identified themselves as Witnesses or Mormons or Adventists. They asked Moshe if they could speak with him. Moshe's smile progressed from the teenagers to the adults and back to the teenagers.

"You haven't had much success in this neighborhood, have you?" he asked them. Their silence was affirmation enough. "You go from house to house, and some of us are willing to listen, some not, but even those of us who listen are not greatly moved. Am I right?" Again the confirmation of silence. "We either have our own faith traditions, or we resent being peddled faith door to door. So why do you think it is that your church requires you to do this, to walk through neighborhoods and knock on doors?" He had their attention, even if they did not respond.

"Let me tell you a story about one of the great teachers of my tradition. His name is Reb Nachman. He used to say that when a person teaches about God, it's as if he is shining a direct light on the person he is teaching. He can't know how much of that light is being absorbed or what that person is learning, but some of the light is reflected back toward him. He hears his own words and weighs every one of them. Each word he speaks sharpens him in his own tradition. Now do you understand why your elders want you to go from house to house? You may or may not have any effect upon the person you are addressing, but every word you speak sharpens you in your own tradition."

The adults behind the teenagers nodded their confirmation.

"Now," Moshe continued, "if you would like to learn more about Reb Nachman, why don't you come in? I would be happy to share some of his stories with you."

The adults whispered some words to the teenagers, who thanked Moshe for his time and abruptly turned to go on their way.

The Order of Questions

The story was okay, Stephanie thought. It was different, coming from him, but okay. She learned from it. There was so much she could have learned from her uncle Al, if he had only told his stories. He was selfish, she thought. Or afraid.

Sidney said, "Moshe taught me that the first speaker in any group is most likely to be a man. There might be forty women and ten men, but the first to speak would be a man. He didn't venture as to why that might be. The phenomenon disturbed him. He said men often spoke with such certainty, from the aspect of *Gevurah,* they tended to suppress the involvement of the women. To counter that, he thought to begin the learning with *hevrusa* study, learning in pairs. Then women and men would be primed equally, one as likely to raise a hand as the other.

"But it didn't work."

"Are there questions?" Moshe asked as a way of bringing the class together again.

A graying man in the front row was the first to raise a hand. He spoke without waiting to be called upon. "When it says that you can't expound before three, does that three include the teacher? Or is it a teacher and three students?"

The question was clear, concise, and admitted an answer. It was a question the rabbis had asked.

Moshe had his answer ready. "Some say the three includes the teacher, some say it doesn't. It doesn't make any sense to me that the three would include the teacher. Then the one would include the teacher as well, and you would have one person teaching himself or herself.

"Consider what we learned from Reb Nachman. In order to learn from reflected light, there has to be another person present to bounce the light off of. So the teacher can't be included. When it says not more than three or two or

205

one, my understanding is that the text means three, two, or one other than the teacher."

That was the end of the answer. Some questions opened doors into worlds, and some into closets. Worlds were meant to be explored, but closets were also important. There was inventory to take, extraneous material to clear out.

The Order of Creation

Another man raised his hand. "What is meant by the Work of Creation and the Work of the Chariot?"

Moshe's response was immediate and sharp. "The Mishnah mentions three things: Sexuality, Creation, and the Chariot. So how come you ask only about Creation and the Chariot? Why didn't you ask me what is meant by Sexuality? Why don't you ask about Sexuality, too?"

That brought smiles from some and frowns from others. Moshe's words, while laced with humor, had been piercing nonetheless. Moshe continued unperturbed. "The answer is that all three have to do with sexuality. It's just a matter of degree. You have to be careful how you talk about sexuality. According to *halachah,* Jewish law, you may not do so in an irresponsible fashion. If that is true about that which arouses our emotions, how much the more so when it comes to matters concerning Creation and the Chariot!

"Creation is also a matter of sexuality. After all, how do you create, other than through sexuality? The Work of Creation is about how God created this universe, and there's some sexy stuff in that."

He turned from the questioner to the class at large. "Tell me, according to the first chapter of Genesis, what does God create on the first day?"

"Light and dark," came the correct response.

"God separates the light from the darkness. And on the second day?" Moshe didn't wait for an answer. "God separates the waters below from the waters above. And on the third day? God separated the dry land from the waters."

He paused before continuing, implying a break between the first three days of creation and the last three.

"On the fourth day, God went back to finish the work of the first day. God made the sun, moon, and stars for the day and the night. On the fifth day, God finished the work which had been started on the second day. God made the fishes for the waters below and the birds for the waters up above. On the sixth day, God finished off the third day, making animals and humans to inhabit the dry land.

"So, you see," Moshe spread his arms wide, "day one is connected to day four, and day two to day five, and day three to day six, and in the middle you have . . ."

"It's a menorah!" proclaimed someone who had guessed the meaning of Moshe's spread arms.

"If you like. A menorah," Moshe agreed. "Or"—he drew a Jewish star on the chalkboard—"a Star of David. Six points, six days of creation, one over against the other, and in the middle . . ."

"Shabbat," came several voices. Others said, "Shabbos."

In this fashion, without having to ask, Moshe learned how many Jews were present.

"Shabbat," he agreed, using the Sephardic accent. "Shabbos," he agreed again with those who still used the European pronunciation. "And what did God do on Shabbat?"

"God rested."

"Rested? Where did you ever get such an idea? God had sex!"

If any mind had been wandering, it snapped back at that moment. Moshe sat on the table, his feet swinging below.

"Shabbat va-yi-nafash," he said. "Shabbat. God withdrew, sat back, and then va-yi-nafash. Nafash, from nefesh, one of the words for soul. God poured soul into the universe. In the first six days, God created a framework to contain soul. When the framework was ready, God created soul and poured it into the universe. 'Shabbat va-yi-nafash.' God sat back and created souls.

"How do we human beings create souls? We have sex. Now when God has sex, it's not the same as when we have sex. But if sex is the act of creating souls, that's what God did. Now, what do you do on Shabbos? How do you celebrate it?"

No one responded. They were afraid to answer. "Candles, bread, wine," would have been an obvious answer. No one dared suggest it.

"You have an oneg Shabbat," Moshe said. "Do you know what the word oneg means? A delight. You have a Shabbat delight. Oneg is one of the euphemisms for sex in rabbinic tradition. Ta-anug—delight, pleasure, sex.

"What happens on Shabbat? The tradition is that extra souls descend. Husband and wife take on extra souls. The husband takes on the aspect of the Holy One Blessed Is He, and the wife the aspect of the Shechinah, Blessed Is

She, the presence of God within space and time, and they have sex, a holy union, symbolically reunifying the masculine transcendent with the feminine immanent."

The stillness in the room was palpable.

"Now when the Rabbi says after the Friday evening service, 'The sisterhood invites you into the social hall for an *Oneg Shabbat* . . .'"

Laughter exploded out of the silence.

"Why haven't we ever heard anything like this before?" a questioner interrupted.

"'Matters of sexuality may not be expounded before more than three persons,'" Moshe quoted from the text. "'Nor the Work of Creation before more than two.' We may not say such things openly. But you are all paired off, responsible for each other. I am expounding here only before two. Now, please, take some time and review with each other what you have learned."

The room resonated at once with the response. Moshe descended from the table to sit by his wife.

Rivkah's Concern

Stephanie felt Sidney waiting. It was for her to continue, but she had not yet righted herself.

In all the previous tellings, Sidney had begun with the four who had descended to Paradise, all the warnings, and then the model of the kabbalist. That was the way Moshe had begun the lesson himself.

For Sidney to change Moshe's order . . . The very thought astonished her.

On one hand, Sidney's originality should be applauded, that he would take a chance and do something on his own. But this wasn't the place for it. He had made the lesson more difficult than it needed to be.

She did have something to add, and this she needed to do herself. The interaction between Moshe and Rivkah she did not want to leave to Sidney.

Stephanie gathered herself, brought to consciousness the last words of Sidney's story, and continued, "While the class learned, Moshe sat with Rivie. That was part of the learning as well."

"How are you doing?" Moshe asked.

"I'm doing fine," Rivkah said. "I may not be able to wait until *Shabbat*. But I don't know how the class is doing. Aren't you being a little hard on them? That poor fellow who asked about creation . . . You got away with it, Moshe, but if you had answered me like that, I don't know if I would be back next week."

Moshe nodded. "I'm teaching too much from *Gevurah*," he acknowledged. "I'll be more careful. How am I really doing? Is there anything new here, anything you haven't heard me teach before?"

"The creation menorah. I hadn't heard that before. Did you make that up, or did you get it from somewhere?"

"I don't remember," Moshe answered.

"Maybe Jews should have menorahs on their roofs instead of TV antennas," Rivkah joked.

"It's not a bad idea," Moshe agreed.

"What about the Chariot? You didn't answer the fellow when he asked about the Chariot. You let that slip."

"You noticed that? I wanted to do some work with creation before I talked about the Chariot."

"Now conversations like this may not seem like serious learning," Stephanie added, "but something was happening there, because Rivkah remembered every such exchange well enough to tell me about them later."

The Chariot's Garage

Sidney continued the teaching.

"The Work of the Chariot," Moshe said.

With these words he brought the energy back to center. "The foundation of the Work of the Chariot is the first chapter of the book of Ezekiel. Ezekiel has a vision. It, too, is a sexy experience, but just as the Work of Creation is more profound than matters of human sexuality, the Work of the Chariot is more profound even than the Work of Creation. What was it that Ezekiel saw? Ezekiel witnessed the innermost process of creation of souls, something that cannot be related by reason alone, but only hinted at through visionary experience. This is something to learn only one on one, and then that one has to be especially qualified, to have insight, the text says. Even more than insight," Moshe added. "We're not ready yet to explore matters concerning the Chariot. In a few weeks, perhaps."

"So," Sidney concluded, "Moshe put the Chariot in the garage, out of sight."

The Woman Who Raised Her Hand

Sidney said, "Some months later, when Moshe and I were well into the discipline of learning together, I had some reason to recall the question of the first woman to raise her hand. This was her question: 'Why is it so bad to ask what is below and what is above?'

"I asked Moshe if he remembered the question. He asked me if I remembered the woman. The woman, he said, was more important than the question. I told Moshe I didn't remember the woman's name. He said she didn't tell us her name, but she told us a lot about herself. I hadn't quoted her fully. She had also asked, 'Why shouldn't we be able to ask any question we want?'

"She was angry. Her questions had been suppressed too many times, maybe by her husband, more likely by a parent. She wasn't about to tolerate any such suppression from God, or from Moshe, as God's representative. So she asked her question, and she signed it with anger. It was an angry woman who asked an angry question. Moshe answered her question, but he also responded to her anger. Answering the question was easy. Answering the anger was more difficult.

"I learned from Moshe when we are confronted with an angry person and we don't know what caused the anger, the best thing to do, if we have to respond, is to respond with a story."

On the blackboard Moshe had drawn a large letter *BAYT*, closed to the right, open to the left, thick above and thick below, the line below protruding just a tad to the right. "This is the letter *BAYT*," he explained. "It is the first letter of the Torah. It is with the letter *BAYT* that God begins the process of creation. In the Torah it is written without the dot in the middle.

ב

BAYT

"There's a wonderful story in the *Zohar*. The *Zohar* is the big book of Jewish mysticism, written in the thirteenth century. Each of the letters comes before the Throne of Glory and asks God to begin creation with it. 'Me, me, me!' each letter says. Now if the *ALEF* came first, it wouldn't be a very long story, because, after all, *BAYT* is the second letter of the alphabet. So the story begins with the last letter and works its way backwards. Each letter makes its case, and each letter is turned down for one reason or another.

"There are some wonderful lessons to be learned from the letters. *SAMECH* comes forward and says, 'Begin with me. I stand for Support. I could be the pillar of the universe. I could hold up everything.'

"'Indeed you could,' God answers. 'But look who comes after you, the *NUN*, which stands for *Noflim*, those who are falling down. If I took you away, who could the *Noflim* lean against? Who would be there to support them?'"

Moshe wiped his glasses and changed his tone of voice as a way of indicating parentheses in the body of his answer. "I used that in a eulogy once," he digressed. "It was a eulogy for a woman who had been president of National Hadassah. That's *National* Hadassah, not a local chapter. You understand how competent such a woman must have been? Can you imagine how many people were at her funeral?" Heads nodded.

"Other than me and the funeral director, there were two people at her funeral. Two. She died when she was ninety-six years old. She had Alzheimer's. She had outlived everybody except a great-niece and the woman who had taken care of her the last twenty years.

"The niece was angry, very angry. 'What is the purpose of such an existence?' she asked me. So I told her the story from the *Zohar*, of the *SAMECH* and the *NUN*, the support for those who are falling. For seventy-six years her aunt had been the one to give the support, a pillar of strength, holding the world up on her own shoulders. If you had an instrument that could count *mitzvahs* per second, she would have been off the scale."

The expression *mitzvahs per second* produced some smiles, but not everyone knew the meaning of *mitzvah*.

"Good deeds," Moshe translated. "A *mitzvah* here is a good deed. Consider how many fallen she had lifted up, how many good deeds she had done. This woman's aunt had been a veritable *SAMECH*. But for those last twenty years she had been among the fallen. She hadn't been able to do a single *mitzvah* in all that time. But what she had been able to do was to enable her niece to do a *mitzvah*, and her attendant. So two souls became *SAMECH*s because of her.

211

"What I was attempting to do was to infuse into those twenty years some sense of purpose. With purpose, pain becomes bearable. Purpose can defuse anger. I don't know if I succeeded or not, but I had an obligation to try.

"That's just two of the letters," Moshe continued. "The story goes on, backwards through the alphabet, until finally the letter *BAYT,* the second letter of the alphabet, comes forward and asks, 'Begin with me. I stand for *Brachah,* for Blessing.' And God says, 'It would be good to start the world with a blessing.'"

When it seemed Moshe was done with the story a student asked, "What about *ALEF?*"

"That's just what God asked. God turned to the *ALEF,* the first letter, and said, 'Why are you so silent?' The *ALEF* responded, 'It wouldn't be right for me to come forward and ask now that you have already made your decision.' God said, 'Because of your humility, when I speak to the people at Sinai, I will begin with you.' So *ALEF* is the first letter of the ten commandments. Even more than that, *ALEF* becomes the sound that begins every utterance, when you speak a word with awe. *ALEF* is a silent letter. You open your mouth and the sound that you don't hear before the word is spoken is *ALEF.*

"Prepare to say something." Moshe opened his hands by way of invitation. "Now open your mouths and hear the *ALEF.*"

Throughout the room, mouths gaped open.

"Now for the *BAYT.* The letter *BAYT* is closed above, below, and behind. From this the rabbis teach that you don't ask what is above, below, or behind. You proceed only in the direction of the opening, into the words of the Torah itself. The Torah has in it all you will need. There isn't anything to be gained by asking what is above, or below, or behind."

Moshe waited and wondered if anyone knew the Hebrew alphabet well enough to find the flaw. When no one spoke, Moshe enlarged the opening for an objection. "There's a problem here. There's another letter of the Hebrew alphabet that would have served this purpose just as well, or better."

It was an Asian gentleman who raised his hand and offered, "The letter *KAF.*"

Moshe, to his credit, showed no evidence of surprise.

Sidney responded to the unasked question. "Yes, I was the Asian gentleman. From the outset I knew something extraordinary was happening in that classroom, but I didn't know what. With that one word, that one letter, *KAF,* I announced my intention to find out. I became a player in the process, whatever it was going to become."

"Yes, the letter *KAF*," Moshe continued. He drew the letter *KAF* on the board next to the letter *BAYT.*

כ

KAF

"The *KAF* is also closed above, below, and behind. But note the difference." He pointed to the tiny projection backwards at the bottom of the letter *BAYT.* "You see this? This is here for the student who has the *hutzpah* to challenge the rabbis and say, 'Oh yeah, well if that's so, why didn't God begin creation with the letter *KAF*? It's closed above, below, and behind too!' This little pointer at the bottom of the *BAYT* is for that student. Such a student is permitted to ask such questions, what is above, what is below, what came before. But if you don't have the imagination to ask such a question, or the courage to challenge authority in such a way, then be satisfied with the words of the Torah. They will guide you well enough. There isn't anything to be gained by stepping over the boundaries.

"So it's not for everybody, this study. Judging from the size of this class you might think there is a lot of interest in the Kabbalah, but the truth is that most people don't care. They don't ask questions like these. They are satisfied with the words of the Torah, as much as they know of them. How the world came into being, what its purpose is, what is above, and what is below, none of that is of any concern to them. There's nothing driving them to take the elevator up to the fourth floor to spend a few hours pondering the answers to such questions. You are a self-selecting group. There's something in you that isn't satisfied with conventional wisdom, and you want to step over the line and learn more.

"Tradition tells us we do not push people over the line against their will. Whatever belief they have that sustains them, it's their belief. It's not for us to knock out the pillars that hold them up, just because we see structural flaws in their support system. They have to ask the questions themselves. They have to be willing to ask, to risk, to change. So the rabbis put barriers in the way. They tell you not to ask. Most people are satisfied with that. They don't ask.

Others say, 'Who are they to limit my growth?' and they ask. There's a place for them, too. At the moment that place is here on the fourth floor.

"Take a moment please to work with your study partner. Why are you asking? Why are you here? Is there someone in your life who puts limits on your growth? Is there a line you are told not to cross? Why do you cross it anyway? And if you don't like any of my questions, ask your own and answer it. We'll take a few minutes."

Danger

"Would you tell the Paretzky story here?" Sidney asked Stephanie while the students were immersed in their learning. He had to repeat the question before she heard it.

"Why didn't you begin with the four who descended to Paradise?" she asked in return. "The Paretzky story belongs there."

"I thought I would shake the order up a little, make it fresh. It was becoming too much rote."

"That was a difficult beginning. I like it better the other way."

"Why is the order so important?"

"Not for me," Stephanie defended. "For the students. I could care less what the order is. But it would be easier for them to follow."

"But you do care," Sidney pushed.

Stephanie turned her back on him to bring the class to order. She said, "When I began to learn the tradition from Moshe, he reminded me, when done at depth, it might be dangerous. I had difficulty accepting the idea that meditation could be dangerous, even after Moshe had shared with us what had happened to Jaime at Princeton. I heard the words, and as awful as they were, they did not register.

"One morning when I was visiting with Rivkah I found Moshe so immobile on a deck chair, I checked to be sure he was breathing. An hour I sat with him, fearful to touch him, fearful to leave. When his eyes opened, they were focused on me.

"'I was afraid for you,' I told him. 'Why do you do that?'

"Moshe laughed, and said, 'You're not the first to ask me that. Paretzky asked me the same thing.'"

"Why?" Dr. Paretzky had asked.

Paretzky wanted Moshe to continue for a Ph.D. The rabbinic thesis was a natural opening. Moshe already had a foot inside. Kabbalah was to be the academic ground of the future.

"What would you do?" Moshe answered with a question of his own. "Let's say you find a manuscript in the archives. Nobody has read it in centuries. You read it. It's a discipline that will bring you before the Throne of Glory. It teaches the secrets of the universe, the purpose of creation. It leads to fulfillment, completion, ecstasy. What would you do?"

"You know damn well what I would do. I'd translate it and compare it and footnote it and publish the damn thing and make a big name for myself, as if I needed one, thank you. I know you could do that, if you wanted to. And you, what do you want to do? You want to take that damned manuscript and skip off down the yellow brick road. I'm asking you why. There's a whole world of scholarship about to be opened, and you can be the one to do it. But if you go skipping off down that yellow brick road, nobody's going to have a damned thing to do with you.

"Damn it, Katan! A scholar has to have some distance from what he studies. You can't be a blooming mystic and a scholar of mysticism. You know that. You have to choose one or the other, to study or become an object to be studied, and I know which one you've chosen, and I ask you again, why? Why choose the harder path? What makes you do it?"

He didn't know why. Paretzky was not about to let him go without an answer. Why?

Moshe's breathing slowed. His focus narrowed. He envisioned the letters of the name of God, a technique he had learned from the texts. His body relaxed. "Why?" he asked himself, his own voice asking, not Paretzky's. "Why? Why do I do this?"

The business of the day fell behind. Why? Paretzky would not let him go without an answer. He was at sea, in the Gulf of Tonkin. The ship rolled in the troughs. The corpse wore its helmet. He had but a glimpse of it. Why? Why this image? What in this image was an answer to his question, to Paretzky's question, "Why?"

"Because I'm going to die," Moshe said, astonished at his own words. "Not right away. There's nothing wrong with me. Whenever. When I'm 120. It doesn't matter. I'm going to die. I know it. I accept it. It's a given. I want the answers. I want to know what I'm here for. It's what I came to this school to learn, and I haven't learned it yet. That's why."

Paretzky accepted the answer. It was the truth.

•

215

"Paretzky understood it," Stephanie said. "Even now I'm not sure I do, so I keep telling the story, hoping I will."

That was a canned response from previous tellings. It wasn't true anymore. She did understand it, not fully, but somewhat. She couldn't quite articulate her understanding, but her parents and her uncle Al fit into it. They were going to die, and knew it. In Poland each had come to that awareness, though at different times.

Those stories had to be told. She needed to know them, but they would never tell them.

What did she know? For thirty years Al had delivered the letters to her mother. How had he done that? Her father disliked Al, in Poland, in Miami. For thirty years Al delivered the letters, her father never knew. It came as a surprise when he was going through his dead wife's closet and found the hatbox. He knew what the letters were, knew how they had been delivered. Al's address was on each envelope, and a return address, to London, Arlington, New York, San Francisco. He hadn't read them, but knew how to return them. He could have thrown them away, but he didn't. Why not?

A story began to develop. It didn't spring forth whole, as the grandmother story had. This began with bits and pieces, from what was known to what was not.

Every Thursday her mother went to Al's shop to buy a magazine. How did Stephanie know it was Thursday?

She knew. She heard it in her story. Her mother made lunch on the hot plate, as she did every day, in the back of the store. After lunch, before going home, she stopped by Al's to buy a magazine. "I'm going to buy a magazine," she said every Thursday.

"I wish you'd stay away from Al," her father said. "I still don't trust him."

"I'm buying a magazine. I don't pay any attention to Al. He doesn't pay any attention to me." That was the truth.

Every Thursday afternoon her mother bought a magazine. It didn't matter which magazine. She didn't read it. She chose one at random, put it on the counter, turned aside. Why did she turn aside?

She didn't want to see Al insert a letter. No, she didn't want to see Al, didn't want to speak with him. Her husband had forbidden it. Why did he forbid it?

Her father didn't trust Al, even in Poland. Why not?

Perhaps he spoke badly about Al because her mother had been in love with him before the war, had been torn away from him to marry the jeweler's son.

216

She did as her parents had asked, because, after all, that's the way such things were done. Was her father still jealous of Al after all these years?

That's where the story ended, for the moment. There was more, but Sidney was about to tell the Truth.

Where was the story coming from? How did she know these things? Were they true? Did it matter?

Truth

Sidney wrote the Hebrew letters אמת large on a legal pad and placed it in the middle of the deck. *"ALEF MEM TAV,"* he said, reading from right to left in the Hebrew order. "Moshe drew these on the chalkboard. His Hebrew calligraphy was better than mine. He wrote the letters as they appear in the Torah scroll. This is the best I can do."

$$\text{ת} \quad \text{מ} \quad \text{א}$$

TAV   *MEM*   *ALEF*

"*ALEF, MEM, TAV,*" Moshe said, pointing to each letter. "*EMeT,* the Hebrew word for truth. Do you know what truth is?" he asked the students.

Moshe circled the *ALEF* and the *TAV.* "*ALEF* is the first letter of the Hebrew alphabet. *TAV* is the last letter. It's like saying the truth extends from *A* to *Z.* That's the truth."

Moshe circled the first two letters. "What do these two letters spell? *EM?* What might *EM* mean?"

"Mother," someone ventured.

"Yes. Mother." Moshe circled the last two letters. "'*MeT.*' What do these last two letters mean?" He waited for a response. "Death," he volunteered at last. "Mother, birth. From birth to death, and that's the truth. So truth goes from *A* to *Z,* from birth to death."

Moshe circled all three letters and placed different vowels below them. "Don't read '*EMeT,*'" he said. "With these vowels the same letters can be read '*AMooT,*' and what does *AMooT* mean? It means, 'I shall die.' And that's the truth.

"If you are here to learn the truth, that's where you begin. I shall die. If you are not prepared to accept that, you're not likely to learn anything here.

217

That's where all truth begins, with the acknowledgment *I will die*. If you have such *hutzpah* as to think everyone else dies but what does that have to do with you, there's not much that can be learned. So . . ."

"But reincarnation," a voice interrupted. "You don't really die. You come back again." Moshe looked up into the eyes of a young woman, pale blue eyes, a sad demeanor. "You believe in reincarnation, don't you?" she pleaded. "I know there's reincarnation in the Kabbalah."

"We'll get there eventually," he promised. "We'll talk about reincarnation. In this lifetime," he joked, but her mood did not lighten. "Not right now, though. I hear your concern. I won't forget. I don't think you'll let me. Okay?"

The young woman nodded, though clearly it was not okay. She wanted reassurance at once. The notion of personal death was terrifying to her. Moshe wondered about that. She was so young to have such fears. "What's your name, please?"

"Emily."

"We'll look at reincarnation before we're done. I promise. It's just important to take things in order. I know it looks like I'm rambling all over the place, but there is some method to the madness, and we're just not ready for reincarnation yet. Is this okay, Emily?"

This time it was a little more okay, but Moshe made a mental note. Emily would bear watching.

"*EMeT*," he pronounced as he pointed to the letters on the board. "*AMooT*. I shall die, and that's the truth. It's only because it's the truth I can play games with the letters like this. We have to be very careful with such games, because you can use coincidences with letters to prove anything you like. Anything at all. I could prove I'm the Messiah, or that the world will come to an end next Tuesday. Anything at all. So the rabbis have established certain rules. Coincidence can be used only to reinforce a truth that has already been established by some other means.

"I know I'm going to die. I recognize that as the truth. So if I like, I can explore the letters within the word *EMeT* and discover there something to make me think more deeply about this truth.

"Anyone who attempts to convince you of a truth just because of some coincidental relationship is a charlatan. There's nothing there but smoke and mirrors. It's illusion. However, if the truth has been established first, then the smoke and mirrors can be used as a device to hammer it home."

The room was quiet. Moshe was fearful he had offended someone in making his point. How many present subscribed to some New Age tradition

based on coincidence? The *I Ching*? Astrology? Shamanism? Had he just offended everyone in the room? "I'm not saying there is no value to coincidence. What makes a coincidence meaningful is that it is based on meaning
which has already been established. The meaning here is the truth. The coincidence illuminates the truth."

There was still no response. "Let me give another example." Moshe circled the letter *ALEF* in *EMeT*. "This is the letter *ALEF*. Note how it is made.
One long line on a diagonal, and two short segments." Moshe drew one long
vertical line, and beside it two short lines.

ו ׳ י

YOD   YOD   VAV

"These are the component fragments of the letter *ALEF*. They are letters
themselves. This long one is a *VAV*, the short ones are *YOD*s. Now there is a
system of ascribing numerical value to each of the letters of the Hebrew alphabet. *ALEF* is the first letter. It has the value of one. *BAYT* is the second letter. It has the value of two, and so forth. If you count it out, *VAV* has the value
of six, and *YOD*, ten. So if you count up the *VAV* and the two *YOD*s, that
makes twenty-six. So *ALEF*, which has the value of one, also equals twenty-six."

יהוה

HEY VAV HEY YOD

He wrote the name of God on the board. *YOD HEY VAV HEY*. "This is
the four-letter name of God. Let's see what its numerical value is. *YOD* equals
ten, *HEY* is five, *VAV* is six, another *HEY* is five, and the total is . . . twenty-
six. So, we have an equation."

Moshe wrote this equation on the board:

ALEF = *YOD*+*YOD*+*VAV* =26 = value of *YOD HEY VAV HEY* = God = ONE = *ALEF*

"So, the letter *ALEF* which has the numerical value of one is made of component letters which have the numerical value of twenty-six, which in turn is
the numerical value of the name of God. God is One, which is the numerical
value of the letter *ALEF*. So, God is One. Neat."

219

It was clear the class thought the equation was neat as well. "But I haven't proven anything by this," Moshe added. "If I did not know God was One already, this in no way would constitute a proof. But since I know God is One, this is neat. It makes me consider the oneness of God from a different perspective. It creates a feeling, a bit of wonder and awe. There's nothing wrong with that. But it isn't a proof."

Moshe erased the board and continued speaking with his back to the class. "I've taken a lot of time to explain what the Kabbalah isn't. It isn't magical combinations of letters and numbers. There are lots of such combinations, but they are not magic. They're frosting on the cake. Window dressing. The cover on the book. It's time now to see what's in the book, or in the store, or how the cake is baked. Ready?"

They were ready.

"Good. We'll take a few minutes to review with our study partners, then we'll begin."

"Letters."

How did her mother read the letters?

She carried her magazine back home, climbed the steps, made tea, sat down to the small table in the kitchen. Only then did she open the magazine. Maybe there was a letter. One week in four, maybe five, maybe six, there was a letter. Stephanie was so sad she had not written more often. Or longer letters.

If there was a letter, her mother read it, then read it again. It was the best story, the only story in the magazine. She folded the letter carefully, put it back into its envelope, went to the bedroom closet to add it to the collection.

She had a stepladder in the closet, to reach the hatbox on the back shelf in the corner, an old hatbox.

If there was no letter in the magazine, she still made the trip to the closet, to read the old ones. They had been fingered and read many times.

The Assistant

The review done, Stephanie said, "Rivkah told me that she had not the slightest notion that the teaching was intended for her. She heard everything Moshe was saying, but at the same time was taking her assigned responsibility seriously. She was monitoring the class, not at all sure what she was looking for."

220

"So, what do you think?" Moshe asked his assistant.

"Emily will bear some watching."

"Yes. I picked that up, too."

"Do you see those two?" Rivkah pointed to a couple sitting in the rear. "Norman and Marsha Plotkin. You've met them. He's a surgeon. I see him occasionally on the sixth floor. She does something at the art museum. The Asian fellow sitting next to them? His name is Sidney Lee. A big shot at Freeman March. He's on the hospital board. His picture is on the wall by the first-floor conference room. You've got quite a group. I guess you never know."

"You never know," Moshe agreed. "Will you do some work for me? Will you watch out for Emily?" Rivkah nodded. "Anyone else you see need watching?"

Rivkah scanned the room. "Maybe the fellow in the plaid shirt. He doesn't have a study partner. He didn't react well when you were talking about dying."

"I think, sometimes, there are two kinds of people who come to these things. Those who are afraid they are going to die and want to find a way to avoid it and those who know they are going to die and want to find out what to do with their life while they have it."

"What category do I fit in?" Rivkah asked.

"Social worker," Moshe answered quickly.

The Kabbalist

On the legal pad Sidney drew Moshe's picture of a kabbalist. He drew it gracefully, with an economy of strokes. The body of the kabbalist was a box, a receiver with two dials. The head, a satellite dish, the neck, a pole connecting the dish to the receiver. Two legs extended from the box, each ending in a sandal.

Students leaned forward to see it clearly.

"A receiver," Moshe said. "That's all a kabbalist is. A receiver. First a kabbalist has to have his head or her head turned in the direction from which the signals come. If your head is pointed in the wrong direction, don't expect to receive very much. And if there's something over the face of the antenna"—Moshe drew a dotted line in front of the satellite dish—"not much is going to get through either. This dotted line is pride. That's all it is. Pride. It's like having a sheet of aluminum foil over the antenna. All you receive is a reflection of yourself.

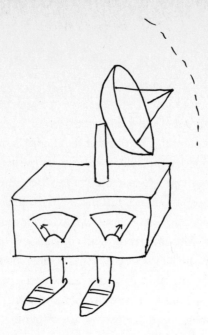

"The signal comes down into the receiver. Two things happen here. One"—Moshe drew a needle in one of the dials of the box—"background noise has to be reduced. And then"—he drew a needle in the other dial—"the signal has to be amplified.

"That's a kabbalist. That's all there is to it. First, get your head on straight. Second, remove the layer of pride. Third, reduce background noise. Fourth, amplify the signal so you can hear it with some certainty.

"The first step is done through learning. Through argument and study. Taking out notions you hold precious concerning the world, God, and the way they work together. Dispensing with notions that are clearly false. Replacing them with notions that may not be correct but are at least more consistent.

"The second step, reducing pride. Understanding one's true measure over against the scope of the universe. Accepting how small one is, but also how great. Objectivity.

"Third, reducing background noise. Meditation that serves to relax, to remove oneself, to move under the surface to calmer waters.

"And fourth, to amplify the signal. If there is a broadcast from Creator to creation, to hear it, to accept it, to allow it to move you, to transform you.

"That's all there is to it."

"Which part of the drawing do you think is the most important?" Sidney asked.

The students began to argue, some choosing the antenna head, some the receiver body.

Sidney said, "Moshe and I discussed his model many times. Every time I referred to it, he suggested a different part to be the most important. He had no steady answer. I'm not sure if it was arbitrary, or according to his mood, or some combination of the two."

"Or something else entirely," Stephanie added, her contentiousness rising.

Sidney continued, pointing to the bottom of the drawing. "This was Moshe's response at the Institute."

"Here's where the important work takes place. Birkenstock sandals. Everyone thinks kabbalists wear Birkenstock sandals, and besides, they're easy to draw." Moshe looked down at his own feet. He was wearing tennis shoes. "So, not all kabbalists wear Birkenstock sandals. Just most of them. When the signal comes in, and when you reduce background noise and amplify the message, two things happen. The most apparent thing is that you walk differently in the world. You can't walk the same way anymore. Your direction changes. So one thing to consider right away is that if you are comfortable in the way you are walking, maybe you shouldn't be studying this. Because if you do, you'll be walking differently. Understand?"

He looked about, as if expecting a question, and then affected surprise when no one asked. "Ahhh, I see. You are here to learn *about* the Kabbalah, not to *learn* the Kabbalah itself. Yes, you're right. You can learn *about* the Kabbalah all you want and not have to change the way you walk in the world. But I have to let you know, while you may learn something about the Kabbalah here in the next weeks, my real intent is to teach the Kabbalah *itself*. To give you what you need to get involved in it, to do it.

"You know what it's like? It's like platform diving, like those athletes in the Olympics who climb up fifty feet or so and jump off into a pool. You can learn about platform diving, study the books, look at the pictures, read up on the records. Or you can learn how to do platform diving. You understand the difference? In only one of them do you get wet. Here my intent is to get wet. This isn't a college course about Kabbalah like I used to teach at the university. This is the Institute of Expanding Light. You don't come all the way up to the

floor just to learn about Kabbalah. Here you get wet. So I have to make
know right away, if you get wet, you don't walk the same way in the
and that's just the half of it.

"The other half is this." Moshe tapped the pole connecting the antenna
to the box. "The signal that gets amplified affects the feet and the way
you walk. It also affects how you turn your head and the way you think. I
said at the beginning that you have to have your head turned in the direction from which the signals emanate or you don't receive much. Well, you
can get it only so straight yourself. The most you can expect to do is to
have it more or less in the right direction. But what happens when the signal is amplified is kind of a spiritual feedback. Something comes back up
the pole here and turns your head slightly, in a way you could not have turned
it by yourself. If you like, it's an act of grace. The end result is you think
differently.

"So consider the consequences of what we learn here. The end result,
you walk differently in the world. You think differently. Your belief system, your very assembly language that determines how you consider Creator
and creation, all of this is likely to undergo change. Are you willing to risk
that?"

He waited for questions. The Asian gentleman was quick to raise his hand.

"At this point I become a part of the stories," Sidney said. "I have no choice."

I raised my hand. "Isn't that true about anything you study?" I asked. "Whatever you learn is going to change the way you approach the world."

"There's change, and then there's change," Moshe responded. "If a hospital buys a new piece of equipment, and the staff learns how to use it, treatment changes. But the philosophy of the hospital doesn't change. The
hospital continues much as it had before. Only the department that received
the new equipment is affected, and even then, marginally, or rather, mechan-
ically. But if you make a change in the philosophy of the hospital, that changes
everything. Every department is affected. Every person, every patient. Everything.

"Studying the discipline of Kabbalah is much like that. It has the capacity
to change everything.

"Everything," Moshe said once again, more to himself than to his students.

"Discipline was important to Moshe," Sidney said. "When he spoke the word, he underlined it. He was a drill instructor with a class of recruits. His first task was to teach them discipline. That explained his *Gevurah* aspect, somewhat. Not completely."

"Do you understand what I mean by discipline?" Moshe asked into the silence. "The end result of discipline, any discipline, is the same. The end result is grace. Can you name a discipline? Any discipline?" The class had become too timid to answer, so the question became rhetorical.

"High jumping is a discipline," Moshe answered. "Ballet is a discipline. Karate is a discipline. Piano is a discipline. All disciplines. The end result of all of them is grace. All of them produce the same result. The high jumper can soar to heights unimaginable, and she does it gracefully, seemingly without effort. The ballet dancer, the karate master, the pianist. All of them. Basketball, archery, automobile racing . . . It doesn't matter what it is. Each of them requires study and practice. Each requires a master teacher, a *sensei*, a *maestro*, a coach. Different names, all the same, each to his own discipline. Study alone won't do it. Practice alone won't do it. Both are required. Each has its own rules, its own arena, its own uniform, but in each the end result is the same, the ability to do something that is inordinately difficult with apparent ease. To soar through the air and slam dunk. To play a Rachmaninov piano concerto. To hit the bull's-eye time after time. Such masters make it all look so easy. Such grace.

"Do you know what grace is?" Moshe continued, obviously another rhetorical question. No one responded. "Grace is the act of an agency outside of oneself that enables a person to reach a goal one could not reach by one's own power alone."

He said it as if he were reading from a dictionary, but no dictionary defines grace in such a way. That definition of grace was in itself an act of grace, for the definition had come whole to Moshe at that instant, from outside of himself, through himself. Those who had brought notebooks were writing. "Say it again, please," one asked.

"Grace," he repeated. He tapped the antenna, the head of the kabbalist, drawn on the blackboard. "The kabbalist cannot turn his head precisely. He can turn it only more or less in the right direction. But as he does the discipline, as he reduces the barrier of pride and brings in the signal, as he amplifies it and removes distortion, as an act of grace, the action of an agency outside of himself, the antenna is adjusted, aimed better, so the signal is received better, and the process continues. Grace, an act of an agency outside of oneself that enables a person to reach a goal one could not reach by one's own power.

"Grace is the end result of every discipline. Ask the athlete how he did it. It doesn't matter what the *it* is. Broad jump, marathon, boxing—whatever. The response is, 'I don't know. I felt something lifting me, carrying me, enabling me to reach a place I never reached before.' Grace. An agency outside of oneself enabling one to reach a place one couldn't reach alone. The physical manifestation of it is the ability to do with apparent ease something that is ordinarily very difficult. But that ability comes from an agency outside of oneself."

The surgeon from the sixth floor cleared his throat and ventured a question. "What is it that the kabbalist can do that's so difficult?" he asked. "We can see what the high jumper can do, hear what the musician does. What does the kabbalist do?"

For a moment Moshe appeared suspended, separated from the class. The surgeon had dissected him away from the body of students. It was apparent there were multiple answers, that he was taking his time in the selection.

"The high jumper, the musician, they work in different departments," he began, "different expressions of life. The kabbalist goes to the very core of life itself, its purpose, its direction."

Before continuing, he erased the portrait of the kabbalist from the board and replaced it with a flat line. "High jumping." He made a curved line, a sine wave, which oscillated gently above and below the flat line. "Most people can high jump only this amplitude. The disciplined high jumper"—he made a sharply accentuated sine wave, much taller and deeper—"jumps this. Most people have musical ability only within this range." He indicated the flatter wave. "The disciplined musician's ability extends to this range. At peak moments, even beyond. Now for the Kabbalah. The undisciplined person lives within this range." He pointed to the flat wave once again. "The kabbalist has a much broader amplitude, open to much more of the experience of life. The highs are higher; the lows lower. He contains more, retains more. The exposure is greater. He acts on his soul to a greater height and depth. The Kabbalah works on the very fabric of life itself."

"You learn how to live better," the doctor suggested.

"Yes," Moshe agreed. "You learn how to live."

"We began with a text, and we'll finish with a text," Sidney said as he passed copies left and right. "This one is a warning."

> Our Rabbis taught: Four men entered Paradise (PaRaDiSe—פרדס)— Ben Azzai, Ben Zoma, Aher, and Rabbi Akiba . . . Ben Azzai looked and died. Of him Scripture says: *Precious in the sight of the Lord is the death of His saints.* Ben Zoma looked and became demented. Of him Scripture says: *Hast thou found honey? Eat so much as is sufficient for thee, lest thou be filled therewith, and vomit it.* Aher became estranged. (Only) Rabbi Akiba departed in *shalom.*
> —*Talmud Hagigah 14b*

Stephanie glanced at the words she had expected to see earlier. "Some warnings are worth taking seriously," she said. "*Open Trench,* for example. If you are riding a motorcycle, a sign proclaiming *Open Trench* you will take very seriously."

She had heard the warnings from Moshe, had come to respect them. Even so, knowing an open trench is ahead is no guarantee of safety. Even with a warning, one can fall into it.

As Sidney completed the lesson, her mind drifted back to her motorcycle ride with Moshe. Had the suggestion to experience that ride been innocent? Or had she known there would be an open trench into which she was all too willing to fall?

There were different kinds of danger, she recognized, fearful lest her blush be noticed, but all attention was on Sidney. The entire lesson had been about sex. She hadn't until then admitted it. The Kabbalah was sexy. It made the unbalanced vulnerable.

What had thrown her off-balance? She searched for an answer, found only her anger.

Sidney completed the lesson.

"We finish with some warnings," Moshe said. "You will have to decide what to do with them."

The room was in disarray. Chairs had been moved from orderly rows as study partners had shifted, then shifted again from groups of twos to fours. The first lesson was nearly at an end, yet the energy of the class was still very much present. "The text speaks about these four great rabbis—Rabbi Akiva,

Ben Zoma, Ben Azzai, and Aher—truly great rabbis, teachers from the second century, who desired to do this study and peek into paradise."

Moshe wrote the words big on the chalkboard.

PaRaDiSe
פרדס

"This is the Hebrew word for orchard," Moshe continued. "They desired to peek into the orchard. We are taught that one died outright, one went crazy, something strange happened to the third. Only Rabbi Akiva descended in *shalom* and ascended in *shalom*. Do you know what the meaning of *shalom* is?" His aspect was more inviting and allowed for answers.

"Hello," ventured one student.

"Good-bye," suggested another.

"Peace," said several others.

"That's all correct," Moshe agreed. "*Shalom* has many meanings. It comes from the root for wholeness, complete, perfect. When we say hello, good-bye, or peace in Hebrew, we are wishing the other wholeness, completion, perfection. Fulfillment.

"Here the word *shalom* means *safety*. Rabbi Akiva descended in safety and ascended in safety. He was the only one to make the descent and the ascent and stay whole. The others didn't. They descended and came back damaged. In one case, the rabbi didn't come back at all. He died.

"We have other warnings like this in the tradition. It is said that once a rabbi came from Jerusalem to Babylon to teach. Jerusalem was where this stuff was learned. When he opened his mouth in the academy of Babylon to speak about these things, a wasp flew into his mouth, stung him, and he died. It was said afterward it was appropriate he should die. These things should not be taught publicly."

Moshe paused and looked about the room. "That's why I check carefully for insects before I speak," he joked. Into the laughter he said, "I once asked an Orthodox kabbalist who taught openly about these things how he could do so, considering the warnings and prohibitions. He told me in the time when the warnings were written, the spiritual level of the people was so high that, if one should be careless with a spark of insight, throwing it where one might not be ready for it, the whole community might go up in flames. But today, the spiritual level is so low, one could teach like a flamethrower and be lucky to get even a trace of smoke.

"The spiritual level of this class may not be as high as in Jerusalem of the third century, but it isn't as low as in the general population either. There will be some sparks thrown out here, and it is appropriate to take the warnings to heart. Consider what happened to Ben Azzai, Ben Zoma, and Aher. As for me, I surely consider what happened to the teacher from Jerusalem. I don't take it lightly. Neither should you."

Sidney said, "The lesson was done. Before Moshe could vault from his table, my friend Norman Plotkin raised an administrative matter. The Institute catalogue said the course would be for four weeks, but five dates had been given; five Thursdays, not four. He wanted to know if there would be five lessons or four. Other students at once expressed their desire for five. Moshe was suddenly at a loss. He had planned for only four. He put the decision off by saying that, if any students were left after four weeks, they would decide then if they wanted another session or not. With that he left his table, but before he could reach the door, he was beset by those who needed to see him, to speak with him, whose urgency was so great they could not wait until the next week."

CHAPTER 7

Those Who Ask for Others

"One thing I learned from Moshe early on in our work together," Sidney said, "is that when we are asked to help someone else, we enlist the person who asks to become the primary helper himself. We are no more than a catalyst in the process."

As the classroom emptied, several students gravitated toward the teacher. The man in plaid was the first to speak, his need so salient the others soon left him alone.

"Do you remember me?" he asked. "Harvey Klein. It was Harvey and Marsha when we were at Temple Shalom. You bar-mitzvahed my kids. Steven is thirty years old now. Lives in Tennessee. Memphis. Sells computers. Stacy is twenty-eight. She's the reason I'm here. I'd like you to go to see her. I really wish you would." Harvey Klein nearly came to tears.

"I'll wait outside," said Rivkah.

"It's all right" Moshe said. "Do you remember my wife, Harvey?"

"Mrs. Katan." Harvey nodded. "It's good to see you again, too."

Rivkah had permission to remain, but she left anyway.

"Harvey and Marsha. The names are familiar," said Moshe.

"You were wonderful for Stacy then," Harvey continued. "Right after the bat mitzvah, Marsha and I separated. You had Stacy come back week after week to help with the kids just beginning their lessons."

"I remember. Petite. Thin. Dark hair?"

"Blond now."

Moshe had trained nearly five hundred children for Bar or Bat Mitzvah in his five years at Temple Shalom. During the few weeks before the celebration the bond between Rabbi and student became intense. Hebrew phrases were polished, presentations mastered. The Torah service was choreographed. The family was assured and comforted. The moment the celebration was complete, Moshe's attention drifted ahead to families deeper into the calendar.

Moshe dreaded the words, "Rabbi, do you remember me?" He hardly ever remembered. "Rabbi, you bar-mitzvahed me fifteen years ago, twenty years ago, so many years ago. If it weren't for you, I wouldn't be Jewish today, I wouldn't be happy today, I wouldn't be alive today. Do you remember me?" Most often Moshe could not remember. "You were the most important person in the world to me, Rabbi. Do you know my name?"

What could he say?

"It's kind of you to recognize me. I'm sure I've changed in these twenty years. But you've changed so much more! When I knew you, you were still a kid, but now you're a man, a woman. Forgive me please, if I don't remember."

Sometimes they forgave him.

Sometimes he did remember. He remembered Stacy, her bat mitzvah, more trauma than celebration. She had been suffering through the dissolution of her parents' marriage, and with the separation the day after the bat mitzvah, he couldn't let her drown in the calendar, so he rescued her for a few more weeks. "Where is Stacy now?"

"Stacy is a patient in the Addiction Treatment Unit at the hospital. She's been an addict since she was seventeen. I think this is her last chance. I'm really frightened. Would you see her?"

Would he see her? Moshe was the volunteer Jewish chaplain at the ATU. Every Jewish patient was asked if he or she wanted to see a rabbi, and if so, it was Moshe who was called. He received few calls. It wasn't that there were so few Jewish patients; it was that so few asked to see a rabbi.

"What makes you think I can help?" Moshe asked.

"She knows you. She'll listen to you."

"What do you want me to tell her?"

Harvey Klein had not expected that question. "I don't know."

"If you were a rabbi, what would you tell her?"

Again, a pause. "I don't know. I'm not a Rabbi."

Moshe heard the uppercase R. "I know you're not a Rabbi, but what do you imagine a rabbi might say, a Jewish spiritual counselor might say, that I might say, that would help?"

"I don't know. I think just you're being there will help. If she knows you care, that will help."

"Thank you. But you said she would listen to me. What is it you imagine I might say she would listen to?" Moshe was not about to let him off the hook without a struggle. The first step had been to lead him from relating to an uppercase Rabbi to lowercase rabbi; the next step, to empower him, the father,

231

as a conduit for spiritual guidance. "What words or ideas do you think I could convey that might help?"

"I don't know." Harvey became restless in his resistance. "She needs something. I think you can give it to her."

"Why did you come to the class? Why not just call me and ask me?"

"I saw the ad in the paper. I saw what you were teaching. I wanted to hear you and be sure you were the right person to help."

"Do you think I'm the right person?"

"I think so."

"So now that you've found I'm the right person for Stacy, how about for you? Are you going to come back to the class?" Harvey paused to consider. "I'll offer you a deal," Moshe proposed. "You come to class; I'll visit Stacy. It's not fair she should learn some spiritual discipline and you shouldn't. If you want to be of assistance to her, you need to learn, too."

"A deal," Harvey agreed, sighing his relief. "Thank you." He turned to leave.

"Harvey. One last thing. Is there anything you want me to tell Stacy?"

Harvey paused. "Just one small thing. Tell her I love her. And tell her I'm afraid for her."

"'Just . . .'" Moshe repeated. "That's no small thing. I'll tell her."

In the Porsche, on the way home, Moshe asked Rivkah if she remembered the Kleins.

"I remember Stacy," she said. "You had her over to the house a few times after her bat mitzvah. I remember there were family problems."

"If I saw her around lunchtime tomorrow, do you think you might sit in with me? Your being there would probably help. You might even find it interesting. Some of the things I teach in class you might get to see in practice."

Clergy Emergency

"Moshe Katan may have given up the rabbinate," Sidney said, "but the one perk he did not give up was his clergy parking sign. It was a white plastic sign with blue letters. On one side it read CLERGY OFFICIAL BUSINESS, on the other CLERGY EMERGENCY. The only place he ever used it was at the hospital, and then only when he was visiting a patient in the Addiction Treatment Unit, not when he was meeting Rivkah for lunch. The day after the first lesson,

232

he did both. He had lunch with Rivkah, and then, together, they went to visit a patient."

The hospital was a maze of buildings and bridges. The elevator off the main lobby took Moshe to Four Pavilion and the social work office, where Rivkah was waiting for him. A walk through the orthopedic floor led to a bridge across the avenue to the Merton Tower. Four Tower was respiratory. The stairs behind the nursing station brought him to Three Tower, the ATU.

"Good morning, Joyce," Moshe said to the back of the large woman seated at the desk.

She swiveled around, looking sternly over her half glasses. "Good morning, rabbi. We haven't seen you in a while. How ya doin'? And Mrs. Katan. Nice to see you again, too."

"I'm doin' okay, Joyce. How are you?" Moshe responded, mimicking her accent, a game he had played with her for more than a decade.

"No better than usual, thank you. Who you here to see?"

"Stacy Klein. Rivkah is going to sit in with me if it's all right with Stacy."

"Stacy." Joyce checked her schedule. "Oh yes, here it is. Stacy is just finishing group. Why don't you go down to the chaplain's office? I'll have her meet you there." Joyce unlocked the desk drawer and searched for a tagged key. "Be sure to bring it back before you leave."

"When have I ever forgotten, Joyce?"

"August 14, 1987."

"Just checking, Joyce. Just checking. Someday you'll forgive me, and I can go to heaven clean."

"Not a chance, rabbi. Not a chance." Joyce was semiserious. On her floor, keys were the symbol of ultimate authority.

Moshe stopped at the cooler to fill a paper cup with water and carried it carefully to the chaplain's office. "It's not because I'm thirsty," he told Rivkah. "I almost always have good use for it in the first session. You'll see."

The office was tiny. A small desk, two chairs, a floor lamp, and a bookcase nearly filled the room. He struggled to extract the chair from behind the desk. Desks served him well for learning, but not for counseling. The cup of water he put on the windowsill behind him.

"Stacy," he said to the young woman who hesitated in the doorway. "I'm Moshe Katan. Your father asked me to come."

"I remember you, Rabbi" she said. "You haven't changed much."

"This is my wife, Rivkah. Rivie is a social worker here in the hospital. Would it be all right with you if she observed our meeting? She's learning some of the things I do, and this might be helpful to her."

Stacy shrugged her assent.

Moshe smiled. "You've changed a lot. I wish I could say I remember you, too, but to be honest, I wouldn't recognize you. You've grown up. You were *Parshat Yitro*. You read the Ten Commandments."

"Fifteen years ago." That made her twenty-eight years old, but she looked forty.

Moshe invited her to sit. He sat in front of her almost knee to knee. Rivkah removed herself to a corner. She had a vague notion she was being painted in.

"So, Stacy," Moshe began, "what can I do for you?".

"I don't know." She leaned back in her chair, pretending she was at ease, but her arms were folded across her chest.

"Your father asked that I come to see you. You didn't ask, did you?"

"No," she said, shaking. "It was his idea."

"They asked if you wanted to see a rabbi, and you said you didn't?"

"I didn't think a rabbi could help."

"If you had said yes, they would have called me. Did you know that?"

"No."

"If you had, would you have asked to see me?"

"I don't know. I don't think so. I haven't had anything to do with Judaism for a long time."

"Last time I saw you I think you were in the tenth grade. There was a kid I wanted you to tutor, but you didn't want to."

"Around then I didn't want to do anything."

"What happened?"

"I finished high school, somehow. Went to college. I'm a lawyer, did you know that?" Moshe did not know. "I've never worked at it. But I finished law school. Passed the bar. I went to Oregon and lived there for a while. What have you been doing?"

His eyebrows registered his surprise. Few addicts at her stage in recovery had the presence to ask him about himself. "I left the Temple a long time ago," he answered. "I've been working a little, here and there. You haven't married? Any relationships?"

"No marriage. One relationship. It's still on, more or less. Depending."

"Depending on what?"

"On what I do here."

"What can I do to help you with that?" There was no response. "Let me put it another way. Imagine for a moment I could work miracles. What could I do for you?" She didn't answer. "You don't believe in miracles?"

"No."

"But we're just imagining."

"I don't think imagining is going to help."

"Try anyway."

"You want me to imagine you can take away my addiction? You can't take it away."

"Not even if I were a miracle-working rabbi?"

"No."

"Why not."

"Because it's forever. This isn't the first time I've tried. I'm sorry. This wasn't my idea. I didn't ask to see you."

"So the addiction is forever. It's permanent. Nothing can get rid of it."

"Nothing." She was adamant. The strong denial allowed her to relax her body. She unfolded her arms and shifted her weight in the chair.

Moshe pointed to the bookcase. "Like that glass there. You see it? It has ripples." The glass was Moshe's contribution to the bookcase. Other chaplains had donated Bibles, prayer books, spiritual texts of various sorts. Moshe had contributed a rippled glass. He held the glass up to the light. "Ripples. You see them? They're on the inside of the glass." Stacy nodded. "If they were on the outside of the glass, perhaps I could polish them and get rid of them, but they're on the inside of the glass. It's hard to reach in there. So I guess they're permanent. Nothing can get rid of them. However, if I pour water into the rippled glass . . ." Moshe retrieved the paper cup from the windowsill and poured the water into the glass. "The ripples disappear." Indeed, the ripples disappeared. "A miracle, maybe?"

"What happened? Where did they go?" Stacy leaned forward to look more closely.

"They're still there. You just don't see them. What makes the ripples is that the glass is thick in some places, thin in others. Light passes through thick glass and thin glass differently, so you can see the ripples. But when I fill the glass with water, it's all the same thickness, and the ripples seem to disappear. It would work for scratches, too. If the inside of the glass were scratched, and I filled it with water, you wouldn't be able to see the scratch. It looks like a miracle."

Stacy examined the glass, still wondering where the ripples went.

re scratched, Stacy," Moshe said gently, pouring words through the
t of access. "Like the glass. It's just like you said. It's permanent. A
nent scratch, inside, where you can't polish it away. That scratch will al-
be there. If only somehow we could pour water in, it would fill in the
scratch, and even though the scratch was still there, you wouldn't be able to
see it. Or feel it. It would be like the scratch had disappeared.

"Now imagine if I had a cover over the rippled glass, and I tried to pour
water into it. It wouldn't work, because the cover would keep the water out.
The miracle you need is to have your cover removed, so the water can get in."

"What water?"

Moshe shrugged. "Okay, so it isn't water. It's healing. Imagine God is trying
to pour healing into you, and it can't get in because you have your cover on."

"What if I don't believe in God?"

"Then believe in healing. Here, look." Moshe pointed to a scab on the back
of his hand. "I cut myself a couple of days ago. It's healing. How does it know
to do that? The doctors don't do it. It seems to do it all by itself. If it had been
bad enough, I would have come here, and they would have stitched it up. That
doesn't heal it. It just helps the healing go faster. I could keep it from getting
healed, if I wanted. I could let it get dirty, infected. That would slow it down.
But all things being equal, the skin somehow knows what cells have to grow
where so that in a few days this scab will fall off, and I won't even know I was
ever cut. It's as if there was some law that says, 'Wherever there can be healing, there will be healing.' This healing works whether I believe in it or not. I
have very little to do with it. But the cut you have is on the inside. You can
keep the healing out all too easily. If you could learn how to take the cover off,
then the healing could find its way in and fill in all the scratches. As long as
that healing was inside you, you wouldn't be able to see or feel the scratches."

"How do I take the cover off?"

"That's what they teach here. The first step is to recognize that such healing is possible, that you can't do it yourself, that the cover is there, that you
want to take it off. I guess that's more than one step. But that's the hardest
part. After that, the rest will come pretty naturally."

"So all I have to do is take the cover off?"

"Well, no. Even for this glass, you see, water evaporates. So I'd have to
keep adding water, or the ripples would appear again. And for you, what happens is the cover keeps growing back. So you have to learn not only how to
take the cover off once, but how to keep it off. That's a lot to learn."

*Just leave yourself open to the light
of God — see if it heals*

236

"How do you know the healing is there?"

Moshe pointed to the scab on the back of his hand. "It's that obvious."

Need-to-Know

Sidney tapped the back of his own hand. "It was a tactical situation," he said. "That's the way Moshe spoke about it. Visiting someone at the Addiction Treatment Unit was like going to general quarters. There was a similar urgency. He had no more than half an hour to focus on the target and make an impact. He drew from all of his experience, more from his Navy training than from the seminary.

"Moshe claimed the Navy schools were the best he ever went to, better even than MIT. Not the Officer Candidate School, but the tactical schools—air control, intelligence, the advanced training he took in Georgia and California after he was commissioned.

"He learned the inner secrets of aircraft and submarines. Most everything he learned was classified. There was no homework, so late afternoons were spent not in study but at the pool, evenings at the officers' club. Alcohol was the food of choice. Mornings students and instructors arrived to class on time but bleary-eyed.

"The instructors had developed a motivation that proved invaluable. 'Some of what we teach is nice-to-know,' they said, 'some is need-to-know. If you do not know what is nice-to-know, you may not do well on the exams. If you do not know what is need-to-know, you are going to die.'

"That was excellent motivation.

"At the ATU, Moshe was the instructor. No nonsense. There wasn't time for it."

"This is need-to-know," Moshe said.

"But I don't believe in God," Stacy challenged.

"Your cuts heal anyway," Moshe responded.

"But I don't believe."

"You need to believe? You need to know how it works before you'll let it work?"

"Yes."

"Do you know how a car works? Do you know how a television works? Do you turn it on anyway?" No response.

"There is no God," Stacy challenged after a moment.

237

"Why not?" Again, no response. "There is no God," Moshe suggested, "because if there was a God, how could a God let Stacy suffer so much? How could a God let Stacy's parents break up right after her bat mitzvah? If there was a God, how could a God let this happen or that happen? Go ahead and fill in the blanks, Stacy. Whatever you like. Go ahead and put it in there. All of it boils down to, if there was a God, how could this happen to me? Or to us? Something like that.

"When you look at the world from the center out, when you put yourself at the center of the world, anything that makes you uncomfortable seems bad. You ask, how could this happen to me? But there's another way of seeing the world. Take yourself out of the center. See yourself from above, a Stacy moving around in the world with everything else moving around, too. Not at the center. At the center, everything moves around in relation to Stacy. But seen from above, you become just one person moving around with everyone and everything else. Stacy's life begins here"—Moshe indicated a point in the air—"and moves around and around, up and down, and eventually ends. And on the way it meets and collides and intersects and interacts with all these other points.

"Two ways of seeing things. Stacy at the center, and the world revolves around Stacy. Stacy in space, and Stacy is a moving part of the world.

"What I'm telling you now is need-to-know, Stacy. You have to learn this if you want to live. You have to learn how to view yourself and the world this other way. It's not a natural thing to do. It has to be learned. Your life depends on it."

"Need-to-know," Stephanie heard at the beginning of Sidney's story. That was all she heard of it. There was so much she needed to know. They wouldn't tell her. She knew Sidney's story, the stories about the Navy. Those were nice-to-know for her, not need-to-know.

She needed to know about her parents in Poland, and Al. Her mother had married the rich jeweler's son. He had a house, in a beautiful neighborhood. A maid, and Rosenthal china. He sold it all.

His brother Stephan also had Rosenthal china, and a house in a beautiful neighborhood. He didn't sell the china. He didn't sell the house.

What did Uncle Al do in Poland? All the conversations they had together in the shop, she must have learned something about Al in Poland. He wasn't a doctor, a lawyer, none of the professions. He wasn't a businessmen, a banker.

Uncle Al always had a position about everything, whatever was happening in the news, a news store, papers, and magazines. Uncle Al had a position.

He had a position, in the Jewish community. He was a councilman, a leader.

A leader who made the decision to remain in Poland. Al had a position, to stay in Poland and weather the storm. Her father didn't listen.

They were political enemies, her father and Al.

That was part of the story. Stephanie knew it, was certain of it. It was a lot of work, digging out a story. There was more, not very deep, but that was enough for the moment.

Dead Reckoning

Sidney said, "A story from the Navy is useful here."

Lieutenant Kayten had been an operations officer during his tour of duty in the Gulf of Tonkin. He supervised the enlisted men who maintained and manned the equipment in the Combat Information Center. In the CIC there were two displays, radar and the DRT, the Dead Reckoning Tracer. Eight hours a day, in two four-hour watches, Lieutenant Kayten sat at the radar console. The antenna turned on a mast above him. He was the center of the world. Aircraft appeared as electronic marks moving toward him, away from him, always in relation to him. Each electronic mark was labeled, known or unknown, friendly or bogey. The electronic marks inched across the radar screen. Each inch on the screen was twenty miles in the air. Closing speeds were in the neighborhood of a thousand miles per hour. With the touch of a button or a voice command he could dispatch a friendly aircraft outbound at the speed of sound to confront an inbound unknown aircraft and, if necessary, remove it from the sky before it could reach the center of the screen. All that mattered was that no hostile aircraft should reach the center of the screen, or even get within two inches!

A surface threat was treated differently.

Early one morning at 0200 hours, general quarters was sounded throughout the ship. The piercing sound of the boatswain's pipe awoke everyone. As if the shriek was not enough, urgent words followed: "General quarters! General quarters! This is not a drill! All hands man their battle stations! General quarters! General quarters! I repeat, this is not a drill!" and, again, the urgency of the boatswain's pipe.

An unknown surface target had been detected by radar, thirty miles away and closing. The image was plotted on the radar console, but also on the DRT. The Dead Reckoning Tracer was a light table. Tracing paper stretched across it. A dot of light projected from below up to the paper represented one's own ship. As the ship moved through the ocean, the dot of light moved across the paper. A technician marked the dot from time to time as it inched across the table. Everything else in the ocean, moving or unmoving, was also marked on the table. One line represented one's own ship. Another was the shore of Hainan Island to the east. Haiphong, on the coast of North Vietnam, was marked to the west. The unknown surface target was plotted northwest, moving erratically.

It was at the DRT that the situation was evaluated. Like gods, the officers stood above the world, watching the movement of all of the ships in the ocean. Here a ship might appear, and there, disappear, either out of range, or removed by missiles or gunfire. It was from the DRT that the decision was made to engage or not. Was the threat real? Lives depended on the evaluation.

On the DRT one's own ship was but another track along with all of the other tracks visible in the world.

On the radar console, one was at the center of the world, and everything else in the world moved in relation to that center.

The radar console presented a subjective view of the world; the DRT presented an objective view.

The officer who sat at the radar console became alarmed, and then more alarmed as the target closed. "In missile range!" he declared.

At the DRT the situation was less alarming. "Wait," Lieutenant Kayten suggested. "He's no threat yet."

"In gun range!" the radar officer shouted. "We can get him with our guns!" A message confirmed that fire control had acquired the target.

"Wait," Lieutenant Kayten suggested again from the DRT. "Still no threat."

"The captain needs a recommendation," the executive officer proclaimed. "I need a recommendation. Speak to me!"

"Shoot!" said the radar officer.

"Wait," said Lieutenant Kayten.

The executive officer looked over the shoulder of the radar officer, saw the target, and then turned to the DRT. Lieutenant Kayten traced for him the erratic path. "No threat yet," he repeated.

To the bridge the executive officer said, "Recommend guns locked on and tight." To Kayten, he said, "You had better be right."

Four hours they watched the track of the unknown surface target. Was it a torpedo boat? A fishing boat? It hovered at extreme torpedo range. To be sure, they might take it under fire. Three hundred lives were at stake aboard the Navy

240

frigate. Maybe four lives aboard a fishing boat, if that's what it was. Four Vietnamese or Chinese lives on a fishing boat that had wandered too far from port.

"Or nothing at all," Lieutenant Kayten ventured. "It doesn't move like a boat. It might be some garbage floating in the water." '

The ship remained at general quarters, all battle stations manned, until daylight. Radar traced the target, fire control locked on. At daylight the target vanished from the screens. There was nothing there, no torpedo boat, no fishing boat, no garbage. Nothing. They had been tracking an electronic anomaly all night. There was no threat, nothing to be destroyed, other than the night's sleep. The crew not on watch returned to bed for an hour or two.

"You were so certain," the executive officer said to Lieutenant Kayten. "What would you have said if you were at the radar console?"

Lieutenant Kayten shrugged. "Shoot," he admitted. "It's all a matter of point of view. From the inside looking out, it was a threat. But from here looking down, nothing."

"It's all a matter of point of view," Sidney repeated. "We all have the radar. We walk around at the center of our universe and see everything in relationship to ourselves. But not all of us have a DRT, the ability to see ourselves objectively, from above."

Moshe continued his session with Stacy.

"There is a skill to learn," he told her. "How to get above yourself and look down. What will you see? You'll see a Stacy down there, who was emotionally damaged through no fault of her own, who has a disability, an addiction. She gets pushed around in the world, banging into people here and there. Over here is where Stacy is born. Here's where she had her bat mitzvah. Here's where she got hurt, and here and here. Here she is now. And she has a long way to go, hopefully, before the track ends.

"When you stay up above and look down, you see how awesome things can be. You can look down at Stacy. Take a look at her body. See the thousands and thousands of things that have to work together in that body so it can live and breathe and move about. How does a body like that come to be? Is it just chance? What's the purpose of it all? Is this lifetime we trace in the air just a random walk? Or is it going someplace? When you're up here looking down, you begin to ask questions like that. What is this? What is it for? Where did it come from? Where is it going?

"You used to ask questions like that. Back when you were a kid. Kids ask.

"I have this theory, Stacy. Kids are really concerned with God. They ask all sorts of smart questions. But when they come out of sexual latency, they go into theological latency. Sex becomes important, and God doesn't. People as a rule don't become interested in God again until their parents become ill and begin to die. Then they begin to wonder what it's all about. That doesn't happen until you get to be forty or fifty nowadays. But sometimes something happens to shake up a person, and you begin to start thinking about these things early. Maybe there's a death or a trauma or something. In my case Vietnam had something to do with it. In your case it's an addiction. They're both life-threatening.

"It's time to come out of theological latency, Stacy. Your life depends on it."

Stacy was still for a while. "They talk a lot here about a Higher Power. I don't know what that means. I'm jealous of the Christians. They seem to know what it means. I don't."

"But you want to?"

"I'd like to."

"That's a first step. It's time for me to go. Should I come back?"

She nodded. "Please."

Moshe stood to leave. "Oh, your father asked me to tell you something. He asked me to tell you he loves you and he's afraid for you." Moshe was not surprised when Stacy began to cry. "I'll be back next week, Stacy. There's a lot of work to do. I know it's hard. I wish you well."

"Once Moshe took me for a ride in his Porsche," Sidney said, "into the mountains. He said that driving the Porsche was like being at the radar console, not at the DRT. When he was at the wheel of the Porsche, driving fast, he was at the center of the world. Everything moved around him. That was a tactical situation, not strategic. Decisions had to be made at every instant, life-or-death decisions. To turn, to brake, to accelerate. To pass or not to pass. He loved it, to be released from the Dead Reckoning Tracer and to live for a while in the immediate world.

"When one is suddenly in extremis, right at the edge of a life-and-death situation, one doesn't think about death. Only life. There isn't time to consider what will happen at the end of the road, only the road itself. But when one has the time, when one takes the time to look down from above and see oneself on the road, then one sees the beginning of the road, and oneself moving along it, and the end of the road as well. When one takes the time, the end of the road becomes a certainty.

"Maybe that's why," Sidney suggested, "they call it the Dead Reckoning Tracer."

242

CHAPTER 8

Seeing and Not Seeing

 Back in the living room Stephanie introduced the last lesson of the morning. "Rivkah had done some homework," she said. "She had taken careful notes of the first Institute lesson and had made an outline which she had reproduced for the students. She thought Moshe would be pleased with it. He said he was pleased, but Rivie perceived some agitation.

"'The outline is okay?' she asked Moshe.

"'Yes, yes, it's fine,' he responded.

"Rivie didn't know what to make of that. Tradition teaches there are no wasted words. One 'yes' would have been enough. 'Yes, yes' meant something else entirely."

Moshe and Rivkah arrived early at the Institute and found the room set up wrong. Moshe grunted his displeasure and turned from the room in search of help.

The bookstore was still open. "Can you assist us?" he addressed the woman behind the counter. "I need a chalkboard and a table. We have to set up the big room differently."

"I'm the only one here," she responded. "I can't leave."

"Well, where might they be? I'll go get them."

"All the rooms are open. Feel free to look around and take what you need."

They found a room intended for movement, a rail running the length of a mirrored wall. "I like this," Rivkah said. She leaned forward and attempted to raise her leg above the bar. "I used to be able to do that," she said.

The next room had a massage table. "Come on, Moshe, we have a few minutes. Right here." She indicated an area behind her neck. When he did not turn to her, she said, "I guess I'll have to come back tomorrow and get a real massage. Have you ever been here during the day?"

He was in no mood to respond.

"Here," Rivkah said as she entered a small seminar room. "The chalkboard." Together they rolled it into the corridor. They assigned two arriving students to push and drag the board to the big room.

"Where could the table be?" Moshe asked the doors before him. One led to an office. Another, in spite of what the woman at the counter had said, was locked. He rattled the door. "No table. No time. Let's go. I want to get started."

They returned to the big room. The students had pushed chairs aside to make space for the chalkboard. Behind the chalkboard was the table. "Where did you find that?" he asked the students.

"It was there," one said. "Is it okay? Do you want us to put it somewhere?"

Moshe had them move the table and the chalkboard to his liking. "Was it really there?" he asked Rivkah.

"I don't know. I wasn't looking for it."

"Is it possible I came into the room and didn't see it? It was there all the time?" He shrugged. "Let's begin."

The room was three-quarters full. "You lost some students since last week," Rivkah advised him.

"That's okay."

"You keep up like this, you won't have any left by week four."

"There are too many anyway."

She stepped back from him. "Moshe, why are you so uptight? Are you still thinking about what happened at Princeton?"

"Maybe." But he wasn't thinking about Princeton. He was thinking about Rivkah, that she couldn't get her leg up over the bar in the mirrored exercise room. Rivie thought it nothing more than a lack of exercise. Moshe saw in it something else.

Stephanie had set the stage for Sidney, a new setting. The students understood Moshe to be distracted, anxious. That was adequate, all they needed to know. The stories could go uphill from there.

Sidney had an opportunity to redeem his opening for the second lesson. Moshe's teaching that night at the Institute had been dry, dull. Sidney, so faithful, so pedantic, had followed his teacher's example. In previous tellings he had been even more dry, more dull.

Learning from a teacher what not to do was surely as valuable as learning what to do. Sidney had shown some originality in the first lesson, albeit misplaced according to Stephanie's opinion, changing the order of the *Mishnah* texts. Stephanie prayed Sidney had a new beginning for the second lesson.

No such luck.

Sidney said, "Moshe was so immersed in the World of Formation, he had been blinded in the World of Action. His concern for Rivkah was so overwhelming, it had obscured something as massive as a table. It was with some confusion he began his teaching."

"We begin with this room," Moshe said. "Take a look around. What do you see? Walls, paintings, windows, floor, carpet, chairs, podium, a ceiling, lights, curtains, doors, electrical sockets, a phone plug. This table.

"Imagine that this room is the entire world. It's the whole universe. That's all there is. Let's consider how this room came into being.

"First there was something or someone outside of this room who wanted a room. Someone decided that there was a need for a room like this and said something like, 'Let there be a room.' That very first thought contained this entire room—the room and everything in it. But you couldn't see everything in that expression. It was all mixed together.

"So what happens next? Next, the one who says, 'Let there be a room,' goes out and hires an architect and an engineering firm to come up with some plans. There has to be a blueprint. Now the blueprint of the room isn't the room, but all the room is going to be is in the blueprint. The blueprint is a better-articulated expression of the room than the original concept was. We've gone from an expression to an articulation. We've drawn something out of that original expression. We can see it more clearly."

Moshe sensed something was missing in his teaching. The ideas were there, but they were not expressed in such a way we could readily grasp them. They were presented without feeling, without energy. It was as if he were talking about inventory on a shelf, without taking it down to show to us. He sensed that and tried to recover. "Have you ever walked into a house under construction and tried to guess what's going to be where? You can make some educated guesses, but it's hard to be certain.

"Now if it's your house, the time has come for you to meet with the interior designer. You need to sit down and explain to him or to her what it is you want your house to feel like."

That did not work for him either. He returned to his original analogy.

"For our room, for this room, we're saying things like, 'I want it to be inviting and warm, but it has to be open and flexible. I want the lighting to be bright, but sometimes I might want to tone it down a bit and change the mood. We need chairs, but I want them to be interesting, not just utilitarian.' So by the time the structure of the room is finished, we have decided on what we need to establish just the right feeling. What colors the wall will be. The texture of the ceiling panels. The curtains. The lighting.

"And then, we go buy the furniture and have it delivered. We arrange the chairs, install the lights, hang the paintings, and wheel in the chalkboard and this table. And we have our room."

"And then we go buy the furniture . . ." Stephanie mimicked internally. Just because Moshe had been teaching poorly was no excuse for Sidney to do so. Sidney was capable of repeating any of the lessons word for word. That didn't mean he had to. He had already taken some liberties with the order of texts. Why not here also?

"Because that's the way Moshe did it," he would respond.

And that's why I'm leaving you, she thought. Moshe's not even around, and you're still letting him do your thinking for you.

For years Sidney had been sitting with one teacher, then the next, every course, new age, old age, any age. He prepared for courses the way he used to prepare for an acquisition, a merger, a contract. It was all he had to do with his time. He was becoming a professional nudge. He was a nuisance in each venue, didn't experience any growth, bar this last experience, and maybe that only because Moshe had become as desperate as he was.

God, Sidney! she wanted to scream. What has happened to you? You used to be so sharp!

Outside he appeared the same. Inside he was decaying.

What We Know of the Builder

Stephanie attempted some *tikkun,* some repair, to recapture the interest of the students. She said, "The Sunday before the second session Rivkah and Moshe had walked in their neighborhood. They had ventured into a house under construction to sit among the struts and beams, making guesses. Where was the kitchen going to be? The bathrooms? The bedrooms?

"As they sat in the skeleton of the house, the owner arrived. Moshe and Rivkah introduced themselves and did their best to explain what they were doing in his embryonic home. Was it really trespassing in a house that was only half-built? 'We were just making guesses,' they told the new owner. He had been kind enough to show them around, but not happy about it.

"They were quiet together as they walked back to their own home until both began to speak with the same thought. They would welcome their new neighbor with hallah or a cake and try to start the relationship over again. They were embarrassed, to be discovered like that in the bare bones of a half-built house. It was like walking in on someone dressing."

Sidney said, "Moshe told me he had intended to make their own home, not the classroom, the model for creation. He thought if he made the analogy personal, he might involve Rivkah more. The episode with the table had distracted him."

Stephanie was quick to add, "I think there was a lot more distracting him than the table, and it wasn't just his concern for Rivkah. I think he was having doubts about the whole manipulative process. It's one thing to formulate such rational plans, but when you put them into action, the emotional results aren't always what you expect, either on the subject or on yourself.

"Do you think it would really have made much difference if he had used their home instead of the classroom?" she asked, more of Sidney than the students. "Rivkah didn't care much for any of these models. She knew well enough what a room was. She knew what a house was. She knew how to build one. She didn't have any need to break the building of a house down into its basic components. That was Moshe's thing. If Moshe thought that by using a house analogy he might involve Rivkah more in his teaching of the Four Worlds, he was wrong."

Sidney continued with the teaching as it was given. He distributed a text introducing the vocabulary of the Four Worlds.

The Four Worlds

Emanation	*Atzilut*
Creation	*Bri-ah*
Formation	*Yetzirah*
Action	*Asi-ah*

Moshe asked, "Why did the creator of this room create it?"
As answers were volunteered, he wrote them on the board.
"To make a profit."
"To have a place to teach."

247

"To satisfy his ego."

"To fulfill his destiny."

"Out of some anal-retentive desire."

The answers were as varied as the students.

Moshe added his own. "Because he had a need to do so. There is no creation without a need on the part of the creator." He paused, wondering if any of us would make the logical leap, and seemed not to be surprised when I raised my hand.

"Excuse me, rabbi," I interrupted. "If you are saying the beginner of our room had a need for a room, that means the beginner of the room lacked something." Moshe nodded. "So if the beginner of the room lacks something, that means he isn't complete, he isn't perfect." Moshe sat still. His feet stopped swinging. I continued, "Now that may be appropriate for a man who is building a room, but if you are making an analogy to a god creating a universe, are you telling us this god isn't complete, he isn't perfect?"

"Would that bother you, Mr. Lee," Moshe responded, "to think of this god as less than perfect?"

"I've always been taught God was perfect."

"Could you entertain for a moment the idea of an imperfect god?" he challenged me. "How would that make you feel? Would it bother you?"

"You're asking me how I feel? I don't feel about God. I think about God."

"And you think that God is perfect?"

"That's what I've been taught."

Moshe paused for a long time, as if not certain which train of thought to follow. He looked toward Rivkah, back to me. "We'll return to this," he said. "First we need to learn some vocabulary."

"There are four stages in the creation of our room. First we have the desire, the will, the urge, which results in the concept, the original expression of 'Let there be a room.' The room emanates out of the will of the creator of our room. This stage in the process of creation is called the World of Emanation. The Hebrew word for the World of Emanation is *atzilut*.

"The room is then defined by certain principles. The principles must exist, and they must be constant; otherwise, the room cannot exist. This is where we consult the architects and engineers. This is called the World of Creation. In Hebrew, *bri-ah*. It's a world of constant principles.

"The next stage is to establish the feeling of the room. Here's where we call in the interior designer, and we talk about feelings. It's very hard to pin feelings down. We talk with our hands a lot. We want the room to feel like this, or like that. In the World of Creation, we can nail things down in blueprints. But in the World of Formation, that's what this stage is called—the World of Formation, *yetzirah* in Hebrew—everything is in flux.

"When we get down to the World of Action, things become real again." Moshe banged on the table. "This is the World of Action, the fourth stage of creation. In Hebrew, *asi-ah*. The World of Action is the empirical world. The world of things. It's the table and the chairs. Physical things. But none of these things would have come into being without having been projected through the other three worlds. Each of them has its origin first in the will of its creator, then in the World of Emanation, the World of Creation, the World of Formation, and only then in the World of Action.

"Learn the vocabulary," Moshe advised his students. He used the break to sit with his wife. He was off-balance. He needed to hold her hand.

The Curse of Blessings

"That was when Moshe began to take Sidney seriously, the exchange about the perfection of God," Stephanie said, then paused. "Or it's when Sidney was seriously beginning to get under Moshe's skin.

"While the students were learning, Moshe wanted to know more about Sidney. Rivkah told him he was somebody important at Freeman March, on the hospital board of trustees. That's all she knew. They might have met Sidney once, at a party in the Plotkins' home when Norman had been chief of staff of the hospital."

Moshe did not remember the Plotkins, let alone Sidney.

"'He asks tough questions,' Moshe told her.

"'He's the only one who's asking,' Rivkah responded, 'and he has to interrupt to do so. You're not leaving any space for questions. "Learn the vocabulary!"' she mimicked. 'You are so intimidating, Moshe! What's going on?'

"He knew he had to change the flow of his teaching. He wasn't concerned with losing students. He was concerned with losing Rivkah. He needed direction, so he closed his eyes, breathed through the four letters of the Divine Name, and surrendered for the minute or two he had remaining in the break. When he returned to the surface, he knew the beginning of the story. He didn't know all of it, but as he told it, the rest of it streamed through him and out to the class.

"The story worked. It drew Rivkah back.

249

"And me, too," Stephanie added, another afterthought intended for Sidney. "It's his stories that kept me engaged, not his teaching. I put up with his pontificating in the World of Creation only because I knew that his stories would follow. Why couldn't he simply teach the stories?"

"It was his work in the World of Creation that generated the stories," Sidney answered. "Without the work, no stories."

"Whatever," Stephanie said, unconvinced. "This is the story."

There was an officer of the law, a recent graduate, proud as you can imagine, in his uniform of blue with brass buttons and gold epaulets. He wore a hat with a plume and a sword with a gold-and-ivory handle. He was as pompous as could be. He was arrogant and bold and callous. Every letter of the alphabet served only to demonstrate his authority and exalt his being.

One day he was walking his beat and heard a commotion in an alley. He ventured into the darkness, and there in the distance saw a man in rags. "Come forward," he commanded. "Come forward now!" But the man in rags did not come forward. "I am an officer of the law, and I command you, come forward!"

The man in rags did not move. He shifted his weight from one foot to the other and spoke, "I don't know what I'm going to do with you."

"Do with me?" the officer of the law mocked. "Do with me? You don't do with me! I do with you! I am an officer of the law, and I command you to come forward."

"Now I know what to do with you," the man in rags said, and as he spoke, he drew his sword. "Now I know what to do." Without further word he moved to attack.

The officer of the law drew his own sword in defense. "Stop that!" he ordered. "Put your sword down right now!" But the man in rags did not stop. The officer of the law had to parry thrusts left and right. "Stop!" he said again, but to no avail. The officer of the law was forced to retreat.

When it seemed the man in rags would prevail, he lowered his guard, and what the officer of the law had intended as a parry became a thrust. His sword ran through the man in rags. "I didn't mean that," the officer of the law said. "I didn't mean to hurt you. Why didn't you stop when I ordered you to? Why did you attack me?"

The man in rags waved the words away. "I am leaving you," he said, "and as I do, I put upon you the Curse of Blessings."

"What do you mean?" asked the officer of the law, now quite confused.

"The Curse of Blessings. Every day you must say a new blessing, one you have never said before. On the day you do not say a new blessing, on that day you will die."

The man in rags closed his eyes. The officer of the law looked about for help. There was none to be found. When he turned back, the man in rags had disappeared. He was gone.

"It was a dream," the officer of the law thought. "Only a dream. I imagined it."

The time was late in the afternoon. The sun was setting. As much as the officer of the law tried to ignore his experience, he could not. The Jewish day ends with the sunset. The officer of the law felt his body growing cold and knew from the chill that his life was leaving him. In a panic, he uttered these words of blessing. "You are blessed, Lord our God, ruler of the universe, who has created such a beautiful sunset." At once warmth and life flowed back into him. He realized, with both shock and relief, the curse had been for real.

The next morning he did not delay. He woke with words of blessing. "You are blessed that You allowed me to wake up this morning." His life felt secure the entire day. The next morning he blessed his ability to rise from his bed, the following day that he could tie his shoes.

Day after day he found abilities he could bless. That he could go to the bathroom, that he had teeth to brush, that each finger of his hands still worked, that he had toes on his feet and hair on his head. He blessed his clothes, every garment. He blessed his house, the roof and floor, his furniture, every table and chair.

At last he ran out of things to bless, so he began to bless relationships. He blessed his family and friends, fellow workers and those who worked for him. He blessed the mailman and the clerks. He was surprised to find they appreciated the blessings. His words had power. They drew family and friends closer to him. Word went out that the officer of the law was a source of blessing.

Years passed, decades. The officer of the law had to go farther afield to find new sources of blessing. He blessed city councils and university buildings, scientists and their discoveries. As he traveled through the world he became in awe of its balance and beauty and blessed that. The more he learned, the more he had to bless. His life was long, and he had the opportunity to learn in every field.

He passed the age of one hundred. Most of his friends were long gone. His time was relegated to searching for the purpose in his life and the one source from which all blessing flows. He had long since realized he was not the source but only the conduit, even that realization welcomed with a blessing that sustained him for yet another day.

As he approached the age of 120, he considered that his life was long enough. Even Moses had not lived longer. On his birthday he made a conscious decision to utter no new blessing and allow his life to come to an end. Still he could recite old blessings, and throughout the day he reviewed them, all the blessings for his body and his possessions, for his relationships that spread throughout the world, for the awesome beauty and balance of creation, and for the deep resonance, the pulse of purpose that pervaded his very being. But no new blessing passed his lips.

As the sun was setting, a chill progressed inward from his extremities. He did not resist it. In the twilight a figure appeared, the man in rags. "You!" the officer of the law exclaimed. "I have thought about you every day for a hundred years! I never meant to harm you. Please, forgive me."

"You don't understand," said the man in rags. "You don't know who I am, do you? I am the angel who was sent a hundred years ago to harvest your soul, but when I looked at you, so pompous and proud, there was nothing there to harvest. An empty uniform was all I saw. So I put upon you the Curse of Blessings, and now look what you've become!"

The officer of the law grasped in an instant all that had happened and why. Overwhelmed, he said, "You are blessed, my God, ruler of the universe, that You have kept me alive and sustained me so I could attain this moment."

"Now look what you've done!" the man in rags said in frustration. "A new blessing!"

Life flowed back into the officer of the law, and he and the man in rags looked to each other, neither of them knowing quite what to do.

"Moshe had no ending for his story," Stephanie said. "The story had come through him only that far. It was enough, though. It encompassed all Four Worlds. Take a moment, pair off, retell the story, see how much you can find in it."

The students paired off. Stephanie fell back into her own story, as much as she had discovered of it.

Al had a position opposed to her father's. Her father advocated leaving Poland. They ridiculed him and his fears. He was preaching the flood to the generation of Noah, and nobody listened. They ridiculed him.

He sold his house for such a low price, and the Rosenthal china, piece by piece. No, as a set. Her mother saw it leave as a set, in boxes.

He sold all the clothes they couldn't take with them.

The jewelry he would have kept. The diamonds. But when they arrived in New York, they had nothing, and in Miami, even less.

What happened to the diamonds?

Al encouraged her mother to stay behind, not to leave. When her father learned of it, he ordered his wife to have nothing more to do with him. Not a word. He ordered her.

That's the way things were done, then.

The story was difficult. She didn't like it. Why hadn't her father thrown away the letters? If he had thrown away the letters, she wouldn't have to be troubled with such stories.

The Four-Letter Name of God

Sidney continued the lesson.

"Four Worlds," Moshe said and waited until the noise in the room dissolved into quiet.

"There are four letters in the name of God. It looks like this." He wrote the name of God vertically on the chalkboard, the *YOD* on top, the *HEY,* the *VAV,* and another *HEY* at the bottom.

י

ה

ו

ה

"When I write it vertically like this, you see it looks like the stick figure of a person. Can you see that?" Instead of pointing to the chalkboard, he turned to face the class and modeled the name of God. "See my legs and pelvis. They're in the shape of a *HEY.*" He straightened his back. "And my spine, it's in the shape of a *VAV*. And my arms and shoulders, an upper *HEY*. And there"—he rolled his eyes upward—"just above my head, the dot of the *YOD*.

"If you think of the name of God like this, you can see how we might be made in the image of God. A simple meditation you can do at home is to look at yourself in the mirror and imagine the name of God written there. You can see the image of God inscribed in yourself. When you move your arms and legs, you see the letters of the God name moving.

"You can try it right now, if you like. Stand up and face your study partner." We pushed our chairs back and stood. "Now look at your study partner and see in him or in her the letters of the Divine Name. Move your arms and legs just a little. Imagine the letters of the Divine Name shifting, as if they were being moved by a gentle wind."

For a few moments we swayed, like a kelp forest in Pacific waters. Moshe compared the experience to a scuba dive off the coast of San Diego. Anchored in the ground, the bodies of divine letters extended and reached for the light above.

"The bottom *HEY* corresponds to the World of Action," he said. "It is anchored in the ground. It is an active letter. It moves around in the world. The *VAV* that ascends up your spine conveys feelings. It is a passive letter. It corresponds to the World of Formation. The upper *HEY,* your arms and shoulders, is used for creating. It corresponds to the World of Creation. It, too, is an active letter. And the *YOD* just above your head, the World of Emanation. That's where the creativity emanates from. You might say that the *YOD* and the *VAV* are the brain and the cord, the central nervous system, that convey the creative impulses to the arms and shoulders, and the fulfillment of creativity to the legs and the hips."

We swayed gently, feeling the presence of God course through our bodies, tracing the letters of the Divine Name again and again.

This was good for Stephanie. She joined with the students, losing herself in the letters. There was no hurry, she thought, no urgency. She needn't be so agitated. She traced the letters, breathed through them, hoping that Sidney was doing the same and taking his time. Too soon his voice intruded.

"We did not have this luxury in the classroom," he said, "to become lost in the letters even for a short time. In such a large group there must always be one person out of synch with the experience." Stephanie considered Sidney the person out of synch at that moment. Better to be quiet and let her and the others lose themselves in the letters. But no, he had a responsibility to return to his schedule, his order of the day, his agenda. "It was a woman with a most grating voice," he continued, "who brought us out of a meditative state."

"Is the *YOD* the same thing as the third eye?" the woman asked, snapping the reverie. Like a whip, the longer the reverie, the sharper the snap.

It took Moshe some time to respond. He did so with equanimity, no rancor in his voice. "I don't know. I'm not certain what the third eye is."

"The third eye . . ." she attempted to explain, but Moshe stilled her explanation with a raised finger.

"A moment," he said. "Just a moment. The only thing I know is a little bit about the Kabbalah. I really don't know much about any other spiritual tradition. I don't know if the *YOD* in the World of Emanation parallels the third eye or not. You will have to make that determination yourself. I'm sorry."

Moshe waited for his apology to be absorbed.

"What I can do, if you are willing, is to teach you a simple breathing meditation on the letters of God's name and the Four Worlds." She was willing. All of us were willing.

Breathing

Sidney turned to his wife, an apparent apology, seeming to understand he had intruded into her meditation. He had closed his story with an opening for her. Stephanie accepted it. She remained seated and addressed the students. "I once spent a week in Massachusetts learning something of Buddhist meditation. I did little more than breathe, following the path of my breath around my lips and nose. Moshe taught me the *YOD HEY VAV HEY* breathing in a few minutes. That few minutes seemed to contain the substance of the entire week I did with the Buddhists, if substance is the right word. On the other hand, perhaps the technique would have made no impression on me if I had not had the benefit of the Buddhist training."

"Sit down please and find a comfortable position. Don't cross your legs or your arms. You can do this with your eyes open, if you like, but most people prefer to close their eyes."

Moshe surveyed the room. Only Sidney had his eyes open.

"There are four parts to the breathing cycle," Moshe continued. "You bring the breath in, you hold it, you let the breath out, and then there is a moment without breath before the next one comes in. When you bring a breath in, you might imagine that it comes down to the lower *HEY,* around the hips and all the way to the toes. When you hold the breath, you might imagine it ascending up the *VAV,* rising up the spine. When you exhale, it is as if the breath were rising around your shoulders and coming down your arms and out from your fingertips. When there is no breath within you, you might focus on the *YOD,* a point just above your head.

"Breathe in slowly. Imagine the breath descending. It might help to know the words for breath and soul come from the same root in Hebrew. The breath descends to the lower *HEY.* Hold your breath. The breath ascends through the *VAV.* Exhale. It's as if the breath rises around the shoulders and comes out the fingertips. *YOD.* No breath in you. And breathe in again . . .

"Three or four breaths. That's all you really need. This can be a meditation in itself, or preparation for something deeper. You breathe in all the way to your toes. The toes relax. The legs relax. You feel the breath rising. Exhale through your fingertips. Concentrate on a point just above your head."

A Tepee

When the students on the deck had finished with their breathing exercises, Stephanie said, "When I asked Moshe if there was any connection between the *YOD HEY VAV HEY* breathing and the Buddhist tradition, all I got was a shrug. It wasn't that Moshe didn't know about Buddhist meditation. He was conversant with most spiritual disciplines, old and new. Most of what he had learned, he had learned from Reb Hayim himself. But Moshe said there wasn't much to be gained from comparing one spiritual discipline to another. Both suffered as a result. It was better to teach from the strength of each without reducing one to accommodate another.

"But I heard Reb Hayim compare disciplines. He told this story of a conference of spiritual leaders he had attended in Denver.

"Those willing to risk the journey and the sharing came from distant places and different traditions to sit and learn. One morning Reb Hayim ascended to the roof for his morning prayers. With the mountains outside, why should he be confined to his room? So he climbed the stairs to the roof, wrapped himself in his huge striped wool *tallis,* strapped the leather *tefillin* to his arm and head, and declared the glory of God from the mountains. At the completion of his prayers, he observed a Native American in traditional garb finishing his prayers on a colorful blanket. As Reb Hayim wound the black-leather straps of his *tefillin* tightly about the cowhide boxes, the Native American gathered feather and bone and rawhide. Not a word was passed, but a conversation had taken place."

"That's not where the tepee comes from," Sidney continued. "Moshe did not like it when we called his diagram of the worlds a tepee, but a tepee is what it looked like."

He drew on the legal pad what did indeed resemble a tepee. "This," he said, "is Moshe's representation of the worlds."

Moshe explained, "You might think of the top part of the triangle as the World of Emanation. The point is the very origin of the concept of the room. It was a singular expression of a need.

"As soon as it was expressed, it began to dissipate. As it descended into the World of Creation, it began to collect into different categories. Structural engineering. Lighting. Financing. All necessary to the room.

"Down a little lower, in the World of Formation, you have color and texture, the feeling tone of the room.

"At the base, in the World of Action, you find things, things you can touch. Chairs you can sit on.

"A question. Where would the loss be greatest if this process stopped somewhere along the way?"

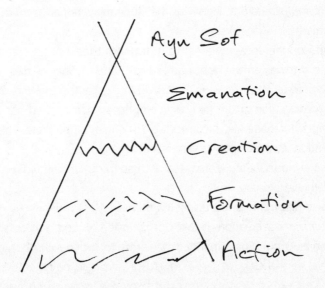

"At the bottom. In the World of Action." That was the consensus answer.

"Right," Moshe agreed. "Here in the World of Action.

He pointed to the top of the triangle, the World of Emanation. "If the room is stopped here, all that has happened is that the beginner of the room changed his or her mind. Big deal.

"Now if you don't change your mind, if you go out and hire an architect, all you've lost is the fee for the architect. Each stage of the process of creation calls for greater and greater expenditure of energy and resources until you finally get this room in all of its physicality. The World of Action is where the action is. You might argue it's the most important of the worlds. It's where things happen."

Moshe lifted himself back to the table, swung his legs, perused the room. "Are there questions? Before we go on, we need to have a working notion of these Four Worlds, how one flows from the other.

"The World of Action is doing. Formation is feeling. Creation is knowing. Emanation is being.

"Let's take a moment. Ask each other questions. Be sure this is set. And then we'll go on."

The legal pad with the tepee had made it around the circle to Stephanie's hands where it rested as Sidney uttered his discourse. No, Moshe's discourse. There was nothing original to Sidney's Kabbalah. She had seen the diagram of the tepee any number of times, but had never before truly considered it.

"It's wrong," she said to Sidney as the students were paired off in study.

"Why wrong?" Sidney asked.

"There's an inherent wrongness to it. It doesn't feel right." That wasn't an answer, but she was on the right path. "Here! Look!" She pointed to the two sides of the tepee. "Up above is God. Within the tent is creation. But there's nothing on either side of the tent, only emptiness, neither God nor creation."

The emptiness made her uncomfortable. It could not be there. This explanation of creation was wrong in its very essence.

"It's only a model," Sidney said, "something to put down on paper, a way of explaining the vocabulary."

Stephanie heard his words, dismissed them.

"No, if there is a creation, it takes place inside of God, not outside. Imagine an infinite God." She expanded her arms to include all of space. "Now imagine within this God a desire to create, a single point of purpose. No sooner does it exist as a single point, it explodes, expands outward in every direction, and becomes space and time, infused with purpose. Then you have God on the outside, the creativity and purpose of God on the inside, and no emptiness."

They were both quiet for a while. The buzz of the students continued around them.

"Where did you learn that?" Sidney asked.

"I don't know. It was just there. This is wrong." She waved the legal pad.

"It's something to consider, but I don't know how I would draw it on paper."

Stephanie was suddenly angry. "Everything doesn't have to be reduced to paper! Don't you see this solves your problem about the imperfection of God? Were you serious when you challenged Moshe about that, or was it just to hear yourself speaking?"

Sidney appeared more confused than defensive. "How does it solve the problem?"

"It's like this," Stephanie said, a teacher explaining to a slow student. "Outside of the expanding creation you have a God that is beyond space and time. Within the creation you have us, you and me. If creation exists, then God is imperfect. Creation is still meeting God's needs, and anything that has needs lacks something, and anything that lacks something isn't perfect."

"That's my point," Sidney said.

"But consider God from beyond the creation, a God that is beyond space and time. From His perspective, the world came into existence, existed, and went out of existence in the blink of an eye. Time doesn't pertain there. God has already been perfected by His creation. It's only because we're inside of creation that we can consider God imperfect.

"You see it? God is perfect and imperfect at the same time."

"I have to think about this," Sidney said.

"Good," Stephanie added.

She was angry with herself. She had referred to God in the masculine: *His* point of view, *His* creation. She thought she had dismissed a masculine notion of God long before, but when she got close, there He was again.

The Vocabulary of Soul

Sidney distributed the text. He said, "You are fortunate to have these. This is what Moshe wrote on the board for the students to discuss. His handwriting was not the best."

Emanation	*Atzilut*	Yod	*Being*	Hayah
Creation	*Bri-ah*	Hey	Knowing	*Neshamah*
Formation	*Yetzirah*	Vav	Feeling	*Ruach*
Action	*Asi-ah*	Hey	Doing	*Nefesh*

"Do you know how many words the Eskimos have for snow?" Moshe asked to bring the class back to order. "You learn a lot about the experience of a people from its language. I heard once the Eskimos have something like twenty different words for snow. In the Hebrew of the Kabbalah, you will find five different words for soul. Four of them I've written here on the board. *Nefesh* is soul in the World of Action. It's the motivating soul of the animal in us. *Ruach* is the soul of feeling in the World of Formation. *Ruach* means wind or spirit. *Neshamah* is the soul in the World of Creation. Intellect, if you like. And the spiritual soul, the very essence of being, is the *Hayah,* the *being* part of the human being.

"These are not separate one from the other. There is only one soul that comes from the Creator, but there is a different name for it in each of the worlds. The point above the *Hayah* where the soul is united with the infinite is called the *Yehidah,* the *singularity,* or the *union* with the transcendent."

"Who's on the other side of that singularity," I interrupted.

Moshe paused for but a moment and responded, "*Who's* on first," quoting from the classic Abbot and Costello routine. "*What's* on second. Later, Mr. Lee. We'll explore the other side later."

"I was being mischievous," Sidney confessed. "I knew he had some special agenda. I knew he would not brook any divergence from it, but I couldn't resist. My statement was a statement, not a question: 'Who was on the other side of that singularity.' It was a reference to the *Zohar*. Most anyone else would have asked, 'What is on the other side?' When I said who, Moshe was caught for a moment. Either he had to explain the text from the *Zohar,* which he didn't want to do, or he had to ignore me. So he quoted from Abbot and Costello and set the matter aside for the moment.

"Moshe had mentioned a story from the *Zohar* in the first lesson. During the week I found an edition in English. I had surely not become learned in the *Zohar*. I had barely finished the prologue. Still I knew enough to confuse him, and

I must admit I enjoyed it, playing the Asian gentleman who knew not only the Hebrew alphabet but also something of an arcane Jewish mystical text.

"The *Zohar* was written in code. It hid its secrets behind coded images. It played tricks with words. Its commentary to the question, 'Who created these?' referring to the wonders of creation was, "Yes, that's correct. *Who* created *these*." The word *who* became a reference to God. The Hebrew letters for *these* and *who* combine to form an anagram of one of the Hebrew words for God.

"This was not the deepest secret of the *Zohar*, but it was deep enough to let Moshe know the game was on. By quoting Abbot and Costello, he at once acknowledged it and put the matter aside so as not to be distracted from his purpose."

Purpose

"Four levels of soul, corresponding to the Four Worlds." Moshe resumed his theme. "Remember where the action is." He tapped the base of the triangle. "Here, in the World of Action. It is here that the work is done.

"A kabbalist might understand the world in this way. There is an imperative to the development or creation of things that can hold an ever-increasing amount of soul. As soon as these things are formed, soul descends into them. Soul itself is not defined by space or time. It is transcendent. But the creation, this universe, has the capacity of holding soul within its boundaries temporarily, and, while it is captured here, it interacts with other—with things, with other souls—and it grows, or it is refined, or purified. When the body that holds the soul in this world fails, the soul leaves and returns to the One who sent it into this world to begin with. The purpose of creation might be thought of as *soul refinement*."

Emily raised her hand. "And if a soul doesn't finish its work in one lifetime, it returns in another life to complete the work?"

"If you like. There is surely a doctrine of reincarnation within the Kabbalah. There is the notion that each soul comes into this world to complete just one refinement, and, if it fails, it comes back again for another chance. The difficulty, of course, is to know just which refinement you have to do."

Moshe paused to consider. He swung his legs into the moment of silence. Reincarnation presented problems. There was indeed a doctrine of reincarnation within the Kabbalah, and it was not much different from Eastern notions, as best he understood them. The difficulty was people had a tendency to find the doctrine of reincarnation reassuring. Kabbalists were more likely to find it unsettling. It was apparent Emily needed reassurance, either that her life would go on, that she would have another chance, or that she would be reunited with a loved one. She was unaware that from the perspective of the Kabbalah, the purpose of this life, the goal, was to complete the work, perfect the soul so she need never be recycled, never have to return. Another life was not a reward, rather a penalty for imperfection.

To rely on reincarnation for another chance was to surrender the imperative to complete the work in this lifetime. To rely on reincarnation for a renewal of relationships with deceased loved ones was to abandon the search for new relationships with new loved ones in the life remaining. Both were anathema to the rabbis who insisted on *mitzvot,* the fulfillment of commandments and the performance of good deeds, and continued relationships to the very end of life. So, while the doctrine of reincarnation was embraced within the Kabbalah, it was not taught to the masses for fear it would be misunderstood. Moshe saw no purpose in teaching this directly to Emily. He chose a different approach.

"Shall we take some time for another story?" Moshe surveyed the faces. Clearly the class was ready. "This is the worst story I have ever heard. I tell you that in advance."

The Worst Story

"There was once a great rabbi, the sage of his age. A more righteous person was not to be found in his generation. He gathered his disciples about him as he was dying, looked at each in turn, smiled, and breathed his last. A few days later, his chief disciple had a dream. In his dream, the *rebbe* was returning to be recycled into this world. *'Rebbe!'* the disciple said in alarm. "Why are you coming back? You lived the most perfect of lives! What is there that could possibly have been left undone?' The *rebbe* smiled at the disciple in his dream, and said, 'Do you remember when I was dying and you and all of my finest students gathered around my bed? Do you remember when I looked at each of you, and then I closed my eyes and smiled? Well, in that moment, I reviewed my entire life, and I saw that any opportunity there had been to learn a word of Torah, I had learned. And any opportunity there had been to do a *mitzvah,* I had done it. With that I breathed a sigh of satisfaction, and my soul left my body.' The disciple in his dream asked, 'So *rebbe,* where was the imperfection?' 'In that moment of satisfaction.'

"That," Moshe told the class, "is the worst story I have ever heard." And that story told more about the rabbinic notion of reincarnation than any lecture he could give.

"It's not enough that I should tell the story. Take a few moments now and retell the story to each other and share what you might have learned from it. Stories have the power to transform, not so much hearing the story, but telling the story. So please, pair off, and tell the story again to each other."

The class divided into pairs. Rivkah went to learn with Emily.

A Better Story

"I'll tell you a better story," Moshe resumed. "Shall we do one more?" No one dissented.

"There was a *Hasid,* a Jew faithful to his *rebbe,* who wanted nothing more than to be with him for Rosh Hashanah. He harnessed his horse to his wagon and began the journey. The afternoon before the Holy Days began, a wheel fell off his wagon. He realized he would not be able to fix it before the Holy Days started at sunset, so he resigned himself to remain in the field by the side of the road for the two days of Rosh Hashanah. When the Holy Days were over, he fixed his wagon, proceeded into town, found the *rebbe,* and broke down in tears, explaining to him what had happened. 'So,' the *rebbe* asked him. 'What prayers did you say when you were by the side of the road?' 'Oh *rebbe,*' the *Hasid* answered, 'I did not know what to pray, so I said to God—*ALEF, BAYT, GIMMEL, DALET* . . . I prayed all of the letters of the alphabet, and I said to God—Look, I may not know how to arrange these letters into the proper prayers, but surely you do. So I give you the letters and ask you to arrange them.' 'Ah.' The *rebbe* sighed. 'We knew something profound had happened, because there was a moment in our prayers when all of the gates of heaven were opened, and it must have been your prayer in the field that did it.'"

The class liked this story better than the first.

"The first time you hear a story like this, you hear what happens. You hear it in the World of Action. But hearing it once is not enough. The second time you hear it, you hear the feelings. You hear it in the World of Formation. You feel the pain of our *Hasid* when he realizes he can't be with his *rebbe* for the Holy Days. You feel his heart break in his prayer.

"Now the third time you hear the story, you hear it in the World of Creation. You hear the essentials of what it is teaching. You know that a broken heart is the place from which prayers are heard. But there are secrets in the story. The letters of the alphabet are not a simple person's prayer. There are secrets in the letters. They are the basic building blocks of creation. They are also the basic building blocks of meditation. If you know the prayers for the Holy Days, you know that many of them are acrostics—*ALEPH, BAYT, GIMMEL*. All the way through. It's easier in Hebrew to do acrostics on the alphabet. There aren't any bad letters. In English you have *X, Y, Z*. What do you do with those? But in Hebrew, when a kabbalist recites the alphabet, it's like a review of the very process of creation. What better meditation to do on Rosh Hashanah, the anniversary of the creation of the world? So when you hear this story in the World of Creation, you hear a meditation on each letter, so each letter of the Hebrew alphabet becomes a key to opening one of the gates of heaven.

"And then you hear the story a fourth time. In the World of Emanation. The fourth time the story is beyond words. You become the story. There is no separation between you and the story. When you become the story, you feel a need to tell it to someone else. Each time you tell it, you learn it a little better, in each of the worlds.

"Do you remember the story? Then I give you a homework assignment. In the next week tell the story to someone else. Not someone in this class. To someone else. You'll see how much you learn from it.

"Take a moment. Review the elements of the story. Consider who you might share it with. And then we'll do some more with the four worlds."

Stephanie said, "Rivkah was concerned about Emily. She had retold both stories to her, but Emily was not able to repeat them back, even with coaxing. She thought Emily was going to be a problem.

"Moshe was concerned more with Sidney. He wanted to know what Sidney was after. He thought Sidney was going to be a problem.

"Rivkah was not aware of the nuances of the exchanges between Moshe and Sidney. She thought his questions were good.

"'Very good indeed,' Moshe agreed. 'He keeps me on my toes.'

"'Then good for him,' Rivkah said. 'He'll make you reach a little higher.'"

"One more," Sidney said to his students as he distributed another text. "Moshe himself knew it was an overload, but the lesson was important, so he added one more, and so will we. In the first session, Moshe had mentioned Paradise, but he didn't tell us how to get there. At the end of the second session, for those of us who were engaged, he did."

PaRaDiSe

P = *P'shat*	Narrative	Action
R = *Remez*	Metaphor	Formation
D = *Drash*	Allegory	Creation
S = *Sod*	Secret (Spiritual)	Emanation

"I want to talk about Paradise," Moshe said, and quickly had our attention. "I mentioned Paradise last week. The four who descended into Paradise, but I didn't explain how they might have done it. There is a technique of learning Torah through the Four Worlds that brings one into the very presence of God.

"Consider this. If the Torah emanates from God, if it is the word of God, then it may be possible to follow that word back to its source. The road map is the word itself. PaRaDiSe. P-R-D-S. *P'shat, Remez, Drash, Sod.* Studying Torah in such a fashion leads to Paradise. Some say that studying the Torah in this fashion *is* Paradise."

He used the story of the Red Sea as an example.

"You're all familiar with it. The children of Israel have been enslaved for centuries. Moses comes along and tells Pharaoh to let the people go. Pharaoh refuses. There are ten plagues. Moses and the children of Israel head for the sea. Pharaoh's armies chase after them. They are pinned against the sea. A pillar of cloud separates the two camps by day, a pillar of fire by night. An east wind blows all night. Maybe it's a low tide. The Israelites are traveling light. They get through the sea. The Egyptians are following in chariots. The wheels get bogged down. The wind stops blowing. The sea rises. The Egyptians are drowned. The children of Israel emerge safely on the other side. That's the Red Sea story in the World of Action. *P'shat.*

"Now, another reading. The children of Israel are trapped in the tightest of places. The Hebrew for Egypt, *mitzrayim,* means a very tight place.

Taskmasters are set over them. Moses comes before Pharaoh and takes a stick and inserts it into the River Nile. Blood issues forth. There is a first plague, and at the end of each month another, so that the tenth plague brings nine months to full term. The waters of the Red Sea break. The children come forth out of the tight place. And the taskmasters, who had held the children captive within the tight place all that time, come forth after them, and perish. So the birth of the children of Israel, and the crossing of the Red Sea in the World of Formation. We use a metaphor of childbirth. It's as if we had insemination, pregnancy, labor, breaking of the waters, emergence of the newborn, the death of the placenta. The Red Sea story in the World of Formation. *Remez*.

"Wait." Moshe raised a hand to halt the murmur of incipient questions. "There is more. There is no creation without an issuing forth. The very creation described in the first chapter of Genesis is an issuing forth. God says, 'Let there be light,' and there was light. God separates the light from the darkness. God creates the waters, and separates the waters so that the dry land appears. This is the process of creation in Genesis. And here in the book of Exodus? The creation of the people of Israel is described in the same terms. Light and darkness, the pillar of fire and the pillar of cloud. The sea, the splitting of the sea, the appearance of dry land. The children of Israel are created in the exodus out of Egypt. There is no creation without an exodus.

"Do we have an artist here?" Several hands were raised. "As long as you are working on a painting, or sculpting a piece of stone, it is attached to you. It is not a creation until it goes into exile from you, until it is separated from you. When it stands apart from you, it is a creation. When it is attached to you, it is only a part of you.

"So the children of Israel are separated from Egypt and become a people. The world is separated from God and becomes a creation. So we have the framework for beginning to understand the passage through the Red Sea in terms of the World of Creation. *Drash*.

"Now, the World of Emanation. If the first reading of the Red Sea told us what was happening, and the second what it feels like, and the third the model of creation to learn from it, wouldn't it be nice if the fourth reading would bring us into the presence of the Creator itself?

"Do you remember the fourth reading of our story? In the fourth reading you become the story. So it is here. In our fourth reading we become the text of the Torah. We examine the text. We search it for clues, for a pathway through the worlds to the very presence of the Creator. And this is what the rabbis found.

"In the fourteenth chapter of Exodus, verses 19, 20, and 21 each have seventy-two letters. Seventy-two letters is an especially long verse. To have three such verses together is out of the ordinary. Not only that, the three verses are the most numinous, God-active verses in the entire story. They describe how the angel of God illuminates the night to make a barrier between the camps of the Egyptians and the Israelites, and then, the very splitting of the sea.

"In these three seventy-two-letter verses the rabbis find the seventy-two letter name of God. If you have done your math, you know that seventy-two is four times eighteen, eighteen being the numerical value of the word for life in Hebrew. Life, if you like, extended through the Four Worlds. In the deepest Kabbalah, these three verses become a meditation, a doorway to the World of Emanation. *Sod*."

Moshe looked at his watch. "Any questions?"

A student asked. "Where can we learn this meditation." Moshe gave him a reference to a volume in the bookstore. The student continued, "Is it all right if we try the meditation by ourselves?"

"Be my guest," Moshe answered. "When we get deeper into the course there will be some meditations not to do alone, but at this stage, feel free to practice whatever we learn in class."

"I raised my hand one more time," Sidney said. "Again I could not resist. It tied everything together for me, even as I knew it would tie Moshe into a knot, I am such a nasty person. I raised my hand."

"Yes, Mr. Lee," Moshe said.

"You've given us the example of the Red Sea. Can the *PaRaDiSe* system of learning be applied to any section of Torah, or does it work only with a few of the stories?"

"Supposedly it works with any Torah text at all," Moshe answered.

"If I choose a story," I pressed, "could you give us the Four World understanding?"

"We really have no time."

"Maybe Moses and the burning bush?"

Moshe looked again at his watch. "We could do it, Sidney, but there isn't the time. The important thing is that we know of the technique, that we see how a text can be deepened through the Four Worlds.

"What we have done is enough for a night. Next week, the ten *sefirot*. If you think four *worlds* is a lot, wait until we learn ten *sefirot*. Thank you very much."

With that the class ended abruptly.

A Burning Bush

"That last exchange between Sidney and Moshe was not lost on Rivkah," Stephanie said. "On the way home she wanted to know what it was all about."

"He was telling me something," Moshe said.

"Something about Moses and the burning bush?"

"Something about me."

"What does he know about you I don't know?"

"Nothing. You know everything about me. I'm the one who didn't know it. He made me aware of it. I am so stupid!" Moshe slapped the steering wheel.

"Tell me about Moses and the burning bush."

"You know the *p'shat*," he began. "Moses is raised in Pharaoh's palace as a prince of Egypt. When he's forty years old, he sees an Egyptian beating up a Hebrew slave. He kills the Egyptian and runs for his life to Midian, marries the daughter of the priest, works as a shepherd in the desert for the next forty years. That's when he has the encounter with the burning bush, a bush that burns and is not consumed. God speaks to him out of the burning bush and tells him to confront Pharaoh and get the Jews out of Egypt. That's the *p'shat*.

"The *remez*. What is a bush that isn't consumed? It's a very strange word in Hebrew, this bush. It's not the ordinary word for bush. You can stretch the word a little and make it into the word for hatred. Resentment would be better. Resentment is something that burns and is never consumed. Moses has been angry for forty years. He's angry he has to wander around in the desert tending sheep. Remember, he had been a prince in Pharaoh's palace. As long as he was angry, he could never see the bush. He was never willing to confront it. There's a commentary that the bush was there every day, and Moses walked by it without ever seeing it. He was blinded by his own anger. Then, finally, he was willing to confront his anger. That's when God was willing to speak to him.

"And the *drash*. The *drash* is where he went to find the bush. The Hebrew translates to 'the back end of the desert,' but another way of reading it is 'beyond the place of speaking,' to the place where one is willing to confront reality in the realm of symbols and archetypes. The realm of angels. God is revealed through angels, which make themselves known in symbolic form. These symbolic forms are all about us, if we are only open to them.

"And the *sod*. Moses takes off his shoes. Why would anyone take off one's shoes with fire burning on the ground? The exposure must be complete. What does Moses gain as a result of this risk? A name of God. He learns God's name. *Eh-yeh Asher Eh-yeh*. 'I am what I am.' That's what God tells him to say to the elders when he returns to Egypt, so they will believe he's truly been sent by God. What kind of proof is that? If the elders know that name for God, big deal if Moses knows it, too. If they don't know that name for God, why would they believe what Moses says? The secret is the God name is in itself a proof of God. 'I am what I am.' Understand the word *what* as an equal sign. I am *equals* I am. God's name and God's essence are the same. To understand this fully brings one into the presence of God. Moses is the best Kabbalah teacher of all time. He teaches the elders the God name, and they share in his experience and know it to be true.

"That's Moses and the burning bush in the Four Worlds," Moshe concluded.

"Sidney Lee knew all of that?" Rivkah asked.

"No, not everything. What he probably knew was the teaching of Moses passing by the burning bush every day in the desert without seeing it."

"What did he intend to teach you?"

"Something about myself. At the beginning of the lesson he saw me looking for the chalkboard and the table. The table was in the room all the time, and I didn't see it!"

"Lunch," Stephanie announced into the silence.

She asked students to assist her. Lunch was Caesar salad, tuna fish, whitefish salad, bread and rolls, fruit, cookies, beverages, all set as a buffet on the kitchen counter. The dining-room table offered room enough, but most chose to take their meals outside.

After lunch was rest. Some slept. Some found themselves space on the deck to meditate, Stephanie among them.

The stories had moved Stephanie, not the teaching. She had the one insight into the nature of creation and cherished it mostly because it was something that Sidney hadn't considered. That insight wasn't about to change her life, but the stories might, the ones she knew, and even more the ones she suspected she was on the verge of knowing.

The story of the officer of the law had been stunning the first time she had heard it, but, on retelling, it didn't improve. It remained at best an allegory for the worlds. The story that had touched her the most was the worst story in the world, the *rebbe* who returned in a dream to his disciple.

Did the *rebbe* return, or did the disciple discover the story within himself? Or did it matter?

Might her mother return and fill in the blanks in her story?

Stephanie shifted in her chair, followed the path of breath as she had learned from Moshe, allowed herself to fall, descend, to meet her mother.

Was it her mother she saw? A young woman, younger than she had ever seen her. Or an imagined mother? If imagined, she could add wrinkles, change the dress.

Stephanie tried, but couldn't. The image of her mother was more than she could manage. She thought to turn away, but there was no turning away.

"The ridicule was the most difficult to bear," she heard in Yiddish, "even more than parting with the china."

Stephanie closed her eyes more tightly. That didn't help. She opened them. That didn't help either.

Again she heard, "The ridicule was the most difficult to bear, more than parting with the china."

What did that mean? As soon as she asked herself the meaning, the image of her mother was gone.

The ridicule had been difficult to bear. They were the only ones leaving among their family and friends. The times were troubled, but the troubles would soon be over. That was the word on the street. But her father had made a decision to leave. He sold the house. He sold the china. The ridicule of his family and friends was the most difficult of all.

Stephanie had an image of her father, the young man, strong enough to stand up to his parents, his older brother, to say the time had come to leave. Her father had been a Noah preaching to the generation of the flood.

No one listened. He must have been so strong, so certain, so determined! It must have been that way. Only he and his wife left. Everyone else remained behind.

How could she reconcile that image with a father who sat all day on the stool behind the counter, who wore his *yarmulke* like a dunce's cap?

"What happened to you?" she asked aloud. "What happened?"

CHAPTER 9

Theology

The students gathered around Stephanie on the deck for the beginning of the third session. "It was Rivkah's day off," she said. "Moshe had some *hutzpah* suggesting she accompany him to the hospital, but she did. Not because of Moshe, but because of Stacy. She liked Stacy."

The clergy's spaces were filled. Moshe wheeled the Porsche slowly through the parking lots until he found a space half a marathon length from the Tower building. On the way back through the maze of concrete blocks and grass berms they walked by the clergy's spaces. Neither car had a clergy card in the window. One, however, had a bumper sticker. LIFE'S A BITCH, AND THEN YOU DIE!

"At least this one has a theology," Rivkah said.

Questions

Stacy was waiting for them in the lounge. The lounge had a billiard table, a card table, a wall full of books and games, and a popcorn machine. The popcorn was free, but Moshe used to complain that, even so, popcorn was the world's most expensive food, if one considered dental bills. He scooped himself a bag anyway.

"Hello, Stacy. I'm sorry I'm late."

"Hi, rabbi. Hi, Mrs. Katan. Thanks for coming."

"My privilege, Stacy. Let's get to work."

They walked down to the clergy office. Moshe used his key, opened the door, pulled the chair out from behind the desk. He and Stacy sat down, almost knee to knee. Rivkah settled into her space in the corner.

"So? How has your week been?" Moshe began.

"Better."

"Better doesn't mean good, does it?"

272

"No. But better is better than worse."

"What do you need to make it still better in the next week?"

Stacy sucked in a deep breath. "I need to know how it works. I know"—she held her hand up to keep him from interrupting her prepared speech—"I remember what you said. I don't know how a TV works, and it works anyway. But this is different. *They* all seem to know how it works." She waved her hand to indicate the census on the floor. "*They* believe in their Jesus, and Jesus saves. And that's all there is to it. What do *we* believe, rabbi?"

That was more of a challenge than a question.

Moshe settled himself for a moment before responding. Stacy's need was substantial. "First thing, Stacy. I hear your question. But I would like you to ask *me* the question, rather than the rabbi. My name is Moshe. I think you'll do better hearing the answer from me than you will from the rabbi. Okay?"

"I don't understand."

"Call me Moshe and ask the question again. 'What do we believe, Moshe?'"

"What do we believe, Moshe?"

This time there was more question and less challenge.

"One more time. This time as if you really think there might be an answer, and maybe I can help you find it."

"What do we believe, Moshe? How does it work? Where does the help come from? They seem to feel it. I don't feel it."

This time it was all question, no challenge. She had asked the question in such a way as to admit an answer. Sometimes the tone of a question might impede the answer. Moshe glanced toward Rivkah, to see if she had caught the nuance, closed his eyes, and searched for an appropriate response.

Answers

Sidney said, "Once Moshe had a question that tugged at him so deeply, he flew across the continent in search of an answer."

A decade before, when Moshe Katan was immersed in his studies, when the Havurah was smaller, when the demand on his time was less, he had found himself perplexed. A few phone calls had located Reb Hayim at a retreat center in upstate New York. A few more calls, and Moshe was en route to join the retreat for an extended *Shabbat*, Friday through Sunday.

"Shalom, Moshe, how good to see you!" Reb Hayim came from across the room to embrace him. They wrapped themselves in each other. "So, how is Rivie?"

"Good. Good. We're both well."

"Let me finish here, then we'll talk." Reb Hayim returned to the grouping about the coffee table to resume his discourse. Moshe sat in the outer circle, closed his eyes, found the thread of the teaching, and followed it to its conclusion.

After the session, sitting alone with Reb Hayim, he expressed his need. "I'm uncomfortable with the way I address God. It's become a problem for me."

Reb Hayim raised his eyebrows. It was his way of asking about the last phrase spoken. The eyes themselves stayed focused. Only the eyebrows moved. The bushy white beard, the arms folded comfortably on the paunch under the *Shabbos* robe, even the feet perched on the ottoman, all stayed still.

"A problem," Moshe backspaced. "Enough of a problem to warrant a visit. I've been working hard." Again the eyebrows. "*Ma-aseh Beraysheet* this time," he added to identify the nature of the work. He had been doing meditations in the Work of Creation rather than in the Work of the Chariot. "It's made me sensitive. Once, when I was at the gym, after a workout, I was in the hot tub, I began to cry. I realized how far away I was. How impossible it was to know anything. I didn't even know how to refer to God anymore. King doesn't work. Father, mother, parent doesn't work. I felt so empty. So far away. I sobbed like my heart would break."

Reb Hayim cleared his throat by way of apology for speaking. "So, what kept your heart from breaking?"

"When I finished crying, I looked up through the window and saw the branches of the trees swaying in the wind. It was as if I could see each individual leaf. It was so beautiful. It was so beautiful."

"The beauty compensated for the pain of separation?"

"The beauty made it bearable, but I've been in distress ever since. My prayers don't flow anymore. I read the texts of God the King or God the Father, and they're distant to me. It's as if they are written for some other time. So I figure, since I've been working with a *havurah,* and a *havurah* is based on a model of friendship, that perhaps the way to relate to God now is as God the Friend. But I suspect that's not right either. Can you help me?"

As Moshe voiced "God the Friend," Reb Hayim raised a hand, a reflex to ward off danger. "Not the Friend, Moshe. Friends are fine for people, and you are a wonderful friend. But that's not the word for the relationship with

God. Not yet. I understand what you're asking. It's like this. God the King was okay when we related to God primarily in *asi-ah,* when we saw God active in the world, doing plagues, stopping the sun. But after the destruction of the Second Temple, when the paradigm for the way we related to God shifted, King wasn't enough anymore. God became our Father, our King. *Avinu malkenu.* We experienced God more in *yetzirah.* We wanted a relationship. We stopped sacrificing animals, a worship of action, and we started offering words, a worship of relation. Now what you're telling me is that you're leaving *yetzirah.* You're entering a new paradigm. You're entering *bri-ah,* and you need a new way of relating to God. But not Friend, Moshe. *Haver* and *havurah* go together just fine. But that's not yet the way for you to relate to God. *Haver* has the root *HET VAYT RESH,* the root for *joining.*

"It's like this." Reb Hayim held out his hands rolled into fists, one low, the other high above it. "Here you are in *asi-ah,*" he said as he shook the lower fist. "Here's God the King, way up above you." He shook the higher fist. "That's as much intimacy as they could stand back then." He opened his hands, the lower one palm up, the upper one closer and palm down. "Two thousand years ago we entered the age of *yetzirah.* We wanted a relationship. One hand is still above the other, but closer. The relationship isn't that of ruler to subject but parent to child. Now, here's what friend looks like." He made rings of his index fingers and thumbs, and looped one ring through the other. "Joining. This is for when you're ready to leave the world. When the joining happens, you are at risk. You may not be able to separate. You may be drawn out of this world prematurely. Have I ever told you the story of why the Baal Shem Tov stopped traveling at night?"

"No, *rebbe.*" The Baal Shem Tov, Rabbi Israel ben Eliezer, was the founder of Hasidism, the eighteenth-century expression of kabbalistic discipline into daily life.

"Then I'll tell you." Reb Hayim settled back into his chair. "The Baal Shem Tov in his later years did not require much sleep. He would lie awake beside his wife in bed at night, and he would travel through the worlds. He would descend through *asi-ah* to *yetzirah,* and then deeper still to explore *bri-ah.* One night he reached a barrier, the gate to the world of *atzilut.* He began to negotiate his way through when a voice came from the other side. 'Rabbi Israel,' the voice said. 'Be careful. If you come through here, you cannot get back.' So the Baal Shem Tov retreated and returned to his body. The next night he was traveling again, and again he reached that gate, and again the voice spoke to him, 'Rabbi Israel, be careful. If you come through here, you cannot get back.' This time the Baal Shem Tov's desire was so great, the pain of separation he felt was so great, he began to negotiate the barrier. That's when his wife awoke in bed and found the body of her husband growing cold. She shouted, 'My husband, come back to me!' Her cry penetrated through all of the worlds. The Baal Shem Tov heard it and returned. It was said after that the Baal Shem Tov no longer traveled at night.

"So, Moshileh, you be careful. Don't be so quick to go to the place of joining. This world was created so you should be in it for a while yet. There's plenty of time left before you start the joining."

Moshe leaned forward. "Reb Hayim, I hear the warning, but what paradigm do I use to relate to God in the place where I am now?"

Reb Hayim laughed "You are not the first to be there, Moshe. Go call the *havurah* together. I'll be out in a few minutes, and I'll tell a story. You'll find the answer in the story."

Reb Hayim's Story

"This is Reb Hayim's story," Stephanie said. "Reb Hayim told it as an answer to Moshe's question. Moshe told it to answer Stacy's. It was not exactly as he had heard it from Reb Hayim, but then the story Reb Hayim had told was not exactly as he had heard it from his teacher. I'm told it goes back to the Opter *rebbe,* one of the early masters. But who knows where it came from originally. The story went from teacher to student. Each absorbed it in his own way and transmitted it to each receiver differently. No two tellings were ever quite the same."

"You'll find the answer to your question in this story," Moshe began. "But you won't find it by hearing the story, Stacy, only by telling it. So if you want to hear the story, I need a promise you will tell it to someone within the next week. Better still, tell it to several people. The more the better. Okay?" She nodded.

Moshe closed his eyes and rocked gently in his chair as he recalled Reb Hayim closing his eyes, rocking gently in his chair. "This is the story," he began.

There was a *rebbe* who had the power to pronounce blessings, and the blessings would come true. Do you understand how powerful such a thing is? How many students such a *rebbe* would have? How many people would line up outside his door for the privilege of receiving a blessing?

The blessings the *rebbe* would give might not be exactly the blessing a person was asking for. What he would do was to look deeply into a person's soul, see the need of the soul, and pronounce a blessing to meet the person's needs, not necessarily a person's wants. But, for most people, that was good enough. So the *rebbe* had a lot of students, a lot of visitors.

One day some students came to the *rebbe* and told him there was another person in town who also had the power to pronounce such blessings.

"Who is that?" the *rebbe* asked. "The bartender," the students replied.

"The bartender? Really? I didn't know the bartender had any learning at all."

"We don't think he does, *rebbe*. But we watch him, and he gives blessings, and the blessings have about them the same power that your blessings have."

"This I have to see," the *rebbe* said. He changed into ordinary clothes and went to sit in the tavern and watch the bartender. He found the bartender was an ordinary man, of no apparent learning, but as his students had said, he had the ability to give blessings of true power and penetration. Day after day the *rebbe* sat in the tavern, studying the bartender in wonder. *Shabbos* approached, and he thought to watch the bartender during the Sabbath, because if the bartender was a hidden *zaddik,* a hidden righteous person, he would not be able to hide his light on *Shabbos.*

At the conclusion of the Sabbath the *rebbe* still had noticed nothing out of the ordinary. He approached the bartender, and said, "My friend, I have been watching you all week. I am the rabbi."

"Oh, Rabbi, forgive me, I never realized who you were!"

"Please, that's not important. I've been watching you, and I've seen you have the power to give blessings that come true. Did you know that?" The bartender did not know that. "I didn't think you knew. It took me years of study and meditation to learn how to pronounce blessings like that. How is it that you know how to do it?"

The bartender answered, "Rabbi, forgive me, I don't know. I'm just a simple man."

"You have no great learning you are hiding? You are not one of the thirty-six hidden righteous ones? Have you ever done a *mitzvah,* a good deed, so great as to be worthy of special merit? Have you ever talked with God, prayed so intensely you feel you have had an immediate response?"

To each question the bartender shook his head from side to side, but to the last he said, "Maybe."

"Would you tell me about it?" the *rebbe* asked.

"Well, it's like this," the bartender said.

The Bartender's Story

I have a terrible temper. Because of my temper, my business wasn't doing well. Someone would come into the tavern. Maybe there was something about him I didn't like, something he said, or the way he looked. I'd lose my temper, start shouting. Sometimes I'd even jump over the bar and punch the guy out. And that wasn't good for business.

Things got so bad, my wife told me I should take a partner. If I had a partner, she thought, things would get better. But I know me. If I took a partner, sooner or later I'd lose my temper and punch out the partner and that would be the end of the partnership. So I didn't listen to her.

Things got worse and worse. I was having trouble providing food for my family. Finally, I couldn't stand it anymore. I went out to the backyard and broke down and cried to God. I said to God I didn't know what to do. My wife wanted me to take a partner, but I knew me and my temper, and I couldn't take any human partner. So I told God, "I make you my partner. From this day on, you're my partner. I'll give you fifty percent of the profits, then ten percent of my share, because, after all, you're God."

And ever since then things have been better. I've been giving God his fifty percent, and ten percent of my share, and even so, I'm making three times what I used to even in the best of times.

The Rebbe's Question

The *rebbe* listened intently to the bartender's story. When the bartender had finished speaking, the *rebbe* asked, "So, what happened to your temper?"

"What happened to my temper? What do you mean what happened? I've always had a temper. I still have a temper. I will always have a temper!" The

278

rebbe raised his eyebrows asking for more. "It's like this," the bartender continued. "Someone comes into the bar. I don't like the way he looks. I want to jump over the bar and punch him out, but I can't do it. I have a partner. So I hang in there and hang in there, and finally I figure out what it is that I don't like about this guy, and I say, 'By God, what you need is such and such!'"

"That's a blessing!" the *rebbe* said. "Because you and God are partners, what happens is that when you need help, God provides it. You can't control your temper yourself, so God adds the strength you need, as long as you're open to receiving it. And as for the blessings, when one partner pronounces something in the name of the partnership, the other is obliged to fulfill it!"

Investment

Moshe opened his eyes and sat up straight. "That's the story, Stacy. It works like this. God creates this universe for a purpose. You are a substantial part of that purpose. God has a lot invested in you. Do you know how much it costs to produce a body like the one you are in? Don't even think in terms of dollars. It takes millions of years.

"What if you had an expensive car, one you'd worked years to get, and a piece of it broke down? Would you throw the car away or get it fixed?

"You're like an expensive car, and a piece of you is broken down. The piece where you became an addict. God doesn't throw the car away. God's willing to pour a little more energy into the car to keep it going as long as it can. In this case the car has to be willing to receive the help God's willing to give. This car has a mind of its own.

"Some cars might say, 'Hey, I broke down. I failed. I'm worthless. I'm not worthy of being fixed. My driver must hate me. My driver wants nothing to do with me.' And every time the driver tries to help the car, the car turns away. That's got to be pretty frustrating for the driver.

"The driver is saying things like, 'Look here, car, so a piece of you is broken down and you're not a hundred percent anymore. But you're one hell of a car, and if you will only let me help, we can benefit from each other's company for a good many years yet. Let me fix the broken piece. It's not expensive. If it breaks down again, I promise to fix it again. But what I want from you is that you don't turn away from me anymore so we can do the work we have to do together.'

279

"A piece of you has broken down, Stacy. God's not angry about that. God's saying we used to have a partnership, of sorts, but now you've turned away. If you turn back, the partnership is waiting for you. God provides the strength. You and God together go about the business of refining your soul. And your business will be three times better than it ever was, even in the best of years.

"Now, will you be able to tell someone the story?" Stacy nodded. "Who will you tell it to?"

She mentioned the name of one of the counselors. Moshe managed not to smile. That counselor had heard the story dozens of times already, but to her credit, she always appeared to be hearing it for the first time.

"Anyone else?"

"I don't know. I'll find someone else. I'll find several people. I'll tell the story a lot."

"Good for you. Any questions?"

"This is my last week in the unit. It's all the insurance will cover. Will I see you again?"

"That's up to you," Moshe answered. He wrote a phone number on a memo pad. "This is the number of the Havurah office. You can ask to be put on the mailing list."

"You're the rabbi there?"

Moshe laughed. "No, there I'm just another Jew. I stopped being a rabbi some years ago."

"How do you stop being a rabbi?" Stacy asked, her eyes widening with astonishment.

He shrugged. "I don't know. I just stopped."

"Then why do you still come here?"

"It's something I don't want to give up."

"That's not an answer," she pressed him, the attorney speaking, not the addict. "Obviously if you're here, you don't want to give it up. But how is it you choose to be a rabbi here and not anywhere else? Why here and not there?"

Moshe looked to Rivkah as if for help. The attorney was badgering a friendly witness. "This is a clergy emergency," he said, remembering the sign he had kept in the glove compartment all those years. "I can't give this up, Stacy. It's a matter of life and death."

"Here it's a matter of life and death but there it isn't? Life-and-death issues stop at the doorway of the hospital?"

"No, but the urgency is here. Outside, the urgency isn't so great."

"So it's not life and death out there. Once I leave here my life is no longer in jeopardy?" When he had no response, she continued, "Thank you for the story. I'll tell it to someone this afternoon."

Moshe Katan was dismissed.

Discomfort

"Discomfort in one world ripples through all the others," Stephanie said. "No world is separate to itself. They are all interconnected."

Moshe and Rivkah walked together through the parking lots in search of the Porsche.

"I like her," Rivkah opened the conversation. "Do you think she'll be all right?"

Moshe shrugged. "Maybe. She seems determined enough. If she can begin to surrender her notions of a vengeful, judgmental God, her guilt might dissipate. She might no longer feel shame for failing her Father in Heaven. If she's lucky, she'll get angry at her divine Partner for making her with such a deficiency and letting her languish so long. If she's even luckier and the anger gets out, maybe healing can get in."

"It's a matter of luck, then?" Rivkah urged him on.

"I don't know. It's not all luck. There are things she can do. She can tell the story. That's key. The more she tells the story, the better her chances are."

"Are you worried about her?"

Rivkah's questions annoyed him. "Worried? No. I don't think so. There's not much more I can do, in any event. She'll be out of the hospital in a few days."

"Out of the hospital, out of mind?"

That was not the way it was with Rivkah. She followed her families out of the hospital and into their homes. The hospital was only the beginning of her work. She was committed to her families throughout their recovery from illness or grief.

"Why do you continue to do this, Moshe?" Rivkah pressed. "What do you get out of it?"

He had no immediate answer. "Where's the car?" he asked.

Rivkah pointed. "That way. So why do you do this? Why is your name still on the list as Jewish chaplain? What do you get out of it?"

"Maybe it's reinforcement for me," Moshe began. "Maybe I do it so I'll have another chance to tell the story to a new audience."

"Are you okay, Moshe?" Rivkah stopped by the car.

"Of course I'm okay. Why?"

"Is there some reason why you need to tell the story?"

"I always need to tell the story."

"But no particular reason right now? Everything is all right?"

"Everything is going just fine."

Rivkah shrugged her disbelief. "I guess you're not hungry."

Moshe looked to the hand in which he held the bag of popcorn. He had not eaten so much as a single piece. Until that moment he had forgotten it was there. He stood by his Porsche, one among myriad cars, no trash receptacle in sight. He had lost his appetite for popcorn. He did not want to bring it into the car with him. He could not dispose of it.

"Give it to me," Rivkah said. "I'll hold it for you."

"Give them to me," Stephanie heard her mother's voice. "I will hold them for you."

She looked about among the students for her mother. Sidney was already standing, preparing to bring the students inside for the next set of stories.

"Give them to me. I will hold them for you."

Her mother was not to be found on the deck. Stephanie closed her eyes and looked for her mother inside. "Give them to me. I will hold them for you."

They had sold everything for cash, used all the cash for the papers and tickets to get to America. Everything for cash, carrying only what they could bring with them. The clothes on their back, one bag each. And the diamonds.

He was a jeweler. He sold the china, but not the diamonds. Diamonds did not demand much space.

"Give them to me. I will hold them for you."

Her mother held the diamonds as they set out west from Poland. Across Germany.

Stephanie wondered how it was she had never before imagined that passage across Germany just as the war was about to begin.

She wasn't ready for that.

She stood and followed Sidney into the living room.

CHAPTER 10

Evolution of a Story

Sidney invited the students to stretch and brought them back into the living room for the stories of the third lesson at the Institute. "Let's see how much we're willing to risk," he said. "This is a song of Reb Nachman." Sidney began to sing.

All the world is just a narrow bridge, just a narrow bridge, just a narrow
  bridge.
All the world is just a narrow bridge, just a narrow bridge.
And above all, and above all, is not to fear, not to fear at all.
And above all, and above all, is not to fear, not to fear at all.

When the students had ventured far enough into the song, Sidney said, "Moshe began the third session at the Institute with this tune. He was going to teach about exposure and balance. To sing is to risk something. It is an offering. You don't know how it is going to be received. Is there anyone here who would like to risk a solo?"

None of the students in the living room seemed eager.

"Moshe asked the same question in a much larger class," Sidney continued. "There was one volunteer. Harvey Klein. But he didn't want to sing the song. He wanted to tell a story. He had heard a story and had promised to share it. Would it be all right for him to tell it to the class? It was a story about relating to God as Partner.

"Moshe vaulted from his table to sit by Rivkah. Rivie wanted to know if it was a setup, if Moshe had primed Harvey to interrupt with a story. Moshe proclaimed his innocence. He surely knew which story Harvey was about to tell, but he had no notion of how it had grown in the past few days."

Harvey extracted himself from his chair. He seemed too big for the room. He was tall, six-three, maybe six-four, but the measure of the man was more than his height, and Harvey had grown since the course began.

283

If Harvey had been uncomfortable in his chair, he was more so on his feet. He glanced about for a place to deposit his body and, with a grin, lifted himself onto the rabbi's table and began to swing his feet. The class laughed. Moshe smiled.

"There was once a rabbi," Harvey began, "who would visit people in the hospital and give them blessings. He would look into their eyes, and the blessings he gave were so powerful the person hearing them just knew they would come true.

"This rabbi had a lot of students. One day, the students came to him and said there was someone else in the city who could give blessings like that. The rabbi asked who it was, and they said it was a lawyer. The rabbi couldn't believe any lawyer could give blessings." That drew another laugh. The class was with him. Harvey closed his eyes and committed himself to the story.

"'This I have to see for myself,' the rabbi said. So the rabbi went down to the courtroom to watch the lawyer in action. The students were correct. She had the power.

"When she was about to leave the courtroom, the rabbi stopped her, introduced himself, and asked if they could talk for a moment. They went down to the coffee shop and the rabbi asked her if she knew she had the power to give blessings. She didn't know that. The rabbi asked her if she was a learned person, or if she was a righteous one, or if she had made it a practice to talk with God. She said no, but then she said that maybe, once, she had talked to God. The rabbi asked her to tell him about it.

"'Well, it's like this,' she began. 'I'm a drug addict.'" Harvey closed his eyes more tightly to check the tears. "'I used to have a successful practice, and then I began to use cocaine when my work would get me stressed out, and things really began to go downhill. My practice got worse and worse. My boyfriend left me. My family was fed up with me. They kept saying I should get a partner. If I had a partner, things would go better. I shouldn't be in practice by myself. But I knew as soon as my partner would find out I was a user, that would be the end of the partnership. Finally things got so bad, even I couldn't stand it anymore. I went out to my backyard. I didn't have the strength to stand. I fell down on the grass and began to cry out to God . . .'" Harvey paused, settled himself, and continued. "'I cried out to God and told God everything that had happened. I told God my family thought I needed a partner. Even I thought I needed a partner, but I couldn't take a partner because I was using drugs and couldn't stop. So I said to God, "You be my partner. I'll give fifty percent of the profits we make to charity as long as you're my partner."

"'Ever since that moment,' she told the rabbi, 'things have been good. My practice has gotten better and better. I give God his fifty percent, and with the half I have left, I still make twice as much as I used to.'"

Harvey opened his eyes and looked about. He thought to end the story there. It was not an unlikely place for an ending, but Moshe urged him on. "What about the lawyer's addiction?" he asked Harvey.

"Oh yes. That's what the rabbi asked the lawyer. She said, 'I used to be an addict. I'm still an addict. I'll always be an addict.'

"'So what happens when you get stressed out?' the rabbi asked.

"'When I get stressed out and I want to use drugs, I say to God, 'Hey, partner. I need some help right now. And I feel the help.'"

Harvey stopped once again, thinking the story complete. He looked to Moshe who raised an open palm, willing to receive still more. Harvey closed his eyes again, as if to rediscover the most hidden words.

He lifted up the conclusion of the story. "Then she added, 'I hang in there, and I see what it is about my client that stresses me out, and I wait for the right moment, and I tell him, "By God, do you know what you need?" and I tell him what he needs.'

"'That's a blessing,' the rabbi said. 'And because you and God are partners, when one partner signs a contract for the sake of the partnership, the other partner is obligated to fulfill it.'

"That's the story," Harvey Klein concluded, still not certain he had finished it. "That's the story as best as I can remember it."

The class was so still, he wasn't sure how the story had been received. He vaulted from the desk, imitating the rabbi once again. No one laughed. If he had seemed awkward on his feet before, after the story, he seemed more so.

Moshe rose from his chair, stood before him and said, "*Yosher koach*. You did it well, Harvey. You did it well." Moshe opened his arms. "May I? For a risk like that you deserve a hug." The two men embraced.

Moshe turned to the class. "Maybe we'll take a couple of minutes in pairs and retell the story to each other, so we won't forget it."

The class erupted into its sharing. Moshe returned to his seat by Rivkah.

"Now Rivkah had heard the same story twice," Stephanie said. "The first time it was a story told to Stacy which she had overheard. She liked the story, but had not learned it. This second time it was Harvey telling the story, and he was telling it to her, as well as to the rest of the class. This time she had both heard it and learned it. It was easier for her to learn from Harvey than from Moshe.

"'He told it well,' Rivkah commented when Moshe sat beside her. Each of us will tell it differently, she realized. After some moments she added, 'How would an oncological social worker tell it?'

"The door opened. Emily entered and looked about the room as if she had never seen it before. 'You have an opportunity to find out,' Moshe told her.

"Rivkah rose to the challenge of Emily. Moshe walked about the room, listening to the echoes of the story. He returned to his table, started the pendulum of his legs, and prepared to resume his teaching, but hesitated, uncertain of his direction.

"He saw that Rivkah had not returned to her seat. For whatever reason she had chosen to remain by Emily. Perhaps that was it. He attempted to fathom whatever was causing Emily's discomfort so that he might teach into it.

"He had learned from Reb Hayim how to teach into sources of discomfort, healing needs indirectly. He could see Emily's discomfort, even from a distance, but could not perceive the need at the root of it.

"Rivkah stopped talking. Finding Moshe's eyes on her, she came directly to the table to tell him Emily wouldn't listen to the story because it was the wrong story. She didn't need a partner; she needed a miracle.

"'What kind of miracle?' Moshe asked.

"'I don't know,' Rivkah answered. 'She wouldn't say another word.'"

Stephanie paused for a moment and closed her eyes. When she opened them, she said, "I once asked Moshe where his stories came from, those he created, not those he heard from his teachers.

"' I don't create anything,' he demurred. 'The story is always there in potential. When I have a need for it, I surrender to the need, and the story becomes kinetic.'

"In the class, at that instant, Moshe needed a story about a miracle. He didn't know what kind of miracle. A generic eclectic miracle. I don't recall what his transition was, how he introduced this story to the class, but I do remember the story. I will always remember it. He had never told it before, had never heard it before. He surrendered to his need, opened his mouth, and this story came out in response to Emily's unspecified need.

"I don't know how he did that. He just did it."

There was a young prophet named Elijah who had just graduated from the school of prophets and started out on his own, traveling through the countryside, looking for opportunities to exercise his trade. He was in the miracle business.

He came through a village and found there a woman who was very unhappy. "Why are you so unhappy?" he asked.

"Because all of my friends are married, and I am not," she answered in tears.

"And how is it that a beautiful young woman like you is not married?"

"Because I'm not beautiful," she complained.

Elijah reached into his bag and found a mirror. "Look into this, and you will be beautiful," he instructed her.

She looked, and indeed she seemed to herself beautiful. Therefore, she was beautiful. In short order she found a man who could see her beauty, and she was married.

When she told the people of the village about Elijah and his mirror, they dismissed it. "It was just a self-affirmation," they said.

The next year Elijah returned to the village, and again he found the woman unhappy. "Why are you so unhappy now?" he asked.

"Because I have no child. All of my friends have children, but my husband and I have no child."

Elijah reached into his bag and withdrew a small piece of parchment upon which was written a prayer. He told her to recite the prayer every morning and evening. Soon she became pregnant and had a son.

When she told the people about Elijah and the prayer, they dismissed it. "It was just a relaxation exercise," they said.

The next year Elijah returned to the village, and again he found the woman unhappy. "Why are you so unhappy this time?" he asked.

"Because my husband was laid off from work. We have no money and nothing to eat."

"Nothing at all? Do you have anything in your refrigerator?"

"Only one can of beer," she said.

Elijah instructed her to fetch all of her buckets and barrels, and to borrow buckets and barrels from all of her neighbors. When she opened the one can of beer, it poured and poured and filled all of the buckets and barrels. She and her husband went into the micro brewery business and did well.

When she told the people about Elijah and the can of beer, they dismissed it. "It was just a can of compressed beer," they said.

The next year Elijah returned to the village, and again he found the woman unhappy, unhappier than ever. "What is the matter now?" Elijah asked.

"Our son is ill," the woman cried. "He is close to death."

Elijah went into the house and found the son was not only ill, indeed he had died. He stretched himself on top of the young boy. When he stood, the boy stirred and came back to life.

When the woman told the people about Elijah and her son, they dismissed it. "It was just CPR," they said.

Well, Elijah was fit to be tied. He had facilitated four perfectly good miracles, one to get her a husband, one to get her a child, one to get her a livelihood, and one to give life back to her son. All of them were good miracles, but the people of the village had dismissed them.

"I'm going away," he said, "and I won't be back until people appreciate a good miracle when they see one."

With that he summoned a fiery chariot out of heaven. It landed on the village green, and, in the sight of everyone, carried him off into the sky. Ever since he has been roaming space and time, searching for people who appreciate a good miracle.

Now, what do you think the people of the village said when they saw the fiery chariot lift him up into the sky? Did they think it was a miracle? No. They said, "It was just a UFO."

The purpose of this story is to teach you how to see a miracle. There are two words to learn. The first you've heard several times. The second you haven't heard yet at all.

The first word is *just*. The word *just* puts blinders on you, so even though it introduces a miracle, you are unable to see it. Instead of the miracle, you see *just* this, or *just* that. It keeps you from looking into the depth of anything. Your eyes never open in wonder.

Anytime someone tells you to "*just* do something," what they are doing is asking for a miracle, and they don't know it. An example. A child always has a messy room. His parents ask, "Why can't you *just* keep your room neat?" What they are asking for is a miracle. They are asking the child to change his inner nature, just like that. What is the proof? The parents themselves provide the proof. What if, without being asked, the child should clean up his room? When the parents come to see it, what do they say? "It's a miracle!"

There is a word we can use instead of *just,* but it's in Yiddish, not English.

The word is *ta-keh*. It has no meaning in itself. What it does is alert you to the words that come after it. They describe a miracle. The word *ta-keh* draws your attention to the miracle. For example, if I should point to a tree, and say, "Now that is *just* a tree," the tree is a miracle, a breathing, living miracle, but because of the word *just,* you won't see it. The word *just* puts blinders on you so you can't see the miracle in the tree. But if you know some Yiddish, and now you do, and I should say, "Now that, *ta-keh,* is a tree," you would look at the tree in wonder, and you would see the miracle.

There are miracles about us all the time, if we could only, *ta-keh,* see them.

Exposure

Stephanie said, "The story was a miracle. Rivie tried to get Moshe's attention, to let him know what a wonderful story had come through him, but Moshe was already beyond the story. He was searching for a connection to the topic of exposure. That was where he was going. Some twenty minutes of class time had already expired, and he hadn't even begun to take the first step, other than to sing Reb Nachman's 'All the World Is Just a Narrow Bridge.' Harvey had told his partner story. Then Elijah somehow had appeared."

Sidney said, "The Elijah story was like an angel. The purpose of some angels is to make connections. This story was rooted on one hand in Emily's desire for a miracle and on the other hand in Moshe's desire to teach the levels of exposure. Moshe knew that. It took him a moment to follow the path from Emily's need to his desire.

"We waited patiently for him to return. We were in no hurry. Something awesome was about to happen. We all knew it. The gates of heaven were open.

"What came through caught me by surprise."

"All the world is just a narrow bridge," Moshe continued. "*Just* a narrow bridge. So we know now that what follows the word *just* must be a miracle. The narrow bridge *is* the miracle. That we stand on it and survive is the miracle." He vaulted from his table. "How wide do you think that narrow bridge is?" he asked. "Stand up and see." We stood. "Put your feet one in front of the other." We did so. Immediately some of us put our arms out to keep balance. "That's how narrow the bridge is," he said. "The bridge is as narrow as the ground underneath our feet. Do you feel the exposure? Do you understand what exposure is?"

There was no consensus of understanding.

"Imagine you are visiting the Grand Canyon. The bus pulls up, you get off, and you look into the canyon for the first time. It is awesome. You feel awe. Suddenly you realize how great, how awesome, how wonderful, how full of wonder the world is. You knew it before, but you hadn't felt it like this. It's worth what you paid for the trip. You walk closer to the edge, and at a certain distance, the awe turns toward fear. What distance is that? It's different for each of us. It's where we begin to imagine ourselves falling off the edge. There's no real danger. It doesn't require any more skill than what you are doing right now, standing upright on your feet. But the exposure has increased. If you get closer still, that feeling of fear moves toward terror. That may not come until your toes are right at the very edge of the canyon and the ground begins to crumble underneath your feet.

"The Hebrew word for this kind of awe is *yirah*. The word for this kind of fear is *yirah*. And the word for this kind of terror is *yirah*. It's all the same word. How that word is understood depends on the exposure. And how close you can get to the edge of the canyon without being consumed by fear and terror depends upon your balance. We're going to be talking about balance tonight. But before you sit down, perhaps experience a little more exposure.

"Look at the carpet in front of you. Imagine a line just ahead of your toes, and imagine that's the edge of the Grand Canyon. Now look down at the pile of the carpet and imagine the tufts are boulders two thousand feet down. See if you can experience the exposure. No? Lean forward a little. A little more.

"Thank you. You can be seated now." Some of us expressed relief as we pulled back from the brink and returned to our seats.

Moshe remained standing, one foot in front of the other.

"Okay," he announced. "Balance. Here I am standing on my narrow bridge. I think the ground all around me is stable, but all I know with any degree of certainty is that the ground underneath my feet is stable. I can't be sure about the ground around me. I don't know what's under the carpet to the right or to the left. My experience tells me it's all right to stand there, but I don't really know. I can't be certain. It means having some faith in God, that the laws of nature will remain constant. It means having some faith in the building code and the ethics of the contractors." Several students chuckled. "Faith is when we relinquish control. We have faith in those who engineered and built this building. Otherwise, we would never venture to the fourth floor. But we don't stop to consider it an act of faith. We like to imagine that we are in control. But we're not.

"That may be what Reb Nachman means by his narrow bridge. We're not in control. We may walk around under the illusion we are, but we are utterly dependent on the divine building codes that keep everything in order, that keep this carpet as it is, so it doesn't turn to Jell-O when I step on it. So Reb Nachman tells us to give up the illusion, to open our eyes. We don't have to go to the edge of the Grand Canyon to feel the exposure. We can feel it right here.

"Use your mind's eye to strip away the walls of this room and understand how high you are off the ground.

"Imagine yourself on the edge of a sphere spinning at a thousand miles an hour. That's how fast this floor under my feet is moving as the Earth spins, me standing exposed on top of it.

"When you begin to think like this, to strip away the illusion that gives you a sense of security, you begin to feel the exposure. Then you are on the narrow bridge, and your very existence becomes a miracle."

"Until that moment," Sidney said, "I had thought my goal in life was to be secure, free from want, free from concern, and for the most part, I had attained it. I was surely among those who lived in the illusion of security. No longer. Moshe had done something to me with his stories and teaching that night. He had stripped away my certainty. My sense of security had been shattered.

"I had never been so exposed, so frightened, so uncertain as I was at that moment."

Balance

"Moshe hardly ever used the word *meditate* in his teaching," Sidney said. "When people would ask him to teach a meditation, he would say, 'You want to meditate? Okay, let's meditate. Two, four, six, eight: everybody meditate.'

"Then he would tell a story. We would descend into the story and lose all sense of space and time. Sometimes I would emerge from such a story and find his eyes on me. As soon as he saw I had returned safely, his eyes would turn to someone else rising to the surface.

"Moshe taught meditation. He rarely called it meditation."

"Reb Nachman tells us not to fear at all. How do we do that? We do it through balance." Moshe put his hands out wide. "I'd like it even better if I

291

had a balance beam, with weights on either end. Then I could hold it and feel secure on my narrow bridge.

"Here's a way of putting out a balance beam. If you like, you can close your eyes and follow this story along with me."

Moshe returned to his table. "Imagine a little girl or a little boy at a summer camp. There are rules. The rules are you can't go out of your cabin at night. But this little child breaks the rules and sneaks up to the playing field in the dead of night. As she wanders out onto the field, she looks up at the sky. It is *sooooooo* big! There are *sooooooo* many stars! Her pace across the field begins to slow. She looks up in awe and wonder and begins to feel very small. She sees a shooting star, and she is suddenly afraid. She begins to shake and feel cold. She's afraid that a shooting star will fall on her! She is so small, the sky is so big. She is so little, so unprotected, so vulnerable. Can you feel that?

"As she becomes accustomed to that feeling, she does something without really thinking about it. She puts her hand up toward a star, to see if she can touch it. Pretty soon she is jumping, trying to touch that star. She's running around leaping, leaping for the stars. It's as if the stars are an extension of her. Imagine that she grows so her head is up in the stars, they adorn her like so much jewelry. Can you feel that?

"On one hand we are so tiny. We are insignificant. We are vulnerable. We are exposed, afraid. On the other hand we can relate to the stars, no matter how far away they are, even at the ends of the universe. On one hand we are a speck of dust. On the other we can relate through all space and time.

"These are the two ends of our balance beam. They are connected. We are both at the same time, and we can move our feeling and experience from one end to the other. Try it, if you like. Feel the exposure on the left, the exultation on the right."

He allowed time for that experience, then offered another. "Or you might try it like this. Imagine a speck of dust, a mote of dust, floating in the sunlight. It has no control, it is almost nothing. It is smallness incarnate. It is the feeling of the little girl when she senses her exposure underneath the stars. Imagine the speck of dust striking the smooth surface of a pond, ripples emanating out from the center forever and ever. The ripples are your creativity, your children, the impact you make on the world, that emanates out of you to the ends of space and time. So on one hand you are tiny, insignificant, but on the other, your ability to relate has an impact throughout space and time. Two ends of the balance beam."

Moshe did the exercise himself as he spoke it. He felt himself a mote of dust so small, the heat of the sun moved him at will. He felt the coolness of striking the pond, and the ripples emanating out of him.

"I am not two separate people," he affirmed. "You are not two separate people. Each of you is one person. You are not two separate entities. There is one balance beam with two ends. If you find the right place toward the center, you can keep your balance. So there are three points to note on this balance beam. There is the end to the left, the end to the right, and the point toward the center where you grab hold. That becomes the foundation of your balance."

Above a circle at the bottom of the chalkboard, Moshe drew a balance beam bending under a weight on either side. He drew a circle to his left which he labeled *Hod*. The circle he drew to his right he labeled *Netzach*. The circle he drew in the middle of the beam, above the lower circle, he labeled *Yesod*. In the lower circle he wrote *Malchut*.

"These Hebrew words are nice-to-know," he said. "The feeling, the experience you just had is need-to-know for anyone who wants some balance in the pursuit of Jewish mystical discipline. I'm putting the Hebrew words up here because you will find them in so many books in the bookstore, so you'll be able to relate what you learn here to what you read there.

"*Malchut*," he tapped the lower circle, "is generally translated as *kingship*. You might understand it as the land over which you rule. That land extends to no more than the ground underneath your feet, your place out on the narrow bridge. That's the extent of your rule. The balance beam above has three names attached to it. This beam"—he tapped the board—"is a continuum of energy. If it is interrupted, the result is a personality disorder. Imbalance to this side, toward *Netzach*, results in grandiosity; to this side, toward *Hod*, inferiority, low self-esteem.

293

"*Hod* is usually translated as *majesty*. How should we understand this? Your true majesty in this vast universe extends to no more than a mote of dust. Something like that.

"*Netzach* has two meanings. It means *eternity* and *victory*. Your eternity and victory is your ability to relate through space and time.

"Balance comes not from the mastery of the vocabulary, but from the extension of the balance beam. With practice, with exercise, you can extend this beam farther and farther, out to the left and out to the right. Your balance becomes more secure.

"That's the first stage. We'll take a moment for review."

"Review."

Stephanie reviewed the little she knew. Her father had been a jeweler, the only one among his family and friends to leave Poland just before the war. He sold the house, the china, was subject to ridicule. He and his wife took only what they could carry, a suitcase each, the clothes on their back, and the diamonds. Her mother carried the diamonds.

"Don't go," she heard. That would have been Al, speaking to her mother. "Don't go." Al who had a position in the community, and later a position in the camps which he would never talk about.

Stephanie began to tremble. She didn't want to know Al's story.

Her parents left by train into Germany. It was easier to consider that than Al's story. The train stopped at every station, and at every station soldiers, officials in gray suits, took them from the train to the platform to check their papers. The papers were correct. Correct wasn't always enough. Sometimes it took a diamond.

Stephanie didn't want to pursue that story either. She meditated on *Hod* and *Netzach* and searched for a secure balance.

Agitation

Stephanie said, "Moshe had begun that section of teaching in a balance emanating out of the Elijah story. Moshe didn't so much tell a story as became the story. That's why his stories were so powerful. And as for meditation, Moshe didn't lead a meditation; he himself did the meditation, and the words flowed out of his experience. That's why his meditations were so powerful.

"While he was doing the story meditation of the little girl at camp, he was in balance. And as he talked about the mote of dust, he was also in balance. But

294

as soon as he left the stories and turned to the chalkboard to explain the Hebrew words, his balance left him.

"Rivkah knew that. Moshe had been agitated before the session, and without the stories to guide him, he was agitated again. When he came to sit beside her, he looked about for something that was not there."

"What are you looking for?" Rivkah asked.

"A glass of water."

"Would you like me to get you some water?"

"No, I don't want water."

"What's going on Moshe? Is it Emily?"

"No, it's not Emily."

"What is it, then? Something to do with *Hod* and *Netzach*?"

He started abruptly, a memory bursting at the surface. "The Royal Arches, Rivie. Do you remember the Royal Arches?"

They had been climbing in Yosemite. The Royal Arches was the name assigned to the rock face behind the hotel. Moshe and Rivie had taken a course in rock climbing and had advanced to their first climb in the valley. Each climbed with an instructor. Many hundreds of feet above the valley floor they had come to a crack in the rock. The way across the crack was by means of a tree that had fallen years before. The log was rotting away.

"The leader goes across the log and ties in," they were told. "Then you follow. But be careful. There isn't any real protection here. If you go off the log, there's twenty feet of exposure. You'll hit the rock face before I can stop your fall." Moshe's instructor walked across the log like it was a four-lane highway.

Moshe waited until he heard the words "On belay!" chanted from the other side.

"Climbing!" he shouted, but crawling was more like it. Rivkah and her instructor watched him try a first step onto the log. He withdrew, started again, and dropped to all fours. The wind swept down the crack and the log shook. He inched across.

"Do you remember the Royal Arches?" Moshe asked.

"Yes. How could I forget?"

"Do you remember the log? On the far side of the log? Some climber with a sense of humor had stuck a metal flag labeled *Danger*. On the far side!" Rivkah nodded. "I was so angry," Moshe continued. "That climber was making fun of me. I had a notion to go back across the log and traverse it again, standing up, but I couldn't bring myself to do it."

"What brings the Royal Arches to mind now?" Rivkah asked.

"I wonder how I would do today, if my balance would be up to the task?"

"That log must be long gone by now."

"It's a *Hod* thing," he surmised. "I never felt smaller in my life."

"Or it's a *Netzach* thing," Rivkah said. "That's what I was thinking as you were talking. We have no children, Moshe, nothing to ripple out from us to the edges of eternity. We're out here alone."

"*Hod* and *Netzach*," Moshe agreed.

"We have each other," Rivkah said.

"We have each other," Moshe agreed again.

Parenting

Moshe drew another balance beam above the first one, with a circle on either end, and one in the middle.

He turned from the chalkboard to the class. "Imagine this," he said. "Imagine you are on your narrow bridge, and you extend your balance beam. To the left is insignificance; to the right, posterity. On the left you amount to nothing; on the right, the ripples you make go out forever. You hold it right here, balanced in *Yesod*." Moshe held his imaginary balance beam at the level of his groin. "*Hod* is associated with the left leg; *Netzach* with the right leg. The balance point in the middle is *Yesod*. You begin to feel pretty comfortable. The terror has retreated into fear, and the fear into awe. From your perch on your narrow bridge you feel secure.

"Now"—Moshe reached over his head and tugged at the shirt between his shoulder blades—"imagine that you reach behind yourself and pull out another self and this second self stands on top of the shoulders of the first self that is standing on the narrow bridge and thinks it is secure. Suddenly you find yourself shaky again. It's like a high-wire act in the circus. One tightrope walker has another on his shoulders, and he walks out onto the wire. We need another balance beam.

"Let's go back to our little girl who sneaked out of her camp cabin at night and has wandered up onto the playing field. Imagine you are in a hot-air balloon a hundred feet above the little girl. She can't see you, but you look down and see her. The first reaction is, 'Hey, what are you doing out of your cabin at night? Don't you know you're not supposed to be out here?' You lay down the law. That's your first reaction. Or, at least, that's my first reaction. But then I

Tiferet

Gevurah   Hesed

Yesod

Hod   Netzach

Malchat

see her leaping to catch a star. She runs and jumps and runs and jumps, and my heart goes out to her. Yeah, I know, she's not supposed to be out of her cabin. But on the other hand, she's so cute, the way she reaches up for the stars."

Moshe turned to the chalkboard. "Look at this," he said. "When you are laying down the law, you are here, looking down on the girl who is afraid, sneaking out of her cabin." He labeled the circle in the upper left *Gevurah*. "*Gevurah*," he said, "is translated as *might, greatness, power*. Understand it better as constancy. The law is the law is the law. It's positioned here above the little girl who's breaking the law."

He shifted to the other side and labeled the circle in the upper right *Hesed*. "*Hesed* is the name attached to this end of the second balance beam. Understand it as mercy, kindness, compassion. Notice that *Hesed* is above *Netzach*. Our heart goes out to the little girl when we see her in the *Netzach* mode, reaching up for the stars.

"Now we have the poles of another balance beam, a higher balance beam. To the left we have constancy; to the right, compassion. The left is hard-edged; the right, soft.

"This is the way we act as a parent. It's the way we supervise our employees if we're a boss, the way we teach if we're a teacher, or relate to our campers if we're a counselor. Sometimes we lay down the law; sometimes we're lenient. The proper mix of the two sides together is the expression of love."

Moshe turned to the chalkboard and labeled the center circle, between *Gevurah* and *Hesed, Tiferet*. "*Tiferet*," he said, "is the appropriate combination of constancy and kindness. *Tiferet* is love.

"Now the key is the word *appropriate*.

"Let's say a student comes to you unprepared. He's been procrastinating. He doesn't care. The response is from *Gevurah,* from constancy, from judgment. Let's say the student comes unprepared not because of procrastination, but from a true inability to handle the work. The response is from *Hesed,* from kindness. You take time to give the student additional instruction. You have patience. At least I hope you do.

"Notice also the exposure. The student has to come before you. There is risk involved. Exposure. It's not an easy thing to do.

"The desire now is to extend this balance beam out as far as one can. We are creating an array.

"Do you remember our model of the kabbalist from our first meeting? The kabbalist had an antenna for a head? Well, stretching ourselves out like this is like unfurling an antenna. We want it out as far as we can get it. The first balance beam is associated with our lower body—left leg, right leg, groin. Our second balance beam is associated with our upper body. *Gevurah* with the left arm. *Hesed* with the right arm. And *Tiferet* comes from the heart."

Moshe stretched out his arms. "As far as we can go. This now, if you hadn't figured it out already, this upper balance beam is in the World of Creation. The lower balance beam is in the World of Formation, feelings, how we regard ourselves. And our feet, where we walk in the world, are grounded in the World of Action.

"This again"—he stretched his arms even farther—"is the World of Creation."

Moshe returned to his table. "I will tell a story," he said. "You have a choice. You can hear the story and enjoy it. You can hear the story and learn from it. Or you can become the story."

The Little Girl Who Wanted to Say the Sh'ma

"It's my turn to tell the story," Stephanie said.

"But first you need to know something of Moshe's aspect," Sidney interrupted. "Moshe sat on his table. His legs stopped moving. His eyes closed. He was silent so long, I became alarmed. I realized he had begun to tell his story, but was doing so inside, not outside. He was becoming lost, sitting on the table. He was losing himself in deeper worlds.

"Now something had changed in me. In the first two sessions I had delighted in offering a challenge, playing the devil's advocate, but in this third session my earnest desire had become to help, no longer to challenge, but to assist him, to push him further. I wanted to learn from him, needed to learn from him, to go where he had gone. But there he was before me, gone where I could not follow, and I was afraid for him.

"I had seen Buddhist monks in similar states. Soon he might be unreachable. So I spoke up and suggested we prepare for the story with a *niggun*. Perhaps singing the *niggun* would help. His eyes opened, and we began to sing 'All the World Is Just a Narrow Bridge.'

"His legs began to swing again. I felt better when I saw that."

Stephanie looked to Sidney to be sure he had finished. "You done?" she asked, and then turned to the students. "This was Moshe's way of teaching *Hod, Netzach, Gevurah* and *Hesed.*"

There was a rabbi, who taught in a *yeshivah*. It was one of those rare places in the world where Kabbalah is still learned. He was among the great teachers in his generation. It was said of him that he had the power to take a person out of his body and to move him through the worlds. One day he gathered his students together and told them he was leaving the *yeshivah* to take a liberal congregation in New Jersey.

The students were dumbstruck. That their rabbi would leave the *yeshivah* was shock enough, but that he, an Orthodox *rav,* would condescend to go to a liberal pulpit in the suburbs, this was beyond belief. But he told them there was little challenge teaching Kabbalah in the *yeshivah*. The real work had to be done in the suburbs of New Jersey. He could not be deterred from his path. He interviewed at several congregations and assumed the pulpit of the most liberal, where the challenge would be the greatest.

From the very beginning, the rabbi was miserable. Nobody prayed. Hardly anybody came to services, and even those who did come did not pray. They mouthed the service. No prayers were uttered.

He tried to nudge them from their disservice with stories. He told them of the Baal Shem Tov who once came into a town and went from synagogue to synagogue looking for a place to pray, but in vain. At the last place the *shamas,* the person who was watching the door came out to him and asked why he hadn't entered. The Baal Shem Tov responded he couldn't come in because the building was full of prayer. What he meant was the words of prayer were falling

299

from the people's mouths and piling up on the floor, so there was no room for the Baal Shem Tov to enter. The rabbi told this story, and the people loved it. They even understood it, but they never even considered beginning to pray.

Several months into his first year, the rabbi approached his board of trustees and asked for a favor. He would like everyone in the congregation to come to the synagogue on a Sunday morning. Everyone. Man, woman, and child. He was going to teach something very important. The board of trustees hemmed and hawed for some time, even though they knew they would give in. The rabbi was very persuasive. The word went out some weeks in advance. When that Sunday morning came, the synagogue was full.

He told them he wanted to teach them just one prayer. The prayer was the *Sh'ma*. It was the most often recited prayer in the Jewish liturgy. He told them if they could learn to say even one prayer with the proper intention, it would unlock all other prayers. Even if just one person in the congregation could learn to say the prayer, with that key the person could unlock the hearts of all the others, and all would be able to pray.

The rabbi said they would begin without using the name of God. Instead of *Adonai,* the Name of God, they would say *Ado-shem*. Instead of saying *Elohaynu,* which means *our God,* they would say *Elokaynu*. This was because the rabbi did not want to misuse the name of God. He would save it for the moment they were able to pray with proper intention. Then he began to sing the *Sh'ma* in a melody they had not heard before.

Sh'ma yisra-el, Ado-shem Elokaynu, Ado-shem ehad. Hear O Israel, the L-rd is our G-d, the L-rd is One.

Over and over they sang it. The congregation learned the new melody quickly. The sound increased, stronger and stronger. They sang it for the longest of times, until the men began to look at their watches. The energy dissipated. It was gone. The singing stopped.

The rabbi said he was very sorry. He had hoped they would succeed, but they had not succeeded. Perhaps he would think of something else to try. He told them they could go home.

Sheepishly the congregation stood and left. Soon the synagogue was empty, except for one little girl who approached the rabbi and asked him why he had never once let them sing the *Sh'ma* with the real names of God. The rabbi told her the congregation had not been ready to use the real names. She asked what it meant to be ready. He asked if she really wanted to know. She said she did. He asked her again if she really, really wanted to know. Suddenly she remembered what she had heard about this rabbi, how he was supposed to have the power to take you out of your body and move you through the worlds. She looked into her heart and knew she really did want to know. It was not easy for her to say yes, but yes was what she said.

"And that's where our story really begins," Stephanie said. "You can listen and learn, or you can come along. The choice is yours."

Students found comfortable positions for themselves. The story within the story began.

"Sit here," the rabbi said to the little girl, indicating a seat in the front row. He himself sat on the steps opposite her. "Close your eyes." She closed her eyes. "Breathe now, slowly, deeply. Breathe all the way down to your toes. Feel the breath as if it were coming up your back and around your shoulders and out through your fingertips. Turn your palms upward. It might be easier." She turned her palms upward. "When you've finished a breath, concentrate on a point just above your head, and then take a breath in again, all the way down to your toes." The little girl did her breathing. Down to her toes, up her back, around the shoulders and out her fingertips, above her head and down to her toes. Soon the rabbi said to her, "You'll feel a little tug, but it won't hurt. Just keep on breathing." So she kept on breathing, and she did feel a little tug. The rabbi told her, "Tell me now, what do you see?" She had no awareness of opening her eyes, but she could see.

"I see you," she said. "You're sitting there on the steps right in front of me." She looked farther. "I see the sanctuary." She turned around. "I see me sitting in the first chair. I'm smaller than I thought I'd be."

"When you're out of your body like this," the rabbi said, looking right at her, "you don't have to stay on the floor. If you like, you could go right up to the ceiling." She looked upward. To look was to go, and she found herself floating at the very top of the sanctuary. The rabbi looked right at her, and asked, "What do you see?"

"I see you sitting down there looking up at me. And I see a little me sitting in that first chair."

"You know," the rabbi said, "when you're out of your body like this, you don't have to be kept in by ceilings. You could go right through the roof if you like."

She tested by pushing her hand through the roof, and the rest of her followed into the sunlight above the synagogue, up above the trees. The rabbi was looking right at her. He asked, "What do you see?"

301

She answered, "I see the roof of the synagogue. I see the trees. I see birds and clouds and the sky."

"You know," the rabbi said, "when you're out of your body like this, you can go through the roof and above the trees, and if you like, you could go up as high as the clouds."

To look was to go, and out she went, as high as the clouds. The rabbi looked at her, and asked, "What do you see?"

She answered, "I see the town. I see the school. I see the pond and the river. I see my house. I see the synagogue, and, I think, inside the synagogue I see a tiny, tiny me."

"You know," the rabbi said, "when you're out of your body like this, you can go through the roof and up above the trees, and out to the clouds. If you wanted, you could go out to the very edge of the atmosphere."

To look was to go, and out she went, out and out to the very edge of the atmosphere. The rabbi looked right at her, and asked, "What do you see?"

In the softest of voices she answered, "I see the curve of the earth. I see the ocean and mountains. I see clouds and lakes. I think I see my town. And the synagogue must be there, and in that synagogue the tiniest, tiniest me."

"You know," the rabbi said, "when you're out of your body like this, you can go through the roof and up above the trees, out to the clouds and to the very edge of the atmosphere. If you wanted, you could go out into space, to the very center of the universe."

To look was to go. She went outward, slowly at first, by the orbit of the moon, out through the solar system, beyond the planets, into the galaxy and beyond to the void of space, drifting by galaxy after galaxy, myriad upon myriads of stars, to the very center of the universe.

After the longest time she heard the voice. "What do you see?"

She did not know how to answer, or even if she would be able to respond. Her mouth dropped open in awe. Words seemed beyond her.

"How do you feel?" came a whispered question.

"Afraid," she whispered back.

"Why afraid?"

After an eternity the words rose within her. "How will I get back?"

"Are you ready to come back?"

"Yes, but how?"

"Ask."

She opened her heart to ask, but even before she knew it was open, she felt a gentle wind move her, slowly at first, then faster and faster through the myriads of stars, through the galaxies to her own galaxy, down through systems to her own solar system, by the planets toward her through the orbit of the moon to the edge of the atmosphere, through the clouds, by the tops of the trees through the synagog into her body in the first chair.

When she opened her eyes she saw the rabbi looking right at her. "What did you learn?" he asked.

"I learned that the universe is very big and I am very small," she answered.

"What else?"

"I learned that as small as I am, I can move through the entire universe."

"And what else?"

"That as big as the universe is, there is only one law that governs all of it. It all moves together."

"And what else?"

"That as awesome as that one law is, as frightening as it can be, and as small as I am, it still cares for me."

"Ah," sighed the rabbi. "Now *you* can sing the *Sh'ma*."

Together they sang, "*Sh'ma yisra-el, Adonai Elohaynu, Adonai ehad.* Hear O Israel, the Lord is our God, the Lord is One."

Stephanie sang. The students in the living room sang. The momentum of the *niggun* grew and multiplied. The clear melody split into harmony, which made it all the more one.

"I remember once with Moshe," she said after the singing had ceased, "we were singing like this. It seemed like the singing could go on forever, that all we needed to do was to continue for another ten minutes, fifteen at the most, and the Messiah would come. But we looked at the clock and saw it was time for lunch. So we stopped."

Sidney said, "We're just about at the end of our time here. There is another balance beam to talk about, and in truth another and another and another. But these two will have to serve to keep us on our narrow bridge for the moment.

"If you like, take some time now to debrief with your buddy. Moshe ended his third session in the same fashion, asking us to debrief in pairs. While others began the sharing, I watched Moshe. He looked about him as if he had left something on his table. There was nothing there. Several students tried to thank him, but he was oblivious to them, so they stopped trying."

CHAPTER 11

Stephanie realized with a start that she was lost. She didn't know what story came next. The first lesson, then Stacy Klein. The second lesson, the second visit to Stacy Klein. Sidney had just finished the third lesson. What came after that? The fourth? No, there was something before, but for the life of her, she couldn't recall what it was.

What happened after the third lesson? Any special events? Rivkah had caught some of Moshe's discomfort. She didn't know the source of it. She suspected it had something to do with not having children, but when she raised the subject with Moshe, he was not willing to talk about it. End of story.

When Sidney asked the students to stand, stretch, and said they would continue down in the study, Stephanie had the answer to both of her questions—what the story was, and why she didn't remember.

The story was all about Sidney.

Sidney had already introduced himself into the body of the stories because of his interaction with Moshe during the lessons. Sidney liked to be a player, no matter the situation. He asked sharp questions or made pointed remarks that intimated that he, Sidney, somehow knew more than the speaker. Stephanie hated that.

Sidney often did know, if not as much as the lecturer, a significant amount. He prepared for a lecture as he would for an exam, reading up on the subject and the speaker as well. Even for a performance Sidney prepared, listening to recordings, reading old articles and reviews.

Sidney had a story to convey about how he, Sidney, had become an intimate of Moshe the kabbalist. She had heard his story only once, in the living room, during an early cycle. Perhaps Sidney felt her disdain, for thereafter he moved that story to the study, out of her hearing.

This time she was a participant. She was as prepared for Sidney's story as she would be for an exam. She knew the subject and the speaker well. She was ready.

God help Sidney, she thought.

Sidney assembled the students in the kitchen before descending to the study. "It was my first visit to this house," he said.

"It was our first visit," Stephanie corrected.

Sidney seemed surprised by the interruption. He continued, "Moshe had given me good directions, even to the point of telling me where it was safe to turn around should I pass by the entrance. I had resolved not to miss the turn from the road, but did so anyway. It is difficult to find the turn at night.

"I remember being concerned about where to park, so as not to obstruct the two vehicles in the carport. I remember how the red and purple streamed through the stained-glass window. That was the only illumination at the entrance. The lamp in the fixture by the door was out.

"The kilim rug in the foyer was the same as it is now. He warned me to be careful of my footing . . ."

"He warned us," Stephanie interrupted again.

"He warned us. He brought us not through the living room, but here into the kitchen. Rivkah asked if we wanted anything to drink. I wasn't thirsty."

Sidney paused. When Stephanie had nothing to add, he said, "The kitchen was not as orderly as we see it now. Some of these pans"—Sidney indicated the copper saucepans hanging from the rack above the butcher block island—"were in the drain on the board resting on top of the evening dishes. I complimented Rivkah and Moshe on their beautiful home. They received the compliment graciously."

Sidney looked about to be certain all the students were present.

"Then Moshe and I descended to his study, and that's where we'll continue."

In a queue they descended the stairs. Sidney indicated appropriate places to sit. Some found folding chairs, some the floor. None sat in the chair before the large desk, or in any of the three chairs around the table. Sidney chose one of them for himself. Stephanie sat in the corner, on the carpet, near the far bookcase.

"Moshe taught that one learns of a creator through his creation. I recall my first impressions of this room. It was much as you see it now. The charts may be different"—Sidney indicated the wall of corkboard covered with bar charts—"but the impression was essentially the same. The bookcase was as empty as you see it now, one shelf of poetry, mostly Walt Whitman, another with texts on technical analysis of markets. The desk was clean. The curtains drawn back from the windows, just as you see them. The brush outside was thicker, pressed in almost to the glass.

"On this wall"—Sidney indicated the bare grass cloth behind him—"there used to be a painting. I paid little attention to it at first. The charts intrigued me more. And the books, or rather the lack thereof. And the globe. And the large monitor on the desk. I was making guesses, learning as much as I could from the impression of the room."

Sidney closed his eyes and raised the tone of his voice slightly to indicate the shift from narrative to story.

"What can I do for you, Sidney?" Moshe began.

If I had known what he could do for me, or even been able to articulate what I wanted of him, I would have done so. I wasn't at all certain why I was there, so I spoke about the room instead. "I expected perhaps a map of the *sefirot*," indicating the bar charts of market performance. Some were printed, some drawn by hand.

Moshe said nothing.

I turned around to examine the painting. It was a powerful piece by an artist I did not know. A triptych, a pieta in the middle, two women instead of Mary and Jesus, both nude, one with a hint of wings comforting the other. To the right, another woman on a field of blue, also nude, emerging as if from a cocoon. To the left, the same woman inverted, on a field of red, as if being crushed by the cocoon. Rikvah didn't like the painting. You can still see on the wallpaper where it used to be.

I found the work challenging and told Moshe so.

Moshe said nothing. He let his sandals fall and pulled his jeans-covered legs up to the edge of his chair. He embraced his knees with both arms. "What can I do for you, Sidney?" he repeated.

"I don't know."

"What do you know?"

He wasn't making it easy for me, but then I deserved that. "I'm sorry if I make the classes difficult for you. I don't mean to."

He laughed. "Of course you mean to. You go to a lot of trouble just so you will be able to. What Kabbalah do you know? Where did you learn?"

"I know very little," I confessed. "I had an introduction to the Kabbalah through a mutual friend, Rabbi Hayim Ostracher."

"You know Reb Hayim?" Moshe was surprised.

"It's not so much that I know him. I met him once, heard him speak. He mentioned your name, but you had already stopped teaching." Suddenly I knew what it was I wanted. "I want to travel," I said.

"Reb Hayim told you how I use that word?"

"Yes."

"Why would you want to travel?"

I couldn't answer at once and was thankful he did not press me. When the silence stretched on, he said almost in a whisper, "Out loud, Sidney. Think out loud. It doesn't have to make sense. Just start, out loud."

"I want to travel," I repeated, curious to see what words would come next. "I want to . . . I need to . . ." I knew what he wanted me to do, to surrender to the process, to let the reasons surface, one after the other. Too much of my intellect stood in the way.

"I want to, I need to," he repeated, encouraging me to continue.

"I need to . . ." I closed my eyes. That made it easier. "I need to . . . know. I need to . . . learn. I'm hurting." The word surprised me. "I need to know why I'm hurting. I'm hurting, and I don't know why."

When I opened my eyes, he was looking at me, beyond me, not seeing me. He was pondering. I was hurting, and he was pondering. I had no choice but to wait.

"Where are you coming from?" he asked when his attention returned.

I didn't know quite what to answer. "Hong Kong, originally," I said. I wanted to please him, to answer accurately. I hadn't been aware until that moment how much I wanted his help. "I was born into a privileged family in Hong Kong. Educated in London. My father was sent to London by the family."

"Sent?"

"An old family with many interests, preparing for the time when Hong Kong would revert to Chinese rule. My father was sent to London, his brother to Los Angeles. Other family members were sent to Canada, Australia, Mexico." I wondered if that answered where I was coming from.

"My mother died when I was fifteen. An automobile accident. At sixteen I went off to college. Is this what you want to know?" He didn't answer. I continued. "The family was preparing me. I was being groomed to remain in London, to supervise the business there. At eighteen I left."

"Left what?" he asked.

"Left everything. Left college. Left the family. Left England. I came back to England and college, but not the family. I chose to study literature. The family had other things in mind for me. That's when I met Stephanie. I took my degree in literature, then followed her to America. She taught at a prep school in Boston. I learned psychology, anthropology. We had children. We had fun.

"We needed money. I went to work for Freeman March. Do you know what Freeman March does? It runs businesses all over the world. I have lots of languages and a business sense bred into me. I did well, got a Harvard MBA, courtesy of the company. Five years ago they moved us here. I was head of North American operations. I sat in an office about four times the size of this room, in a corner of the top floor. Managers brought me their problems. They had problems because they weren't sitting high enough to see the resources available. Usually the solution was no more complicated than moving inventory from one shelf to another.

"I left the company three years ago, retired. I study. I search. I'm not sure what I'm looking for. I realized only a few minutes ago that I am hurting." When the silence became uncomfortable, I added, "That's where I'm coming from."

Stephanie had barely moved as Sidney was speaking. This was not the story he had told months before in the living room. That story had been different in content and tone. Sidney was not hurting in that story. He was bored. He had been there, done that. He had come to learn the Kabbalah because he had already learned everything else. He may not have said so in as many words, but that was the impression his story gave.

That Sidney was hurting was news to Stephanie. Had he been hurting when he sat that first time with Moshe? Or was he hurting now? Or both?

"You make your time at Freeman March sound so easy," Stephanie interrupted. She wasn't going to let him off without some challenge. "You worked your ass off at Freeman March. You fought your way to the top floor. It didn't come easily."

"That's true, too," Sidney said. He turned from her back to his story.

Moshe didn't say anything. Either he was using his silence to provoke me into deeper revelations or he was somewhere else. I waited with him and used the time to examine the room more closely. The bookcase was almost empty, Walt Whitman and a few objects.

"Why Whitman?" I asked.

"Whitman is what involves me at the moment, the evolution of *Leaves of Grass*. The rest of our poetry is upstairs in the library. I keep here only what I'm working on."

308

"No Kabbalah?"

He shrugged. "In the library upstairs. I keep here only what I'm working on."

Again we played our waiting game. This time I sensed that he was waiting to see what else I would notice in the room. "You're active in the markets?" I asked.

"The charts? Beans, oil, and meal."

"Soybeans," I said, to let him know I knew what he was talking about.

"Do you speculate in the markets, Sidney?"

"No, Moshe, I don't. Stephanie manages our finances."

He seemed interested in Stephanie, wanted to know what she did, what she was learning in the class. Again our dialogue lapsed into silence. He was better at silence than I was.

One set of charts seemed out of place. They were drawn by hand. "What are these?" I asked. From his reaction it seemed I had asked a profound question.

"Those are my own analyses of certain spreads. I could have the computer run them for me, but sometimes I find it better to do it myself. My focus is better. Drawing them out like that is a meditation in itself. It makes me more a part of the market."

I stood to examine them more closely. "I see. And this one here?"

Moshe paused. After this there would be no return. "That's a chart of CA125, Sidney."

"I'm not familiar with that market, Moshe."

"It's not a market. It's a marker for a tumor. It's the plot of the progress of a cancer."

I was overwhelmed. I had to sit.

"You?" I asked when I was able.

"No. My wife. Rivkah," Moshe answered.

"So that's what's going on," I said.

"Rivie has been in remission from ovarian cancer for years. I've been plotting the data, watching it from month to month. I don't know that it's active. I only suspect."

"She doesn't know?"

"Even I don't know," Moshe snapped. "I only suspect, and I'm not going to share a suspicion with her when there's no purpose in it." Moshe stood to pull the chart and another from the wall. "Do you see this one? This is November beans. You must be familiar with charts like these, Sidney. What do you see?"

I examined it. "Nothing. It looks like a random walk."

"Between here and here," Moshe said, stabbing at two points, "I made $18,000. I don't know exactly how I do it. I surrender to the chart. I don't observe the market; I become the market. I'm not always right. Maybe two-thirds of the time. Less than that. But it's enough to acquire the occasional Nicastri." He nodded toward the painting behind me.

He laid the CA125 chart on the coffee table. "Now this one. It also looks like a random walk. The oncologist thinks so. She thinks I'm nuts. But what I sense here makes me most uncomfortable."

"This has something to do with your teaching the course?"

Moshe nodded. "Yes. I'm hedging the market. I'm teaching the class just in case."

"I understand the urgency now," I said. "But I don't understand what it is you hope to gain by teaching."

Moshe sat back in his chair, drew up his knees, and embraced them again before answering. "It's not so much what I gain by teaching, Sidney. It's what Rivkah may gain by being in the class. She knows bits and pieces of what I do, but she's never had the opportunity to experience it. Ever since my student days she has been resistant to Jewish spirituality. I can't teach her directly. The class is an indirect way of giving her the foundation she may need, I may need, if at some time . . ." Moshe paused to rephrase his response. "If she should be ill, there may be something we can do together. I'm teaching so she'll have the foundation, just in case."

I processed that, considering my best response. "So, what should we do together? How can I be of help to you?"

There were many other questions I might have asked, Moshe knew. I might have asked what it was Moshe intended to do, what kabbalistic magic he intended to perform, should Rivkah become ill. Such a line of questioning was obvious. It wasn't that I didn't want to know, but I suppressed my curiosity, asking instead what I could do to be of help.

"How deep is your knowledge, Sidney?" Moshe asked me in return. "What have you learned in the Kabbalah?"

"I've read Scholem and Idel," I said. "They've provided a good academic foundation. Steinsaltz for *Ma-aseh Beraysheet*. And for the meditative disciplines, Aryeh Kaplan. I don't have the Hebrew for the Hasidic texts, or the *hechalot* literature you have studied."

Moshe nodded, accepting the foundation as adequate. "In the next few weeks I'll develop the framework of the *hechalot* in the class. If we should do some work together, one on one, it would be good for you to have that framework first. You've learned something about the *sefirot* from Reb Hayim?" I nodded. "It's good you are learning them from me as well. My understanding is somewhat different. The more balance you will have, the better."

"So when shall we begin?"

"Next week. Do the class on the *hechalot* with me, and we'll begin, one on one."

Rivkah and Stephanie were sitting in the kitchen when we ascended from the lower level. Rivkah looked at us, and said, "It looks like the two of you made some progress."

"Yes," I agreed. "We have done very nicely. Your husband is a remarkable man."

She was an attractive woman, dressed in a beige cashmere sweater and jeans. She gave every appearance of being in good health.

Stephanie thought the story had improved with telling, but it still had a way to go. She saw Sidney lean forward to stand, but stopped him with her words.

"Let's stay here," she said. "I have a story to tell. It took place in the kitchen upstairs, but there's not enough room there for all of us. While Sidney and Moshe were talking down here, Rivie and I had coffee in the kitchen."

Sidney sat back, waiting. Even as she began the story, Stephanie had little idea what it would contain.

I changed my mind concerning a drink and asked Rivkah if she had some decaf coffee. She asked if instant would be okay. Instant was fine with me. Within five minutes Rivkah became Rivie. That's about how long it took.

Before Sidney and Moshe climbed back up the stairs we knew everything about each other. I knew where she was from, her schools, her hopes and ambitions. I knew about the congregation in New Jersey and the troubles in New York, her illness and recovery, her marriage and her work. I knew how much she had wanted children, and why she didn't want to adopt.

Rivkah knew I was raised in Miami, went to Tufts on a scholarship, how I met Sidney during my junior year abroad. She knew about Allison and Ada, wanted to know everything about them and their husbands. She had been in the audience when Allison and Alexi had performed in San Francisco the year before. I was so sorry I hadn't known her then, to invite her to the reception afterward. I told her about Ada and Simon. They were together in medical school in Rochester. They were all away, all the children, far away.

She knew I was estranged from my parents, as Sidney was estranged from his. She was so sorry for that. She was so close to her parents, her sister, and couldn't imagine what it was like to be without family.

I wasn't without family, I told her. I had Allison and Ada and Alexi and Simon. My family spread forward, not backward. And it spread out, to Rochester and New York. Spread forward, spread out, but still family.

I learned about Moshe, how independent he was, resisting definition. Sidney had been like that, too. We were attracted to our men for the same reasons.

We talked about those things, but not right away. First we talked about the course, why we were there and doing that. I was there because of Sidney, and I didn't know why Sidney was there. She was there because of Moshe, and she didn't know why Moshe was there. That was the immediate bond. We had that in common.

But what we didn't have in common was that her relationship with Moshe was getting better with the years. When Moshe left the congregation, the uppercase rabbinate, though that's not the way she said it then, the barriers that had grown between them began to come down, and each year now was better than the last.

With me it was just the opposite. When Sidney left Freeman March, only then did barriers seem to come up. We used to do things together, outlandish things. It was an outlandish thing for this girl from Miami Beach and that guy from Hong Kong to get together to begin with. We had wonderful kids and did wonderful things. Freeman March was fun and challenging. We made lots of money. And then Sidney left. Moshe got fired, or voted out, whatever it was. But Sidney left, like it wasn't worthy of him anymore. He had outgrown it.

I think he became afraid of it.

Just when I began taking flying lessons, Sidney became afraid, like a ghost had found him. Maybe that's what it was. A ghost. Freeman March was going to expand their Asian operations. Sidney would have been a natural. They would have sent him. He couldn't have refused. So he dropped out of Freeman March the way a kid drops out of college. We used to fly gliders and scuba dive. We haven't scuba dived in I don't know how many years. But we go to lectures and take courses. That's what we do. We run from ghosts.

I never knew that before.

So Rivkah and I, Rivie and Steffie, had instant coffee and became instant friends. We talked childhoods and husbands. I didn't know why Sidney was taking the course, she didn't know why Moshe was teaching. We were there because of our husbands. We had that in common.

Stephanie had raced through the story. The wake of her own words washed over her. Was that really what had happened in the kitchen with Rivie? They had coffee and become friends, that much she knew. Had they really talked through all of that in such a short time? She couldn't remember.

But it was a necessary story. Sidney wanted the students to know how he and Moshe became friends. They should know also how she and Rivie became friends. But there was more in the story than that.

There was the children, how much she missed them. They didn't need her anymore. Allison and Alexi were on tour, Ada and Simon at medical school. They stayed in touch, but they were gone.

And there was stuff about Sidney she had never put into words before, stuff she had let burst out of its case and only after realized Sidney was present and listening. And stuff about herself, too. Stuff. Pillow-pounding stuff, not material to unravel in front of strangers.

They were both running from ghosts.

They were doing it differently, Sidney escaping inside, in systems of speculation and meditation, and she escaping outside, on motorcycles and airplanes.

Was she correct? It seemed right to her in the moment she said it, but she wasn't sure. She wasn't sure that her story was a story at all. When did a statement, a protest, an exclamation, become a story?

Sidney said, "Let's go upstairs."

CHAPTER 12

Only a Jest

Back in the living room after a short break Sidney said, "I arrived early for the fourth lesson, but Moshe had arrived before me. He was in the bookstore, examining a volume on witchcraft. I asked him what he was looking for. He answered without looking up. 'Magic. Do you believe in magic, Sidney?'

"'Moshe,' I answered, 'I wish I knew what I believed.'

"After he returned the book to the shelf, he said, 'They have more books here on magic than on mysticism. Have you noticed that? Given a choice between magic and mysticism, magic wins every time, at least in bookshelf space. Magic sells.'

"'How do you define magic?' I asked him.

"He answered without the slightest hesitation. 'Magic is the illusion of producing a profound effect without any appropriate cause.' And anticipating my next question he continued, 'And mystical discipline? Mystical discipline is the achievement of a profound effect through an appropriate cause. I just made that up, Sidney, so I wouldn't take it too seriously. Still, if you offer people a choice between illusion and achievement, most will take illusion. Achievement comes at too high a cost in time and energy.'

"When I told him he seemed cynical, he responded, 'I haven't taught any magic yet, have I Sidney? Most of your classmates came here to learn magic, not mysticism.'

"Moshe was on edge. He was about to venture into Princeton material, and the definition between magic and mysticism would become very fine."

Moshe's demeanor was focused and stern. "If you would take out a piece of paper, please, we'll have a quiz." The students looked at each other in confusion. "You think just because there are no grades here that there are no examinations? Take out a piece of paper please. Put your name at the top of it. Put your review sheets and all notes away."

314

He closed his eyes as he walked. "There will be six questions. Number one: What is the Hebrew name for the *sefirah* which means strength or constancy? Number two: What is the correct translation of the Hebrew word *Hesed*? Number three . . ."

"Stop!" "Wait!" "You're going too fast!"

He turned on his heel, searching for the questioners. "Let me repeat, then. Two. What is the correct translation of *Hesed*? Three. What is the name for the balance point between *Hod* and *Netzach*? Four . . ." He paused, waiting for the slower students to catch up. When all eyes were on him in anticipation of the fourth question, he said, "I guess three is enough. Don't bother turning them in. You can grade your own paper."

After the collective sigh, Moshe asked, "The answer to number one is . . . ?"

"*Gevurah,*" several of the students responded.

"Very good. The correct translation of *Hesed* is?"

"Love." "Kindness." "Mercy."

"Also good. Except maybe for love. I'd apply the word love to *Tiferet*. But you are free to do it differently. The truth is I don't know what the correct translation of *Hesed* is, so whatever you put down is all right. And if you didn't put down anything, even better. The answer to number three? What was number three? I forget."

Dr. Plotkin reminded him. "The balance point between *Hod* and *Netzach*."

"Right. The answer is?"

"*Yesod,*" Dr. Plotkin said.

"Also right. Give yourself an A. All of you, give yourselves A's. You've acquired some understanding of the nature of the *sefirot*. Mind you it's a limited understanding. It's my understanding. It's actually my understanding of the *sefirot* from six years ago, which was the last time I taught a course like this. I remember how I taught it then, and it was easier to repeat than to design a new way of teaching it. Will you forgive me? Will you forgive me for giving you a quiz? Thank you."

Moshe turned to the blackboard and sketched the sefirotic tree. He filled in the names quickly. If the students did not already have those names neatly written on their review sheets, Moshe's writing would have been indecipherable. "This *sefirah,* above *Gevurah,* which all of you knew to be the Hebrew for strength, judgment, and constancy, is labeled *Binah. Binah* here means *understanding.*

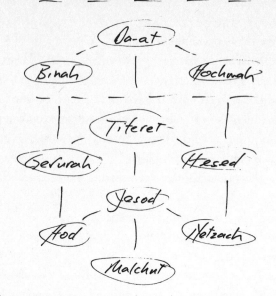

"Now I gave you the quiz for a reason. Since you all got A's in the quiz, you all have some understanding of the *sefirot*. Your *Binah* concerning the *sefirot* has been activated to some degree. How much wisdom you have of the *sefirot* I don't know. That wasn't measured in the quiz. The quiz was a test of understanding only, not wisdom."

Moshe drew a line from *Binah* to a circle above *Hesed*. He tapped it and said, "This is *Hochmah*. *Hochmah* means *wisdom*. Wisdom might be understood to be an intuitive grasp of the concepts. If I were to give you a quiz to examine your *Hochmah* of the lower seven *sefirot,* I might ask you to write a poem about them. Or to tell a story about them. Maybe a story about a little girl who wanted to say the *Sh'ma*."

Moshe drew a circle on the third level between *Binah* and *Hochmah* and labeled it *Da-at*. "Da-at." He pronounced it with the accent on the first syllable. "Operative knowledge. To have *Da-at* of the sefirotic tree, you must have both *Binah* and *Hochmah* of the sefirotic tree, and it must have become an operative system within you, as second nature to you as walking. If you have *Da-at* of the seven lower *sefirot,* you look at anything and everything in the world and see it spread across this entire spectrum. When you start seeing the world this way, when these balance beams become part of your operating system, part of your assembly language, part of your worldview, then and only then do you have *Da-at* of them.

"Now I draw a dotted line here separating the seven below from the three above, because it's easier to talk about these lower seven. The higher you go, the more words fail. See for yourself.

"*Malchut* is identified with the World of Action, where you walk around. That's easy to talk about. It's what you are doing.

"*Hod, Yesod, Netzach.* The World of Formation. How you feel about yourself. It's more difficult to describe with accuracy, but you can get your point across.

"*Gevurah, Tiferet, Hesed.* The World of Creation. It's where you parent. Where you create. The person you are sharing with has to know your frame of reference.

"And then *Binah, Da-at, Hochmah.* Your consciousness, your very being. The World of Emanation. How do you share that? The essence of what you are?

"And there is a higher level still that is beyond the scope of this class. *Keter.* Crown. And then you find words like *Ayn Sof,* which means *without limit.* Beyond space and time. The transcendent.

"The higher I go, the deeper I go, the more likely I am to use a word list rather than a single word. No single word is adequate."

Moshe looked from one blank face to the next. "It's all right," he said. "You don't need to know the vocabulary for where we're going. I'll give you the tools you will need when we get there. Don't be concerned." After a pause he added one more word: "Yet."

Under Pressure

Sidney said, "As soon as he sat beside her, Rivkah reached for Moshe's hand to settle him down. 'It will be all right,' she told him. 'Sing a *niggun,* and it will be all right.'

"Together they observed the study pairs. One student sat alone in the corner. Rivkah was the first to recognize Emily. 'It doesn't look like her,' Moshe said, but Rivkah was sure of it.

"'I thought that was a man sitting there,' Moshe said.

"'It's not a man. It's Emily,' Rivkah insisted. 'Something's going on, but I don't know what it is. I'll take care of her. You concentrate on your teaching.'

317

"Moshe began with a *niggun,* slow and plaintive. He monitored his breathing and left behind the rush of the day. His intent was to open windows of opportunity. That was very different from taking advantage of a window of opportunity already opened.

"When Moshe had visited Stacy in the Addiction Treatment Unit, her window of opportunity was open. Maybe the shutters were closed, but she was ready for change. Moshe did not have to do much work. And if his work failed, she did not have far to fall. She was already at her bottom.

"But for the students in the class, most of us were functioning well. Our windows of opportunity were closed. Moshe was about to use his teaching to open them, or at the very least to create the possibility of their opening, and here, if something went wrong, there was considerable risk. We had a long way to fall.

"It takes courage to step through an open window on the fourth floor. Moshe had no doubt that some of us were up to the task and would attempt it. He had been building a safety net for us through the study pairs, but he still had a few more precautions to take."

Moshe ended the *niggun* with an extended exhale, a long vowel, then a cleansing breath which emitted no sound.

"Okay, my friends, we begin. You have enough of the vocabulary to get started, so let us start. Make sure, please, you have your buddy at hand. We're going into the water." The atmosphere within the room had changed palpably.

"Who here is a certified scuba diver?" he asked as he raised his hand. Rivkah raised hers, and Norman, Stephanie, and I followed suit. "It's time to talk about *Ma-aseh Merkavah,* the Work of the Chariot, the Chariot of God. All of our preparation in *Ma-aseh Beraysheet* has been for this purpose. We've learned, in theory at least, the technique of keeping balance, and something of the experience of the worlds. If we compare this to scuba training, what you have learned here is the resort course. You don't get fully certified, but then you don't get to dive anywhere dangerous either. So please, as we begin to get into this, don't go off diving by yourselves. You are responsible for your buddy. Stay close, check in, enjoy the view. Get a sense, if you can, of what is at deeper levels, but don't go deeper until you're fully certified."

He turned to the chalkboard but saw he had already erased it. He pointed to it anyway. "Now, what is all of this for? The sefirotic tree and the worlds. Hopefully they're engraved in your memory as well as written in your notes.

I've already hinted that through meditation on the sefirotic tree, through the extension of this antenna array, one develops a sensitivity. The sensitivity extends through all worlds.

"In the World of Action, colors become sharper; all of the senses are refined. Nuances in the World of Formation, the emotions, feelings, become conscious. A willingness to be open to new ideas in the World of Creation develops. Spiritual charisma, activation in the World of Emanation begins to emerge.

"Balance becomes a key word, balance on the narrow bridge of Reb Nachman's teaching. The greater the balance, the narrower the bridge can be, the greater the exposure you can stand. The greater the exposure, the greater the leverage. The greater the leverage, the greater the potential for huge gains, and huge losses. Balance becomes all important when the exposure becomes great.

"You all know something now about the worlds. You know as you descend into deeper worlds, the nature of space, time, and soul change. It's very much like scuba diving. At least five of us know that time is experienced differently as we descend through the water. The volume of air that might last us for days on the surface lasts only a few hours at twenty feet, only an hour at sixty feet, only twenty minutes at a hundred feet. To bring something to the surface from great depth requires enormous expenditure of energy.

"So it is also in a mystical descent. Two hours on the surface might seem like twenty minutes at even a moderate depth. What you bring to the surface are words, and to lift them requires a great expenditure of energy. It's a lot of work. Sweat and tears. Sometimes blood, sweat, and tears.

"You don't do such work casually. The exposure is great, similar to scuba diving. A small mistake you might be able to recover from at twenty feet, but at a hundred feet the same small mistake might be catastrophic. So it is also in the type of descent I'm about to describe."

Moshe paused to check the room, to be sure he had their attention and their consent. He looked for Emily, but she was gone. He turned to Rivkah with the unspoken question. She answered it with raised hands and a shrug.

Emily remained a mystery.

The Chariot of God

"For this exercise," Moshe said, "you may want to lie on the floor. I don't know if there is space for all of you to do that, but you can use all of the room.

Talk it over with your buddy, decide if you want to do that. You can do the exercise sitting up, if you like, but my guess is that Ezekiel did it lying on his back."

In short order the carpet filled with a random mosaic of sprawled bodies. Only Rivkah remained in her seat, Moshe on his table.

"*Merkavah* mysticism has its beginning with the prophet Ezekiel back in the sixth century before the common era," Moshe began in his teaching voice. He left the table and, as he spoke, made his way from foothold to foothold of carpet, between the bodies, to the light switch by the door. "Ezekiel, along with the leadership of Jerusalem, had been exiled to Babylon. The holy Temple had been destroyed. The people were distraught. It was as if God had deserted them, and said, 'I no longer want you. I don't want your sacrifices. I don't want your worship. I don't want you.' The people turned to their prophet, Ezekiel, with a desperate need to know if God was still with them, even in Babylon.

"So what did Ezekiel do? Perhaps it was early in the morning, just before dawn. Ezekiel went down to the riverbank, said his prayers, opened his heart, cried, lay back on the grass, and looked up into the clouds. There was a strong wind. The clouds appeared to march across the sky with a will of their own. Ezekiel looked up into the clouds and saw figures there."

Moshe lowered the lights. His speech became softer, the pace of his words slower. Each sentence of words was followed by a sentence of silence.

"He saw the face of an eagle.

"The face of a lion.

"The face of an ox.

"And the face of a man.

"The eagle became the lion.

"The lion the ox.

"The ox the man.

"And the man again the eagle.

"He saw all four at once.

"He saw them with hooves and wings.

"They were angelic forms. They scooped him up and carried him.

"In the center of his vision was a hint of blue, a blue so brilliant, it pulled him toward it.

"Surrounding that distant blue, a wheel, a circle rimmed with eyes.

"As he entered the wheel, the eyes penetrated him.

"They searched and seared every element of his being.

320

"They burned away his body so only his soul remained to vault into the blue.

"There it was buffeted by lightning.

"It was driven under a throne so large it seemed a mountain suspended above his head.

"Below was a cobalt blue and above a brass that burned like fire.

"Higher still were all the colors of the spectrum, so bright they drove his senses away."

Moshe progressed through the vision. He did not lie down, but did the meditation sitting, eyes half-opened. As he experienced the meditation, he spoke it. The words described not some possible experience, but his own experience. The words encouraged others to follow, to share in his process. Because the words came from experience, and not the experience from the words, every word he said was inscribed with truth and certainty. The words had power.

When they ceased, each student followed his or her own path. He did not leave us alone for long, but began to speak softly in his teacher's voice. "The rabbis speculated why Ezekiel ever wrote of his vision. Visions are usually private. They are not shared. The results of the vision may be made public, but rarely the experience itself. My guess is this was a message for us that it is still possible to access the presence of God, even when we are in exile. It was reassuring to the community then, and it is reassuring to us today. If you would be kind enough now to work your way to the surface, check in with your body and then with your buddy, and do some sharing."

"A circle rimmed with eyes."

That was enough to throw Stephanie back into her story. She followed Ezekiel's progression through the circle and phrased a question that made no sense to her.

"Where did you keep the diamonds, Mama? Where did you keep the diamonds?"

Sometimes the papers were not enough, a diamond was necessary. Her mother excused herself from the platform, returned with a diamond, which she passed to her father.

"Where did you keep the diamonds, Mama?"

Moshe continued his teaching. "A puzzle," he said. "A paradox. Who will see it?

"The Temple was rebuilt. Some five hundred years after Ezekiel, the Temple was destroyed again. Worship by sacrifice was no longer possible, so the rabbis developed another discipline, based on Ezekiel's vision, to bring themselves into the presence of God."

On the chalkboard Moshe wrote: *DESCENT, ENCOUNTER, RECONCILIATION, TRANSFORMATION.*

"These four words describe the stages of the *merkavah* process, the Work of the Chariot. Using meditative techniques, these mystics descended through the worlds to approach an inner temple. The size of the temple would be large, awesome. At the gate of the temple there were angels, usually more then one, and usually in multiples of four.

"These angels are not cute little valentine cherubs with bows and arrows. These angels are like Ezekiel's wheel rimmed with eyes. These angels are like the *heruv*," he used the Hebrew for cherub, a more threatening word in Hebrew than in English, "at the Garden of Eden that brandished a fiery sword in all directions. These angels are not something easy to encounter.

"After doing the work of the confrontation with the angels, after reaching some kind of reconciliation with them, access is gained to the door of the temple. Inside, one finds another temple, bigger than the first, with still more angels at its door. The process is repeated, and then repeated again. One goes from encounter to encounter, from temple to temple, each one bigger and more awesome than the last. Tradition has it that there are seven temples, the last one leading to an experience similar to Ezekiel's. This last temple is given as an act of grace. It's as if God himself sends out a coach and four to bring you home.

"That's the framework. What's the paradox?"

It was Norman who raised his hand. "What is contained cannot be greater than the container," he said. "The temple inside the temple cannot be bigger than the original temple."

"That's it!" Moshe seemed surprised anyone had found the paradox so quickly. "But we're not talking about buildings in the World of Action, Doctor. There aren't any physical buildings here. Imagine it like this. Imagine there was something threatening inside of you that was walled off from you, so you didn't have to confront it. It might be something you were not able to handle, some recognition about yourself you weren't ready to cope with. A temporary amnesia to block off something traumatic . . ."

Moshe stopped mid-sentence. He understood what was happening with Emily, but too late. It had been there for him to see, and he had missed it. Emily was gone. What would he do if she returned?

He collected himself and continued with his response. "Let's say you were able to descend to that place and recognize something had been walled off within you. You encounter it, confront it, ultimately reconcile yourself with it. The gate opens. Memories flood in. The walls disappear. Now the universe is larger to you, from your new situation looking out. Your temple is bigger.

"When you look in deeper, you see another matter that has not been reconciled. This matter is more powerful than the first. If it weren't, you would have confronted it first. The very fact it comes second means it is more difficult to resolve than the first. If you had come upon it first, it might have overwhelmed you. Now, however, since you have been tempered and strengthened by the first experience, since all that energy is now free for use, you can bring it to bear on the second temple. And then the third, and the fourth and the fifth. Each one is greater in magnitude than the one before."

The doctor interrupted, "I'm not a psychiatrist, but I think you are talking about something like psychoanalysis."

"There's no conflict there, Doctor. Remember, Freud was Jewish." That drew a laugh from the class. Moshe continued, "The system I'm describing is indeed similar to analysis, but it goes beyond a conventional analysis. It is more than a descent into the unconscious. Only so many of the inner temples relate to the personal unconscious, or the World of Formation as we might call it here. The inner temples are in the realm of the World of Creation.

"What might these temples look like? They might appear as theologies. Theologies limit one's experience of the divine, because every expressible theology is wrong. That's one of the dangers of this work. People may have a lot invested in a given theology. Ultimately, that theology will be exploded."

Moshe checked the room for damage before continuing.

"Do you really think it is possible for us to express in human words that which can contain the Creator of the universe? That we can use human words and human concepts to confine the Divine? In the process of descent, we are disabused of such notions one by one. One theology is replaced by another and then by another. The reason the last temple comes as an act of grace is that there is no way we could achieve it by ourselves. It is beyond words! It is beyond definition! It is beyond us as humans! We are brought into and engulfed by the Divine!"

Moshe stopped. He stopped talking, stopped moving. After that last word, there was nowhere to go. He needed to retreat and begin again. Before doing so, he asked us to learn with our study partners the framework of the temples.

The Bodies of Angels

Stephanie said, "Moshe had been teaching with such passion, he seemed so exhausted, Rivie rose from her chair to help him into his seat. Before she could say anything, he raised his hand.

"'If Emily comes back,' he said, 'go sit next to her. Tell her I care for her, that the rabbi is really concerned for her. She probably won't respond, but be sure to tell her that. If she leaves the room, let her go. Don't go after her.'

"Rivkah asked if he thought Emily was dangerous. Moshe was cryptic in his response. 'Not Emily,' he said. 'Not Emily.'

Sidney added that the mood of the class was subdued. When Moshe returned to his table he did not need a *niggun* to quiet the exchange between study partners. After a few swings of his legs the class was attentive and ready.

"Moshe was teaching the class about the role of angels," Stephanie said. "But, just in case, he was also preparing Rivie for a possible encounter with Emily."

"You hear the word *defense* a lot in psychology," Moshe began. "We defend ourselves against awareness of this or that. We might imagine a fence put in place to keep us from this awareness. What is that fence made of? What does it look like?

"If we were to make a fence to keep an enemy away in the World of Action, it might be made of steel or heavy wooden beams. In the Worlds of Formation and Creation, the fence is made up of the bodies of angels.

"Do you remember the angel, the *heruv,* that stands outside the Garden of Eden? That's a fence in the World of Creation.

"The fences we have within ourselves are no less dramatic. Perhaps we experience something traumatic, something that might overwhelm us. In our model, the life of the whole organism is more important than the existence of any one part. That part of our experience that might overwhelm us is fenced off from us. An angel, more likely a band of angels, flies in and positions itself between our greater self and the experience, and we are defended against it.

"Angels have a very single-minded purpose. A defensive angel is there only to defend and will not move away until it sees its purpose is no longer required. It will stay there forever, if necessary. But what happens is that the organism that needed the defense at an earlier stage in its growth might no longer need it at a later stage. But the angel is still there defending. Keeping it there is consuming a lot of your energy and impeding your growth. You would like it to go away, but how do you get it to go away?

"The way to let it go is to descend to the level of the angel, to equalize the pressure on both sides. The angel has to be encountered on the level at which it is. No amount of looking down on it from above will work. You descend down to the level of the angel. The angel looks at you. You look at it. You can probably see in the appearance and demeanor of the angel some hint of what is behind it. The angel sees you can handle the pressure at that depth. Hopefully you really can handle it. If you can't, you are in some danger. But assuming you can, with pressure the same on both sides, the angel is free to leave. Remember, the angel came at first not to impair you but to save you. So you let it go with appreciation, with thanks for doing its job.

"This is what happens in the encounter process after the descent."

Norman's voice was loudest and most insistent, so it was his question that was heard. "How real is the danger, rabbi? How real can such danger be?"

Sharks

"Moshe weighed the tone of the question," Sidney said, "to determine if it was a challenge or a serious inquiry. He determined the balance to be in favor of inquiry, so he chose to respond."

"Doctor, you know what would happen if you should be scuba diving and ascend from depth while holding your breath?"

"The air in my chest would expand. I would embolize and die," Norman answered objectively.

"You would blow your lungs out," Moshe interpreted a bit more graphically. "The danger here is something like that. You impose something from one depth upon another. You hold a notion so strongly in the World of Action you carry it with you into the Worlds of Formation and Creation. Or you have a dogma you adhere to so strongly you fail to recognize what is happening and interpret danger where there is none. An imagined danger down there is as perilous as a real danger. Or you do not see danger where the danger is real, and there are real dangers. Going down too deep, for example. In scuba diving you get nitrogen narcosis, lose all sense of where you are, and you keep going down until you are crushed to death. There's the potential for that to happen here as well in the *merkavah* descent."

Norman was not satisfied. "Rabbi, you'll forgive me. I understand what might happen, or I think I understand what might happen if a person dives too deeply. What I don't quite understand yet is what it means to hold a notion or a dogma in such a way that it will damage you."

Moshe swung his legs deliberately. "First, an analogy. Scuba diving again. A novice diver is down a hundred feet exploring a wreck. He sees a dark shape looming up behind him, and he imagines it's a shark. He reacts in panic, bolts upward, smashes his face mask against the overhead, breaks the glass. Water rushes in. The panic is compounded. He races for the surface, holds his breath, and blows his lungs out. Or, as you say, he embolizes, and he dies.

"What he didn't know was that the shadow was not a shark. It was nothing more than a loose plank moving in the current, or in the eddy left by his own movement through the water. The false notion is what led to his panic and untimely demise. He descended with a fear of sharks, and sharks are what he encountered.

"Since you are a certified diver, Doctor, I doubt you have a significant fear of sharks. Some respect for sharks, maybe, but not a fear. You could make such a dive safely and return safely."

Moshe addressed the nondivers in the class. "The incidence of shark attacks on submerged divers is minuscule. Dr. Plotkin knows that. The scenario I have been describing would not have happened to him. But it would happen to you, if for some reason you were diving with your lack of experience at that depth."

Another Jest

"Let me give you an example of a false notion that could prove fatal at depth, and it's a false notion most of us hold here in this room. The best way for me to illustrate it is with a little test. Ready?"

326

Moshe was astonished when students began to reach for paper and pencil.

"No. Please. Not that kind of test. The quiz earlier was only to illustrate the difference between *Binah* and *Hochmah*. This will be an oral quiz. We can all take it together.

"I'm going to say a word. Please respond with the opposite. Nothing fancy. Straightforward. A word and its opposite."

Moshe said, "Up." The class responded, "Down."

Moshe said, "In." The class responded, "Out."

Moshe said, "Beginning." The class responded, "Ending."

Moshe said, "Good." Most responded, "Bad." Some said, "Evil."

Moshe said, "Life." The class responded, "Death."

"That's enough," he said. "You see? There's a false notion. On the surface it's trivial. At depth it can be fatal." He paused rhetorically. "Ah, you still don't see it. The opposite of life isn't death. Life itself does not admit an opposite. Life has a beginning and an ending. The ending of life is called death. The beginning of life is called . . . ?"

"Birth," the class filled in the blank.

"Yes, the opposite of death is birth, and the opposite of birth is death. They are the two extremes of the time span of a life. But the opposite of life is no more death than the opposite of life is birth.

"Do you understand? To make death the opposite of life is to empower the notion of death with the same vitality, the same force and energy one attaches to life. But life is a real process. It is empirical. It is palpable. It is the participation of soul in space and time. The emergence of soul we call birth; its departure we call death."

Moshe paused after "death." The word was spoken in the World of Creation. It was an idea, a notion, a concept that hung in the air. Moshe was fearful lest he allow it to descend and become an object of fear. He was afraid to look at Rivkah lest the word attach to her. He singled out Norman for the argument, to keep the "death" at a distance.

"We talk a lot about death as if it were an entity, but it's not an entity. It's a name which is attached to the terminal process of living.

"What happens if we descend, a *merkavah* descent now, not a scuba dive, with a false notion concerning an independent power of death? We may see a shadow looming behind us, assume it is the Angel of Death or some such demonic power, panic, and do the equivalent of blowing out our lungs."

Moshe paused to emphasize his next words, forcing himself fully back into the World of Creation. "Let me make this a little clearer. Any time we separate a polarity and consider one pole an independent entity, we are in danger. The danger may be mostly semantic in the World of Action, but at depth it can be lethal. Notions of good and evil are the primary offenders. If you hold a dualistic approach to reality, that there are separate forces of good and evil, you are in grave danger at depth. That fallacy will do more than create semantic problems. It leads minimally to confusion in the World of Action and maximally to horrors."

"Horrors?" Norman asked, jarred to speech by the unexpected word. "What kind of horrors?"

"Murder. Rape. Genocide. Ritual actions to appease or gain power over the gods of evil."

Norman chose his protest carefully. "I'm not saying those things don't happen, rabbi," he began, "but to blame them on the gods of evil? Murder, rape, and genocide are not ritual acts. If they are to gain power, it's power over their victims, not over the gods. Maybe in the days of human sacrifice murder was a ritual act, but not today."

"Today," Moshe snapped. "Even today."

He did not want to argue the question any further and called a recess.

"Recess."

The word hung suspended before Stephanie, a shark in the water. She was a diver, accustomed to sharks. This one she didn't want to see.

"I'm sorry," her mother said. "I didn't mean for you to know. There was never any need for you to know."

Her mother carried the diamonds. She put them in a soft leather pouch which she had smeared with petroleum jelly and inserted into her vagina. Whenever they came to a stop, whenever a bribe was necessary to lubricate their passage through Germany, she excused herself to the toilet and extracted a diamond.

She passed the diamond to her husband and he presented it to the officer. "My last one," he said. "Please, accept it. Let us go."

On one such occasion the diamond slipped from her hand as she was passing it to her husband . . .

The shark was too dangerous, the shadow too deep. "I don't want to see this," Stephanie said aloud.

Sidney heard her.

"Nothing," she said. "I was thinking about something else, another story. One for Rivkah, not for here. Go on."

328

Sidney said, "Moshe surrendered again to the seat beside his wife. She held his hand, but he did not appear aware of it. His eyes closed, his breathing settled, an athlete resting during a brief time-out."

Moshe returned to his table. "A *niggun*," he suggested. "We need to lighten up a bit." He began to sing, "*We're off to see the Wizard, the wonderful Wizard of Oz.*" He motioned for the students to join in the singing. "*We hear he is a wiz of a wiz, if ever a wiz there was.*"

As soon as the tune developed momentum, Moshe stopped and said, "What if . . ." and waited for the singing to end. "What if I asked you to sing that sixty-four times? Not sixty-three and not sixty-five, but sixty-four times? As part of a meditative discipline? How would you count? Would you make marks on a paper with a pencil? Would you count on your fingers and toes? How would you count so you would have exactly sixty-four, and not remove yourself from the meditation in the process?

"I am going to share with you a powerful tool. It's a device used for descent, and it's a doorway that opens into the deepest of experiences. It's not something to do alone. You do not go through that doorway alone."

He made eye contact with each of us, to make sure we had absorbed that message.

"At the end of Yom Kippur, as the sun is setting, the service closes with a repetition of *Ha-shem hu ha-elokeem*." He used the euphemisms for the names of God rather than the names themselves. "Seven times we're supposed to sing it. How do we keep count? What are we supposed to do? To shout out the number after every repetition, like an announcer in a boxing ring shouting out the rounds? That's digital counting. The very act of counting diminishes the experience.

"Here's an alternative. Imagine a menorah. Remember, a menorah has seven candles. Now we'll sing *Ha-shem hu ha-elokeem* seven times. Each time we sing it, light one candle. When they're all lit, you'll know you've done seven without counting. Instead of counting you will have filled the pattern. You'll see before you a menorah with all of its candles lit."

He closed his eyes, prepared to sing, but opened them when he heard a murmur of confusion.

"What's the problem?"

"The Hebrew," several said.

He had forgotten we were not all fluent in Hebrew. "We'll sing it in English," he said. "Sing *The Lord is God*. Seven times, until the menorah is full."

Together we sang *The Lord is God* to a slow, plaintive chant. By the seventh repetition, most of us had our eyes closed.

"We've done two things." Moshe lifted the words up without losing the image before his eyes. "We've completed our seven, and we are left with a powerful image in front of us. We could use that image if we liked. We could intensify it, penetrate it, descend through it. Consider what might happen if we had completed a pattern of sixty-four. Sixteen lights in each quadrant, and we focused on the middle of the pattern. All of our energy would be in the image. Our focus would be strong. We could penetrate through the central lights and descend to a great depth."

He opened his eyes and scanned the class. "Okay," he said, fully at the surface. "Please, open your eyes if you have them closed and make sure your buddy is still sitting beside you." Eyes opened; smiles surfaced. "That was a simple exercise, a short exercise, and it already had some of you going. Some of you had difficulty. Don't worry about that, please. Some of us are strongly visual; others of us will use different methods of descent. This is just one technique of the *merkavah* mystics."

Stephanie listened to Sidney's story, word for word, letter for letter, nuance for nuance, not so much to learn it, but so as not to fall back into her own story. She wasn't ready for that.

"Some of us are strongly visual," Sidney had said. Patterns of sixteen and sixty-four.

Twelve was a multiple of four. Twelve were the stones on the breastplate of the High Priest. Twelve were the stones encased in Father Porter's watch.

"That's it," she whispered, not so loud that Sidney heard. She understood the breastplate and Tuesday. It wasn't that one of the stones shone more brightly than the others. It was the pattern, a vertical rectangle, three by four. Three across from left to right, then three more down to the bottom, two across to the left, two up, two down the center. One two three, one two three, one two, one two, one two. Twelve. Twelve stones. A pattern around the perimeter and into the depths.

One two three. One two three. One two. One two. One two.

One two three. One two three. One two. One two. One two.

The pattern was important, not the stones. The pattern was the vehicle, the chariot, that moved the High Priest to a place beyond himself, where he could receive from beyond himself.

Father Porter hadn't known the propitious day for the work with Moshe. He followed the pattern and intuited a Tuesday. Tuesday became the day for the work. Whenever the work became difficult, Father Porter held the watch, a connection between one world and the next. He left it with Moshe, for Moshe to learn how to use. Father Porter understood. His understanding was far beyond Moshe's. He was waiting for Moshe to catch up, to catch on, but Moshe never did.

Stephanie found herself astonished. She knew how to use it, and knowing how, she didn't even need the physical object. She could envision it, the breastplate of the High Priest.

One two three. One two three. One two. One two. One two.

What was Sidney saying? She could follow Sidney's story and hold the breastplate at the same time.

"Once a person has begun the process, the guide can accelerate the process by suggestion. The guide is important. You do not do this descent by yourself. You always have a guide, a buddy, anchored in the World of Action. There is exposure here. Wherever there is exposure, there must always be someone to spot you. It's a matter of safety. You would not do heavy bench presses by yourself, or rock climbing, or scuba diving, or gymnastics. You would have someone there to spot you, to look out for you when you were exposed. So it is here. The exposure is significant. So, please, no solitary excursions.

"The person who is traveling, the person who is descending, has the responsibility of reporting back what he or she is experiencing. The report does not have to be in grammatically correct, complete sentences. Often a word or two will suffice. It is enough to keep the guide beside you through the worlds.

"The guide accompanies the traveler, but remains connected to the surface. He can make interventions from time to time, suggestions to push the traveler a little deeper. If there is an option to move one way or the other, and one way seems likely to induce an encounter, even a confrontation, the guide is likely to push that way. At the same time, the guide monitors the breathing, the energy level, even the heart rate of the traveler.

"The work being done is real. Calories are being burned. Sweat and tears are not uncommon. Blood pressure increases." Moshe paused to consider which path to take. Had he frightened us enough to keep us from doing this work without proper safeguards? He chose the lighter path. "It's cardiovascular," he said, "but I wouldn't choose it as a way to lose weight."

We welcomed the opportunity to laugh. Moshe continued, "It takes practice to learn to travel and practice to become a guide. Neither role is undertaken casually. The responsibility is great on both ends."

Moshe held up his hand to forestall questions. "Let me finish my thought. At the deepest moments, some of these mystics would raise up hymns. They would penetrate to the deepest, deepest place and resonate their thoughts and feelings. What emerged was often long lists of synonyms and linked words, as if they could not find a single expression to describe what was happening to them. They used such words to surround their experience.

"Often these words came out in multiples of four, a rhythm the travelers were experiencing. What they said was written down and learned by others who wanted to follow in their path and experience something of what they experienced. Chanting these hymns is in itself one of the techniques of descent, so those of you who have difficulty with the visual, here's another technique that's available to you."

It appeared Moshe had more to say, thought better of it, and stopped. "Okay. Questions."

There was only one. "What is the ultimate goal of this discipline, rabbi?"

Moshe's answer was immediate. "To suspend oneself completely, without distortion, and to be moved by an agency outside of oneself in such a way as to best further the purpose of the partnership of creation and Creator."

Teshuvah

"It was I who had asked the question," Sidney said. "The answer followed so quickly upon my words the question and answer seemed to be a continuous sentence. I was startled.

"Before I could voice my next question, Moshe anticipated it, and answered, 'No, Sidney, I did not just make that up. I made it up a long time ago, and I have considered it carefully, so you can take that answer seriously, if you like.'

"His eyes were alive with delight. He was enjoying this encounter with me. I gave him the opportunity to expand upon it and asked him if he would be kind enough to explain what he meant by *without distortion*. What followed was my first introduction to the deepest meaning of *teshuvah*. Of everything he taught,

332

this was the most important. I'm not sure if the class as a whole understood that, but at the moment, Moshe was teaching only me."

"Imagine a magnetic needle," he began, "a piece of iron that has been magnetized. If the needle is suspended on a frictionless bearing, it will turn. As a result of an agency outside of itself, it will align with magnetic north. Except, of course, if there are masses of iron in the neighborhood.

"If the needle is suspended with masses of iron close by, it will still turn and align itself, but it will not be pointing to magnetic north. It will have a distorted reading, because of the influence of the masses of iron. That's why a ship's compass is boxed. Spheres of solid iron are placed around the compass to compensate for the influence of the iron in the ship. That way the magnetic needle will give an honest reading without distortion.

"Now, let's assume you suspend yourself completely. You leave behind all attachment to the World of Action. You become, like the magnetic needle, frictionless. In the physical world there are invisible lines of electromagnetic force that influence the magnetic needle. In the spiritual worlds there are also invisible lines of force, but these influence the soul. These lines of force are called *teshuvah*.

"*Teshuvah* is sometimes translated as *repentance,* sometimes as *return,* sometimes as *answer*. But here understand it as lines of force that direct the flow of the universe, that underlie the purpose of the universe. As the magnetic needle swings into position because of the influence of the lines of electromagnetic force, so the soul swings into position because of the influence of the lines of *teshuvah*.

"The magnetic needle asks the way to magnetic north, and it is answered by an agency outside of itself. The soul asks the way to spiritual north, and it is answered by an agency outside of itself. But as extraneous masses of iron distort the result for the magnetic needle, there are also sources of distortion for the soul.

"The sources of distortion for the soul are the usual assortment of neuroses and psychoses, of guilt, shame, and irrational fears we bring with us into adulthood. Beyond those we are also burdened by dogmas and false notions. All of these must be encountered and reconciled before a reading can be gained without distortion."

"He was teaching theory, not practice," Sidney said. "It wasn't important to the class to know the theory. They only needed to know the practice. But I'm a horse of a different color. I like to know the premise, the foundation. Later I learned much more from Moshe about *teshuvah*. Tradition teaches it was one of those elements that preceded creation. Purpose precedes any creation. *Teshuvah* and purpose are linked."

Stephanie sat still, breathless, and found herself spinning nearly out of control. On one hand she was angry. Such *hutzpah* of Sidney, to say he had learned so much more, so much more. On the other hand his words echoed: "*Teshuvah* and purpose are linked." Of course. To be moved by an agency outside of yourself. To hear beyond your hearing, see beyond your seeing, feel beyond your feeling. To sense order beyond your order, position without imposition.

"*Teshuvah* and purpose are linked." Surrender to *teshuvah*, know your purpose. Know my purpose, Stephanie thought. And to be free of distortion. To be free of anger. To be free of guilt.

In the next moment she was filled with terror. In another moment she might indeed surrender, and a reality beyond herself might burst upon her. She was terrified, opened her eyes to search about for something solid to hold on to. No wonder Father Porter held his watch so firmly. She saw him clearly before her, grasping it so hard his knuckles turned white. He was afraid for her.

Sidney was speaking, not looking at her. He didn't have a clue, she thought. She might scream for help, but he couldn't help. He didn't have a clue.

Reconciliation and Transformation

"Reconciliation," Moshe said, turning away from me and back to the class. "We use meditative technique to descend to an encounter. We equalize pressure down there. The encounter must be at the same depth as the issue to be resolved. How do you know when the matter is reconciled? It's nice to think the angels just fly away. It's not usually as simple as that. You may have to descend to the same place over and over again until you reach some accommodation with whatever is there. When you can finally sum up the experience in a few key words, you are close to a reconciliation.

"The few words you use are called in Hebrew a *hatimah* which means a *seal*, or a *signature* of the experience. We have in the literature the expression *keter* and *hatimah*. *Keter* means *crown*. The *keter* is what the experience gives to you. The *hatimah* is what you give to the experience. The two together complete the reconciliation.

"It's as if you were working through a difficult problem of logic with some-

334

one who had already been through that problem before. You get into the problem, tug and pull at it, and finally explain it. You haven't finished with it yet. The next time you return to it, it's still murky, but it takes less energy this time to penetrate it. And less the next time, until at last you can sum up the whole problem with just a few words. The summary is the *hatimah*. The nod your study partner gives you to acknowledge your accomplishment is the crown, the *keter*. You then turn the page and move on to the next difficulty."

Moshe tapped the last of the words on the chalkboard. "Transformation. That's the result of the discipline. Once you have entered the temple, once you have reconciled whatever confrontation you have met with as a result of your encounter with the angelic guards at the gate, the temple disappears. It is gone. Another may loom in front of you, but you are forever changed as a result of the work you have done.

"That's the Work of the Chariot, the work of penetrating visions. *Ma-aseh merkavah*. There has been an integration of that which had been walled off from the self back into the self. You are now a larger person. You will walk differently in the world. You will receive differently. You will perceive differently.

"Let me caution you once again. No romantic notions, please. There is no way of determining before this work is begun what the end result of it will be. If you have preconceived notions of what it is you want to become, I suggest you use some other way to pursue those goals. In this process you surrender all notions at the door."

As he erased the chalkboard, he said, "That finishes the four weeks. In truth it was all I intended to teach. You have had an introduction to the Four Worlds, the ten *sefirot,* and the discipline of the *merkavah*. Who has a need or a desire for a fifth session?"

When he turned around, he saw every one of us had a hand raised.

"A fifth session, then," he consented. "We'll do a *merkavah* descent. I will choose one of you to work with, and the rest will follow. But even for the followers, there is risk. This is not something to be taken lightly. There is no reason whatsoever for any of you to do this. I actually encourage you not to come. You've already learned everything you need to know to get started.

"Thank you for your attention and the opportunity to learn with you," he concluded.

The fourth lesson at the Institute ended with awkward applause.

·　　·　　·

That finished the afternoon session.

The students were on their own for dinner. There was no shortage of good restaurants within a ten-minute drive.

Stephanie remained seated. Sidney didn't notice she had not moved until the room was nearly empty.

"Are you okay?" he asked.

She didn't respond. Only the two of them were left under the ceiling fan. He knelt before her.

"Steffie, are you okay?"

"I don't know," she answered. "I honestly don't know."

"How do you feel?"

"I don't know."

"What don't you know?"

"I don't know."

"Where are you, Steffie?"

"I don't know."

She began to tremble. He held her, hugged her, and began to tremble, too.

CHAPTER 13

A Bet

 By nine o'clock all of the students had returned from dinner. There had been some changes. There was a chill in the air. The three long skirts were all in jeans. The white beard had changed his shorts for long khakis. Dress Pants was still with the Donna Karan. That hadn't changed.

Stephanie had recovered remarkably. Sidney had held her until the trembling stopped. She announced she was okay. It was like it had never happened. When Sidney questioned her, she wouldn't talk about it.

Stephanie had dessert and coffee ready for the students in the kitchen and encouraged them to take their plates and cups into the living room for the stories of the fifth Institute session.

"The fifth lesson at the Institute came close to never happening," she began. "Rivie was late coming home from work."

"Moshe was anxious," Sidney added. "He planned to guide a descent as a demonstration in the class. It was important to him that Rivkah should be there, to experience the descent, even if only vicariously, but also to assist him. True, she wasn't a psychiatric social worker, but still he needed her assistance, to monitor the class, to protect against another Princeton incident."

"He was anxious for another reason as well," Stephanie added. "He had one more report to add to the CA125 chart. It wasn't conclusive. Still, it unsettled him. There had been many little things—Rivkah's increasing fatigue, her diminishing flexibility, something in her gait.

"The chart wasn't conclusive, but it made him anxious. There was a lot happening, and he knew the evening ahead would be a challenge."

The dining-room table was open to its full extent and covered with market materials: charts, weather forecasts, USDA reports, and letters from several services to which Moshe subscribed. This was one of those times when the spread of data overflowed from his study. He left the papers where they were and set the kitchen counter with dairy dishes. Rivkah still had not disposed of the meat dishes because, she said, she wasn't a vegetarian, even though it had been some years since they had eaten meat.

Moshe chopped the vegetables for the stir fry. He lifted the cover of the pan on the stove to check the rice. When he heard Rivkah's car turn in from the road, he slid the vegetables from the cutting board into the wok. They were nearly done by the time she reached the front door, but not quite.

"I'm at the stove, Rivie!" Moshe shouted to explain why he could not open the door for her. She let herself in.

"I'm sorry I'm so late," she apologized. "It was hard to get away. We're going to lose Tony tonight, I think." Tony was an eleven-year-old who was dying of leukemia. She caressed Moshe's shoulders in lieu of a kiss on her way to the refrigerator. "I'm really worn-out, Moshe. I don't know if I can make it to the class."

Moshe kept his eyes on the wok. "This is the Princeton class, Rivie. This is the one that could be Princeton all over again."

She struggled to extract the cork from the half-full bottle of white wine. "So maybe do something else. I don't know why you want to do the Princeton thing anyway. You can give your talk on Reb Nachman, or teach vocabulary. It doesn't matter what you do. They'll love you whatever it is."

"This is what I had promised. This is what they're expecting." With a flourish he poured the vegetables into a ceramic bowl. "*Voilà!*" he said. "That's Chinese for *dinner is served.*" Rivie smiled. "This is the class where I really need your help, Rivie. God willing, there won't be anything for you to do. I'll get everyone in a deep trance, and you can vegetate if you don't want to meditate. There won't be many people there anyway."

"Who are you kidding?"

"There won't be many. I've pushed them too hard."

"You'll have thirty people tonight."

"Half that. They'll be scared away."

"Five bucks says there are at least two dozen."

"Five bucks," Moshe agreed. "You're on." He served the dinner and hid his alarm.

338

"I had made my first descent the night before in Moshe's study," Sidney said. "Moshe told me it was to be a simple test, to see how I might do at depth. He was also preparing me to be a better monitor in the class exercise."

"Choose a letter, please, Sidney. Any letter."

I sat comfortably in the chair opposite the Nicastri painting. It was as if Moshe had said, "Take a card, Sidney, any card."

"Which letter have you chosen?" Moshe asked.

"I have to tell you, Moshe? You don't know?"

He laughed. "No, Sidney. I don't know. But you don't have to tell me if you don't want to. It's up to you."

After another few breaths, I responded. "It's an *ALEF*."

Moshe had expected a letter of the English alphabet, but the Hebrew would do.

"What color is the *ALEF*?"

"Blue. Deep blue."

"And the background. What color is the background?"

"A light blue," I said. I was surprised. "A light blue."

"If you want to deepen the experience, you might take a dot of light and engrave the letter. Run the dot of light slowly around the perimeter. Take your time."

Moshe waited. Later he told me he was observing my breathing. I knew how to breathe. Most novices did not, but then I was not a novice at meditation. My stomach extended gently with each breath. My breaths were measured, conscious, and steady.

Moshe exhaled audibly and spoke. He took care to be gentle with his words lest they startle. "You might let the *ALEF* come close to you. If you like, the *ALEF* might be very large, and you very small." He waited a few seconds. "Are you able to see the *ALEF* that way?"

Several more seconds passed before I answered. That alone was a sign both to me and to him I was at some depth. "Yes, I see it that way."

"What do you see?"

"The *ALEF* is very large. Very large. Dark blue, blocking out the light."

"How do you feel, small before the large *ALEF*?"

"Small. Tiny. Insignificant. Fearful."

"If you like, you can reduce the size of the *ALEF* to something more comfortable." Moshe gave me time to shrink my *ALEF*. "How does the *ALEF* appear to you now?"

Again a pause. "Smaller. My height. A few feet away."

"Without touching the *ALEF,* what do you think it would feel like, if you could touch it? Would it be hot or cold?"

"I think it would be cold."

"Would it be soft or hard."

"I think it would be hard. Hard and hollow."

"If you can, bring the *ALEF* closer to you." Moshe spoke slowly and paused between sentences. "You might imagine the *ALEF* only a few inches away. If you like, you might reach out and touch it. How does it feel?"

"Warm. Warmer than I thought. Hard, but solid. Like wood. Solid."

"Not what you expected?"

"No."

Moshe had tested me enough to be certain of my abilities. It was significant that my experience in touching the imagined *ALEF* was different from the experience I had anticipated. "Okay, Sidney. We're going to withdraw from the exercise. Slowly. There's no hurry. Allow the *ALEF* to recede from you. Be conscious of your breathing. As the breath comes down toward your toes, be aware of your toes. As you exhale, be aware of your fingers. Bring movement back into your body."

When I opened my eyes, his eyes were there to greet me. We looked at each other for a few moments without words.

"You visualize well, Sidney," he told me. "If you like, we can begin the real work next week."

I looked to my watch and registered my surprise. "It felt like two minutes." Twenty minutes had passed.

"Next week we'll leave the time open-ended, but we'll start early."

"Is there any urgency, Moshe? Is there something new?" I was asking about Rivkah.

"Nothing new, Sidney. Nothing I can be certain of. This is all just in case. In the beginning you'll be doing the traveling, but soon enough you will be guiding me. I need some practice going deep. I can't go deep without the leverage you can provide."

"Why do you need to go so deep?"

"I don't need to. I need to be able to. Hopefully I will never need to. But just in case." He saw my look of concern. "Don't be worried, Sidney. It will be exciting."

"I'm not worried for me, Moshe. I'm worried for you."

Safety Nets

"I was waiting for them at the door," Sidney said. "I was nervous. Moshe had shared with me what he intended to do, but not with whom he intended to do it. I half hoped and half feared that he might choose to do the work with me."

"Five bucks," Rivkah said, as they entered the large room. "I told you. They come to hear you. They don't care if you say it's dangerous."

"It's too many," Moshe mumbled, more to himself than to her.

Moshe motioned for me to come closer. "I need help from both of you if I'm going to do what I planned. I can't watch everyone in the class."

"Whatever you want, Moshe," I agreed.

"What I'm going to do is to choose one person to work with. I'll invite everyone to join in the descent to a certain level, so they can be involved in what we do. But I don't want anyone dropping over the edge. I want them to stay at a comfortable depth and get a feeling for the work, that's all."

"Who are you going to work with, Moshe?" I asked.

"I thought your doctor friend might be a challenging subject."

"Norman?" I laughed. "I think maybe choose somebody else. If Norman does not understand how it works, it cannot work for Norman. I assure you, Moshe, Norman does not understand how this works."

"Then he's just what I need. A challenging subject who will go deep enough but not too deep. So, will you help me? Will the two of you keep an eye on things? Divide the class between you. Watch for any sign of serious disturbance. Hyperventilating, trembling, anything unusual."

"Moshe," I asked, "the danger, is it really so great? Do we really have to be worried?"

Moshe shared with me what had happened at Princeton.

I considered that. "Would it not be appropriate then to share that experience with the class as a whole?" I suggested.

He looked from me to Rivkah, hoping she might offer some objection. She did not, of course. What better warning than a firsthand experience, even if it caused Moshe to revisit publicly what he considered to be the greatest failure of his life? "You're right," he said. "You're right. I'll do that. But that doesn't change anything. I still need the two of you as safety divers."

"What happens if Emily comes in?" Rivkah asked.

"Emily?" I knew who she was, but had not been aware she presented a problem.

"A young woman we think might be somewhat unstable," Moshe advised me.

"So what do I do if she comes?" Rivkah asked again.

"The same we would have done last week. Go right to her. Let her know I'm concerned about her. Tell her she can stay after the class if she likes, or she can call me during the week. If she leaves, let her go. Don't follow her. Does that sound all right?"

"It sounds okay to me," Rivie answered.

"What if we see somebody else in difficulty?" I asked.

"Tap me lightly on the shoulder. I won't be very deep. We'll decide what to do then. Anything else? Okay, we'll get ready."

Good and Evil

I took a seat on the perimeter to have a good view of the class. Emily was not among the students. I was thankful for that. I felt the work would be substantial enough without a destabilizing presence.

Moshe wrote the key words for the work of the *merkavah* on the chalkboard: Descent, Encounter, Reconciliation, Transformation. The students looked to the board and began their review in pairs without any prompting. He made himself sit on the table. He was anxious. It was difficult for him to sit.

A *niggun* brought the class to order.

"Questions before we begin?" he asked.

One hand rose timidly in the back of the room. It was Emily. My energy had been caught up in the rhythm of the *niggun* so much I had not marked her entrance. I promised myself to be more alert thereafter.

"The nature of good and evil," she said. "Could you explain that?"

Moshe did not seem surprised by the question. "We touched upon it last week," he said, "when we were talking about false notions that could be dangerous at depth. Dualism is the most dangerous of them. Dualism holds there are independent powers of good and evil. But that is not the case. There is only one power, with its good and evil aspects. There is nothing good in creation without some bad, and there is nothing bad in creation without some good." Emily's expression gave no clue as to whether or not she was following his explanation.

Moshe's tone became lighter. "I remember once walking with one of my teachers into a fish restaurant. I told him it was a very good restaurant. 'For us it is good,' he said to me. 'For the fish it is not so good.'" This drew a chuckle from the class. Emily did not laugh. "So bad and good often depend upon the perspective of the viewer."

Moshe pondered Emily for a while in silence, debating whether or not to continue with an essay on the nature of good and evil. Deciding against it, he said, "The bottom line is that good and evil are not independent powers. They are the ends of a polarity, like north and south are the ends of a polarity. You can't have a separate good and evil any more than you can separate the north and south poles of a magnet. Does that answer your question, Emily?"

Actually, that was the essay, the sum total of it. There were a great many Hebrew words and technical terms he might have used, but they wouldn't have added any more about the nature of good and evil than he had managed in those few sentences. I found them stunning, but Emily said nothing. Her aspect changed from attentive to hostile. Without comment she stood and left the room.

Rivkah was already in chase. Moshe caught her eye and held up his hand. She stopped at the door and let her go.

"Anything else?" he asked. The class had witnessed Emily's exit. "It's all right," he reassured them. "Maybe it was something I said. Are there any other questions? No. Then let me share with you something that happened in a class like this six years ago." He pushed ahead quickly to leave Emily's exit behind and introduce a more relevant concern.

"I was teaching at a conference on spirituality at Princeton. There were eighteen students in the class, all of them with substantial knowledge and experience, not unlike those of us here." Moshe waved aside the ripple of laughter. "I was in the process of leading a *merkavah* meditation when something seriously wrong happened to one of the students, a man in his thirties. He had fallen to the floor in convulsions and struck his head against something in his fall." Moshe had the full attention of the class. "He died."

He allowed time for that to register.

"The cause of death was attributed to the trauma of his fall. He had struck his head here." Moshe indicated his own left temple. "The convulsions that led to the fall, there's no certainty as to the cause, but he was likely in a very deep meditation. Everyone was eager to go deep. I had given the warnings. I'm not sure anyone took them seriously.

"After that I decided not to teach the *merkavah* system of meditation again. You'll remember it is intended to be done one-on-one, not one on eighteen, or one on thirty, as we have here. But times have changed. So many Jews have been leaving Judaism in search of profound spiritual experience, I think it is necessary to let them know an experience every bit as profound is available within Judaism. But profound means deep, and deep means exposure. There is no exposure without risk."

Moshe made quick but direct eye contact with every student before continuing. "I don't intend to do the same thing I did at Princeton. First of all, you are all paired up. At least I hope you are. Is there anyone here who does not have a buddy?" He scanned the room again. "Let me ask it differently. Please take the hand of your buddy and raise it. I want to make sure all of you are paired up." After a bit of confusion, all hands were raised.

Norman Plotkin kept his hand up. "May I ask a question?" Moshe nodded. "What was the meditation that you were doing in Princeton? Were you doing the visual counting that you described last week?"

"Yes. Why do you ask?"

"An educated guess. How did it work, what you did?"

Moshe needed a moment to remember. "We did a series of sixty-four. Sixteen lights in each quadrant."

"Your student, the one with the seizure, was most likely epileptic," Dr. Plotkin said. "The pattern of lights is what triggered the seizure. That's probably what it was." Moshe swung his legs below the table and digested that. "He was most likely epileptic," the doctor repeated. "Leading him through the pattern of lights was like taking him to a carnival at night. The flashing lights in the corners of his mind pulled him deep so quickly his body could not adjust. He had a seizure."

"Thank you, Doctor," Moshe said. "You may be right." He did not seem convinced the episode had been an epileptic seizure, but instead of continuing with the matter, turned to address the class. "I don't have time to go around the room taking a medical history, but if you have a heart condition, respiratory problems, blood pressure abnormalities, neurological disorders . . . If there's any suspicion of any reason at all not to do this kind of med-

344

itation, please don't do it. And if in the process of doing it you feel at all uncomfortable, stop. Open your eyes, look around, remember what you had for dinner, or whatever else it takes to reattach yourself to the World of Action, and watch whatever happens from there. Tap your buddy, let him or her know what's going on with you.

"In scuba diving, buddies often ask each other if they're okay. They flash this sign." Moshe made a ring of his index finger and thumb, an *O*, with the other three fingers extended into the semblance of a *K.* "It means, 'Are you okay?' The other buddy responds with the same sign. It says, 'Yes, I'm okay.' If the buddy doesn't respond, he or she is not okay, and it's time to come to the surface."

"The okay sign doesn't always work," Stephanie said. "Once Moshe and Rivkah were diving in strong current on the wall off Grand Cayman. They were a hundred feet deep, drifting, the ocean a cobalt blue around them, the abyss darkening to more than a thousand feet below. He had asked Rivkah if she was okay. She flashed back the sign by rote, even though panic from the exposure had set in. The next moment she was thrashing toward the surface. He reached up to grab one fin and pull her back to him. He engulfed her in a bear hug, mask to mask, eye to eye, until the panic subsided and her breathing approached normal.

"It's important to look into the person behind the sign," Stephanie said.

The Volunteer

"I need a volunteer, Norman," Moshe said.

Norman was startled. "Me? No, I'm not the right person. Work with Sidney."

"Sidney's too easy, Norman. You're just right."

His wife pushed him forward. "Do it," Marsha said. "Go ahead!" The prospect of her husband in the center of the class excited her.

"Why don't *you* do it?" he protested.

"Because I want *you* to!"

Whatever logic there was in that argument, there was no denying it. Norman stood forward. Moshe provided a chair for him. "Thank you," he said, as Norman sat.

"I'll be looking out for Norman, Marsha, but you stay with him, too. If you

345

need to come back, look up and Rivkah will find you. Rivie is going to be keeping an eye on everyone."

"Here's what I hope to do. We'll all begin using meditative techniques we've touched on and even practiced a little. There isn't any hurry. We can take our time. Going through the techniques will be a review of much of the material we've learned. At some point I'll let you know that Norman and I will continue on together. That's when you become observers rather than participants. Follow along with me if you like, but, please, don't go off on your own journey, because there will be no one to follow you.

"Make yourselves comfortable. I don't suggest lying down, but sitting against the wall is all right. Stay in your chairs if you like. Whatever is best for you." Students found their places.

"Moving around and finding a comfortable position is the first part of the exercise. All meditations begin in the World of Action. They begin in the body, with an awareness of the body.

"Be aware of your breathing. As you breathe, be aware of the breath as it comes in. Breathe in as if the breath could reach all the way to your toes. As you hold the breath, you might imagine the breath rising up the spine. When you exhale, it's as if the breath comes around your shoulders and out your fingertips. When there's no breath within you, focus for a moment on a spot just above your head. Then breathe in again."

The Demonstration

I expected what had worked so readily with me was not likely to work with Norman. With me Moshe was direct, and the descent was rapid. With Norman Moshe chose a more circuitous route.

"We'll begin with a meditation on the sefirotic tree. I'll use the language of the early kabbalists. Let the words play over you." He spoke slowly, softly, to induce calm. "Pay attention not so much to my words, but the feeling the flow of words conveys. Allow that feeling to grow inside of you," he suggested.

A voice interrupted from the perimeter. "Once we begin, do we have to keep our eyes closed?" a student asked.

The speaker was unaware they had already begun. Moshe swallowed his sharp response and answered the question. "Whatever is comfortable for you. Most people like to have their eyes closed when they meditate, but you may surely have your eyes open if you like. Throughout this whole process, please do whatever is necessary to make yourself comfortable, without, of course, disturbing the class.

"We'll begin again. Open and close your hands and be aware of the play of your fingers. Recognize how wonderful your hands are, what an incredible piece of machinery. And you have them available to you! Recognize them as a gift, a blessing.

"Wriggle your toes and do likewise. If you have toes, they too are a blessing.

"Feel your clothes. Be thankful for them. We have enough exposure in this world without having to walk around without our clothes. Accept your clothes as a blessing.

"Be aware of your body underneath your clothes. Be aware of how open it is, the abdominal and thoracic cavities, the sinuses, the veins and arteries, the latticework of cells that make up the skin, the spaces and spaces that pervade your body.

"Be aware of the air that passes through your body, not only the air that comes in through the nose and out through the mouth, but the air that passes through the pores of your skin. There is little substance to the skin. Air comes in; air goes out. Air passes through your body, through the holes and holes and spaces and spaces.

"Be aware of the breath as it comes into your body. The words for *breath* and *soul* are from the same root in Hebrew. The soul-breath descends pure from the World of Emanation. It is created in the World of Creation, formed in the World of Formation, and it descends into you in the World of Action. You bring this soul-breath into you, as if it descends all the way to your toes. You hold it as it ascends up your spine. It's as if it exhales around your shoulders and out your fingertips. And then focus on the arrival of the next breath up above your head.

"As you breathe, listen to the words that initiate this meditation.

"I address the sovereign of all worlds. My desire is to descend toward you, to come closer into your presence. I acknowledge it is not because of anything I have done that I should be welcome, that you should pay any attention to me. After all, what am I? What is my size? What is my stature? What is my force? My strength? What can I say before you, master of all worlds? Aren't even the deeds of the heroes like nothing before you? Aren't even the expressions of the wise trivial before a wisdom that creates and maintains a universe? Most of our actions amount to nothing. The very days of our life seem of no significance. The advantage I have over a beast is hardly worth measuring.

347

When I consider myself in such fashion, I approach nothingness. I am about to disappear in my insignificance.

"The feeling associated with this line of thought you might associate with the left leg. The feeling associated with the right leg begins with the word *but*.

"But. However. Nevertheless, I come from a long line of people who have related to you in this fashion. I come from Adam and Noah, from Abraham, Isaac, and Jacob. From Sarah, Rebecca, Rachel, and Leah. As tiny as I am, I relate through my very being back to the beginning of time. And from this point in time, through my own creativity, through my own progeny, I can relate to the ends of time and space. I may be tiny on one side, but on the other, I still make ripples that continue out to the very ends of the universe.

"So I shift my awareness from the left leg and my insignificance, to my right leg and my consequence. Back and forth, back and forth. And I find a point of balance. And from that point of balance I encourage you to whisper the *Sh'ma*, 'Hear O Israel, the Lord is our God, the Lord is One. *Sh'ma yisrael, Adonai elohaynu, Adonai ehad.*'

"From this place now we'll chant a *niggun*. Slowly, quietly." Moshe began to intone a simple melody familiar from earlier classes. They sang for several minutes during which he opened his eyes and made contact first with Rivkah and then with me. All seemed well in the room. Another minute of singing, and he had returned to depth. When he left off singing, the *niggun* soon stopped.

"If you like, imagine a light off to the left. Do not look at it directly. Let it become a certain color. Do not impose a color on it. Let it become whatever color it might be. The center of your attention remains focused ahead.

"If you are able, you might pronounce aloud, in a whisper, what color it is that you see."

Some of the students responded immediately. "White." "Yellow." "Blue." "Pink." Some responses were delayed. "White." And then, "Green."

Norman Plotkin said, "Blue." It had taken him some time to settle on a color, or perhaps some time to bring the word to the surface. Moshe hoped for the latter.

"If you are able, press the light on your left into a shape. Press it into the shape of the number 6. Expend some energy to confine the color into the shape of the number 6." He would have preferred to use a letter of the Hebrew alphabet, but could not in such a mixed class. Letters of the English alphabet did not have as consistent a form as the Hebrew. But the number 6 was the number 6. It was a good, consistent form to use.

"You might take a dot of light and etch the outlines of the 6. Give the number a firm outline." He followed his own instructions, tracing the 6 off to the left, doing every aspect of the meditation even as he described it to the class.

"Inside the outline you have the color and substance of the number 6. What is the color in the background? If you are able, whisper the color in the background, outside the 6, aloud." Again some students responded at once. Other reports of color drifted in at intervals. Norman Plotkin said, "White. No, gray."

Moshe adjusted the color of his own 6 to blue, the background to gray. Wherever Norman Plotkin went, Moshe would go. "Note the boundaries of the 6. Make them sharp, if you can, clearly defined. If you are able to, let the 6 be in the middle of a Jewish star, a six-pointed star. If you like, you can let the star replace the 6. The star is a 6. You might trace the triangles of the star, and see that the 6 and the star are the same. If you can, in a whisper, count the triangles." Moshe listened to the counting in the room. Norman Plotkin counted very slowly, one through six.

"The star is to the left. Your attention is toward the center. To the right, an image that reminds you of love and warmth, something from your own experience. Let an image of love and warmth fill the right. Your attention is toward the center. The star is to the left. Take your time. As much as you can allow it, let the image choose itself. When you are ready, and there is no hurry, a whispered word or two, to identify the image, just loud enough for your neighbor to hear it."

Moshe's eyes and his being remained open and receptive to Norman's response.

Words came slowly from the perimeter of the class. "Mother," was mentioned several times.

"Candles," Norman said.

In a gentle voice directed at Norman, Moshe asked, "Which candles?"

"*Shabbat* candles. *Bubbie*." Norman reported in these few words an image of his grandmother lighting *Shabbat* candles.

"Feel the warmth emanating from this image. Absorb it. Your attention keep focused ahead. To the left are the hard edges of the star and the number 6. A star is a star. A 6 is a 6. A star is a 6. The edges are sharp. To the right an image of warmth. Maybe *Shabbat* candles, a grandmother with a covering over her head. A smile for a grandchild. A compassion which is always available. To the left, a 6. Two times three is six. If you answered seven on a math test, you were wrong. You got no credit. You got a zero. But your grandmother would console you. She would comfort you, care for you. Even if you got a zero. To the left is the never-changing star, the *6*. To the right, warmth, a compassion that is always available. Focus in the center, hold both images at the same time. If you like, we can say the words of the *Sh'ma*. 'Hear O Israel, the Lord is our God, the Lord is one. *Sh'ma yisrael, Adonai elohaynu, Adonai ehad.*'"

Moshe waited some time after the last word had faded away. "I'm going to recite sixteen words," he said. "If you are able, whisper them after me. As you do, arrange them in a pattern. With each word, complete a square, and then place each square in a corner of your vision. When all four squares are formed in all four corners, you will know we have finished the list of sixteen."

Moshe began his list, pausing a few seconds between each word.

True	Consistent	Upright	Faithful
Correct	Established	Beloved	Cherished
Delightful	Pleasing	Authentic	Accepted
Awesome	Mighty	Beneficent	Beautiful

As Moshe focused on his own squares, his eyes closed, but with the last word they opened again, somewhat distant, but still aware of Norman. This was not his descent. He was only the guide and had a responsibility to Norman and a roomful of students in addition.

"Norman," he said without wavering in his focus. "Tell me please, what do you see?"

Norman took his time in answering. Moshe had chosen Norman because he was trained in science. He would be cautious, certain of his responses. "I see the squares," Norman responded. "Four squares."

"What color are they?"

"They're just the outline of squares on a black background. The outlines are all different colors. The colors don't stay still."

"Do you see the inside corners of each of the squares, where the corners come to a point?"

"Yes."

"Can you connect them to make a central square."

The "Yes" came after several seconds.

"How does this central square differ from the other squares?"

"It has no borders. It's darker. Its black is blacker."

Moshe adjusted his own image to match Norman's. "If you are willing," he said, "the two of us will go deeper. As for the rest of the class, please stay where you are. Do not go off by yourself. My suggestions now are for Norman alone. Share what he is experiencing if you like, but do not go off by yourself.

"Norman, are you willing to go on with me?"

"Yes."

"How do you feel about entering that dark square?"

"Nervous. A little anxious. Apprehensive."

"Can you still recall the star to the left and your *bubbie* lighting candles to the right?"

"Yes."

"Is that a balanced place? A stable place?"

"Yes."

"If I mention them again, you will be able to get back to that place. Even if you are imbalanced, you can rely on them for support. You can bring them back again, just as you have now. Okay?"

"Okay."

"Are you still anxious about going into the black square?"

"Yes."

"Are you willing to do it?"

"Yes."

"How shall we go in?"

"Headfirst," Norman said. "Like into a dark pool of water. Like when I was boy diving in the quarry."

"After you," Moshe said. Norman's body trembled with the impact of the water. Moshe checked Norman's breathing and closed his eyes.

"What do you see?" he asked.

"My room." Moshe refrained from asking which room, knowing that Norman would tell him when he was able. "My bed. Railing. So small."

"The room you were in as a small child?"

"Yes."

"What's happening in that room?"

"Nothing. I'm just there. Nothing's happening."

Moshe allowed time for something to happen. Nothing happened. This was a critical time. He had to balance his desire that something should happen against patience, waiting for the experience to ripen. At the same time he had to keep his own mind balanced, unobscured by the thoughts of his own day. It was difficult for him to know when to speak. "What's outside the room?" he asked with a certainty he did not feel.

"The corridor. My sister's room. To the right. Through the wall."

"Is there something to do there?"

"No. She's not there. Wait. Wait." The tone of Norman's voice changed. Moshe opened his eyes partially, to watch Norman, but simultaneously stayed in the experience. "I'm sinking!" Norman was alarmed. "I'm sinking through the floor. I don't believe this! I'm sinking through the floor!"

"What's underneath you?"

"The living room. I'm sinking into the living room. I'm in the living room." Beads of sweat formed on Norman's forehead.

"What's happening?" Moshe asked.

"Nothing. Nothing's happening."

Again Moshe waited for something to happen. Again nothing happened. Again he had to be patient and hope he spoke at the proper time. "What do you see?"

"I see the witch picture."

"Which picture?"

"No, the *witch* picture. Above the fireplace. I used to be afraid of that picture. I used to be afraid to come into the living room at night. The picture scared me. The witch picture."

"Is there any work to do with the witch picture?"

"No. I'm not afraid of the witch picture anymore. Scotty just brushed against my leg."

Moshe waited for an explanation. When there wasn't one, he asked, "Scotty?"

"Cocker spaniel. Scotty. Has a leash."

"What does Scotty want?"

"Wants me to walk him. I have the leash. Outdoors. I'll take him outdoors." Norman frowned. His body shifted in the chair.

"What's happening."

"The door is open, but I can't get him to go out. He won't let me take him outside."

"What does he want?"

"He wants me to follow him."

"Where?"

"Into the kitchen." Norman gasped and paled.

Moshe noted the shock, the change in breathing. He said nothing. The fewer words said at this depth, the better.

"My mother. Mixing bowl. Looking at me." The words came up slowly, phrase by phrase. "Housedress . . . Purple . . . She mixes the batter . . . Looks at me . . . Waiting . . ."

After a long pause, Moshe said, "For?" The one word was said as gently as he could pronounce it.

Tears streamed from Norman. His chest heaved with sobs. "Her eyes. Her eyes." Moshe placed a handkerchief in Norman's right hand. He took it, but made no attempt to use it. "Her eyes," he repeated. "Like she's been waiting a long time. She smiled at me." After some time his breathing settled.

"Do you want to do more?" Moshe asked him. Had they been working alone, he would have kept him at depth for another encounter.

"Enough," was the one word response. "It's enough."

"If you like, you can reach for the star and the candles."

Norman lowered his head, his shoulders rolled forward. "I have them."

"There is no hurry. Take your time. Be aware of the star to your left, the candle to the right. Find a balance between them.

"Monitor your breathing. Be aware of each breath as it comes in, as it goes out. Each breath brings you a little higher, a little closer to the surface. Check in with your toes. Check in with your fingertips. Exhale. When you are ready, come back."

Norman opened his eyes and looked at Moshe for several seconds without blinking. "Astonishing," was his first word. He looked down at the handkerchief in his hand and used it to wipe the remnants of the tears from his cheeks and the perspiration from his forehead. "Astonishing," he repeated.

Certain Norman was fully back, Moshe turned to Rivkah and to me. We each gave him the okay sign. Students were returning about the class. One was snoring gently. Rivkah went to wake him.

"What was astonishing?" Moshe asked.

"It was all astonishing. Scotty, most of all. My dog. I tried to lead him out the door, but he wouldn't go out. I couldn't understand why he wouldn't go out. He had his leash on. Why would he have his leash on if he didn't want to go outside?"

"The leash wasn't so you could lead him. It was so he could lead you. What does an angel look like, Norman?"

Norman did not answer the question. "My mother died when I was in my twenties," he said. "I never really forgave her. That's what she looked like, in that purple housedress. She was a wonderful cook. Mixing batter in a bowl.

All these years, I never forgave her. It was like she was waiting for me to come and forgive her for dying. I thought Scotty would take me outside."

"Where did Scotty go after he led you into the kitchen?"

"I don't know. After I saw my mother, I didn't look for him." Norman closed his eyes, as if looking inside to see where his dog went.

Moshe brought him back with a question. "Can you tell me about the painting in the living room. The witch picture. Was it really a picture of witches?"

"No. It was an abstract painting my parents liked. I was afraid of it for years. But I got over it. Afterward I used to call it the witch picture."

"That was the *hatimah,* the seal for that experience. That wasn't where the work had to be done. You had finished that before."

"That's right. The work was in the kitchen." Norman's eyes lost their focus.

"Be careful, Norman. You're going back."

"The way my mother looked at me. She was so patient. There was so much love in her eyes." He looked down at the handkerchief. "Thank you," he said as he returned it.

Moshe stood, stretched, and turned to the class. "Everybody is back all right? Good. We'll take a few moments now, and share with each other."

Norman returned to his seat beside Marsha. She beamed at him. She was so proud.

Rivkah and I joined Moshe at the table. "Very impressive," I said. "Very, very impressive."

Rivkah was more reserved. "This is what you used to do with your clients?"

Moshe nodded. "Something like this."

"What's the difference between this and conventional therapy?"

"Can you wait a minute or two? Someone else is bound to ask."

She smiled. "I can wait. Even if it was conventional therapy, I agree with Sidney. It was impressive. It's one thing to teach the theory. It's another thing to show the results in the laboratory. *Yosher koach*." She used the expression one says to a person who has fulfilled a religious duty.

Moshe called the class back to order without a *niggun.* "Comments and questions," he said flatly, all business.

Skeptics were usually the first to speak. "Did you prepare Dr. Plotkin before the class?"

"Norman, would you answer please?"

"This was a surprise to me. I had no idea I was going to be the subject."

The skeptic would not let it go. "Do the two of you know each other outside the class?"

Moshe answered. "My wife tells me we've met at a cocktail party. I think that's the only time." Norman nodded his agreement. The skeptic seemed satisfied she had uncovered the trick.

"Any other comments or questions?" Moshe asked.

"How is this different from other forms of psychotherapy?"

Moshe smiled but refrained from looking toward Rivkah. "It may be similar in many ways, but ultimately the intent is different. The purpose is not so much to increase function, but to learn the purpose behind function. It may be that some work of reconciliation has to be done first in the personal unconscious before one descends to the archetypal level of the World of Creation, but it is in the World of Creation that the most significant work will take place. This was a first experience, so it was in the World of Formation.

"Note the form of the experience. We descend to a temple, the home of Dr. Plotkin's childhood. There was an angel in the form of a very single-minded dog. There was an encounter, a reconciliation, and perhaps a transformation. That will take some time to see. The matter may not be finished yet. Dr. Plotkin might return to that experience several times more before it will be resolved. Then, if he should continue the discipline, there will be more encounters waiting for him at deeper levels.

"Other comments or questions?" He turned toward Rivkah to see if his answer had been adequate. She shrugged, not completely satisfied.

Moshe nodded in the direction of a raised hand. "Do you always get such clear results in the first session?"

"This wasn't the first session. It was the first descent with Dr. Plotkin, but we have been preparing for this for four weeks now. We have been working steadily in the framework of *Ma-aseh Beraysheet,* the Work of Creation. I have spent four weeks priming us, sharpening us to provide a fertile ground for this experiment. If someone comes in cold off the street, this is not where we start."

"Where do we go from here?" was the next question.

Moshe turned to Rivkah, who produced a sheaf of bibliographies.

"What if we want to do this *merkavah* mysticism ourselves?" a student asked as the papers were circulated.

"I've given every warning and disclaimer I can think of," Moshe said. "Ultimately what you do with this information is up to you. I would not do it alone. With a little effort you can find a situation that will provide some balance. There are some organizations listed in the bibliography. They have retreats and conferences, and some have regional chapters. I suggest you write to them for information." He looked at his watch.

"It's hard to bring a course like this to an end," he continued. "No matter how much earnest work we do, the expectations are always higher. But that's the nature of the work itself. We may get a taste of heaven, but the taste doesn't satisfy us. It leaves us hungry for more.

"Please, let's understand we've done as much as we could do in our five weeks together. Be happy for what we've learned and eager to learn more in other settings. We were all of us blessed in our coming here. Let us now be blessed in our going. And, if you like, we'll end with a *niggun*."

He led them in an upbeat version of Reb Nachman's "All the World Is Just a Narrow Bridge." His heart wasn't quite in it. The *niggun* did not exactly fall flat, but then it did not end the class on a significant note of uplift either. When the singing stopped, the applause was scattered, the leave-taking awkward. Moshe remained on his table so that those who had a need to thank him could do so.

I was the last to come forward. "Thank you, Moshe. Thank you very much. I'll see you on *Shabbat*. Stephanie and I thought we might come by to experience your *minyan*. If that is permissible?"

"It's more than permissible, Sidney. We look forward to seeing you."

With that I left. Moshe and Rivkah remained behind. They were not in the elevator with me when it descended.

Not Emily

"The work of the evening wasn't finished." Stephanie assumed the narrative. "On the way home Rivie asked Moshe what he would do now that the course was over.

"Will you start taking clients again?" Rivie asked.

Moshe kept his eyes on the road. "No, just Sidney. He's not exactly a client."

"What is he, then?"

"I think he's a friend. We have a lot to learn from each other."

"Why now?" she asked. "Why have you gone back to this work now?"

356

He shrugged. "It seemed like a good time."

He turned into the driveway, came to a stop, and backed into the carport.

"Why is this time better than any other time?" she continued, as they walked toward the front door. The path was illuminated by a half-moon and the light that spilled out of the open curtains.

Moshe was saved from a response by a figure that rose to confront them out of the shadows near the front door.

"Hello, rabbi," the figure said.

Rivkah reached for Moshe's arm. "It's Emily," she said.

Moshe looked carefully at the young woman before them. "No," he said. "No, I don't think so. It's not Emily."

CHAPTER 14

Not Emily

Stephanie told the story without interruption.

She looked like Emily. She was dressed in jeans with a Western belt, a loose-fitting man's dress shirt, a large sack hanging from her shoulder that was a feed bag for an animal or a fashionable facsimile. She wore athletic shoes of a radical design.

"It's not Emily," Moshe said. She pressed the bag closer to her side. "Where's Emily?"

"Inside," the woman answered. "How did you know? Emily said you were smart. What you said tonight didn't seem very smart, though."

"Emily's inside?" Rivkah asked, looking toward the window.

"Not inside the house," Moshe said to her without taking his eyes from the woman. "Would you like to come in and talk about what I said tonight?"

"Yes. That's why I came."

"What's your name?"

"Francine."

"What do you have in the bag, Francine?"

"What business is it of yours?"

"The bag is not my business. You are welcome to come in the house. The bag is not. If you put the bag down, you can take it with you when you leave."

Francine was of a slight frame. Moshe outweighed her by more than fifty pounds. He was standing close enough to reach out and take the bag by force, but the last thing he wanted was a physical confrontation. He was not at all certain he would have the better of it. Francine waited, as if hoping he would make an attempt to wrestle the bag from her. When he did not, she settled it on a pile of rocks in the planter by the window. "Let's go," she said.

Moshe motioned to Rivkah to open the door. Francine followed, and he came close behind. They walked deep into the large room. Newspapers from the morning were scattered over the coffee table. "Sit here, please." He directed Francine toward an oversize reading chair.

"Can I get you anything?" Rivkah asked both of them. The laws of hospitality encompassed even such strange behavior.

"Does she have to be here while we talk?" Francine asked.

"It's her house. It's her decision, not yours," Moshe said.

Rivkah looked to Moshe for direction. "What's going on?"

"Francine needs help, but I haven't worked with anyone like Francine in a long time." He turned to Francine. "That's for your information, too. That's something for you to consider." To Rivie he said, "If we started to do some work now, it's likely to turn into a marathon." He checked the time. "It's ten-thirty. We'd likely be up all night."

Rivkah looked at both of them. "What was this thing with the bag? Why did she have to leave it outside?"

"I don't know what's in the bag. Will you tell us, Francine?"

"It's not your business. You said so."

Moshe shrugged. "There might be something dangerous in the bag, Rivie. I don't know. I didn't want to take a chance. That's why I asked her to leave it outside. But I don't think there's any real danger to us here."

Rivkah paused before speaking. "Moshe, I think I have an idea of what's going on. I don't know what my role is in this, if you need me, or want me to stay. You have to let me know."

He wanted her to stay. "It would help, but it's up to you." He pulled a Windsor chair across the carpet and sat down a few feet in front of Francine.

"I don't want her to stay," Francine said.

Moshe leaned forward and repeated firmly, "It's not your decision." He turned to Rivkah. "Can you get me some coffee?" He didn't ask Francine if she wanted any.

Rivkah walked toward the kitchen.

"Francine, do you want to tell her what's going on?" Moshe asked.

"No, you tell her. You tell her what you think is going on."

He changed the subject abruptly. "Who do you work with?"

Francine was taken aback by the question. "What do you mean?"

"Who is your therapist? Who told you about me? Who told you to take my course at the institute?" Francine did not answer. Moshe continued, "If you want to go any further, I need permission from your therapist to work with you. I want to call her, or him, whoever it is."

Francine laughed. "It's not her decision!" she repeated, mimicking Moshe. "It's not her decision. She has nothing to do with this."

There were two therapists who treated dissociative disorders of this kind.

359

Only one was a woman. "Rivie?" he asked toward the kitchen. "Would you please bring my book and the phone? Thank you."

He asked Francine, "Why did you come here tonight? Why didn't Emily come?"

"Emily is too timid. I couldn't believe she went to the class, even. That's not like Emily. Emily is a sit-at-home type. Emily is in deep trouble with Harry for asking those questions."

Rivkah returned with the phone and his book. Moshe looked up a number and dialed.

"Who are you calling?" Francine asked.

"Phyllis Bergman."

Francine was startled. "How did you know?"

"I've been through this before." Into the phone he said, "Phyllis? Moshe Katan. I'm sorry to call so late. I have a visitor at my home. The names are Francine and Emily and Harry. Does that sound familiar?" The names were familiar. "It was Emily who took a class I gave on Jewish mysticism at the Metropolitan Institute. Is it all right if I work with her a little? She was my student. I feel an obligation." After another moment, he said, "Thank you," and hung up. "So Phyllis didn't tell you about me. Who did?"

"Charlotte."

Moshe raised his eyebrows. "Charlotte? I haven't seen her in years. How is she? Where is she?"

"She's well. That's not her name now, but it's what she told me to tell you. She said you would recognize it. She was one of my counselors in Chicago. She told me when I was ready I should look you up."

Rivkah returned with two cups of coffee. Moshe took one. Rivkah kept the other. "What's causing this?" she asked.

"I'm not sure yet, but if she's coming to me, it's probably because of some involvement with a satanic cult," Moshe said.

"Satanism? Be serious," Rivkah protested.

"I am being serious. I didn't believe it either until I worked with a young woman who had broken away from them as a teenager, but it was already too late. The damage had been done." Moshe sipped his coffee. "Did something like that happen to you, Francine?"

"Something like."

"Satanism is real?" Rivkah asked. Her hands tightened on her coffee cup. "The things they say about it really happen?"

"They are all too real, and they really happen. And for those who survive

360

the experience, those who escape, the results are all too often catastrophic." He spoke to Rivkah, but he kept his eyes on Francine. "Do you recall from the class I talked about angels forming a defense to wall off memories of a traumatic experience? In this case, the experience is so severe that one entire personality is walled off from the next. The person fractures into many personalities. Some of them function very well. Some not so well. Is this what's going on, Francine?"

"Pretty much."

"What do you do for a living?"

"Emily is a librarian at the university."

"I bet Emily has a Master's degree in library science."

"Ask her."

"You've been to the clinic in Chicago?" For Rivkah's information he added, "There's a clinic in Chicago that specializes in these cases." To Francine he continued, "And Charlotte is a counselor there? Will you be in touch with her? You'll send her my love?" Francine nodded.

Rivkah asked, "How did you get involved in this, Moshe?"

"Do you remember when I was developing the *merkavah* stuff? Phyllis came to learn with me. I can't remember who referred her. Someone in the Havurah. She thought the *merkavah* techniques might be useful. She began to send me some of her clients for the spiritual side of the work. Sometimes I'd come in late and tell you it was another tough one. I couldn't share exactly what it was with you. I'm sorry. It goes even beyond confidentiality, if word gets out and the cult finds the client."

"If you suspected Emily was part of a satanic cult, why didn't you tell me?"

"I wasn't sure. How could I say anything unless I was sure? It would be *lashon ha-ra*. That's the Hebrew expression for slander," he explained to Francine. "I suspected what was going on, but I couldn't talk about it."

"Thank you," Francine said sincerely.

"What's going on here now?" Rivkah asked.

"Probably an attempt at a reconciliation. It will be very different from the work we did with Norman. There may be something to learn from it, if you would like to stay and observe. It's up to you, Rivie. It's likely to be a real roller-coaster ride."

Francine's affect changed in the chair. The muscles on the left side of her face tightened. Her back arched, her shoulders lifted. The pattern of her breathing deepened. "Get the fucking bitch out of here now!" It wasn't Francine's voice at all.

Rivkah nearly dropped her coffee. Moshe was shocked himself, even though he had expected it.

"It's not your decision, Harry." Moshe's voice had no anger in it, only sadness and compassion. To Francine he had spoken sternly; to Harry he spoke with kindness.

"I don't want her here. You get her out of here now!"

"It's Rivkah's decision to stay or to go, Harry."

Harry's features relaxed. Francine returned. "What just happened?" she asked.

"Harry came for a brief visit," Moshe told her. "Only a few seconds. He's not pleasant."

"I don't know if I should stay," Rivkah said as she sat down, making a commitment.

Francine said, "Harry doesn't like it that I'm here. Emily is in deep trouble. I don't know if Emily is ever going to be able to come back. I've always been able to stand up to Harry before, but this time, I don't know. I'm afraid."

"How afraid?"

"Really afraid. I don't know if I can do it."

"You had a lot of courage to come here like this on your own, Francine, to wait for me by the door."

"I had to. It's not for me. It's for the little ones."

"The children?" He kept his eyes forward, but spoke for Rivkah's benefit. "Are there children inside? Are you the one who takes care of them, Francine?"

"Yes. I'm afraid for them. I'm the one who stands up to Harry. I don't know what would happen to them if anything happened to me."

"Why did you choose this time to come here?"

Francine began to cry. "Because Harry is getting stronger. I don't know how much longer I can hold out, and the children are afraid. I called Charlotte. She told me to come. She said you could help me. Would you? Please?"

Rivkah spoke. "May I ask something?" Moshe nodded. "The children are infantile personalities?"

"The children are children. They broke off as children and never grew up."

"All of these people are inside her? None of them are real? All of them are imaginary?"

"Just the opposite. None of them are imaginary. All of them are real."

"Who is listening to what we're saying right now?"

"All of them."

"Even Harry?"

"Even Harry."

Rivkah paused to consider that. "Charlotte is real, though. I mean, there's another person, in another body, who is Charlotte."

"Yes. It seems Charlotte is in Chicago."

"I don't know how you tell what's real from what isn't real."

"It's all real, Rivie. Every bit of it. Do you want to help me in this? I can really use your help. I'm tired. I can use all the energy you can lend me. Just your being here gives me support."

"If it's all right with Francine."

"I can use her help," Moshe said to Francine. "It's been a long day for me. Is it all right if she stays? She's asking you. It's your decision now."

"It's all right."

"Let's get to work, then. Rivie, would you turn down the lights please. And some more coffee?" He pulled his chair closer to Francine so their knees were almost touching. Her chair was deep and low. It would not be easy for her to raise herself out of it. The Windsor chair was hard and high. "Make yourself comfortable, Francine. We don't want a muscle cramp getting in the way."

Francine shifted her weight in the chair.

"Were you in the class when we taught the breathing techniques? Do you remember how to use the letters of God's name and inscribe them on your body?"

"I'm afraid to do that."

"Why?"

She bit her lip. "I don't think the letters of God's name belong on me."

"I can see them there," Moshe told her. "Look. I can trace them."

He made a jab in the air above her head for the *YOD*, outlined the *HEY* before her arms and shoulders, drew the *VAV* in the air in front of her chest, and traced the lower *HEY* around her hips and legs.

Rivkah returned with coffee from the kitchen in time to see him tracing the Hebrew letters of the divine name in the air. "Are you doing an exorcism?" she asked in disbelief.

"Just the opposite, Rivie. Just the opposite. We're going to do an *innercism*, aren't we, Francine?"

"I'm scared," Francine said, ignoring the question.

"Can you feel the letters of God's name traced on your body?"

363

"I'm afraid to."

"Breathe in, Francine. Breathe in, and imagine the breath coming down through your lungs all the way to your toes." Francine closed her eyes and inhaled. "Hold the breath, Francine. Hold the breath. Let it rise up in your chest, and now exhale, breathe it out through your mouth, slowly, slowly. Don't hurry to take another breath. Now, breathe in again, all the way down to your toes."

Rivkah placed the full cup of black coffee next to Moshe and sat in a chair to the side. Moshe observed Francine's breathing cycle. On the eighth breath he spoke. "I have a question for Emily. Would you let her come forward please, or send the question to her?" He did not wait for a response. "I want to know why Emily is so interested in reincarnation. Can you tell me that?"

Francine shifted slightly in her chair. She began to cry, gentle tears. "Because I'm dying. I've really screwed up, and I'm dying, and I want a chance to do it again."

"Emily? Is that you speaking?"

"Yes."

Moshe refocused his energy to address Emily rather than Francine. He recalled the timid Emily who raised her hand in the first session and spoke to her. "Emily, for you there is most certainly reincarnation. You can be sure of that. If you surrender yourself, you will not be lost. All of you, every bit of you, will be gathered up and cherished, and you will have just the opportunity you ask for. You will have your forgiveness and the opportunity to do things differently. I know it is frightening for you to surrender. It must be terrifying. It will take a lot of faith, a huge faith to allow that to happen."

In the next twenty minutes Emily expressed her fears again and again, each time to be met by reassurances. The energy of her fears decreased, the strength of her faith increased, and Emily was gone. Francine announced it.

"She's with me," Francine said in Francine's voice, from Francine's aspect softened somewhat by the inclusion of Emily. "She's in me," she corrected herself. "What do I do now?"

"Who else is listening? Who else is close?"

For two hours Moshe invited personalities to surface, to be cherished, to be strengthened. Several were folded into Francine. Occasionally a child was in the chair, terrified, crying, alone, abandoned. Moshe motioned Rivkah to come forward. She spoke to the child and caressed her. Her voice was soothing, her touch reassuring. The child's trembling quieted, and the child became still.

"I'm tired," Francine said. "I need to rest."

"Five minutes," Moshe told her. "Five minutes. I'll wake you in five minutes."

Francine curled up in the chair. She had the appearance of a young girl, peaceful in her sleep.

"I've never seen anything like this, Moshe," Rivkah whispered to him in the kitchen. "I've heard about it. I'm not sure I ever really believed it."

"No whispers," he said aloud. "I don't want any of them to think there's a conspiracy here. They're welcome to hear anything we have to say."

"But she's asleep."

"Francine's asleep. I don't know about the rest of them."

"How many are there?"

"I don't know that either."

The dishes were in the sink. He washed; Rivkah dried.

Rivkah asked, "How many clients like this have you seen?"

Moshe laughed. "I could say a hundred, but Francine is the fourth. It feels like a hundred though."

She did not find his answer humorous. "And you never shared any of this with me." She held up her hand so he would not interrupt. "I know. It's a matter of confidentiality. But even so, you might have let me know something about the nature of the work."

"Rivie, I couldn't. People might be looking for her, people who would kill her if they could find her."

"Even so. I don't like the feeling you're keeping something from me."

Moshe had no response to that. He finished the dishes in silence. "We have to get back to work. She's sleeping. We're not. The heavy work is still ahead of us."

"What more do we have to do?" she asked him.

"What we've done so far is to work with whatever was close to the surface. She was ready to do all of that. It could have happened with Phyllis in the course of therapy, or spontaneously when she was by herself, as much as she is ever by herself. Or that any of us is by ourselves." He closed his eyes to focus on the work at hand. It was not a time to wax existential. "She's marshaling her forces, getting ready for what we're about to do."

"So what is it we're about to do?"

"Pay a visit to Harry. That's what this is all about. She was afraid to face that encounter alone."

They returned to the living room. Rivkah picked up the newspapers and neatened the area, a sure sign she was perturbed. Moshe sat back in his chair and waited impatiently for Rivkah to finish.

"Francine," he said gently. "It's time to go back to work."

She stirred in the chair and uncurled. "What do we do?" she asked, looking first at him and then at Rivkah. She smiled at Rivkah. "Thank you," she said, but did not make clear who was speaking or why.

"We begin again with the breathing, with the letters of God's name."

The letters fit more easily this time. There was less resistance. Moshe led Francine through the letter *HEY*. She fixed herself on the letter *VAV* and pulled herself away, leaving her body behind as she yearned toward the second *HEY,* the entranceway to something like a corridor, a tunnel, a cave, a temple.

Francine was a good subject. He had expected that. All of them had been good subjects. It was a quality necessary to survive the experiences of their childhood. From each such client he had learned more about the satanic cult. To break away from it required the greatest courage and resourcefulness. To stay away from it required unflagging will and determination. Those who had the strength to escape were fearful for their lives ever after.

Should he have shared the nature of his work with Rivkah, he asked himself. Rivkah was angry with him. He could feel her anger. It was distracting him.

"What do you see?" he asked Francine.

"The entranceway is like a mine shaft. Wooden beams above and on both sides."

"How do you feel about entering?"

She bit her lower lip. "There's nowhere else to go."

Moshe surrounded himself with the image of the letter *HEY*. He used it as a barrier against Rivkah's resentment, to no avail. There was no way he could have shared his experiences with her, he thought. It was unfair of her to ask. It was unfair of her to be resentful. Whenever he took risks, he did it by himself and spared her the exposure. That's the way it had been with the commodity markets. She might have joined him, but she had cut him loose. So he went on by himself.

"How do you feel?" he repeated.

"Frightened. Alone," Francine responded. After several seconds, she asked, "Are you down here with me? I don't feel you nearby."

Damn it all, he thought. She was so sensitive. She could pick up the slightest nuance. "No, I'm not that close," he answered truthfully. "Stay there, wait for me to catch up." He felt he was diving under pressure, rushing for the bottom, unsure of his equipment, not having made the proper safety checks.

After the panic on the Cayman wall, Rivkah joined him only for dives at shallow depths. The deep exposure was not for her. She had no right to be angry with him. She had no right to be resentful he had hidden himself from her. He had not hidden. It was she who had not joined him. He had not hidden, but also, he knew, he had not shared. He opened his eyes and looked at Francine. She was suspended, waiting for him. "Rivie," he said, "I need you to come with me. I can't do this by myself."

Rivkah had her eyes open. Her glance at him was not kind.

"Francine needs us together," he said. "If we're not together in this, I can't help her."

She turned toward Francine and made her decision. "What do I have to do, Moshe?"

"Do just what she does. Do the breathing. Image the letters. Move through them." He shifted his chair to be closer to Rivkah and held her hand. They used to hold hands when they drifted alongside shallow coral reefs in the Bahamas. "Deeper still," he encouraged her. "Francine is waiting for us, and she's deep."

He pulled the letter *HEY* about him again, felt its security, left it behind heading for the depths, pulling Rivkah along with him. "We're here," he told Francine after several minutes. "What do you see?"

"The opening to the mine. I've been waiting. It stays the same, wooden beams above and on each side."

"How do you feel?"

"Nervous. Anxious."

"Look into the depths of the mine. What do you see?" He expected a flower, with many petals, an aggregate object, a collective of some kind.

"A dot of light," she said.

"What color is the light?"

"Pale blue. Maybe green."

"I can image a pale blue light. Maybe green. Rivie? How about you?" He squeezed her hand. She squeezed back. "Rivkah is here, too, right beside me."

"That's good," Francine said.

"What would it take to move closer to that light?" he asked her.

"I would have to go into the mine."

"How do you feel about going into the mine?"

367

"I don't know."

"A word list. When I think about going into the mine I feel . . ."

"When I think about going into the mine," Francine began, "I feel determined. Anxious. Afraid. Resolved. Little."

Moshe waited for more words, but none followed. He said, "I'm going to repeat the words. Remain focused on the entrance to the mine while I repeat them. As you hear them, decide which words go together. These are the words: *determined; anxious; afraid; resolved; little.* Which words go together?"

When the words had fallen into place, she answered, "*Determined* and *resolved.*" She said them as if she were determined and resolved. "*Anxious, afraid,* and *little,*" she added in a small voice.

Moshe leaned forward. "Add some more words to determined and resolved. Feel that feeling as if it were over to the right."

Francine responded, "*Determined. Resolved. Courageous. Set. Must. No choice. Now.*"

"And add some words to *anxious, afraid* and *little,* and put that feeling over to the left."

"*Anxious. Afraid. Little. Small. Trembling. Whimpering. Tiny.*"

"Now stretch the feelings out, far to the left and far to the right. On the left you feel tiny, insignificant, afraid. On the right you feel powerful, courageous, determined. Imagine a pole that connects the two feelings. Imagine you're holding that pole, right in the middle, so it's balanced. How does it feel to be holding such a pole?"

Francine's forehead wrinkled. Her back straightened and her chest came forward slightly. "Balanced. Stable."

"Can you hold that feeling and take a step forward?"

"Yes."

"Another step?"

"Yes."

"Are you ready now to move into the mine, closer to that blue light?"

"Green. It's green now. Yes. I'm ready."

"Let us know what you see." Moshe relaxed back into his chair. He squeezed Rivkah's hand and received a squeeze back. They had developed a sign to signify okay. He closed his eyes to intensify his focus on the entrance to the mine, the wooden beams above and on either side, and the green light in the distance.

"There's nothing except the green light," Francine reported. "I'm getting closer to it. It's like an oval jewel, cut like a diamond. A green diamond. The light that comes out from the center of it is a pale green."

An oval jewel cut like a diamond. Moshe envisioned it along with Francine and knew he had an image suitable for the work.

"Focus on the center of the jewel, Francine. What is the shape of the center?"

"Oval."

"And around the center, what shapes do you see?"

"All different shapes."

"And what are the colors of the different shapes?"

"Different."

"Francine, can you focus on each of them in turn? Choose one, if you can, and tell me about it."

"One is blue." Through half-opened eyes, Moshe saw her forehead wrinkle. "A little dull."

"What is its shape?" he asked.

"Squarish."

"What color is the one next to it?"

"Yellow. A dull yellow."

"You seem uncomfortable looking at the shapes this way."

"Yes. They're dull. Flat. No light comes from them."

"Where does the light come from, Francine?"

"From the center. The green oval."

"Can you look into it? Could you go inside it, and look out from the inside?"

After a substantial pause, Francine answered, "Yes. It's very big inside. I didn't realize it would be so big." Her body uncurled somewhat in the chair.

"Can you see the blue square and the yellow shape from the inside looking out?"

"Yes. They have a lot more light. They're much brighter."

"Can you turn yourself toward the center of the jewel? What do you see?"

"It's so big." The words held awe. "There's light all around me, patches of different color."

"How many different colors and shapes are there, Francine?"

She shook her head ever so slightly. "I don't know. Too many to count."

"How many jewels are there, Francine?"

"Just one." The answer came immediately.

Moshe chose words to reinforce the learning. "Many facets," he said. "Just one jewel. Many expressions of the same person, when viewed from the center looking out. Many different persons, dull persons, when viewed on the outside looking in. Am I describing your experience correctly?"

"Yes."

"If you like, you might move back and forth and see it better. Move out to one of the shapes, and feel what it is like to be there on the outside."

Francine shifted her position in the chair. "I feel the blue shape."

"How does it feel to you?"

"It feels *Mary-ish*."

Had he not been so tired, Moshe would have pursued that. He did not know what *Mary-ish* meant but was satisfied Francine did. "What do you see from the blue shape? Can you see the other shapes?"

"No."

"The blue shape is all by itself?"

"Yes."

"Can you return to the center of the jewel?" Francine's balance shifted again in the chair. "What do you see from the center of the jewel?"

"Lots of colors. Lots of shapes."

"From the center you can see lots of colors and lots of shapes. Each facet of the jewel is different. One is *Mary-ish,* one is *Emily-ish.* If you are out there, you think each one is independent of the next, but here in the center, you see that they are all facets of the same personality. Can you see that?"

"Yes."

"You know that for a certainty."

"Yes." She began to laugh.

"Why are you laughing, Francine?"

"I just realized something. I'm *jewel-ish*. I'm learning from a *rabbi,* and I'm *jewel-ish!*"

Moshe felt a squeeze from Rivkah. "That's the *hatimah,*" he said. "That's the word you can use to remember this experience. You feel *jewel-ish*. Now, if you're ready, look around the jewel. Is there a part of it that doesn't have color? Is there a part of it that you can't see clearly?"

"Yes."

"What do you imagine is there?"

"I know what's there. Harry."

"Why don't you want to see Harry?" She did not respond. The question was too complex. He chose another. "How do you feel about moving toward that area?"

"Afraid. I feel afraid, angry, mad."

"What are you angry at?"

"Harry."

"Are you afraid of Harry or angry at Harry?"

"Both."

"Are you more afraid or more angry?"

"Angry. I'm more angry." There was surprise in her voice. "I'm angry at Harry."

"Why are you angry at Harry?"

Francine's body tensed. She was in apparent distress. Moshe felt Rivkah incline forward to help Francine. He squeezed Rivkah's hand to restrain her. "Why are you angry at Harry?" he asked again.

"Because of what he did."

"What did he do?" Moshe waited for a response. "What did Harry do? Francine, can you tell me what Harry did?"

"No," she whispered. "Harry is very bad. Very, very bad. Harry is dangerous. I think we'd better stay away from Harry."

"Where is Harry, Francine?"

"There. The dark one. Between the blue and the yellow." She turned her head from right to left. "Right there. The dark one."

"Can you move toward the dark, Francine?"

"Don't want to."

"Move toward the dark, Francine. I have a question for Harry." There was a risk in this, Moshe knew. He had only so much energy and was using it up quickly. He needed Harry to respond soon. "Harry, what did you do?"

Francine's nose wrinkled up as if she could not bear the smell. The muscles of her neck stood out in cords. The edges of her mouth pulled back as if a metal bit had been placed between her teeth. The voice that issued from her throat was muffled. "Who the fuck are you, asshole?"

"What did you do, Harry?" Moshe asked gently. "What did they make you do?"

"Who's the bitch, asshole? She'd eat you alive if she could, you know that? The way she feels, she'd eat you fucking alive."

Moshe felt Rivkah's squeeze of alarm. He reached over and caressed her one hand in both of his. "What did they make you do, Harry? Why is Francine angry with you?"

"Why is the bitch so fucking angry with *you,* asshole?"

"I know why Rivkah is angry with me, Harry," Moshe said evenly. "Why is Francine angry with you?"

Harry laughed. "Francine's angry with me because she didn't stop me. She knows she didn't stop me. She thinks she's so fucking good, but she just sat there and watched everything and never did a fucking thing to stop me. She's angry because she knew I'd tell you. She cut me off and left me out here, the fucking bitch."

Francine spoke up. "I had to! I had to! He's the one who killed her! I had to cut him off! He'd kill again!" In a calmer tone she added, "He's evil. Pure evil. I cut him off so he couldn't kill again."

"What does he look like, Francine. Tell me what Harry looks like."

Francine squeezed her eyes together until tears were wrung out of them.

Moshe repeated his question. "Tell me what Harry looks like. What do you see?" She shook her head violently back and forth. Moshe pressed, "What do you see, Francine? What does Harry look like?"

"Me." She forced the single syllable out through clenched teeth. "Harry looks like me."

"Is Harry all evil, Francine?"

"I don't know."

"Are you all evil, Francine?"

"I don't know."

Moshe exhaled a long breath. Only then was he conscious he had been holding it. "What color is Harry, Francine?"

"Pink."

"Not dark anymore?"

"No."

"How do you feel?"

"Tired. Very tired."

"You did it, whatever it was, whatever they made you do, and you cut off the part of you that did it, so you didn't have to face it. That way you could say Harry did it, not you. Is that what happened, Francine?"

"Something like."

"You tried to cut off the bad and throw it away, but the bad isn't all bad, is it? And the good isn't all good. Do you know what a bar magnet is, Francine?" She said nothing. Moshe went on. "Do you think you could cut off just the south pole of a bar magnet? Do you know what you'd have then? You'd have a big magnet and a little magnet. They would both have a north pole and a south pole. And the little one would look just like the big one, just smaller. Do you understand, Francine?"

Francine continued to cry. The tears came gently, without effort.

"You're strong enough now to accept this. You can bring Harry back in. Harry's lonely out there. That's why he's so obnoxious. You weren't strong enough, back then, to resist what they did to you. You're strong enough now."

"I didn't kill anyone. They did it," she said.

"Who's speaking?" Moshe asked.

"Me. Us. Harry's with me. We didn't fucking kill anybody. I didn't kill anybody. I watched. They made me watch. They took my baby. They made me give them my baby. They made me watch."

Moshe felt Rivkah tense. She tried to pull away from him, but he held her hand tightly. It was not yet time for her to go to Francine. Later Rivkah could comfort her and console her, but not at this depth.

"They made me watch while they killed my baby. They made me watch."

Again Rivkah tried to pull her hand away. Again he held it. He opened his eyes, looked at his wife, found her glaring back at him with such a profound anger that by reflex he opened his hand and let her go. He saw she had not been trying to go to Francine. She had been trying to pull away from him. It was all he could do to focus on the work at hand, to bring it to an orderly close. "A little bit more before we come back to the surface. Are you still inside the jewel?" Francine nodded. "How does it appear to you?"

"The light is blue now. There's a lot of light. The facets are shining."

"Are you ready to come back?"

"Yes."

"Look up. What's above you?"

"Light."

"If you like, you might surrender to the light."

Francine Harry Emily and the children surrendered to the light and began her ascent. While Francine floated up into the light, Moshe kept his eyes closed in an attempt to manage the pain.

Sidney waited for the students to recover and then taught this story of the Baal Shem Tov.

Sometimes when a client would come for counseling to the great *rebbe,* the Baal Shem Tov, the client wouldn't know exactly why he came, and the Baal Shem Tov wouldn't know either. The client might have rambled on and on forever and ever trying to focus, but the Baal Shem Tov had no patience for that. Instead the two of them would learn Torah together. When you learned words of Torah with the Baal Shem Tov, you descended through world after world.

What was hidden on the surface was revealed at depth.

How did that happen? On the surface, the client and the Baal Shem Tov were separate entities. As they descended through the worlds, space became compressed, and their very beings overlapped. At that moment the Baal Shem Tov had insight into his student and understood his concerns and needs with certainty. Nothing could remain hidden. At that same moment the student might have had similar insight into the *rebbe,* but usually the student's concerns and needs were substantial enough to mask whatever direct insight might be gained.

When the Baal Shem Tov and the student returned to the surface, the *rebbe* knew how to respond and what course to take.

That was how the Baal Shem Tov counseled. Moshe had made use of the technique himself, but in his eagerness to help Francine, he had forgotten what happened when partners ventured deep together.

When he opened his eyes again to Rivkah, she was still glaring at him. He had invited her to dive beside him into the depths of Francine's experience. At depth, all borders overlapped. He and Francine and Rivkah had overlapped with each other. When Francine had begun the process of resolution, when she was no longer in danger and no longer an object of concern, Rivkah had been free at depth to pursue her own course. She had asked again the question that had gone without satisfactory answer week after week. "Moshe, why are you teaching this material now?" She had looked into him, and at that depth, nothing could be hidden from her. In a flash, she understood.

"It's because of me, isn't it?" were her first words to him. "You taught the whole course and engineered this whole thing because of me."

That Stephanie had completed her story about Emily and Francine had been an act of Olympic fortitude. From the point she mentioned the jewel, the story was on automatic, flowing out of her, while the greatest part of her was following the diamond as it bounced on the platform at the train station. She had divided, dissociated, become two separate people, telling two stories at the same time, one to the students, the other, a story for later, for Rivkah, should she find the courage.

Sidney's discourse about the Baal Shem Tov she hadn't heard. She knew all too well Rivkah's recognition of Moshe's manipulation, all the feelings associated with it. She had too much going on to deal with that again.

The diamond fell from her mother's hand and bounced on the platform of the train station. The guards saw it. One picked it up and held it to the light.

"This is very pretty," he said.

"You don't need to know this story," her mother interrupted. "Stephanie, pay attention to your husband. Go somewhere else. You don't need to know this story."

It was too late. The story was there. But there was something she needed to do first. She needed Father Porter's watch. She reached for it, held it in her virtual hand, opened it, counted the stones, all diamonds, one two three, one two three, one two, one two, one two.

"So, do you have any more?" the guard said to her mother. Her mother said nothing. He slapped her. "Do you have any more?"

They took her mother and father inside the station, an empty room, searched her mother. They searched her handbag, her luggage, stripped her of her clothes. They spread her on a table and found the diamonds.

"If this can come out, then this can go in," one of the guards said. And then another, and another.

They let them continue out of Germany, her mother and father. They arrived in New York, with nothing. Eviscerated. Nothing at all.

Al had been lucky. He had been sent to the camps.

CHAPTER 15

Numb

"There are different qualities to numbness," Sidney said. "Ask any anaesthesiologist."

Once Francine had backed safely onto the road, Moshe turned to walk down the fire trail toward the lake. The footing on the dirt path was treacherous. The earliest emanations of dawn were not enough to make the flashlight unnecessary. At the edge of the water he raised the pistol and ejected the clip into his hand. One by one he flipped the rounds into the water. He heard the splash as each struck. The empty clip followed the rounds. He was about to heave the pistol after it when it occurred to him to check the chamber. He pulled back the slide. The round that had been readied for firing catapulted back over his shoulder and fell to the ground. It took him a few moments to find it. When he did, it joined its comrades in the lake. The pistol itself made a big splash. He could only imagine the ripples in the darkness.

Rivkah was asleep in bed when Moshe returned. He was too agitated to join her. His sense of time had been disrupted by the events of the night. He left the bedroom, gathered his *tallit* and *tefillin* from the armoire in the living room, and ventured out onto the deck to *daven.* The black rawhide noose cinched down tightly above his left biceps. With each of the seven coils on his forearm he imagined a color of the rainbow. When the spectrum merged to white, he turned his attention to the *tefillin* for his head, placing the leather box between and above his eyes. He extended his left hand and bound the rawhide strap around the middle finger with the words, "I betroth myself to you, I engage myself to you."

The shadows were pronounced in the early-morning light. He lifted himself with blessings and psalms, meditated on the words of the *Sh'ma,* and in his recitation of the *Amidah,* paused at the petition for insight and knowledge, suspending himself, leaving himself open to receive direction. Without any certainty he closed his prayer. Still wrapped in *tallit* and *tefillin,* he sat in a chair to ponder the day. There he fell asleep.

When he awoke, his arm was numb. Rivkah was gone.

Sidney continued when Stephanie shook her head, indicating she was not ready to tell the next story. "If Moshe was numb after that night's experience," he said, "Rivkah was much the opposite. She was aware."

Rivkah had called from the hospital and left a message on the machine that she would be home late. Moshe prepared *Shabbat* dinner. Rivkah returned home with barely enough time to shower and change before candle lighting. When she came to the table, he had the candles ready and waiting for her. He said the blessing over the wine. They sang the songs that welcomed the Sabbath queen and her retinue of angels. They had no guests that night. They sat down to dinner alone.

Moshe had struggled all day to find the right words to open the dialogue, but had not found any. He closed his eyes and began.

"I don't know."

"What don't you know?"

"I taught the course because I suspected something, because I saw something in your test results. I don't know that there's anything there. I showed what I saw to Dowling, and she thinks I'm nuts. But it scared me, and that's why I taught the course."

Rivkah digested that. "So what's the connection? What's the connection between something wrong with me and teaching a course on the Kabbalah?"

He chose his words deliberately. "The course was a way for me to sharpen myself, and for you to acquire some tools, just in case you should need them."

"So I'm right. You taught the course because of me."

"Yes. For me, too, but because of you."

Her self-control did not keep her cheeks from becoming flushed and her voice from rising. "What do you think you're going to do? Say some magic prayers and make it go away? All of your prayers, all Reb Hayim's prayers, all the prayers in the world didn't do a damn thing last time!"

"I wasn't teaching prayers, Rivie. I'm not saying prayers won't help, but that's not what I was teaching. I was teaching balance in the face of exposure. If it should come back, we would both need all the balance we could possibly find. Now I don't know that it has come back. All I know is that I was scared, and I needed some balance. For me. And if you learn something in the process, what harm is there in that?"

"Why not just tell me what you were doing, and why you were doing it?"

The answer seemed so obvious to him. "Why should I scare you? The odds are that there's nothing wrong with you. I was the one who was scared. The whole course was just in case. I needed it first of all for myself. And yes, I hoped you would come along. I wanted to share with you some of the things I've learned. But I never meant to do you any harm, Rivie."

Rivkah pushed what was left of her dessert away. She played with her napkin. "I've been thinking about it all day, Moshe," she said evenly, without looking at him. "You didn't do me any harm. But I don't like this feeling that you're hiding things from me, that you know something I don't know that affects me, and that you're not sharing it with me." When she did look up, the anger was back in her voice. "I didn't like it last night with Emily, that you were hiding your experience from me. That you had worked with women like her before. It was like you had been hiding it from me for all these years. What we did last night might have been dangerous. I didn't have a clue as to what was going on. For all I know, she might have had a gun in that bag of hers." She saw it in his eyes. "Damn it, Moshe! She did have a gun in that bag, didn't she?"

"Rivie, it's not like I had any opportunity to tell you!"

Rivkah pushed her chair back, ran to the bedroom, and closed the door firmly behind her.

After several minutes he stood, cleared the table, and did the dishes. When the last dish had been put away, the table wiped down, the lights turned off, he went to the bedroom door. It was locked. That door had never been locked before. "Rivie," he said. "Rivie, let me in."

When he tried the knob again, the door opened. She was under the covers. Crumpled tissues littered the floor by the bed.

"I love you," he began this time. It was a better beginning. "If I've hurt you in any way, I'm sorry. Everything I've done, whether right or wrong, has been because I love you. I don't like the notion of sharing with you things that scare you, if there's no reason to scare you." His words seemed to be acceptable.

He continued, "You know how I hedge in the commodity markets? I take a position, just in case something bad might happen? Well, what I've done here is the same. I've taken a position just in case something bad might happen. I don't know that anything bad will happen, Rivie. That's the bottom line. I truly, honestly, don't know."

She looked up at him through red eyes. "But I know, Moshe."

378

"What do you mean?"

She wrung a pillow in her hands. "In the last few weeks I've lost five pounds. I was so proud of myself. I wasn't even trying to, and I lost five pounds."

"Why didn't you tell me?"

"Because I probably had guessed why." She put the pillow down and smoothed it. "I went to Fowler today. That's why I was late. He saw something. They're going to do a biopsy on Monday."

The Minyan

"There's something we haven't told you," Stephanie said with a sudden burst of energy. "You don't get to choose your stories. They choose you. You surrender to them, they come up, sometimes whole, sometimes in pieces. Sometimes they're finished, packaged with a pretty bow. Sometimes they finish you by trimming off unnecessary bits and pieces. You should know that. Moshe told me that. Told us that. I'm not sure I quite believed him. I believe him now."

She looked toward Sidney, into Sidney, knew his story, but that was for later. There was a different story for the moment.

Stephanie said, "After I married Sidney, I pretty much gave up on Jewish life, probably because I felt my parents had given up on me.

"I had come with Sidney to the Kabbalah course not because of its Jewish content but to be with Sidney. Still, I enjoyed the course and looked forward to it from week to week.

"I became curious about the Havurah. After I got to know Rivkah, more curious still. We talked a bit during and after the classes, but her schedule was such that, after our coffee together in her kitchen, we didn't have time together one-on-one. So it was with a bit of curiosity about the Havurah and a desire to spend some time with Rivkah that I accompanied Sidney to the Havurah *Shabbat* morning service, something they always referred to as the *minyan*—the quorum for prayer."

"Rivie doesn't usually come for the *davening*," Moshe said. "She may be here later for the Torah discussion. Let me get you situated." From a cardboard box he withdrew two prayer books. "We like to *daven* around tables. It frees our hands, and it's a place for our *humashim*. You'll see that people bring their own. Everyone has a favorite Torah commentary."

"You do your services here every Saturday?" I asked.

"Every Saturday."

"What about the High Holidays? Where do you meet then?"

Moshe pointed upward. "We rent the sanctuary. The rabbis in their wisdom fixed the calendar so that the first day of Rosh Hashanah and Yom Kippur could never fall on a Sunday. That way we always have church space to rent."

"How convenient," I said.

"It's because of *Shabbat* and Yom Kippur," Sidney explained. "On *Shabbat* one would not be able to make adequate preparations for the fast day if Yom Kippur were to fall on a Sunday. It would be a hardship."

Moshe's eyebrows went up a notch. "I'm impressed," he said to Sidney. "What have you been reading?"

The leader began singing the opening hymn, *Mah Tovu,* and that pre-empted any answer.

We sat together. Moshe started us on the right page. The leader had chosen an upbeat pace. The melodies had hints of jazz and reggae. Within a few minutes all of the seats were filled, the tables covered with books. The volume of the singing rose, harmonies erupted. Moshe had been sitting by us but soon submerged underneath the cover of prayer.

After an hour, the service done, the leader began to read from the Torah. Each time the door of the vestry opened, Moshe looked up to see if it was Rivkah. The Torah paraded among the members, carried by a young woman who had celebrated her bat mitzvah with the *minyan* the week before. As the Torah was readied for reading, the service leader leaned over to Moshe to ask in a whisper if his friends could be called for an *aliyah*. "Sidney's not Jewish," Moshe said, "but Stephanie is. You can call her."

The first *aliyah,* the honor of being called to the Torah, was for newcomers. Three people, myself among them, were called. The leader improvised a *mishebayrach,* a blessing of welcome, for those of us new to the *minyan*. I was nearly in tears. I had not been a participant in a service since attaching myself to Sidney.

The second *aliyah* was for a couple who had become grandparents for the third time. They stood for the reading, recited blessings, and were blessed in return with a *mishebayrach,* a blessing, for their new granddaughter, that she should grow to become the pillar of a family of her own, learn much Torah, and accomplish many wonderful deeds.

The third *aliyah* was for those in need of healing, either for themselves, or for someone close to them. The tradition of the *minyan* was that those who stood for the *mishebayrach* for healing would say for whom the blessing was intended, so that members of the community might know who was in need. Rivkah was not there to stand for herself, and Moshe, without her permission, did not stand for her.

The progression of *aliyot* continued. Moshe no longer looked to the door. The Torah discussion was lively. He did not participate in the arguments, but I did. It is my nature to participate in arguments.

At the conclusion of the services Moshe apologized to us for Rivkah's absence. "She usually comes for the Torah service."

"Next week, perhaps," I said. "I've been looking for something like this for a long time."

Moshe had no small talk to offer, nor did he stay for the *kiddush,* the blessing over the wine, with the *minyan.* He was the first to leave the vestry.

His behavior bordered on the discourteous. I wasn't upset however. I was worried about Rivkah without quite knowing why.

Rivkah at Home

"Rivkah hadn't come to the service because the bridge between them was still too narrow to cross," Stephanie said. "That bridge is constructed of words, and not enough words had been spoken."

Rivkah was in the kitchen when Moshe returned from *Shabbat* services. She had prepared the *Shabbat* meal. The table was set.

"Good *Shabbos,*" Moshe said, and kissed her. "The table looks beautiful. Just the two of us?"

"Just the two of us."

"Sidney and Stephanie Lee were at the service." He looked up, hoping to catch her eyes, but she was not looking at him. "I missed you. I hoped you would come."

"I thought about it. I couldn't bring myself to go. You would have wanted me to stand for a *mishebayrach*. I don't think I could have done that. I thought I would stay home and make a nice lunch for us." At last she looked up at him. "I don't know when I'll be able to do this again."

381

Moshe lifted the cup of wine and sang the blessing. Together they went to the kitchen to fulfill the ritual of washing their hands. Returning to the dining room, Rivkah uncovered the hallah and sang the blessing for the bread. They ate for a while in silence.

"Moshe, do you understand why I couldn't come to the service?" When he didn't answer, she continued. "I couldn't stand up for a *mishebayrach*. I'm not ready yet to let people know I might be sick. You didn't stand for me, did you?" He shook his head. "They don't work anyway." He was not certain what the pronoun referred to, but he was hesitant to ask. "I'm not saying it's not a nice custom. But it's not as if they really work. It wouldn't have made any difference. The cancer is there or it isn't there. If it is there, no amount of prayer can make it not there."

He wasn't about to argue with her. Not then.

Grammar

"According to tradition the letters of the Hebrew alphabet were in existence before the world was created," Sidney said. "Otherwise, how could creation have taken place? God created by speaking. If the alphabet had not existed, how could there have been any words? It is said that whoever understands the secrets of the Hebrew letters, understands the process of creation. And whoever understands the process of creation can make changes in the process of creation."

Monday Fowler did the biopsy.

Monday night I came to the house to learn. Stephanie had asked if she could come but had been put off with an excuse. Rivkah was resting in bed. Moshe and I descended to the study.

"Where would you like to begin, Sidney?" Moshe asked when I was seated.

"Moshe, I would like to begin by learning Hebrew."

"Learning Hebrew?" he asked in surprise. "Do you want to be able to pronounce it? Understand it? Speak it?"

"I want to be able to read Hebrew with understanding. I already know the alphabet. I want to be able to read the Torah in the original. I don't know how else I can learn the Kabbalah deeply without having a command of Hebrew."

Moshe laughed. "Commanding Hebrew won't work for the Kabbalah, Sidney. The Hebrew will have to command you."

His quick reversals always made me smile. "I understand. But first I have to open myself to the language. Then the language can open herself to me. Where do I begin?"

Moshe considered his response. "Two things," he said. "One, register for the introductory course at the university and get as much time as you can in the language lab. They'll teach you modern Hebrew, but there isn't that much difference between modern and biblical. Knowing one, you'll be able to get by in the other. As for biblical grammar, we'll find a way to teach you that. And two, pick a letter. Any letter. We'll begin relearning the alphabet in a way that matters."

"*HET*," I said with barely a moment's delay.

"*HET*," Moshe repeated, rolling the initial letter into a guttural.

"*HET*," I repeated, mimicking his accent.

Moshe drew the letter on a legal pad. "This is the way a *HET* is usually drawn. Two *ZAYIN*s side by side with a bridge at the top. But a kabbalist is more likely to draw it like this." He drew a *ZAYIN* and a *VAV*. "*ZAYIN* has the numerical value of seven. *VAV* has six. Together they make up thirteen, which is the value of the Hebrew word *ehad*, which means one. So in the letter *HET* drawn like this you have an implicit symbol of the unification of the name. This is important because the *HET* is a *hupah*, a marriage canopy. Two are made into one under the marriage canopy, so you would like your *HET* to be a vehicle for unification."

ZAYIN VAV

HET

Moshe drew the *HET* again, in outline form, using the combination of a *ZAYIN* and a *VAV*. "Take the pen," he instructed me, "and trace the outlines of the letter until you have mastered it."

I traced the letter several times. Moshe handed me a fresh pad. "Now trace the outline from memory." I drew a passable *HET*.

"Good," Moshe said. "Sit back, close your eyes, and trace the outline of the letter *HET* in front of you. Make it a large letter. Work your way around inside of it. Learn it like a new neighborhood.

"Pull the letter down around you. Wear it like a comfortable coat. This is the letter *HET*. It will protect you from wandering off the path. It's the place where the two become one. It will keep you focused on the one. It will provide you with balance."

Moshe led me through the *HET*, deeper and deeper. An hour later, we surfaced, exhausted, and rested a few minutes in silence.

"Thank you, Moshe, for introducing me to the letter *HET*."

"You are welcome, Sidney. Now, I have a favor to ask you. It will be my privilege and pleasure to work with you and guide you in your work. What I need from you is for you to guide me occasionally. Circumstances now are such that I need to be able to go deep. Very deep."

"Circumstances, Moshe?"

Moshe sighed. "Rivkah had a biopsy this morning. The pathology is not back yet. But it doesn't look good, Sidney. It doesn't look good."

Due Diligence

"I hammered Sidney until he told me," Stephanie said. "I knew something was wrong with Rivie."

They returned home from the doctor's office, their heads spinning with data about stem cell replacement, destruction, and regeneration of the immune system; Taxol, the latest miracle drug, made from the Amazon yew trees; shark cartilage, a treatment intended to take advantage of the shark's extraordinary resistance to cancer; and myriad other facts and figures about blood transfusions and reverse isolation, everything Dowling could pour into them in an hour.

I was waiting when they arrived, me and my motorcycle.

384

I had made a conscious decision to take the Harley instead of the Jeep. I had the black-and-orange bike parked in front of the house so it would be the first thing they would see as they came into the driveway. My eagle-adorned leather jacket only compounded the image. I walked forward from the front step to meet them. "I was riding up in the hills and thought I might come by to see if there's anything I can do."

Rivie's eyes went from me to the motorcycle. "What do you mean, anything you can do?" she asked.

"I had a friend who had ovarian cancer two years ago. There was a lot to do. I thought you might need some help."

Rivkah looked to Moshe for an explanation.

"All I told Sidney was you had a biopsy, and it didn't look good," Moshe said to Rivkah. "I needed to explain to him where I was at. I didn't tell anyone about the malignancy. How could I? I didn't know until this morning."

There was too much for her to comprehend all at once. My guessing about the cancer. The motorcycle. The leather jacket. "What happened to your friend?" Rivie asked, cutting to her primary concern.

"She died."

For a moment it was as if a car had gone off a cliff in an action movie. We waited to hear the crash from the ravine below. When there was none, I continued. "I wasn't the primary caregiver. Another friend was, but she spoke with me every night and told me what was happening and what she had to do. I figured if you're going to be sick, I'd better get over here right away. I like what Sidney is doing with Moshe, and I liked our coffee together. I'd like to share more. I don't want to lose you. You're going to need someone's help to get through the next few months, and it might as well be mine." I extended my hand, making it as difficult as possible for her not to make a decision in my favor.

Rivie looked at my offered hand as she tried to connect a disparate chain of logic. Me in the leather jacket, the motorcycle, I knew about the cancer, the patient died, Sidney's friendship, instant coffee, and a simple sense of urgency. I was betting on the irresistible sincerity that linked them all together.

"I guess you're right," she said. "There isn't any time to waste." She surrendered her hand to mine. "I'll take whatever help you can give me. Come in, please, and tell me what I need to be thinking about."

Moshe opened the door for us. Rivie looked askance at the motorcycle one more time.

Sidney said, "Within a few days Rivkah was referring to Stephanie as a god-send. They were together most every day, on the phone when they were not together. There was much to do in preparation for Rivkah's treatment. By the next *Shabbat* they had settled on a course of action."

Rivkah accompanied Moshe to the *minyan.* Stephanie left the shuffling of chairs to others and came to greet her. They sat together, away from Moshe and me, and no doubt annoyed their neighbors as they talked throughout the service.

During the reading of the Torah, at the *aliyah* for healing, Rivkah stood, and Stephanie stood beside her. Before the *mishebayrach,* Rivkah asked if she could speak.

"Some of you remember back to the early days of the Havurah when I had ovarian cancer. I've been very fortunate all these years to be healthy, but I'm sad to say the cancer has returned." Alarm and concern erupted around the tables. "In the next few weeks and months I'm going to have a very aggressive treatment. I feel fine right now, but in a little while I'm going to be feeling sick. So I have a favor to ask of you." She reached out for Stephanie's hand. "This is my friend Stephanie Lee. Steffie is going to be helping me through this. I know all of you would like to do what you can to help, and there will be a lot you can do, but I would like all of that help to come through Steffie. She's the gatekeeper. She'll know how I am, what I need, what there is for you to do."

Stephanie squeezed Rivkah's hand and turned to the *minyan.* "Thank you," she said. "First I want to tell you how fortunate Sidney and I are to be here. We've been looking for a community like this for a long time, and you've made us feel welcome. Secondly, I want to brief you a little on what's going to be happening. Rivie and Moshe have a new telephone line. That will be where to call if you have any questions concerning Rivie's health. Mostly you'll get an answering machine that will give you an update. You can leave messages there, and we'll get back to you as soon as we can. The other thing is we need type A positive blood. If you are able to donate in the next few days, we need to know that. I need to know that. Please, let me know." She held up a stack of papers. "I'll distribute these after the service, and we're going to mail them out to the entire Havurah. It has Rivie's new phone number on it, and my phone number, and all the information you'll need to donate blood, where to go, and what to say to make sure the blood goes to the right place."

The leader of the service looked to Moshe for permission to pronounce the *mishebayrach*. He thought, perhaps, Moshe might like to pronounce it himself, but Moshe nodded to him to proceed. He said the words with all of the *kavannah* he could muster. He made no errors. It was a clean blessing.

"After the service the four of us came back here," Sidney added. "Stephanie talked about the *minyan*. She wanted to know who everyone was. Moshe led the grace after the meal. The two women went to the deck to talk some more, leaving us to clear the table. I asked Moshe if this was all right, Stephanie's intrusion into his family affairs. I wanted to be sure he knew this was Stephanie's idea, not mine. He said Stephanie was a blessing for both of them. While the women talked, Moshe introduced me to the fundamentals of biblical grammar."

The Strawberry Vine

"We lived more in their home than in ours," Stephanie said. "Often we spent the night. Sidney learned with Moshe in the study. He learned the lessons all over again, and asked all the questions he hadn't asked in class, and challenged all the challenges. He and Moshe went deep together, very deep. Within a few months, they were speaking Hebrew.

"Moshe taught me as well. Sometimes Sidney taught, and Moshe observed Sidney's teaching. Sometimes I saw Moshe's eyebrows rise as he heard something new, then he would retreat inside himself to ponder the discovery.

"Mostly I learned from Rivie. She talked about her life before Moshe, and with Moshe, her work at the hospital, and her relationships with members of the Havurah. Moshe and Sidney sat in with us from time to time. Moshe spoke of the same episodes from his point of view. They were tying up loose ends in such conversations, he said. That work was important, because it freed more energy for the process of healing.

"We were optimistic in those first months. It was very exciting. After the regeneration of Rivkah's immune system, the CA125 marker was ten. We were ecstatic. Thirty-five was normal. Two weeks later it was twenty, then thirty, forty, fifty. After that Rivkah's depression deepened with each increase."

387

Moshe sat with her often on the deck. It became hard to draw words out of her. When he was able, the words were often angry. "What happens when I die, Moshe? And why am I asking you? As if you know. As if you could tell me.

"If there is a God, Moshe, why do things like this happen? I must have done something very bad to deserve this. What did I do, Moshe? Do you know?"

When the pain began, she withdrew even deeper.

One afternoon, Moshe returned home from Ferrell Bower and found her wearing earphones, listening to a tape. "Reb Hayim sent me something," she said. "Do you want to hear it?"

He nodded. She pressed the rewind button and turned on the speaker so they could listen together.

Reb Hayim's voice filled the room. "I'm so sorry I can't be there with you, Rivie, and with you, too, Moshe. I can only imagine the pain both of you are experiencing. I have not been well myself lately, and my doctor wants me to stay in Jerusalem. I don't know when I will get to your area of the world next. That's why I'm sending you a tape.

"Here's a story I learned a long time ago from a Sufi friend. I want to share it with you. It's a good story for both of you. Moshe, I don't know that you've heard this story from me before. Maybe you have. Maybe from somewhere else. The story has a name. It's called 'The Strawberry Vine.' Are you ready? It's not a long story, but it requires a lot of concentration.

"Once there was a man who loved to climb mountains. You'll forgive me, Rivie. When I tell the story, it's a man who climbs the mountains. I like to think of myself, when I was younger, when I used to climb mountains. In France, when I lived there, in the Alps. In a few minutes this story will belong to you and you can change it however you like.

"So, this man, he loved to climb mountains. One beautiful day he decided to make an ascent by himself, an easy climb, just for the exhilaration of it, a few moments of pleasure. He put his hands on the cool rock surface, found his holds, and up he went. In a few seconds he was up twenty feet. In a minute he was a hundred feet high. He paused to look out over the tops of the trees, and up to the sky, and farther up the mountain. Up he went, climbing easily, two hundred feet, three hundred, five hundred.

"The day was glorious. He felt the breeze and the mist coming off the falls. He might close his eyes for a few seconds and bathe in the warmth of the sun.

When he opened his eyes, the green of the valley below him was glorious, glorious. He was in love with the rock under his feet, the sky above, the trees below. What a wonderful day!

"He looked at the rock face to see where to go next. There was a traverse across the face, a simple traverse. He could do that safely, he thought, and he started across, placing his feet carefully. Without warning, a piece of shale gave way under his feet, and he found himself sliding down the face of the rock, then falling over the edge.

"Instinctively, he reached out and grabbed a vine. The vine stopped his fall. He found himself in shock, swinging on the vine, ten, twenty feet down from the edge of the cliff.

"Can you feel that? The shock of suddenly finding yourself in such a precarious situation when you thought everything was safe?

"When the shock wore off, he examined his situation. He was dangling on a vine. The rock sloped away from him. He could not touch it. He looked up and knew he would not be able to make his way back up to safety. He looked down, and there was a thousand feet of empty space below him. The realization dawned on him he was going to fall. He could not hold on to the vine forever.

"But he had not fallen yet. He had not fallen yet.

"After a while you get used to anything, you know? After a while he got used to hanging on the vine, a thousand feet high. It became easier to hang on the vine. He could use less strength than he thought. He had more energy for other things. But what other things are there when you're hanging on to a vine a thousand feet high?

"He could pay better attention to the world around him. He felt the breeze and the mist on his face. The blue of the sky was deeper than he had ever known. The beauty of the mountains and the valley nearly made his heart explode.

"He could hear the beat of his heart, feel the pulse in his neck. He was aware of the breath coming in through his nostrils. There was so much to do there on the vine. He never could have imagined there would be so much to do.

"At last he looked at the vine itself, the brown cords that were strong enough to hold him, the green leaves, the red strawberries. It was a strawberry vine, and he had only just seen it. The strawberries were ripe.

"Now this is the story, Rivie. This is the whole story. Everything up to this point is to prepare you for this. He took one of the ripe strawberries, and he put it into his mouth, and he tasted it.

"What did that strawberry taste like? How did that strawberry taste to him?

"Can you taste it? Can you taste the strawberry? Can you feel it in your mouth, on your tongue?

"What would it be like to taste everything like that? To see everything with that man's clarity? To hear things, see things, feel things like that?

"That's the story. If I could be with you in person, this is the story I would share with you. I'm sorry that right now this is the only way I can do it.

"I love the two of you dearly. Let me finish now with a *mishebayrach* . . ."

Rivkah pressed the stop button. Moshe opened his eyes and saw the tears on her cheeks. He found a tissue to wipe them.

"It's such a beautiful story," she said. "I've listened to it maybe ten times."

"What about the *mishebayrach*?" Moshe asked.

"I don't want to hear it. I don't believe in *mishebayrachs*. The story I believe in. I can feel the story. The story helps. What do you think, Moshe? It's a good story."

"It's a good story," he agreed. "If it works for you, it's a very good story."

Too Much Exposure

Each time Stephanie told the strawberry vine story, she returned to those long months with Rivkah. Together they had listened to the recording many times. Rivkah would descend into the story, and Stephanie into Rivkah, a conscious attempt at enhanced empathy, to feel the pain, the concern, the restrictions, the focus.

It was Sidney's time to step forward and tell the story about his conversion. That was among his favorite stories to tell and Stephanie's to hear. But Sidney paused longer than necessary, then said, much to Stephanie's surprise, "This is a new story. I have named it 'Too Much Exposure.' It's about a motorcycle ride."

Stephanie blushed and checked to see if he was looking at her, but he was not. There was a story to tell about a motorcycle ride, but how would Sidney know it? She had never shared it with him.

Sidney kept his eyes toward the students and away from his wife.

Early on a Sunday morning Moshe was awakened by the sound of a motorcycle. He looked up to find Rivkah dressed in jeans. "What's going on?" he asked. "Where are you going?"

"For a ride," she said. He hadn't seen such excitement in her eyes in weeks.

He helped her with her shoes. Pulling up the jeans had exhausted her.

Stephanie arrived with a present for Rivie, a T-shirt emblazoned with a Harley logo and the caption, "Live to ride! Ride to live!"

Together Stephanie and Moshe accompanied Rivkah to the motorcycle. Stephanie mounted first. Moshe helped Rivie lift her leg over the rear seat. The bike roared and proceeded slowly down the driveway out of sight.

Moshe *davened,* made coffee, and still they hadn't returned. He was outside, pacing, when he heard the sound of the Harley returning.

Rivkah blanched in pain as he helped her lift her leg to dismount. He held her until she was steady on the driveway. "Are you all right?" She nodded. "How was the ride?"

She was out of breath from her effort. It took her some time to answer. "Wonderful! Wonderful! What a rush! I wish I had done that before!"

Stephanie lowered the kickstand and dismounted. The two of them helped Rivkah into the house and onto the sofa. "You try it," Rivkah said to Moshe. "Steffie, take him for a ride." She grimaced as she moved to a more comfortable position and closed her eyes to sleep.

"Come on," Stephanie said to Moshe. "It's your turn. The helmet will fit you. It fits Sidney, and his head is bigger than yours."

He followed her to the bike. "What do I hold?" he asked.

"Whatever is comfortable," she answered.

She started the bike. He climbed on behind her. "Not too fast," he said.

"The only hard part is getting out of the driveway. After that, relax and have a good time."

She stayed in second on the road up to the highway. He held on to the seat behind him. Once on the asphalt, she opened the throttle, the bike roared, leaped forward, and his hands jumped around her and clasped her firmly about the waist. He looked down to the road and was astonished at the pace of the yellow lines dashing underneath them. He kept his eyes forward after that. As he acclimated to the speed, he became aware Stephanie's breasts were resting on top of his arms. He thought to put his arms elsewhere but was afraid to move them.

The ride terrified him. When he dismounted, he was shaking.

"What do you think?" Stephanie asked him. "You ready to get a bike of your own?"

"No," he answered. "That was enough, thank you. This kind of exposure I don't need."

. . .

The students laughed.

Of course Sidney knew the story, Stephanie realized, but from Moshe's point of view. He had never mentioned it before, waiting for Stephanie to share it with him first. But she had never shared it. Surely she had told him she had taken Rivkah and then Moshe for a ride. But she hadn't shared her feelings. Why? Because she was confused by them. Embarrassed by them. She still blushed at the thought of them. Yet Sidney seemed to know, or guess.

Moshe had mounted the bike behind her. She had been so careful on the path to the road, considerate of his fears. But once on the road, was she consciously anticipating what would happen when she rolled back the throttle and drew so deeply on the Harley's torque? Did she know or hope where Moshe's hands would go? Did she want them higher still?

Stephanie knew from week to week the state of Rivkah's body, the degree of physical intimacy it permitted. In the early months Rivkah and Moshe made love purposely. Later when she could not bear his weight, they joined with delicacy, almost at right angles, allowing them to make love with their eyes as much as with their genitals. Sex was still a delight, and playful. Rivkah bought two wigs, one blond and one brunette. When the tumor pain became such that joining was no longer possible, they fell in love again through their fingertips. A month, two months had passed in that fashion by the time of the motorcycle ride. Two months without release, and Stephanie was aware of it.

His hands had been like fire on her ribs, and her breasts burned in the heat. Did Sidney know that? Had he been waiting all these months for her to share that with him, and why had she not?

Throughout their marriage she and Sidney had an honest sexual relationship. Every erotic thought and nuance of the one was available to the other. Such sharing had enhanced their sex life. But this experience Stephanie had kept to herself.

The evening of that motorcycle ride, Rivie asleep and Sidney engaged with Moshe in the study, Stephanie sat in one of the plush chairs in the living room. She was still flushed with the rush of that ride. Her hand dipped between the buttons of her sweater and, with a will of its own, found her breast. The nipple was so erect as to be painful. The orgasm astonished her. It started in her chest and worked its way down between her legs. Her hands followed it. They released the buckle of her jeans, but found difficulty with the tight denim. She wrestled the fabric below her hips, her pelvis not resisting, but rather rising so she had ready access to produce orgasm after orgasm until she thought she might die.

That night she dreamed Moshe had been watching as she writhed. The heat of that exposure flashed into such pulses she screamed out in her sleep. She said nothing when Sidney stirred, choosing to remain within the experience rather than to share with him.

For days after, she burned in Moshe's presence. She felt like a schoolgirl, imagined enticing him, seducing him.

All of this confused her. She didn't find Moshe particularly attractive. More than that, she didn't even like him. She tolerated him for Rivkah's sake. Had it not been for Rivkah, she would have had nothing to do with him. She found him arrogant, stiff-necked, presumptuous, distant.

She was so confused, she could not share her feelings with Sidney. Yet Moshe had shared his feelings with him. He had told Sidney about the motorcycle ride and where his hands had been. If Moshe had been terrified by his own sexual arousal and kept his distance from Stephanie in the days following the motorcycle ride, Stephanie had not noticed, for she, in her confusion, was keeping her distance from him.

She wondered what else Sidney might know.

Conversion

Sidney told his story.

On a Monday morning, just after dawn, a dozen members of the Havurah walked with us to the lake. We wore bathing suits and carried towels and robes. Others carried long poles, a Torah scroll, books, a bottle of wine. Moshe and Rivkah rode with Stephanie in the Jeep. The fire road was pitted, and Rivie winced with each rut they hit. No one had been foolish enough to suggest to her she not make the trip.

Moshe spoke first about a scribe who was about to begin to write a Torah scroll. "What does he do?" he asked. "He gathers all of the equipment he will use to prepare the scroll, the knives for sharpening the quill pens, for cutting the parchment. The inkwell he will use, all of the implements that can be immersed in water, and he takes them with him to the *mikveh,* the ritual bath. There he immerses them, and himself as well, and prepares himself and his equipment for the holy purpose of writing a scroll of the law.

"When a person chooses of his own free will to identify fully with the community of Israel, we prepare him just as the scribe would prepare for his task. The scribe is preparing his instruments for the transmission of Torah. Here we are preparing Sidney to be an instrument for the transmission of Torah. Sidney joins the community of Israel for no other purpose than his love of God, Torah, and the community itself."

Stephanie and I walked into the lake. When I was deep enough for modesty, I stepped out of my bathing suit so there would be nothing separating me from the water. Stephanie attended to me. She held my suit so that it would not float away.

I knew the blessings to pronounce. My Hebrew, while not yet fluent, was adequate to most liturgical tasks. The immersion done, I reclaimed my suit and emerged from the water hand in hand with Stephanie.

A *niggun* erupted among the Havurah members and continued while we dried ourselves and donned our robes.

"A gift from Rivie and me," Moshe said as he placed an embroidered *kipah* on my head.

I declared in the hearing of the community my desire to be a Jew. Moshe pronounced words of welcome in Hebrew and English. I closed my eyes and sang the words of the *Sh'ma*. Moshe embraced me and said the threefold blessing. "May God bless you and keep you. May God's light shine upon you, and be gracious with you. May God always watch out for you and enable you to achieve fulfillment." After each blessing, the community responded, "May this be God's will."

"We give you a new name now. From this time on you will be known in the community of Israel as *Shmuel ben Avraham vi-Sara,* Samuel the son of Abraham and Sarah. May this name become great among us. May you be privileged to learn much Torah, to accomplish many wonderful deeds, just as you are privileged now to stand underneath a *hupah* in marriage."

The chorus of amens gave a way to another *niggun* and a flurry of activity as a large *tallit* was attached to four poles and a *hupah* erected. My bride and I, still in robes, were brought underneath the marriage canopy. "It's time the two of you had a Jewish wedding," Moshe said. Stephanie was crying and smiling at the same time. "You know," Moshe said, "when you cry and smile at the same time, you can see a rainbow."

He read the marriage service and invited members of the Havurah to recite the blessings over the new Jewish union. Rivkah read one of the blessings from her seat in the Jeep. At the conclusion of the wedding, the Havurah formed a circle around us and sang "*Siman Tov U-mazal Tov,*" the traditional song for good fortune.

The morning service began. Eager hands spread the *tallit* from the *hupah* over a picnic table and opened the Torah scroll. I was called to the first reading. I pronounced the blessings and chanted the Hebrew text from the parchment scroll. At the conclusion of the reading, Moshe began the *mishebayrach*. "May the one who has blessed our fathers Abraham, Isaac, and Jacob, and our mothers Sarah, Rebecca, Rachel, and Leah, now also bless Samuel, the son of Abraham and Sarah, that he continue in his path of learning, that he should be an open vessel for Torah, that he should find ways to transmit it to us, that he should have joy in his family, and his new extended family . . ." He left an opening for others to add words of blessing for health, prosperity, long life, a good marriage.

With the service done, coolers and thermoses appeared from the back of the Jeep. The events of the morning were crowned with coffee, bagels, cream cheese, and lox.

Sidney looked toward Stephanie to see if she had anything to add. "It was the most glorious celebration," she said. "I had never been so profoundly moved by the joy and acceptance of a community. Before we took our leave to celebrate our honeymoon for a few hours, we came to Moshe, to thank him.

"Moshe said we should not thank him but the *bayt din,* the rabbinic court that had examined Sidney prior to the conversion.

"'It was close,' Moshe told Sidney. 'But in the end the vote was two to one against.'

"'Against?' Sidney asked. 'Then how were you able to accept me?'

"'Oh, for conversion we were all in favor,' Moshe said. "The question was whether or not we should ordain you a rabbi.'"

The Truth

Sidney said, "Throughout much of the illness there were visitors in the house. Sam, Gloria, Sharon, Barbara, they all took turns staying in the guest quarters. When Rivkah became very ill, Gloria stayed on. Stephanie remained the gatekeeper. She performed her role with such simplicity and honesty no one complained. When Stephanie said enough, it was enough. Even Gloria accepted the limits Stephanie imposed."

Rivkah liked to be out on the deck as much as possible. When it was cold, she asked that she be bundled in blankets and allowed to sit outside. Moshe liked to sit with her. They might sit for an hour without speaking.

After one such period, Rivkah began, "I wish Stephanie weren't married. I would like for you to have someone like her."

Moshe kept his silence.

"After I die, that is," Rivkah continued. "It isn't so hard, this dying. I've made a new friend. Stephanie has been a wonderful friend."

"Steffie is wonderful," Moshe agreed.

"Reb Hayim was right with his strawberry vine. It's like when we used to scuba dive. At the end of the dive, we'd pick out a piece of coral, and there would be more to see in that piece of coral than in the whole dive itself. You know what I mean?" Moshe nodded. "It was the end of the dive. Maybe we appreciated it more."

She remained silent a while. She could no longer speak at length.

"I'm sorry, Moshe. I've been so afraid. I've never dared to go as deep as you."

"That might have been true once, Rivie, but you go deeper than I do now. You dare to do things that terrify me."

"I'm using a lot of what you taught me, Moshe. I thought you might like to know that. When the pain gets bad, I focus on the breathing. I push myself through the letters and leave my body behind. That's what you wanted to teach me."

Again she was quiet.

"You're going to do something, aren't you?" she asked him.

"What do you mean?" he asked in return.

"You're going to do something. I know it. Do you think you can keep me from dying?"

"I love you, Rivie. That's all I can tell you. I love you."

"It's all right if I die, Moshe. It's getting harder and harder. I don't want the pain to get so bad, you know?"

"I think I know."

"I can accept it, Moshe. Denial and anger and bargaining and acceptance. I never did much bargaining. I don't believe in bargaining. Acceptance is a good place to be."

She shivered in the breeze. He rose to tuck the blankets about her more tightly and stayed beside her, holding her hand under the covers.

"Are you going to say some magic words now and make me all better?"

He shook his head. "No, Rivie. I don't know any magic words."

"But you haven't given up looking for some, have you?"

"I think it's easier for you to accept that you're dying than for me. I don't want you to die, Rivie. My heart breaks when I think about it. But it's not my choice, is it?"

"No. It's not your choice." She closed her eyes tightly as she moved to find a more comfortable position.

"What can I do to help, Rivie?" he asked.

"I don't think there's anything, Moshe. I'm going to find out, aren't I?"

"Find out what?"

"What's on the other side. You can only guess. I'm going to know." Her hand tightened on his with surprising strength. "What are you going to do? You're going to do something. I know it. Tell me the truth."

"I'm going to stay with you Rivie. That's the truth. That's all of it. I'm going to stay right here with you."

"It's my choice," she insisted.

"It's always your choice, Rivie."

He kissed her on the lips. They were cold. He shivered.

CHAPTER 16

Descent

 "There came a time when even Stephanie needed help," Sidney said. "Physically, the burden had become too great. Most families would have resorted to a hospital, but there was no way Rivkah would leave her house.

"We needed someone to manage movement and medication, someone knowledgeable enough to reassure us that we were doing right by Rivkah. That's what hospice is for. We pressed Stephanie to get help.

"Stephanie was not one to choose a hospice out of the Yellow Pages. She did her due diligence, consulted with Rivkah, but even so, there was no aide who could be as responsive or caring as family or friends. We had to be satisfied with what we could find. Even family and friends need to rest sometime."

There was still work to do. Even though all his market positions were closed, Moshe had responsibilities in the Havurah. Gloria remained home evenings when Moshe was teaching. When Moshe was at home, Gloria might venture out to the grocery, or, as she was doing that night, walk out into the sunset, down the dirt road to the lake. Stephanie and I had been ordered to take the night off, to go out for dinner, rest.

Moshe passed through the living room to check on Rivie before he descended to his study. The evening attendant looked up from her magazine. "She's fine," she told him. "She's just fine."

"No, I'm not," Rivkah said. "I'm not fine." Her voice was stronger, more focused than he had heard it in days. Only her lips moved. Her body was hidden under the afghan.

"What can I do for you, honey?" the attendant asked, annoyed she should be contradicted. She leaned forward and lifted her reading glasses from her nose. "I thought you were comfortable, darling, I surely did."

Rivkah ignored her. "Moshe, whatever you're going to do, I think you'd better do it now." She did not elaborate.

Moshe did not hesitate. He sat on the chaise beside her. Her hands were cold in his, her eyes weary with pain. She could dull the pain with morphine on command, but neither the pain nor the morphine was tolerable anymore. For several weeks she had been vacillating between the two. He leaned forward to kiss her on the forehead. He longed to hold her to him, but such physical embrace was no longer possible. Gently he put his cheek next to hers, closed his eyes, and kissed her again. "I'll be back in a moment," he told her.

In the kitchen he tapped the number of our mobile phone. "Sidney," he said. "It's time. We need both of you."

He did not wait for us to arrive. He moved the Windsor chair to be next to Rivkah, his right side to her right side. He leaned forward, elbows on his knees, his shirtsleeves rolled high. Rivkah's hand he held between both of his.

His eyes closed, he proceeded by stages to fill himself with the name of God. A single breath, and *YOD HEY VAV HEY* outlined the framework of his body.

With another breath he traced the letters of the divine name underneath his feet. They glowed a brilliant blue.

On his left leg he imaged the letters so that they resonated in his being, each with the vowel *OOOO*, as in pool. *YOOO, HOOO, VOOO, HOOO.* The sounds rumbled in his chest. The light that emanated from the letters was a glowing rose. On the right leg, the letters of the Divine Name descended in pink and whined with the vowel *EEEE*. He drew the letters together, joining them in a glowing orange. Blue under his feet, dark rose to his left becoming orange and blushing to pink on his right. *OOOO* resonating from the left through the groin focusing to *EEEE* on the right.

Moshe made certain of his balance before continuing. His left arm he filled with the four letters. They were pronounced *eloheem* and glowed a warm reddish gold. The right arm blazed in silver, so brilliant it was nearly white. Only the first syllable, *el,* could be spoken there. Together they merged into his chest. The name of God in his heart resonated with *OH,* as in *go. YOH, HOH, VOH, HOH.* His heart glowed yellow and purple at the same time, each color distinct, yellow to the right, purple to the left.

Again Moshe paused to check his breathing and his balance in the worlds, the blue under his feet, the pink, rose, and orange embracing his legs, the red, gold, silver, and white merging in his chest into purple and yellow. A chorus of *OOOO*'s, *EEEE*'s and *OH*'s resonated in his head.

Above his left eye the name of God, *eh-yeh,* "I am," pulsed in yellow and green. It sounded with the vowel *AY* as in *day. AY-YAY.* "I am." It was a name realized through reason. Above his right eye the *eh-yeh* appeared again. He pronounced it with the vowel *AW* as in *awe*. *AW-YAW*. "I am." It was the same name realized through insight. It flashed all the colors of the rainbow. Above his head was the name *asher*, "that." It was an excruciating white. He could not look directly at it. The full name echoed in his head. *Eh-yeh Asher Eh-yeh. AY-YAY ASHER AW-YAW.* "I am that I am." "I Am That I Am." "I AM THAT I AM."

All of this required but a few moments. He donned the names of God with the ease of a professional diver outfitting himself with tank, fins, mask, and snorkel. Quickly. Gracefully. Checking each stage. Certain of balance before descent.

"Rivie, where are you?" he asked. "Take me to where you are, Rivie."

His voice and his aspect were so strange, the hospice attendant fled the room.

Encounter

"We knew we might receive such a call," Stephanie said. "We were ready. It was but a few seconds, and we were in the car and on our way. The attendant was waiting for us at the door."

"Where are they?" I asked.

"In the living room," the attendant said, pointing behind her without looking. "The Rabbi is sitting with her in the living room. I don't know what's going on, but . . ."

We didn't wait to hear the end of her sentence.

The room was filled with the gold of sunset and the incandescent light of a single reading lamp by the attendant's empty chair. Moshe's eyes were closed, as were Rivkah's. Both seemed oblivious to our arrival.

Sidney carried two straight-backed chairs from the dining room. One he put to Rivkah's left for me. The other he placed for himself to the left of Moshe. "Moshe," he said. "We're here."

Moshe did not respond.

Sidney monitored Moshe's breathing and pulse. He asked me to call Frank and tell him to come over right away with his bag. To Moshe he said, "Did you hear me, Moshe? I want to bring Frank in. Is that all right? If I'm going to help you, I need a response."

400

As Moshe exhaled, he brought a sound to the surface. "Hmm," and on the next breath again, "Hmm."

"Thank you," Sidney answered. "I'm right here with you." Sidney closed his eyes and measured his own breathing. "I'm right here with you," he said again, the words paced at a slower tempo. "A word or two, Moshe, if you can, to let me know where you are."

Rehearsal

"We had done what we could to prepare," Sidney said. "We knew nothing could prepare us adequately for the depth of descent Moshe had in mind, but we reviewed likely procedures. Even with that, I was alarmed to find his pulse so slow and so weak."

"So what do you expect to do?" I had asked Moshe one Tuesday evening after guiding him through a particularly deep descent. "I am in awe of where you go, Moshe, but what will you do there when the time comes?"

Moshe shrugged. "I wish I knew. All I know is the work will be done at depth if it's going to be done at all. She will resist it everywhere else, and maybe there as well."

"So let us assume she doesn't offer any resistance. All the barriers are down. What will you do?"

Moshe slipped back under the surface, just a little, to draw an answer closer to him. "I'll do in that world the same as I do in all other worlds. I'll make connections. I make connections for myself, and I coach others so they can make connections for themselves. That's what I do, Sidney. I do it, and I coach it."

I laughed. "Can you tell me what *it* is, Moshe?" Nearly two years had passed since I had used the same tone of voice asking for a definition of magic. Moshe responded to the challenge much as he had then, by reflex.

"First ask what *it* is in the World of Action, Sidney. What does a coach do in the World of Action? What does a basketball coach do, or a judo coach? A track and field coach when he sees an error in technique? He illustrates by action. If he's a good coach, he does so with the most gentle of interventions. He shows the athlete how to make changes, how to connect one motion to another to yield a desired result. He can't force the athlete into the change. He coaches the athlete to make the choice to change."

I knew I had heard only the first part of Moshe's response and did not interrupt.

"Then ask what *it* is in the World of Formation," Moshe continued. "What does the therapist do? The therapist empowers the client to make the connection between a traumatic event and the resulting dysfunction. She does so with the most gentle of interventions. When the client makes the connection, then the client can choose to do things differently.

"And what does the rabbi do in the World of Creation? What do I do when someone comes with a conflicted theology that inhibits growth? I don't ram a new theology down his throat. I pick and pull gently at the notions until the knots unravel and the person can see for himself, or for herself, what the conflict is, and make new choices that allow for greater growth.

"So what happens in the World of Emanation, Sidney? What is *it* in the World of Emanation? I've seen *it* happen once, with Frank's aunt Doris, in the hospital, when she made the choice herself between living and dying. I saw *it* with my own eyes. I know what *it* looks like. Doris made a connection in the deepest of places. I've told you about that experience, but I've never been able to describe how exquisitely delicate that moment of connection was. I have no words for *it*. But if *it* is in the neighborhood, I'll recognize it. What I did for Doris was to show her she had a choice.

"I cannot live with myself, Sidney, unless I do everything in my power to give Rivie that choice, too."

I pondered the answer. Moshe was uncomfortable in the silence. "Did I answer the question?" he asked.

"Not bad, Moshe. Impressive, actually." I was hesitant to continue but did so anyway. "You'll forgive me, Moshe. I don't want to probe where it may cause pain, but let me ask you this. Even the best of coaches can't teach a klutz to high jump. The klutz is not trainable."

I continued in a style that mimicked Moshe. "Even the best of therapists can't work with a client with irremediable emotional damage. The client is not reachable.

"Even you can't make an impact on a dogmatic fundamentalist. The blinders are impenetrable.

"Now, what if you descend and find that there are no connections to be made, that there are no choices? What if the physical damage is irreparable? You've taught me yourself the answer to a prayer which would result in the destruction of worlds has to be *no*. Rivie's disease is so far advanced, Moshe,

402

it's a wonder she is still here. Surely at this stage, even if you descend with her to the very depths, the answer must still be *no*."

Moshe took his lower lip between his teeth and closed so hard, I expected to see blood. When he relaxed and opened his mouth, he said, "Thank you, Sidney. I love you for your honesty. I truly do. The situation is like this." As he responded, he nodded to underline the import of each phrase. "I don't know what the answer is. I only know the question, and I cannot, will not, let it go unasked. I have no idea how anything works, let alone healing. What I do know is there is a lot of healing available in this universe. I thank God for it three times a day. All I can do is ask the question. If the answer is no, then it is no. But I won't know until I ask, will I?"

I considered Moshe's response. "Tell me what you want me to do, Moshe. How can I help you when the time for asking comes?"

Angels

Sidney said, "Moshe held Rivkah's right hand. Stephanie held the left, and my hand rested on Moshe's back. The sunlight faded to darkness. The one lamp in the room cast stark shadows. Words came to the surface rarely. I had to lean forward to hear them."

"Glass," Rivkah said once, with a hint of motion, as if reaching out to touch something to see if it was real. And then again, "Glass," when she found that it was.

Stephanie looked to the coffee table, as if expecting to find a glass there. I shook my head and motioned for her to remain by Rivkah's side.

"Warm?" Moshe asked.

A furrow deepened between Rivkah's eyes. "Warm," she agreed. "Fluid. Thick."

"Do you want to go through it?"

"No," came the response many seconds later. "Afraid." Then after a few minutes, "Company. Children."

"Know them?"

Rivkah moved her head, as if looking from one child to another. "Lost children. Hospital. Gone. Debbie. Ron."

The names were those of children long gone.

"They want?" Moshe asked.

Rivkah trembled. "They float." The afghan slipped from around her shoulders and Stephanie, hastening to raise it, let go of Rivkah's hand. Rivkah's fingers opened in a plea for company. Stephanie reached and grasped them again. "I'm here, Rivie," she whispered. "I'm here, right beside you."

"They want? The children want?" Moshe asked again.

"Me to go," Rivie responded.

Moshe breathed deeply and his next question rode on the exhalation. "And you want?"

"I see you," Rivkah said without answering the question. "I see you. In the glass. Reflection. You."

The doorbell rang. The voice of the hospice attendant reached into the room. "They're in there. All of them."

Frank paused but a moment to take in the scene. He drew the blood pressure cuff from his bag and approached Rivkah to bind it to her arm. I reached out to restrain him. "No, not Rivkah. Moshe." To Moshe, I said, "Frank is here. He'll be touching your arm in a moment. Please expect it." To Frank I whispered, "Gently."

With care Frank bound the cuff to Moshe's left arm. He inserted the diaphragm of the stethoscope, pumped and listened. "Ninety over sixty," he whispered to me, not knowing if it was important or not for me to know.

Moshe and Rivkah were quiet. The intrusion had left a turbulent wake. They waited for the waves to settle.

Moshe resumed the dialogue. "Me? Where?"

"In the glass," came Rivkah's eventual response. She smiled. Moshe could not see the smile. His eyes were shut. He felt the smile through a squeeze of her hand.

"Where are the children?" he asked.

"Deeper. Floating. Looking."

"What do they want?"

She did not respond. Her aspect changed. Stephanie leaned forward. With her free hand she caressed Rivkah's cheek. "We're here with you, Rivie," she whispered.

Frank whispered to me, "Eighty over fifty. What's happening?" I put a finger to my lips. Frank spun the chromed release and the air sighed out of the blood pressure cuff.

We sat in silence, Frank squatting between Moshe and me, Stephanie on the other side, holding Rivkah's hand, caressing her cheek.

At last Moshe asked, "Where are you?"

"Here. Sad."

"And the children?"

For several minutes there was no response at all.

"Seventy-five," Frank reported. "I don't know what's happening, but not much more, I'll tell you that." He looked toward me, but I paid him little attention. I was afraid to remove my presence from Moshe for more than a moment. He looked to Stephanie, but she was focused on Rivkah.

"The children?" Moshe repeated again, perhaps ten minutes later.

"Here. Waiting." Rivie whispered.

"And the glass?"

"Here."

"Become the glass, Rivie. Become the glass. Look back. See what the glass sees."

When the message had time to penetrate, when she was able to follow it, her aspect changed. Her head nearly lifted off the pillow. "Gold light," she said loud enough for all to hear. In awe, she said again, "Gold light in gold light."

Moshe drooped over, his lips close to Rivkah's ear. "Rivie, you have a choice." The words were barely audible.

"Yes," she said. "You in gold light. Me in gold light. You in me!"

"Falling!" Frank said, alarmed. "Bring him back!"

"You have a choice, Rivie," Moshe repeated.

"Yes," she said again.

More loudly, Frank said, "I have nothing here! Nothing! Bring him back!"

I stirred. "Moshe," I said quietly, but with urgency. "We're losing you. We need to bring you back."

"She's gone," Moshe said. He fell forward, unconscious.

Frank and I reached for him, rolled him over on the carpet. "Lift his legs," Frank said. "Get some blood back into him. Moshe! Sidney, help me. Moshe! Lift his legs. I don't know what the hell is going on. Let's get some light." Frank turned and saw the hospice attendant standing in the doorway. "Turn on some lights!" he shouted to her.

Stephanie, still holding Rivkah's hand, had not moved through the entire episode. "She's gone," she said.

Frank and I paused to look across Rivkah's body, not quite comprehending. Frank reached out for Rivkah, put his hand to her neck. "Gone," he confirmed after several seconds. "She's gone. We have work here. Let's do it."

405

His clasped hands thrust firmly into Moshe's chest. He set the rhythm for me to continue, then opened Moshe's mouth to clear the airway and began to breathe into him.

How a Funeral Is Done

"There was so much to do," Sidney said. "Somehow Stephanie continued to marshal the forces to do it."

She alerted the funeral director. She arranged for *haverim* to meet members of the family at the airport. She called the church to rent the vestry space. There would be no charge, the minister had told her, not for the Rabbi. She called the neighbors and asked that one remain in the house for security during the funeral. She sent out for paper plates and cups and plasticware. She ordered deli and pastries. She changed the message on the answering machine to let callers know the time and place for the funeral. She turned off the ringer on the hot-line phone.

The family gathered in the living room and passed their memories around like a balm for pain. I asked questions, wanting to know what Rivie had been like before she met Moshe. Sam and Gloria were eager to tell me. Sharon spoke of a sibling rivalry, and then a closeness they maintained even though separated by a continent.

Gloria withdrew into herself. "She was so beautiful, my Beckie," and began to sob. Sharon and Sam comforted her. Each of them was comforted by the others in turn.

"Who is going to do the funeral?" Sam asked.

"The funeral will take care of itself," I said.

Members of the Havurah came with cars and vans for the family. They arrived at the vestry at the appointed time. The space was full. Concentric circles of chairs emanated from the center of the room. The family sat in chairs reserved for them. Latecomers stood on the perimeter.

At the set time Frank stood at his seat in the second circle and said he would begin the service with the 23rd Psalm. He chanted it first in Hebrew. When he repeated it in English, many voices joined with him. Other members of the Havurah stood to read selections from Psalms and Ecclesiastes.

I rose and said the family had met the night before and had begun the process of healing. I said the pain was great. The memories were the only source of relief. It was time for the community to probe the depth of the wound and begin its healing. I requested that each person turn to a neighbor and share with that neighbor why he or she had come that morning. I asked them to share what they remembered of Rivkah, their experiences together, and now, that she was gone, what it was that they would miss.

Members of the Havurah were accustomed to sharing. Those who were new to the process, those who expected a funeral at which the minister spoke and the congregation was silent, were hesitant to speak aloud of their own pain, their own loss, but they were soon caught up in the energy that filled the room. After a few minutes, I asked that the conversations expand, that in small groups they share with each other their memories and feelings of loss. A member of the Havurah chanted a psalm. The room returned to order.

"We would welcome single sentences," I told the assembly. "Some words now from and for the community."

The room was silent a few seconds until a coworker stood and said, "The sixth floor leans the wrong way without her." She paused as if tempted to say more, but nodded an exclamation point and sat down.

An oncologist spoke. "We sat together on the ethics committee. Now that she's gone we've lost an insight no one else could bring."

"All night when my son was dying, she stayed up with us. I don't think I could have survived the night without her." The woman who spoke was dressed in an elegant black-silk suit.

"The house exploded out of her. I've never had a client express a house that was so much at the very core of her being." The interior designer put his hands to his mouth, as if astonished by the intensity of his own words.

"It wasn't just the house. It was Rivkah herself who invited the Havurah in and nourished us," a young man from the Havurah added.

Stacy Klein spoke. "She taught me about trust and partnership. I would not have learned so well without her."

A woman with sad eyes rose to speak, turning to address the entire room. "When I came from Russia, and all they let me do was manicure, she listened to me and encouraged me to open my business. I never forget that."

"The woman who spoke about her son, I need to say my daughter too, my little Ronnie. I don't know what I would have done without Rivkah. I don't know how we would have managed those last days."

The sentences came more quickly. Different voices, they joined together into disjointed paragraphs, a random association that made a mosaic of

Rivkah's impression on the community at large. The words became a tapestry of her life. They enshrouded her in death.

The last contributor was Francine. She had waited for some long seconds of silence, then stood to say, "She was my savior. She reached so deeply into me, and drew me together. The two of them. Without her, I could not be here. Without her, some of me is not here." She looked toward me, sensing that only I among those gathered was likely to know the full depth of her words.

Frank asked us all to rise for the *el molay,* the prayer for Rivkah's soul. He chanted it in Hebrew and again in English. The funeral director gave instructions for the procession to the cemetery.

"You have so many wonderful people here," Sam said in the car.

"Do you know who that woman was who spoke about her daughter?" Gloria asked.

"No," I said.

"How about the Russian woman?"

"She has a chain of beauty salons."

"They liked her so much at the hospital. I didn't know she worked with so many terminal cases," Gloria said. "I knew she had some, but not so many."

We remembered everyone who spoke and were so immersed in memories we forgot where we were going. Our arrival in the cemetery came as a shock.

"I need to walk with her," Stephanie said. We followed behind the casket and three times asked that it pause on the way to the grave. In Hebrew I recited the psalms I thought Moshe might have chosen.

The attendants lowered the casket into the grave and cleared away the burial machinery. Members of the Havurah read the committal prayers. In turn we took the shovel and, using the back side of it, dropped earth into the open grave. It struck the wood with a finality that could not be denied.

Many contributed their energy to covering the casket with a layer of earth. The community rose to support the mourners in their recitation of *kaddish.* Stephanie counted herself among the mourners. She insisted on wearing the black ribbon, cut, a symbol of the heart torn underneath. She walked with Sharon through the passageway of comforters formed to convey the mourners from the grave to the cars. "May God comfort you among the rest of the mourners of Zion and Israel," many said. Others were generous with hugs and kisses.

I stood among the ranks of the comforters, not that my heart wasn't broken as well, but Stephanie's loss was greater than mine. I had lost a friend. It was as if she had lost a sister.

The family returned home to sit and search for consolation in each other. I returned to the hospital to relieve Barbara, to sit by Moshe's side. He was no longer in intensive care. Life support had been removed. His body continued to breathe on its own.

The doctors said there was no way of knowing when he might come out of the coma, if ever. I held his hand and used all he had taught me in an attempt to reach him, but to no avail.

He was beyond the boundary.

I could only wait. And pray.

CHAPTER 17

It was midnight in the living room.

"Seven days Moshe was in the coma," Sidney said. "Seven days. When the week was up, his eyes opened. He looked at me a while before speaking, as if he needed time to take inventory of his limbs and remember which world he was in. 'I'm here, Sidney,' he said. 'I'm here. It's all right.'"

Sidney's Story

At the end of the thirty-day period of mourning, Moshe and I walked together down through the woods toward the lake. His recovery had been beyond all expectations, as if he had never been in danger. Our pace was rapid, our progress silent. A steady wind whipped at our sweaters. The cut black ribbon Moshe had worn for the month flew like a pennant from his heart. He would have cut his clothes to the skin had he been conscious to do it, but he woke with the ribbon, and the ribbon he kept.

At the lake we found shelter behind a picnic table turned on its side. We sat with our backs against it. The wind blew the water away from us, but where could the water go? It blew out a few feet only to tumble back upon itself and return to shore.

Moshe plucked the ribbon from his sweater. "It's been thirty days," he began. He fingered the torn black velvet. "Thank you for all you've done, Sidney. Without you and Stephanie, this all would have been so much more difficult."

"It was our privilege. My privilege," I corrected. "Stephanie will speak for herself."

"You must want to know what happened in that last encounter. You've been patient. I've been thinking about it a lot, going back through it, trying to find the right words to encompass it."

"It's not for me to ask, Moshe. If you want to talk about it, I'm here to listen."

"She was deep, Sidney. I went after her." Moshe caressed the ribbon, drawing the torn edges together, creating the momentary illusion that it was whole. "I filled myself with the name of God. My body, my eyes, my ears, my nose, just like I've done with you so many times. I went after her. She was waiting for me. No resistance, Sidney. None. She was waiting for me."

A hawk overhead hung in the sky, motionless against the wind.

"She had angels to guide her. The angels came in the form of children she had known at the hospital, children long gone. She recognized them. She knew their names. They came out to her and pulled her deeper." With his free hand he found and tossed a pebble. A small splash, and it disappeared into the lake. "They pulled us deeper. It was as if I could see them, too. I never knew her children, Sidney. She would talk about them, but I never met them. Not until that moment. They appeared as adults in the bodies of children. They had lived entire lifetimes, old in experience, patient. Waiting."

Moshe found and threw another pebble. "*Mayim.*" He pronounced the Hebrew for water. "*Mayim, shemayim,* and *hayim.* Water, sky, and life. The words are linked. They all overflow their boundaries. The *mayim* overflows in two dimensions. *Shemayim* overflows in three. And *hayim* . . ." He did not complete the progression aloud, but I followed without question. "It was like we were diving in a sea of *hayim.* We were so deep. It's hard to describe what I saw. The glass. She saw me in the glass, looking out at her."

Abruptly he turned toward me with an absurd question. "Do you know what a fish is, Sidney? Did you ever dive into a school of fish? Did you ever become one with the fish?" He continued without waiting for an answer. "A fish is a bag of water in a sea of water. That's what it is. Water comes into the fish, through the fish, out of the fish. How much of the water is fish? Is it only the water that's inside the fish? Or the water around it? Is that part of the fish, too? Or the water that comes through it?

"Did you ever imagine how the fish sees you under the water? The fish sees you as a fish, a strange fish, out of its element. A bag of air in the water, pretending for a time to be a fish. A bag of air that wears a fish suit and descends into the sea and lives for a while as a fish." He tossed another pebble into the lake, which swallowed it as quickly as the first two.

"The children were angels in the World of Formation. Now, the glass. At the deepest place, the glass was an angel in the World of Creation." He looked up again toward the hawk hovering above, then to Sidney. "Like a window glass, Sidney. Or a mirror glass. She saw me there. I saw her. Sparkling gold. Red gold. White gold.

"I asked her to look back and see herself. Did you hear me ask that?" I chose not to answer. "She looked back from the glass and saw herself. Gold floating in a sea of gold. Light floating in a sea of light. Life floating in a sea of life. A vessel of soul in a sea of soul.

"The choice was there. She knew it. She could open herself to the flow of life, let it wash through her, clean her, and return. Or she could open herself to the flow of life and dissolve in it, not to return. The choice was hers, just as she wanted. She knew it."

Moshe held the ribbon high. The wind tried to suck it from his fingers.

"What might have pulled her back, Sidney, was unfinished work. The only work she had not yet finished in her lifetime was me. There was still work to do with me, in the one world in which we had not connected. But in that moment . . . In that moment, the work was finished. There was one instant when nothing was withheld, nothing at all. She became one; I shattered. She went on; I returned."

I was frozen into his recitation. I might have reached out to console him. His tears were surely an invitation, but I was caught between his words and held my peace.

"I have work to do," he continued. "I have work to do. But her work was done, and she was gone."

Moshe Katan opened his hand. The wind seized the ribbon and whipped it toward the lake. The hawk, seeing what it took for life below, plunged after it, but finding the ribbon dead in the water, let the wind under its wings lift it back again into the heights.

Stephanie's Story

Stephanie knew she had one story left to tell, but didn't know if she had the courage. She sensed Sidney knew the story. She wasn't going to surprise him, only herself. He had been laying a foundation, reordering the lessons with the emphasis on sexuality, all, she suspected, so her story might be told. Now if she could only tell it.

She was in no hurry. The students were still lost in the poetry of Sidney's story. It was a glorious story. She heard it even as she was searching for her own.

She reached for Father Porter's watch, the breastplate of the High Priest, and panicked when she could not find it.

One two three, one two three, one two, one two, one two.

Where was it? Why couldn't she summon it?

She inscribed the letters of the Divine Name on her body, *HEY* around her legs and pelvis, not difficult even while she was sitting. *VAV* along the spine. *HEY* around her shoulders, down her arms to the fingertips. *YOD,* just above her head.

Again she searched for Father Porter's watch and could not find it.

She breathed through the letters down to her toes, allowed the breath to ascend her spine, exhaled around her shoulders, out through her fingertips.

It was there, but not the breastplate, something more intricate than the breastplate, far more intricate. She had but a glimpse of the full pattern, complete, four groups of four, each separate from the other, and something deep in the center, very deep, heavy. She felt a gravitational attraction that terrified her. She would not go. Not there. She would tell her story, but not from that place.

She closed her eyes against the pattern. That only brought it back, empty, except for the depth in the center.

She took inventory of her emotions to stop her trembling: reluctance, tenderness, love, and awe, then focused on the upper right-hand corner, to give it life and color. She attempted blue, but red emerged. She was not controlling this.

She turned her attention to the bottom right, but it was the upper left that filled, red again. Then counterclockwise, against her will, around the pattern, the distant corners, all red.

Below the first square in the upper right she attempted blue again, but silver flowed, not below but to the left. Silver, counterclockwise, all around.

Curiosity controlled the trembling. Two squares filled in each of the corners, what would happen next? Gold, in the upper right, completing the corner, then quickly, left, down, and right, four completed corners, red, silver, and gold.

Only then her blue, a sky-blue, limitless blue, a blue beyond any horizon she had ever known. A breathtaking blue, through all four corners.

She saw it all, not one pattern of sixteen in groups of fours, but sixteen patterns, one through sixteen, in a pattern of sixteen, with an external energy that flowed clockwise, but counterclockwise internally, both directions at once, running this way and that, flashing with color, involving, intriguing, and in the very center of the sixteen, alone, distant, unique, a single dot beyond color, of such weight and depth, such attraction, she could no longer resist.

It was from that point, summoning every reserve of strength to lift her words to the surface, she told her story.

The evening of the thirtieth day we gathered in the living room, Moshe, Sidney, Frank, and I, for a memorial service, just the four of us. We spoke about Rivie, our feelings for her, how she had died, what we missed, and what we might do now she was gone. Moshe had not had the benefit of the funeral. Sidney recalled all the words that were said. All the words, as if he were reading them from a journal. Every speaker, every word. It was uncanny, like a replay of the funeral itself.

The repetition opened in me a pain the funeral had not. I had too much to do with and about the funeral, but a month later, it was all done. There was no activity to protect me from the recognition of my loss.

We had become soul-sisters, Rivie and I. My life had become so quickly bound up in her life, and her life in mine. I lived her pains, her hopes and despairs. I was opened to a sorrow I had only begun to plumb, as deep as a volcano with a lava of rage bubbling at the bottom.

That night, Frank gone, Sidney asleep, I left my bed to ascend to Rivkah's room. Moshe was sitting at the foot of his bed, in boxer shorts, his feet on the rug, his eyes fixed on the open window, the light of a half-moon filtering through the clouds.

Why did I come to him? At first I thought it was to comfort him, then that he might comfort me. Now as I consider it, I was drawn by a motivation I did not understand. Surely not by sexual desire, more I think by anger, a chance for retribution, an act of religious disobedience.

"Religious disobedience." Stephanie repeated for her own ears, the words startling. She had never spoken them before, never heard them before. An oxymoron: religious disobedience. Was such a thing possible? Yes. That's what she had done.

"An act of loving religious disobedience," she said aloud.

Rivie had died childless.

That thought echoed in my mind. It was that thought, and the inequities it illuminated that drove me.

A *man* should be responsible to be fruitful and multiply? Were they nincompoops who understood Torah in such a fashion? A childless *man* should be brought back to have children? Have you ever heard of such an absurdity?

The *brother* of a childless *man* should lie with his widowed sister-in-law to provide a child in his dead brother's name! Then shouldn't the surviving sister sleep with the widowed husband and draw seed to register in the dead sister's name?

How otherwise could the woman who died childless rest?

This was to be for Rivie, that she could rest in peace, that I would bear a child for her in my last months of childbearing.

"For Rivie," I said. "Please."

I lifted his hand to my breast and turned to him. Only then, I think, did he become aware of my presence.

"For Rivie," I repeated. "Please. For Rivie," not knowing what I meant by the words, only that they were necessary to say.

He turned to look at me. At me, not my body.

I held his hand more firmly to my breast, but he withdrew it gently and stared at it, as if it, of its own will, had committed some offense.

"You have been such a friend," he told me. "I thank you. For Rivie, I thank you."

I began to cry, to sob. He held me. My tears fell on his shoulder. He held me only to comfort me. "Thank you," he said again and again until the moment subsided, and I withdrew.

His understanding was immediate. Mine has come only now. He said, "She has her children. It's okay, Steffie. She has her own children."

All these months have passed, and all the storytellings. This has been the seventh telling. I don't know if there will be more. But this I have recognized only now, with just courage enough to whisper it here, not yet courage enough to roar.

There will be a new telling, from a new perspective. The Kabbalah you have learned isn't complete. It isn't balanced. It came through men, for men.

There is another Kabbalah yet to come, and this one will come through us, through me!

Stephanie was astonished at her own words. Had she really spoken them?

"Yes," Al said. He was bent with age, supported by a cane. "It will come through you."

"Yes," her mother said. She was still the young woman, proud, upright. "It will come through you."

"It's okay, Steffie. It's okay," Sidney said. He was beside her, holding her hand. His touch smoothed the defiance from her face. "It is coming through you," he whispered.

"It is?" she asked incredulously. She reached toward him. His face was golden, his eyes alive, smiling.

"Do you understand now why I sent you the letters?" Her father's voice, but she couldn't yet see him. "Why I sent them? Why I didn't throw them away?" She found him, on his stool. He looked the same, no change. "They were all I had of her, of you, of me. I put us all into your hands." His words echoed as if from an empty chamber. "Would you bring her back to me? Would you bring you back to me? Would you bring me back to me?"

"It is coming through you," Sidney repeated. "Your Kabbalah comes through your heart, Steffie, through your stories. Your stories carry you through all of the worlds. I have been listening, really listening. I have learned so much from you, from them."

"You have?" she asked, still not quite free from the story she had told, the letters and images swarming around her. "Like what?"

"Like the ghosts I've been running from, we've been running from. Like it's time for me to visit Hong Kong. Will you come with me, please? I must go, and I am afraid to go alone."

"First Miami, to see my father. He wants his letters back. They were all my mother left to him, and he entrusted them in me."

"First Miami." Sidney nodded. "I'll go with you. And then you'll go with me?"

"Yes," Stephanie agreed.

After she had settled safely within herself, Sidney turned to the students. "Moshe was gone the next morning, he and his Porsche. He left a note saying he needed to do some driving, reconnect with the road, make some decisions. He is still driving, finding his way.

"The house he left in our care, for the Havurah, for the students who might learn here. He asked that we use it for teaching, that we offer courses in memory of Rivkah. That's what we've been doing.

"We have shared many stories and lessons with you. They are yours now to tell. Remember, you learn not so much from hearing them, but from telling them."

Sidney looked to Stephanie, to see if she would offer the closing prayer. When he saw she was still inside, he sealed the storytelling himself.

"God, you who are filled with compassion, you who reside on high, let Rivie find comfort under the wings of your Divine Presence. Let her soul be resplendent among the holy and pure beings. Source of compassion, gather her close to you, for you are her inheritance, and she is yours.

"As you make peace in the heavens above, please now make peace in this world below, for us—for Stephanie, for myself, and for all others who have the courage to reach into themselves and risk their own stories.

"May this be your will. And let us say, 'Amen.'"

CHAPTER 18

The Eighth Telling

Stephanie was at the cemetery before the gates opened, impatient to be with Rivie. The first of the groundskeepers came, unlocked the gate, let her in.

A fresh pebble was on the bronze plaque, on the left side.

"Moshe was here," Stephanie said, not quite certain how she knew, but certain nonetheless.

She placed her own pebble on the right side, sat on the granite bench, and considered how she might begin.

"Rivie," she said, "I can't wait to tell you my stories. Some you've heard, some you haven't.

"It took me a while to hear them, and even longer to understand them.

"I'm not the same as I used to be. I hope that's okay.

"If I'm messing up, you'll let me know, won't you?"

GLOSSARY

Pronunciation notes: Underlining indicates the syllable emphasized. The emphasis is as the word would be pronounced in this book, not necessarily as it would be pronounced in modern Hebrew. The uppercase H is used to indicate a guttural HET or KAF, as in hupah (Hoo-pah) or baruch (ba-ruH).

Adonai (ah-doe-<u>nye</u>), Lord, euphemism for the name of God

aliyah (alee-<u>yah</u>), the honor of being called up to the ritual reading of the Torah during a service

am ha-aretz (ahm ha-<u>ah</u>-retz), ignoramus

amidah (amee-<u>dah</u>), the prayer said while standing, petition

Ana v'Koach (<u>ahn</u>-a vi-<u>ko</u>-aH), liturgy: "Please and with Strength," an appeal for help, an acrostic of the forty-two-letter name of God

asi-ah (ah-see-<u>ah</u>), doing, action

atzilut (ah-tzee-<u>loot</u>), nearness, emanation

avinu malkenu (ah-<u>vee</u>-noo mal-<u>kay</u>-noo), our Father, our King

ayn sof (ayn sof), without end, infinite

baal shem (bal shem), a master of God's name

Baal Shem Tov (bal shem toav), master of the good Name, good name master; Israel ben Eliezer

bar mitzvah (bar mitz-<u>vah</u>), boy at age thirteen, old enough to be worthy of the commandments

baruch (ba-<u>ruH</u>), blessed

baruch ha-ba (ba-<u>ruH</u> ha-<u>bah</u>), welcome, literally blessed is the one who comes

bayt din (bayt din), rabbinic court

bayt knesset (<u>bayt</u> ki-<u>ness</u>-et), synagogue, literally house of assembly

bayt midrash (bayt mid-<u>rash</u>), house of study

bimah (<u>bee</u>-mah), raised section of synagogue from which Torah is read

binah (<u>bee</u>-nah), understanding, one of the *sefirot*

brachah (bra-<u>Hah</u>), blessing

bri-ah (bree-<u>ah</u>), creation

bubbie (<u>bub</u>-ee), grandma

bupkis (<u>bup</u>-kiss), nothing

da-at (<u>dah</u>-aht), knowledge; one of the *sefirot*

daven (<u>dah</u>-ven), pray

dayan ha-emet (dah-<u>yan</u> ha-eh-<u>met</u>), Judge of Truth

drash (drah-sh), inquiry, teaching

Eliahu ha-navee (elee-<u>ah</u>-hoo ha-nah-<u>vee</u>), Elijah the prophet

Eloheem (el-oh-<u>heem</u>), God

em (em), mother

emet (eh-<u>met</u>), truth

esrog (<u>es</u>-rohg), citron, ritual fruit used on the holiday of *Sukkot*

gevurah (ge-voo-<u>rah</u>), greatness, strength; one of the *sefirot*

goy (goy), non-Jew

goyim (<u>goy</u>-yeem), non-Jews

gragger (<u>grah</u>-ger), Purim noisemaker

ha-shem hu ha-elokeem (ha-<u>shem</u> hoo ha-elo-<u>keem</u>), the Lord is God

hadar ohel (hah-<u>dahr</u> o-<u>Hel</u>), dining room

Hadassah (hah-<u>dah</u>-sah), Jewish women's group

Hadera (hah-<u>der</u>-ah), Hadera, city in Israel

haftarah (haf-tah-<u>rah</u>), section from the books of the prophets read on Saturday morning after the reading from the Torah

hagba (<u>hag</u>-bah), the honor of raising the Torah scroll after it is read during a service *haggadah* (hah-gah-<u>dah</u>), the home service for the evening of Passover, *seder* service

halachah (hah-lah-<u>Hah</u>), Jewish law

hallah (<u>Hah</u>-lah), bread for the Sabbath

Hanukkah (Hah-noo-<u>kah</u>), the festival of Hanukkah, eight days in December

hashatat zera (hah-sh-Ha-<u>tat</u> <u>ze</u>-rah), destruction of the seed

hashmal (Hah-sh-<u>mal</u>), electricity, energy

hasid (Hah-<u>seed</u>), pious person, devotee

hasidus (Hah-<u>si</u>-dus), Hasidism (old pronunciation)

hasidut (Hah-si-<u>doot</u>), Hasidism (new pronunciation)

hatimah (Hah-tee-<u>mah</u>), seal, signature

havdalah (hav-dah-<u>lah</u>), ceremony to conclude the Sabbath

haver (Hah-<u>ver</u>), friend

havurah (Hah-voo-<u>rah</u>), fellowship

havurot (Hah-voo-<u>roat</u>), plural of *havurah*

hayah (<u>Hah</u>-yah), living essence, soul in the World of Emanation

hayim (<u>Hah</u>-yeem), life

hayot ha-kodesh (Hah-<u>yoat</u> ha-<u>ko</u>-desh), holy living beings; class of angels

Hechalot Rabbati (heh-Hah-<u>loat</u> rah-<u>bah</u>-tee), *Great Work Concerning the Temples,* volume of early Jewish mysticism

heruvim (Heh-roo-<u>veem</u>), Cherubs

hesed (<u>Heh</u>-sed), loving kindness, one of the *sefirot*

Hillel (Hill-<u>el</u>), first-century rabbi

hochmah (<u>HoH</u>-mah), wisdom, one of the *sefirot*

hod (hod), majesty, one of the *sefirot*

hora (<u>hoar</u>-ah), Israeli folk dance

humash (<u>Hoom</u>-ah-sh), the five books of the Torah in one volume

humashim (Hoom-ah-<u>sheem</u>), plural of *humash*

hupah (Hoo-<u>pah</u>), marriage canopy

hutzpadik (Hootz-pah-<u>dik</u>), brazen

hutzpah (<u>Hootz</u>-pah), gall

kabbalah (kah-bah-<u>lah</u>), received tradition; Jewish mysticism

kaddish (<u>kah</u>-dish), prayer for mourners

katan (kah-<u>tahn</u>), small

keter (<u>keh</u>-ter), crown, one of the *sefirot*

ketusha (keh-<u>too</u>-shah), Russian rocket

kibbutz (kib-<u>bootz</u>), collective farm

kiddush (kid-<u>doosh</u>), prayer of sanctification of the Sabbath, said over wine

kipah (kee-<u>pah</u>), skullcap, *yarmulke*

lashon ha-ra (la-<u>shon</u> ha-<u>rah</u>), slander

lirot (lee-<u>roat</u>), old Israeli currency, pounds

Ma-aseh Beraysheet (mah-ah-<u>say</u> beh-ray-<u>sheet</u>), Work of Creation

Ma-aseh Merkavah (mah-ah-<u>say</u> mer-kah-<u>vah</u>), Work of the Chariot, Merkavah mysticism

madraygah (mahd-<u>ray</u>-gah), rank, grade

MahTovu (mah <u>tow</u>-voo), O How Good . . . the first hymn of the morning service

malchut (mahl-<u>Hoot</u>), kingship; one of the *sefirot*

mashal li'ma ha-divar domeh (mah-<u>shal</u> li-<u>mah</u> hah-di-<u>var</u> doh-<u>meh</u>), a parable that sheds light on the subject

matzah (<u>mah</u>-tzah), unleavened bread

mazal tov (mah-<u>zal</u> toav), congratulations, good luck

Meah Shearim (<u>may</u>-ah sheh-ah-<u>reem</u>), hundred gates, religious neighborhood in Jerusalem

mehitzah (meh-Hee-<u>tzah</u>), division in traditional synagogue that separates women from men

merkavah (mer-kah-<u>vah</u>), chariot

met (meht), dead

mezzuzah (meh-zoo-<u>zah</u>), scroll fixed to a doorpost

mezzuzot (meh-zoo-<u>zoat</u>), plural of *mezzuzah*

mikubal (mih-koo-<u>bal</u>), kabbalist

mikveh (<u>mik</u>-vah), waters for ritual immersion

minyan (<u>min</u>-yan), quorum for prayer

mishebayrach (mih-sheh-<u>bay</u>-raH), blessing said on someone's behalf

Mishnah (<u>mish</u>-nah), six volumes of rabbinic law from the first two centuries of this era

Mishnah Hagigah (<u>mish</u>-nah Hah-<u>gee</u>-gah), tractate of the *Mishnah* containing laws concerning mystical speculation

Mishneh Torah (<u>mish</u>-neh <u>tow</u>-rah), code of law of Moses Maimonides

mitz eshkoliot (meetz esh-<u>kol</u>-ee-<u>oat</u>), grapefruit juice

420

mitzvah (mitz-<u>vah</u>), commandment

mitzvot (mitz-<u>voat</u>), plural of *mitzvah*

Moshe (mow-<u>sheh</u>), Moses

Moshe ben Hershel (mow-<u>sheh</u> ben <u>hear</u>-shel), Moses the son of Hershel

Moshileh (<u>mow</u>-shi-leh), little Moshe (affectionate)

nefesh (<u>neh</u>-fesh), soul, in the World of Action

neshamah (neh-<u>shah</u>-mah), soul, in the World of Creation

Netanya (neh-<u>tahn</u>-yah), Netanya, city in Israel

netzach (<u>netz</u>-aH), victory, eternity; one of the *sefirot*

niftar (<u>nif</u>-tar), passed away

niggun (nih-<u>goon</u>), repetitive tune

ofanim (oh-fah-<u>neem</u>), wheels, class of angels

olam (oh-<u>lahm</u>), world

oneg Shabbat (<u>oh</u>-neg shah-<u>baht</u>), Sabbath delight

pardes (pahr-<u>dess</u>), orchard; Paradise

Parshat Yitro (par-<u>shaht</u> <u>yit</u>-row), Torah reading from Exodus containing the Ten Commandments

Pesach (<u>peh</u>-saH), Passover

p'shat (pih-shaht), simple explanation

Purim (<u>poor</u>-im), a carnival holiday one month before Passover

Rabbi (<u>rab</u>-bye), teacher of Judaism, Jewish minister

rabbi (<u>rab</u>-bye), Jewish coach

reb (reb), mister

rebbe (<u>reh</u>-bee), spiritual leader

rebbitzen (<u>reh</u>-bih-tzen), rabbi's wife

rehov (re-<u>Hov</u>), street

remez (<u>reh</u>-mez), hint

Rivkah (<u>riv</u>-kah), Rebecca

Rivkaleh (<u>riv</u>-kah-leh), little Rebecca (affectionate)

Rosh Hashanah (row-sh hah-<u>shah</u>-nah), Jewish new year, high holy day

rosh yeshivah (row-sh yeh-<u>sheev</u>-ah), head of a Jewish academy

ruach (<u>roo</u>-aH), spirit, soul in the World of Formation

seder (<u>say</u>-der), ritual Passover meal

sefer (<u>say</u>-fer), book

Sefer Yetzirah (<u>say</u>-fer yet-zee-<u>rah</u>), *Book of Creation*, early mystical text

sefirah (seh-fee-<u>rah</u>), nexus of energy in the process of creation

sefirot (seh-fee-<u>roat</u>), plural of *sefirah*

Shabbat (shah-<u>baht</u>), Sabbath

Shabbat shalom (shah-<u>baht</u> shah-<u>loam</u>), a wish for a peaceful Sabbath

Shabbos (<u>shah</u>-bus), Sabbath (old pronunciation)

shalom (shah-<u>loam</u>), peace, fulfillment, safety, wholeness

Shavuot (shah-voo-<u>oat</u>), festival celebrating the giving of the Torah at Sinai

shaygetz (<u>shay</u>-getz), derogatory term for non-Jewish man

sheitel (<u>shay</u>-tel), wig

shem (shem), name

shemayim (she-<u>mah</u>-yeem), heaven

sherut, (sheh-<u>root</u>), shuttle

sh'ma (she-<u>mah</u>), listen, liturgy: Hear O Israel, the Lord is our God, the Lord is One

shofar (show-<u>far</u>), ram's horn sounded on Rosh Hashanah

shul (shool), synagogue

siddur (sih-<u>door</u>), prayer book

Siman Tov U-mazal Tov (<u>see</u>-mahn toav oo-<u>mah</u>-zal toav), a good sign and good luck; a song of celebration

smichah (smee-<u>Hah</u>), rabbinic ordination

sod (sohd), secret

sukkah (soo-<u>kah</u>), temporary shelter erected for the festival of *Sukkot*

Sukkot (soo-<u>koat</u>), harvest festival

ta-keh (<u>tah</u>-keh), indeed

tallis (<u>tah</u>-liss), prayer shawl (old pronunciation)

tallit (tah-<u>leet</u>), prayer shawl (new pronunciation)

Talmud (tahl-<u>mood</u>) encyclopedic argument of Jewish law completed in fifth century

Talmud Hagigah (tahl-*mood* hah-<u>gee</u>-gah), argument of Mishnah Hagigah

tayglach (<u>tay</u>-glach), honey ginger confection for Rosh Hashanah

tefillin (teh-fee-<u>leen</u>), amulets worn on arm and head during morning prayer *teshuvah* (teh-shoo-*vah*), answer, return, repentance

tiferet (tih-*fer*-et), glory; one of the *sefirot*

tikkun (tih-*koon*), perfection, correction, refinement

tikun ha-nefesh (tih-*koon* ha-*neh*-fesh), refinement of the soul

Torah (tow-*rah*), the five books of Moses, all of Jewish learning

T"U b'Shvat (*too* bish-*vaht*), Jewish arbor day

tzitzit (tzee-*tzeet*), fringes on the corners of the *tallit*

ulpan (ool-*pahn*), intensive Hebrew school

yehidah (yeh-*Hee*-dah), unification, the joining of the soul to the infinite

yeshivah (yeh-shee-*vah*), academy of Jewish learning

yesod (yeh-*soad*), foundation, one of the sefirot

yetzer ha-ra (*yeh*-tzer hah-*rah*), the inclination to evil, the animal appetite

yetzer ha-tov (*yeh*-tzer hah-*tov*), the inclination to good, to resemble the Divine

yetzirah (yeh-tzee-*rah*), formation

yirah (yeer-*ah*), fear, awe

Yom Kippur (yoam kee-*pur*), Day of Atonement, high holy day

yosher koach (*yo*-sher *ko*-aH), acknowledgment of the performance of a religious act

Zohar (*zo*-har), thirteenth-century mystical commentary to the Torah